EXIT LIGHTS

JACOB MOSES

Also By Jacob Moses

THE BIG BASTARD

This book is dedicated to Tracy, my beloved wife.
She is full of unconditional love and support.
Without her encouragement, this novel
would still only be a decade-long dream.

EXIT LIGHTS

1

Tonight was not the first time I had seen the strange spotlight that shone down from the sky, but it was the first time I was able to see what it was shining on. The previous occasions just left me confused because I could see a spotlight shining down, however, where it ended was a mystery. There were always large buildings occupying the space between myself and where the light might be illuminating the ground. Still, I had not simply accepted the fact that I could not see where the spotlight ended. I have traveled many miles trying to discover the end, or maybe the source of the mystery, but it blinked out each time before I arrived.

The source of the spotlights seems to be beyond the limits of my sight. Never has it looked to be coming from a star, aircraft, satellite, or anything else I can see. You're undoubtedly thinking it strange that I would refer to this as a spotlight. However, it was a light from above, and it was shining down with pinpoint accuracy. No light seemed to stray outside the beam itself. At least it was clear to me that it had the specific physics of any spotlight I would see shining from the top of a building or down on a stage, so it just made sense to call it that and it would make it a little easier to explain the phenomena to someone else. Not that I have told anyone of the spotlights I have seen over the last month.

There was something different on this night. This unexplainable thing became more explainable because it had popped up, or shot down, on Michigan Avenue, and I just happened to be walking out of Loyola University on Michigan Avenue when it appeared. From this distance, it didn't merely look like a plain white spotlight from the sky, but rather a light that contained something magical. The essence of the beam was almost blizzard-like. It was as if I was looking at the fuzz on a television screen. Except, at the same time it looked snowy, it also was fully translucent, letting me see everything beyond it quite clearly.

Wait, I should stop for a moment to introduce myself. How could I expect you to buy into what I am telling you when you don't even have a clue as to who I am? I know I have started this off right in the middle of some craziness, but I felt this was the beginning of the story you needed to hear. I will catch you up on this part and then I am going to tell you everything as it happens. You see, in the time since this started, I could see these events were increasing in frequency. And after what I saw this evening, I just have this gut feeling that something big and bad is going to happen and I am likely to end up dead. That is why I am sharing this story with you. I need to tell someone and I don't expect anyone in my life to believe me.

So, my name is Cotter Trespin and I have lived in Chicago all my life. My short black hair is combed to the side and no part of it has turned white because I am seeing paranormal activity. My eyes are brown, not all white, like some demon-possessed man who is beaming spirits into Hell through some form of teleportation. I can also tell you my teeth are fairly straight and all there, hardly even a cavity. I say this because I have no doubt you are thinking I might be down to only a few teeth, like some meth-head prone to hallucinations. But trust me, I have just enough fat on me to dispute any accusations of methamphetamine abuse. I guess my point here is that I need you to know I am not crazy. There is something real happening to me and if I can't make sense of it, maybe you can. Now, I'll get back to the story I wanted to tell you.

The spotlight was a couple of blocks away and on the other side of the street. Still, it was close enough that I could see it was shining on a group of people on the sidewalk, but my instinct told me it was only lighting up one individual. I hurried down the busy sidewalk, weaving between others who were also at the end of their workday on this unseasonably warm autumn evening. In a matter of minutes, or maybe it was only seconds because time seemed to stand still, I was across the street from the thing that had baffled me for weeks, the thing that has me questioning my sanity.

The spotlight was indeed shining on just one person, and as I walked down the street, I could see that the spotlight moved along with this short and round man as I watched him walk in front of the Neiman Marcus building. He stopped at a bus stop in front of Walgreens, so I stepped aside from the foot traffic and positioned myself with my back against a building. As the man waited within a group of other future bus passengers, I had time to scrutinize his features while also glancing up to see if I could see the source of the light. I didn't bother to ask any other passersby if they could see the light. There had been enough shocked looks during past encounters to make it clear to me that I was either crazy or the only person on the street seeing the show.

The light had no obvious origin. It was just a beam that must have been coming from a place my eyes were not capable of seeing, so I focused my attention on who it was shining on. He was a squat, middle-aged looking man with round eyeglasses and a head of hair that, well, had no hair for the most part. Still a distance away, I couldn't make out if the short hair remaining was blonde or light gray, but I could see that there was only hair on the sides, as the top was a large circle of baldness. The man wore a brown suit that looked nice enough to be professional, but not like something that was purchased within the last decade, and perhaps not even the two decades before that. I couldn't see the suit in full detail from this distance, but it seemed like some '80s wool suit and it just added to the cringey feeling I had for the man.

I was so deep into observing the round, wool suit-wearing man that I nearly didn't notice the hooded figure who pushed him from behind. On the fortunate side of things, I did see the individual who pushed him. On the unfortunate side of things, I had to bear witness to the carnage resulting from an oncoming bus, which apparently was not slated to slow down for this bus stop. Perhaps nine times out of ten a bus traveling at the speed of a city street might leave room for survival, but the wheels on the bus made sure this was that one-time chance. The spotlight was extinguished.

I ran across the street and caught myself asking others in the area if they had seen the light. Of course, they hadn't and I quickly decided to keep my thoughts to myself. One glance at the wool-suited-man was all I needed to know he was beyond help. His body and face were twisted to a point that spoke of no coming back by way of stitches, casts or even complicated surgeries. The man was dead, and he had been pushed. Yes, he had been murdered! I began asking those around if they had also seen the hooded person who pushed him in front of the bus, but I could find no other person who recollected the events as I did. In fact, some of those I spoke to believe the man had jumped in front of the bus, like it was a suicide! Instead of trying to understand other perspectives of the incident, I decided I would wait to talk with the police.

After giving them a brief statement, the police had asked if I would be willing to wait for further questioning. It was an hour before a detective in a black suit came around to talk to me. He was wearing a nice enough looking red-checkered tie, but the tail was not tucked into the keeper loop and it always peeked out from behind. I am not a perfect dresser, but I notice those little details, and I can't help but want to reach over and tuck that tail in for a guy. Otherwise, the detective looked a lot like the wool-suited-man, except his hair was a darker brown and he sported a mustache that would have had him suing to join the Massachusetts State Police. I would guess him to be at least fifty, but nowhere near retirement. Of course, that guess is coming from a twenty-one-year-old who has trouble guessing ages, so maybe the detective is well beyond fifty.

When he introduced himself as Detective Banner, I immediately asked, "Did you find anyone else who saw a hooded individual push that man?"

"Not only did we not find anyone who saw the man get pushed, we haven't heard from anyone else that recollects seeing a hooded individual. Now, tell me, what did you mean in your statement when you said a hooded individual? Were you saying it was some guy in a Ku Klux Klan hood or what?"

"What... oh, I think I understand why you asked me that? I guess I just was in shock and it was how it came out, but I meant a hooded sweatshirt. It looked like a plain black hoodie and the hood was up. It all happened in the blink of an eye, and I didn't see much else, but I can tell you the person was wearing a hoodie."

"It happened fast you say, so is it possible that you could have confused that man jumping in front of the bus for being pushed? Because every other witness has at least suggested that he moved in front of that bus on his own accord. Most have gone so far as to say he flat out leapt into the street to get hit intentionally."

"No, even as fast as it happened, it was crystal clear to me that the man was pushed by someone in a black hoodie."

"So do you mean to imply to me that this was a black man?"

"Wait, what? With all due respect, Officer Banner,"

"Detective."

"I already said I didn't get a look at his face. So, no, I am not implying it was a black man. Hell, I don't even know if it was a man or a woman. And, more than just black people wear hoodies and commit crimes, you know."

"I do know that, but here is the issue I am having right now. There is no evidence of a crime here. So while you might not like how I am asking the questions, you are the one who is responsible for me being away from my family tonight to investigate this death. You are the only one making claims that this was not suicide, and I am trying to gain an understanding of your situation."

"Well, I am very sorry to have pulled you out here to do your job, detective."

As I began to walk away, Detective Banner called after me and walked over. "Here's my card, dude. That is my direct line so give me a call if you remember anything else about the hooded individual you saw."

"You mean the black criminal in a hoodie who I didn't see? Or, wait, was it the leader of your local KKK chapter?"

"Whatever, dude. Use the card or don't," and he turned and stomped off.

That guy, was the absolute worst. I mean, dude? What middle-aged homicide detective working in Chicago calls someone dude?

Anyway, there it is. This was the first time I saw where the spotlight actually finished on the ground. Though this has been a confusing time in my life, I have to admit that it was enlightening to finally be close enough to see an ending. Well, given the disturbing thing that happened, perhaps ending isn't the best way to refer to the moment prior to the spotlight flickering out. Or, now that I am thinking about it, maybe because of that, because there was an end to a life, it is the perfect way to refer to this moment. I mean, I can only hope this isn't what has happened every time I have seen one of these lights, but I would say it is reasonable to look at tonight's event as a one-act play. After all, there was a spotlight shining on a scene, and there was a clear conclusion to mark its end.

2

If I plan to be completely honest with you, and I want to, I have to say that I feel like a sack of shit this morning. I would like to tell you that it's not from a hangover, but that is exactly why I am struggling to focus. My parents stomping around the apartment isn't helping my cause either. Yes, I live in my parents' apartment and I don't appear to be going anywhere soon. I somehow gained an Associate of Arts degree from Malcolm X College, but that took me three years. I was pushed by my parents and girlfriend to continue my education. I walked into Loyola University to enroll for classes, but I walked out of Loyola University with a job. You're wondering what kind of job someone with an AA degree can get at Loyola University. I am a custodian. I am so tired of school that I am happy to be a custodian. And I should say, I've gained an appreciation for such work. It's as important, or more important than any other position on the campus.

"Cotter! There is some breakfast left if you want some?"

"Thanks, Mom. Maybe I'll be ready in a minute."

As I walk to my door, I am thinking about how I don't want to go out there right now, but some breakfast might do me some good with this hangover. There's no doubt in my mind that my parents know I have been drinking quite a bit since I turned twenty-one, and I guess they can't say too much since I am of age, however, it does feel a bit awkward to be around them when I have a massive hangover. Maybe I can hide it.

"Good morning, Mom."

As much as I don't want to at this moment, I hug her because it is our custom. She is a loving mother and I have a lot of respect for her. I guess my parents had a change of heart about kids pretty late in the game, because they were in their mid-forties when I was born. They are both retired already. Mom is a plump little lady with short curly gray hair. She is wearing an apron with chickens on it right now and, well, she is wearing it often as she spends plenty of time in the kitchen. I don't think she knows what to do with herself after finishing her teaching career.

She is smiling at me right now and those perfectly placed dimples have come out, she was a real looker in her day, but her smile fades when she says, "looks and smells like you had quite a night."

So much for hiding it, but I am not too proud to beg for pity. "I had a rough time after work. You heard about that man who was hit by the bus?"

"Yes, I heard it on the news last night. What about it?"

"Well, I witnessed it from across the street. It was awful when it happened and what I saw after running across the street was even more horrific."

A shocked and sad look crosses her face and she steps forward to hug me again. "Oh, no! I am sorry to hear you had to see such a thing, Sweetie."

I feel a pang of guilt, but I get over that quickly because it's not like I am lying. Still, deep down, I know I am doing okay after seeing the incident and I was only using it to deflect my shame. I grab the plate she had put together for me and walk toward the study. This is what my father calls it, but my parents have always tried to live modestly, even though they seem to have the finances to live more comfortably. So, my father's study is simply a large walk-in closet with a desk and bookshelf. The door is open and my father is sitting with his coffee and the newspaper. He has put on a lot of weight since retirement and it doesn't fit well on his five-foot, six-inch frame. However, I am glad he started shaving his head. This works much better with his new physique. I had been suggesting this hairdo for years because of his balding pattern, but he just listened in the last year.

Not looking up from his newspaper, almost in an uncaring way, he says, "I heard you say you witnessed this accident I am reading about in the newspaper."

"Yes, I had an up-close and personal encounter."

Now he did look up and I could see the care and concern in his eyes, "Are you okay, Son?"

"Yeah, I am. But, Dad, I have to tell you, I don't know what the paper is reporting but this was no accident."

"Well, I guess I said accident but the paper is suggesting that it was possibly suicide. I guess you saw him jump into the street too?"

"No, the police wouldn't believe me when I gave a statement, but I saw someone push that man in front of the bus. Yet, they say nobody else saw it that way." My father's brow furrows as he sits up a little straighter and listens. "It's crazy to me that nobody else saw what I saw."

"Are you absolutely positive about this? Did you get a good look at the guy?"

"Yes, I am sure of what I saw, but I didn't get any real good look at a face. I couldn't even be sure if it was a man or a woman. The only thing I am sure about is that there was a person who pushed this man, from behind, into the street to be hit by that bus. I am talking about an arms extended shove. I got a good look from across the street and it didn't seem like anything was happening that led up to or provoked the shove. Dad, it was rush hour and there were people all around him. You used to walk the streets during that time every day. You know how busy it can be. And they were just standing with him waiting for a bus. How could nobody else notice such a detail as him being shoved? I must be going crazy or something?"

"I don't think you're crazy, Son. I know you well enough to realize when you are sure about something and it sounds like you saw what you are saying you saw." His face had softened but now he has a confused look. "How did you get such a good look at what happened?"

I don't want him to change his mind about me being sane so I will not be telling him about the spotlight. At least not yet. "What do you mean?"

"I am just thinking if there were all these people around the man at such a busy moment and you clearly saw him get shoved from across the street, you must have either glanced there at just the right moment or you were already looking at this man. And as sure as you've expressed to me that you saw someone shove him, I am guessing you wouldn't be this sure from a glance."

I decide I am going to be as honest as I can without talking about the spotlights. "Well, yes, the man who died caught my attention, so I was already looking at him from across the street."

"What caught your attention?"

I pause. "I guess I just can't say for sure."

"Well, then maybe there was something that happened between this man and whoever pushed him and that is what caught your attention? You were busy walking home from school and maybe you caught something in your peripheral vision that drew your attention but you just didn't see enough of it to have the full picture register?"

Man, my dad is smart. He really knows how to trust his instinct and even without me talking about the spotlight, he realizes how attentive I was to this man. And, yes, my parents think I am studying at Loyola University, not working there. I am not ready yet to tell him that I am not enrolled in college, but I would be willing to tell him about the mystical things I am seeing. It's just that I know he won't believe it and I don't need him worrying about my mental state, so I will just go along with what he is saying so we can button up the conversation. Maybe it's close enough to the truth anyway. "Yeah, that must be why I was looking at this man."

My cell phone is vibrating and I pull it out to see a text message from my girlfriend, Rebecca. *I am sick of waiting for you to be ready to talk. We need to talk today or I don't think I can do this anymore.* My dad is in close enough proximity that I am getting the feeling as I read the text that he is seeing it too. You know that feeling. Like someone isn't necessarily trying to be nosy, but when you just pull your phone out and open a message, even though you don't look at the person to confirm they saw, your senses are telling you that they couldn't help but see what you saw. I generally wouldn't be concerned about him seeing anything that would come across my phone, but here is yet another cause for worry.

"Is everything okay, Son?"

"Yeah, I just need to go catch up with Rebecca. I have been busy lately and to be honest, I guess I have neglected her a bit."

"Give her my best. I have always liked that girl. Your mom and I always pray that you won't do anything to screw that up." He chuckles.

I chuckle too but just so he doesn't feel bad. There is always this pressure to make sure everything stays fine there and it makes me feel guilty, like I must be doing something wrong if she isn't happy.

"I'll tell her you said hi. Bye, Dad."

"Good-bye, Son. Love ya."

"Love you too, Dad."

***

Rebecca had texted me to meet her at the coffee shop near my parent's dry cleaning shop. I don't mean to say that they own a dry cleaning shop, but rather the shop they always use. Anyway, my mom asked me to pick up her dry cleaning. I honestly don't know why she still has anything dry cleaned, especially since she rarely leaves the kitchen. This wouldn't be a big deal for me if the Italian proprietor of said dry cleaning service wasn't so damn annoying. He is always laughing, as if he thinks he's the funniest man in the world. Okay, the truth is, he is pretty funny, but it's not because of his material. What makes me laugh is his accent and how funny he *thinks* he is. But the material, oh my god! He always says the same things.

It looks like Rebecca is running late so I am going to pick up my mom's dry cleaning while I wait. As I walk through the door, I am just waiting for it. With the richest Italian accent, deeper than you'd think his small body could emit, his voice says, "Aye, welcome back, Cotter!" There it is, and a deep belly laugh follows from this short little gray-haired man with a gray handlebar mustache. It's a deep, wheezy chuckle now and I can't help but smile.

"You know, Mr. Zetticci, I don't even spell my name the same as that dumb old show."

"Ah, it was a great show. Johnny Travolta was handsome as ever and almost as funny as me!" Another wheezy chuckle. When he stops, he looks left and right, checking to make sure nobody is close enough to hear his next line. He does this even though the store was empty before I walked in, and I know exactly what is coming next, the dirty joke of the day. "You know what is wrong with 6.9?"

I just get it over with, not exactly questioning his joke. "I don't know."

"The period!" And Ole Zetticci starts losing it before he even finishes the punchline. I humor him and give a half-smile chuckle, but he

11

clearly thinks it's the funniest line ever as he doubles over, holding his arm around the front of his thin waist. Next comes my favorite part and this is typical of a visit to Zetticci's Dry Cleaning. It is my favorite not only because it lets me know my awkward visit here has nearly concluded, but because it always impresses me, and it is arguably the funniest part of his act. Mr. Zetticci goes from doubled over, laughing, to a perfectly postured standing position and says, "seven dollars and fifty cents," as he turns and grabs my mom's clothes, which are hanging directly behind him. Understand this, he never looked at a bill the entire time I was in the store and my mom's clothes were already directly behind him in the front row of several rows of cleaned clothes. I have seen him do this with other customers as I waited and it almost always happens with me. I just pay, shake my head and give a little snicker as I turn and walk away.

As I exit the front door, I am already almost stepping into the outdoor seating of Dark Cravings, Rebecca's favorite coffee bar. I always give her crap about liking the place because there is an establishment of the same name downtown, but it is a gay bar, and I can't help but think that's funny. Rebecca is already sitting with two disposable cups of coffee. Her standard small and a large for me. Having the small doesn't mean she won't have more coffee than it contains, she just has this cute quirk of liking how the small cup feels in her hand. On top of that, she can't finish a cup of coffee before it gets cold to save her life. As she turns, my heartbeat quickens as I see the depth in her amazing hazel eyes. We have dated since high school but I still feel butterflies when I first see her. She says, "Where were you?"

I can't help myself, I am suddenly in a playful mood. "I was in the bathroom and it took three guys asking me if I needed a hand before I realized I was in the wrong Dark Cravings."

I am surprised, knowing that she is not happy with me, when she still lets out a little laugh at my joke. I laugh too and seize the opportunity to bend down for a kiss. Instead, I am left letting out a quiet, "Oof," as she pulls away, and it is now that her demeanor changes to something more like I was expecting. I sit down in the seat nearest to her and go to work mending the wounds I had inflicted, just as I have so many times before. Of course, although I probably know exactly why she is unhappy with me, the dishonest part of me has to play dumb and pry it out of her instead of just owning it and completely being the bad guy, like I should be. As softly as I can, "Wait, what is it that has you so upset with me, Becky?"

"Seriously, Cotter? You've been ignoring the majority of my texts for the better part of a week! And when you have responded, it's with short and sometimes nonsensical replies! And I am just really upset that when my best friend from grade school died after driving drunk last week, you didn't respond to my voicemails until the next day, and that was with a text message that said you didn't have time to see me!" Now she is crying and I truly am feeling like the worst guy in the world. Not only for how she just described me treating her, but also for how I even entered into this conversation with her to begin with.

I can't tell her I was drunk that night and didn't want to communicate with her because she hates how much I have been drinking. Especially given the circumstances of the accident. I doubt she wanted to hear me in the state I was in at that moment. She can even tell when I have been drinking through a text message, so I avoided that as well. And the next day? Yeah, right. As if I was going to be able to console her with a glassy-eyed, booze-smelling hangover. I was probably right not to respond, but that doesn't mean I won't still be nominated for worst boyfriend of the year. I brush some of her tear-soaked long black hair behind her cute little ear and say, "I am so sorry I couldn't be there for you, Sweetheart. I have just been so busy at college."

"Are you flipping kidding me?!" Oops. I thought I was doing that right but I guess I was wrong. She is really pissed if she brought out the "F" word. Yeah, flipping, but she never really swears so this is pretty bad. "Don't treat me like your parents, like I don't know you're not going to school!" I open my mouth to defend myself but she adds, "Besides, I'm pretty sure getting drunk after work every day isn't a custodian's homework. You could have time for me then."

I can see she feels bad about that last remark but I am at least good enough not to try shifting the blame to her. As gently as I can I say, "I don't get drunk every night and I am sorry I let you down. I'd say I won't do it again but you'd know that was a lie because you know by now that it will happen again. I do care about you and the truth is I didn't want to burden you with all my crap." I was not trying to play the pity card but I am getting it anyway and this makes me feel weird inside.

"But, Cott," it sounds like she has softened up a lot because she only calls me Cott when she feels enamored with me, "your crap isn't just crap to me. You can share anything with me. I know I am not perfect, but I'd do my best not to judge and maybe you'd feel better if you try to get stuff off your chest."

"Yeah, I know all that," except she is nearly perfect, "but something I also know is that you know I am not good at sharing my crap with others. And the stuff lately isn't just about the pressure on education from my parents, or figuring life out, it's some crazy crap."

"But you don't have to share with others and I should be put above any such category, so please start sharing with me at least. Also, can we quit calling your stuff crap? I have been constipated for a couple days and the word just adds to all the pain."

I chuckle as she blushes. She really is quite the lady, but she is just very comfortable around me and I love that about her so I say, "Yes, I will stop calling it crap and that was the sexiest thing you've said to me in weeks." We both chuckle at this comment and I am delighted, as I always am to get laughter out of my sweet Rebecca.

3

Two days passed before I saw another spotlight, and then they seemed to come in rapid succession. The first few were some distance away and I did not reach their stage before the light flickered out. One drew me out of the college while I was working. I was not able to see anything from inside, but I felt some unseen force tugging at me. It was as if a marionettist had one of his strings right in my chest and was gently, but forcefully, guiding me towards the door. Once outside and within sight of the spotlight, the force seemed to disappear. I did not think it wise to leave work to chase something that could disappear at any moment, but it felt strange when I went back inside and started working. I was burdened for some time with a feeling that I had done something wrong.

Right now, I am following a spotlight that drew me out of bed in the middle of the night. Much like the instance I spoke of before, I awoke with a sensation that something was tugging at my core, maybe my soul. When I looked out my window, I could see a spotlight that didn't appear to be too far off, maybe just beyond some neighboring apartment buildings. I have just rounded the corner of those buildings and the spotlight appears to be on the opposite side of the Radisson Hotel. Wait, now I am getting far enough to the side of the hotel that it appears the spotlight is shining on the top of the building. Or perhaps, as I begin thinking about the rules of this unexplainable phenomenon, it might be shining on someone inside of the building. As I am telling myself how dumb it sounds inside my head to suggest something like this is governed by rules, there is a glaring answer before me.

A man walks onto the balcony of his hotel room and I can see the spotlight is shining on him. This hotel is dozens of stories high, but this man is on, let me count… the seventh floor. He is far enough away that I can't see much more than a dark head of hair and that he might be dressed in a bathrobe, but it's hard to say for sure. I'm going to get closer and think about going in, however, it strikes me that I don't know why I would have a reason to do that. What would I say if... someone yelps and as I am looking back up, he is off the balcony and screaming now, plummeting straight down. I had been moving towards the building and I am only about fifteen feet away as he strikes the lawn with a sickening thud that I can only describe as a multitude of sounds at once. Ground pounding, tissue splitting, bone-breaking sounds. I feel like I need to throw up but my instinct tells me to look up and I see a hoodie-wearing head peering over the balcony for only a moment before it disappears.

My heart skips a beat, I swallow my dinner again, and I am running for the front entrance of the hotel. This route is bringing me a little closer to the body and I can't help but glance over as I run past. Thankfully, it is dark enough that I don't see much, but a streetlight in the parking lot is hitting the spot just so I can see a glistening twinkle of wetness on a long bone protruding from a leg. Not seeing much in the dark doesn't matter. The thought alone of what I am seeing forces me to swallow my dinner for a third time. Now I am through the front entrance of the hotel and I run to the elevator, but I glance toward the stairs. How am I going to stop this person if I don't know which way he will come down?

"Can I help you, sir?" I glance up to see a woman staring at me from behind the counter.

"Oh, call the police! A man was just pushed from the balcony!"

"What?! Are you serious?"

"Unfortunately I am."

"Well, you call the police. I know CPR." She runs from behind the counter and heads for the door.

I grab her arm as she approaches and she looks directly into my eyes. "Listen, you don't want to see what I just saw out there. He took a terrible and definitely fatal fall. I believe he was on the seventh floor." Her face twists in disgust and she turns, hurrying back behind the counter. I hear her calling 911 as I turn my attention back to the elevator and stairs. My heart is beating fast as I figure he has to be quickly approaching if he is going to come down, and I have no clue what I am going to do when he arrives in the lobby.

Police sirens snap me out of a momentary trance as I stand staring, thinking. At this moment, I am realizing that too much time has passed. What should have been an obvious thought before just now crosses my mind. "Is there a back elevator or stairs?"

"Of course there is. This hotel has multiple elevators and stairways."

She continues talking but I can't hear what she is saying as I have already started running down the hallway. Sure, she could map out the building for me, but I probably wouldn't find them any faster in a hotel this size. I am on the other side of the hotel and see another elevator but it is sitting with doors open. I open the exterior doors on the opposite side of the hall, but I don't see any movement outside. This murderer might already be gone or maybe still slinking down a stairwell. Thinking there are probably stairwells at least at both back corners of the building, I decide to head towards the one that would be furthest from the dead man's room.

I am sprinting down the hallway and as I round a corner, I hear a door slam shut. Now I am approaching an exterior door. My stairwell guess might have been right. I blow through the door so hard that I can hear the door closure break. It was not a quiet exit and in the darkness, I see a figure look back over a shoulder and then immediately start sprinting. I start to give chase but I am already tired. I should have more stamina than this, but I can imagine I have taken a huge adrenaline dump. Even though I can still see the person up ahead of me, it is obvious that I am losing ground. I try to catch my bearings and realize we are running down Lake Street. I think this creep might be trying to escape on the Red Line of the subway. I know there is no way I am going to win this race to the "L", but I refuse to give up. These spotlights have been messing with my life and now this person is messing with other people's lives. I need answers.

I turn the corner and see the person... wait, it's a guy. He was far enough ahead of me that he could be gone by now, but he has turned at the top of the subway stairs and pulled his hood down. We are both just standing here, staring. I can't make out detail as he is well over a block away, but I can at least see that he has shaggy black hair and some facial hair, maybe a shorter black beard. I always assumed it was a man, but now I know for sure. It's not as if I could pick him out of a lineup after a view from this distance, yet something feels familiar about him. He turns and runs down the stairs and I start to run again. As I reach the steps and race down, I first hear and then see the "L" departing the station. I was first confused about why he would stop and even reveal some of himself to me, but now I can see that his intent was to stop me in my tracks. He must not have wanted to chance me reaching the subway before the Red Line departed, so he took a chance and delayed my arrival just long enough to evade me. Now I'm exhausted, no closer to understanding what is going on and I have to make another police report that is bound to look suspicious.

***

I have made my way back to the Radisson and I have had plenty of time to think about how this interview is going to go with Detective Banner. I have no doubt he will be quite curious as to how I ended up at the scene of another death. However, I am surprised as I walk into the lobby and see the only plainclothes officer is not Banner, but a female instead. She looks surprisingly young. I wouldn't expect her to be over thirty and maybe as young as twenty-five. She has dirty blonde hair that I think would fall just below her shoulders if she didn't have it pulled back into a ponytail. She is of average height and thin, but not too thin. She has healthy curves in all the right places. I can see the hotel employee from earlier speaking with her and pointing to me, and as the detective walks over, I see the brightest blue eyes I think I have ever seen. She shakes my hand and says she is Detective Keller.

"I was expecting to see Detective Banner when I got back here."

"Oh? You know Detective Banner?"

"Well, not really. It's just that he was the detective the other day when I gave a statement."

"You needed to give a statement recently? What was that about?"

Damn. I am realizing now that I might have been better off not bringing up the fact that I saw the death of the wool-suited-man. Then again, it might have been more suspicious if Banner found out that I never mentioned it. Regardless, I am now thinking this interview might be more difficult than a second encounter with Banner. "You know, I am going to say right off that I know it's going to seem suspicious to you, but I also witnessed that guy getting hit by the bus."

Her brows twitch just slightly and I am getting the feeling she is becoming a bit more cautious than she was when she first approached me. As she becomes less relaxed and stands up straighter, she pulls her suit coat together and slides one button through a buttonhole so sleekly that it would have been easy to go unnoticed. However, I can't help but notice how the buttoned coat highlights the healthy curves I noticed earlier. I don't see myself as one who freely gawks at women, but she is a true beauty. I try to snap myself out of this brief daze as I literally move my hand towards my chin to close my dropped jaw.

I stop short though and close my mouth, rubbing my hand on my chest and taking a deep breath as I focus again on Detective Keller's unease and say, "Listen, I was across the street when that man got pushed in front of the bus and I was on the ground when this man got pushed from the balcony."

"Why are you getting so defensive if you have nothing to hide, Mister?" She raises an eyebrow and turns an ear towards me while pulling out a notepad as she draws out the mister in question of my identity.

"Trespin. Cotter Trespin. And I am defensive because I know this must feel weird to you because it feels crazy as hell to me. Also, I feel like your judging me and it makes me nervous."

"Well, forgive me, but to say this situation you find yourself in is a coincidence might just be an understatement. Maybe you can just tell me what you saw here tonight while I wrap my head around such a coincidence?" She says coincidence like an exaggerated question. I sense sarcasm that feels condescending, but it also adds to this sense of attraction I can't help but feel. "The front desk clerk said you told her this man was pushed from the balcony?"

I am choosing to ignore her condescension. "Yes, I heard the man scream and when I looked up I saw a man looking over the railing of the balcony."

"Could you give me a description of this man?"

"Well, not from that moment. He was wearing a hoodie with the

19

hood up so his face was completely shado—"

"What? If you couldn't see a face, how do you know it was a man?"

"Like I said, I couldn't give a description from that glimpse, but I got a better look at him as he was catching the Red Line."

"So that's where you've been. I was told there was a witness but when I didn't see anyone standing around I assumed you had just split. Now, how did you get from here to the Red Line?"

I am trying to be as detailed as possible as I tell her all my movements from the hotel to the "L". I also give her the best description I can from the limited look I got of this guy. Detective Keller's mannerisms right now tell me she is listening and not necessarily discrediting my story, but I am also getting a slight feeling that she is just patronizing me.

Now she has finished taking her notes and she looks up at me disdainfully. "Here's the thing about your story, Mr. Trespin. In the time you were away from the scene, we were able to process the room and there were no signs of foul play." I am shaking my head but she continues as she sees my disagreeing look. "No, now just listen. Obviously, you think you saw someone up there, but we can't find any sign of that being the case. The senator had checked in by himse—"

"Wait. That guy was a senator?"

She looks away and takes a breath indicating to me that she regrets her last statement. "Yeah, I shouldn't have told you that so please do not repeat it until a story breaks this news. It's already going to be big enough news as it is. Back to my point though, there is no evidence indicating that there was anyone in the room with the senator or that he did anything other than fall from that balcony on his own. There had been enough alcohol consumed up there to understand easily how such a mistake could happen. Furthermore, there is a slight ledge outside the railing of the balcony just wide enough for a cell phone to potentially land on if it were to be dropped. The senator's cell phone happened to be sitting on that ledge. A combination of alcohol and him possibly leaning over to grab a dropped phone makes a lot more sense than somebody else being in his locked room."

"Wait, the door was locked?"

"Yes."

"From the inside?"

"Well… not the deadbolt or security latch. But the door was locked when officers entered the room."

"Okay, so it was not impossible for someone to have exited that room through the door. You can say all you want about there not being evidence suggesting someone else was in the room, but unless you can tell me something to indicate an impossibility of someone having left that room, I can only tell you that I saw someone else on that balcony!" I am just realizing how emotionally I spoke these last statements. Detective Keller is looking at me with a little more respect.

"Listen, I am not saying I don't believe what you have told me. It's just that I have to report on the facts of what the scene looks like to us. I have taken your statement and you have my word that I will look into what you have told me." As my posture loosens a bit, hers, which had lightened for a moment, stiffens back up as she asks, "I hadn't gotten to ask you, what were you doing here anyway? The front desk clerk didn't think you were a guest, but she wasn't sure since you are in your pajamas."

It is only at this moment that I look down and see that I am indeed in my pajamas. I hesitate to answer as I think about saying I am a guest, but I quickly realize this lie will only make this situation look worse. "No, I live nearby and I couldn't sleep so I was getting some fresh air."

She pulls out her notepad again. "Ah, yes. I haven't gotten your address yet." She is so well polished and professional that I can see how she has become a detective so young, but she sure has made some rookie mistakes during this interview. She might still be relatively new to this career.

"233 East Whacker Drive."

"Columbus Plaza?"

"That's the place."

I think she's giving me the judgmental *how do you afford that place* look as she starts to write it down and adds, "Nice place to live." Suddenly snapping out of her judgmental trance, she looks at me inquisitively. "That has to be several blocks away from here. Why were you all the way over here?"

Though I have done nothing wrong, it is difficult for me not to feel, and probably act, guilty because I know there is more to this story than I can tell anyone. These spotlights are a curse! I have witnessed people die, I feel like I am seeing crazy hallucinations, and now I feel like I am the one doing something wrong as the police are confronting me! I am trying to stay calm but I can feel that my face is flushed. I look around as I tell her, "I guess I just lost track of how far I had walked."

She looks me over from head to toe with every intent of me noticing. "And is it often that you walk so far in the middle of the night in only your pajamas? Sir, you have no shoes on."

Again, a new realization as I look down to see I left so hurriedly at the sight of the spotlight that I not only stayed in my pajamas, but I also spared no time to slip on any footwear. I decide that a bit of honesty might give me more credibility in this moment. "Not often, no. Actually, this is probably the first time I've ever taken a stroll in the middle of the night. I think it was just that it's such a nice autumn night and I got distracted as I was sleepless and decided to take in some fresh air."

"Well, I won't pretend to know what to make of this whole situation right now, but I have more work to do here. I think I have all I need from you right now, Mr. Trespin. Plan on us being in contact with you though. I will have an officer give you a ride home." She turns and speaks to a uniformed officer before she gets on the elevator. Even though I am sure I gave off some feelings of dishonesty and knowing it's her job to try to decipher the truth, I still can't help but feel that she judged me unfairly. Regardless, as she turns in the elevator, I again notice how perfectly curved her body is and those blue eyes are glowing even at this distance, and I can't help it, I like her.

4

I didn't sleep another wink when I finally got home this morning. Maybe that is why I made the decision I am currently regretting. I just sat my parents down and not only told them about witnessing a second death, but I told them the reason why it wasn't just a coincidence that I found myself in those locations. I told them about the spotlights I have been seeing. Mom's jaw is slack and she has this dumbfounded look on her face. Dad looks like he wants to chuckle but is unsure whether I am kidding or not. He catches Mom's concerned look, decides I am not kidding and says, "Son, do you believe this is something physical you are seeing? Or are you saying you have some sort of intuition that is leading you to these locations."

"No, Dad. I am seeing exactly what I told you. I don't mean it as a metaphor and it's not a figment of my imagination. I am literally seeing lights shine down from, well... I don't know where! And, the only two times I have been able to see what they are shining on, the people under the light have been murdered! Then the lights go out as soon as they die."

"Cotter, we have already been concerned about you lately, but this is really scaring me," Mom says.

"Wait, I know things haven't been perfect with me lately, maybe I haven't lived up to your expectations, but this has nothing to do with college or anything else that you've been worried about."

Mom's blue eyes are beginning to twinkle as the tears start to well up. "What about the drinking? Just because we haven't said anything doesn't mean we haven't noticed you seem to get drunk every night!"

Dad puts his hand on her leg and says, "Now, Dear, take it easy. Maybe this is the time to talk about it, but we don't need it all to come out sideways."

I have to admit I am feeling defensive. "So what if I am drinking a little. It's not illegal and I am not hurting anyone." I also have to admit a twinge of denial at this moment.

Dad had calmed Mom a little, but she has instantly lit up again. "You don't think you're hurting anyone!? Look at us! We are constantly worried about you, and look at how your relationship with Rebecca is deteriorating. I am willing to bet your boozing has something to do with that as well."

"You know, sometimes it feels like my parents care more about Rebecca than me." Mom gives a look like she didn't mean to make me feel this way but I wave her off. "No, neither of you know how things are between us. Maybe you don't know as much as you think you do. Besides, I am trying to tell you about something crazy that is happening to me and your questions are about my relationships and drinking habits." Anger is taking hold of me at this moment. "And I don't know what any of that has to do with the crazy shit I am seeing!"

"Settle down, Son. You're upsetting your mother."

"Well, she is upsetting me too!" Dad is standing now and reaches over to put his hand on my shoulder. I slap it away and move towards the door. "I'm not going to college either. I'm working there."

I didn't turn to say this and now Dad sounds a bit angry behind me, "Who do you think you are? Show us some res—"

Mom hushes him, "Just let him go." I am already closing the door behind me but I can hear her begin to sob anyway.

While I don't want to be here arguing with my parents, I guess I don't want to be alone either because I have instinctively pulled out my phone and it is already ringing Rebecca. *This is Rebecca. Please leave a message and I will get back to you as soon as possible, and even sooner than that if this is my Too-Hot-To-Trot-Cott.* Regardless of the mood I am in, her voicemail greeting always brings a smile to my face. Right now is no exception. "I know you're probably in class, but I need to talk. I am heading to Mr. Brown's Lounge if you want to meet me there."

I guess I had better call my boss now. "What's up Cotter?"

"Hey, Mr. Brown." No, I do not believe he has any ownership in Mr. Brown's Lounge. "I'm not going to be able to make it in today."

"No? Why is that, Cotter?"

"I'm just not feeling well at all this morning." This is not exactly a lie.

"Well I have to say, Cotter, it has not been good to see you comin' in late some mornin's and smellin' booze on you at times, and now you're callin' in sick once again. I hope you'd understand if it were hard for me to believe these attendance issues weren't related to alcohol."

"Sir, I have never come into work when I have been drinking. I mean, I never drink in the morning and I have never drank on the job."

"I didn't say I thought you had. Hangovers ain't always just a bad feelin'. They often come with the smell of booze leakin' out your pores. You should know this if it matters to you to not be smellin' like that."

"I didn't know I did, and I am sorry for that, Mr. Brown."

"Okay, Cotter. You are a good worker and I am happy to have you on my custodial staff, but your comin' in late and smellin' of booze has to change or I will terminate your employment here."

"Fair enough, sir. I will get some rest and plan to be in tomorrow morning." What is wrong with me? Though I have only known him for a short time, I respect the hell out of this man yet I am telling him lies.

"See you tomorrow then. But if you feel better later please come in. You know we are already shorthanded."

"Okay, goodbye."

I feel so messed up that I can't imagine going to work right now, but letting Mr. Brown down is only making me feel worse. Good thing I am standing in the doorway of the Mr. Brown that approves of my drinking. This is a place I like to chill in because it's just different from other bars around this part of the city. It's like stepping off the street and into a real Jamaican establishment. I guess I probably feel like I am escaping my life when I go here and I like that feeling, maybe a little too much these days. I order a beer and chuckle to myself as I realize another bit of irony involving Mr. Brown's Lounge and my boss, Mr. Brown. I am pretty sure he is of Jamaican descent. I saw him out to dinner with his father one night and when I was introduced, he totally sounded Jamaican. I guess I didn't give it much thought until now, but Mr. Brown is a skinny black man and his father sounds Jamaican, so perhaps he does own some stock in this joint.

***

It's well after noon now and Rebecca is tapping me on the shoulder. I wheel around on my stool, trying not to lose my balance as I immediately feel the effect of the drinks. This bartender mixes a mean Tally Man. "Cotter, what is going on? You sounded upset in your message."

"Well hello, Sweetheart!" Hearing my voice in my head, I immediately feel like I am in trouble because it is loud and my words are drawn out more than they should be. There will be no pretending like I am not intoxicated.

"What the hell is wrong with you? You're supposed to be working right now, but instead, I find you drunk in a bar. I don't have time for this."

"Ah, come on, my sweet Becca. I've hardly had a few drinks." She glances at the bartender, but I reach up, nudge her chin back in my direction, and wave the bartender away with my other hand while simultaneously realizing nothing can help my case anyway. "How bouts you just have a drink with me, Baby."

There is a tear welling up in one hazel eye and she starts to turn as she says, "I am not going to enable you. If you want to ruin your life, you're going to have to do it on your own." She starts to walk away and I reach for her arm, but she has already moved beyond my reach. Unfortunately, my depth perception at this moment isn't allowing me to realize this and I am grabbing at air. My balance is lost and through the art of slight drunkenness, I gracefully tumble onto the floor. "Are you flipping kidding me, Cotter?" The slip of the flip should tell me how upset she is with me, but I have little ability to understand anything right now.

Rebecca walks back over to scoop me off the floor. Though the tears have now rolled down her cheek, she looks more pissed off than hurt at the moment and I can feel my own tears welling up in my eyes. I think seeing my water wells is why I notice a slight change to her hardening face. Feeling so bad about everything in this moment and having no ability to filter, I just begin to unload everything as the tears begin to drag race down my cheeks. "I am so sorry, Sweetheart! It's just that I saw this guy get murdered. And the spotlights are driving me crazy. And I am letting my parents down, and Mr. Brown. And there is something about this murderer that I can't quite figure out and that is driving me crazy too. And now the spotlights are waking me up at night. It's like I can feel them!"

"Whoa, slow down and get a hold of yourself, Cotter. You're drunk and hardly making any sense." Rebecca is leading me from the bar to a booth in the corner. "I know it must have been hard seeing that guy get hit by a bus, but what do you mean spotlights?"

"I'm not talking about the wool-suit guy on the street. You know, the guy I saw pushed from the balcony last night, or this morning or whatever. The senator or whoever he was."

"What!? I don't know what you are talking about. You saw another person die?"

"Not just die. I saw another guy get murdered. I saw the same person shove that senator from the balcony at the hotel. The same guy with his hood up. The same guy who pushed creepy looking wool-suit guy in front of the bus. Only I didn't see his face then, but last night I did see him, and I think I might have seen him before."

"I can't understand all these ramblings. What do you mean someone fell from a balcony? What balcony?" I can see her mind churning and she seems to be developing suspicions. "You were at a hotel in the middle of the night!? What for!?"

"It's not like that. The spotlight led me to the hotel after it woke me up. And this guy didn't just fall. He was pushed. Then I chased after the hoodie guy and saw his face. But he jumped on the 'L' before I could catch him. Well, I don't think I could have caught him anyway." Another wave of emotion takes over my drunken self and I am almost sobbing now. "I am so sorry, Rebecca. I am sorry for being so distant. It's the spotlights."

"I don't understand. What do you mean, spotlights?"

"They shine from somewhere, I don't know. Then I saw they were shining on people. No, that's not right, like just one person each time. Then this hoodie guy kills them and the spotlight goes out." I can't stop crying. I *am* upset, but too much drinking has me in that embarrassing situation that I am sure to regret tomorrow. "I am sorry I drink too much. Maybe I have a problem or maybe it's these spotlights driving me mad. I am sorry, Sweetheart. And sorry that I was checking out that detective and feeling so turned on and attracted to her."

"What!? What have you been doing? I don't understand you right now. Maybe I don't understand you at all!"

"Wait, I don't know why I said that. It is nothing, I don't even think she is into me."

"What the hell!? Maybe not into you? Are you into her, and who are we even talking about!?"

"No, listen, she is nobody to me. I don't know why I even said that. I'm drunk I think."

"Oh, you think, huh." I can see some serious hurt in her eyes as the tears pour from them. "You're drunker than I've ever seen you and unfortunately there have been many days to compare. You're drunk all the time lately and now you're thinking about other women?"

"No, I am not! It's just this one detective who interviewed me last night."

"Oh, just one woman!? I can't believe you are fucking doing this to me after all we have been through!" Oh shit. This is bad. I have never heard her say that word. What am I doing? I catch myself lost in these thoughts as I realize Rebecca is already most of the way to the bar's front door.

"It's not what you think! I didn't do anything! It was just some super-hot detective I was forced to check out!" She turns at the door and shakes her head with a look on her face that looks so much in pain that you'd think I just put an arrow through her heart. And not a cupid arrow. "I mean, she was just there because I had to get a statement, or, give a statement." I pretty much make this last comment to myself. Rebecca is gone. Yet, all I can see is her face, forever stuck with this expression of pure devastation. Now I notice the bartender and the few patrons seated at the bar looking my way. They are also shaking their heads and their expressions are not far off from Rebecca's. No, I guess they are more like the looks of disgust.

I realize all of this has made me feel a little more sober. I guess there is only one thing to do at this point, so I walk back up to the bar and see a shift change has delivered a not very Jamaican looking white guy to the position on the other side of the bar. "Could I get a Tally Man and a shot of something strong?"

"Sure thing, boss." Before mixing my drink, he pulls out a bottle of really cheap looking tequila, and I don't mean Cuervo. This stuff is labeled Durango. "I don't know why I feel the need to do this, because you just sounded like a true asshole, but this one's on me."

I can't tell if he feels sorry for me or if there is an air of condescension in his statement. "Well, thanks for the gift of bottom shelf hangover assurance." And the shot is down the hatch.

"Oh, I don't think you need any help making your way to the morning hangover." Condescension. It's clear this is not a feeling sorry for me moment. I could object to this treatment, but the shame I am feeling overrides any potential feeling of being wronged by a guy who just gave me a free drink.

There is a tap on my shoulder and as I am wheeling around on my barstool I say, "I am so sorry, Sweethe—" I jump to my feet. "Mr. Brown!"

"Feelin' better, Cotter?"

...

"I would think gettin' rest when you're not feelin' well is something that would happen at home."

"Yes, well...um." I don't see any way I can lie to get myself out of this one. "I actually am not feeling better, sir. In fact, I am feeling much worse now, but I am not sick." Now all of a sudden I feel a pang of betrayal. "Wait, Rebecca called you?"

"What?" His look of confusion turns to realization of what I am asking. "No, Cotter. I am here takin' my lunch break. You understand you leave me little choice as far as your employment is concerned. Despite you being a real good worker, I can't have people callin' in sick when they ain't. Definitely not so they can be in a bar drinkin'. You know I had another employee out today because he attended a funeral, so I've been at the college bustin' it all mornin'. I doubt I need to explain to you my displeasure at findin' you in here, like this." He got up to move.

"Mr. Brown, wait, you have to let me explain."

He waves my words away without looking back as he moves back towards the front door. "No, I don't have to let you explain. I don't owe you nothin'. Anyway, I can't imagine what you could say at this point to change any of this."

"But, Mr. Brown." It's bad timing but I feel the shot of tequila getting me back into my previously acquired drunken state and my thoughts change to things much less important at this moment. "Do you own this joint?"

He turns and looks at me with a look that seems to combine surprise with utter disdain. "No, Cotter, I do not own this establishment and don't bother showin' up to work in the mornin'. You're fired." He is already out the door before I can raise any objections, but he was right anyway. What could I say to him at this point?

Wheeling back around to the bar, I see that my friendly bartender has not only finished mixing my drink, but he is currently pouring another shot of tequila. This time, however, the shot is gliding silkily out of a bottle of Patrón. I look up at him and he says, "Don't worry, this one is also on me." Now he is looking at me like I am the saddest sap he has ever seen in his life. Now it *is* a feeling sorry for me free shot, but it doesn't feel any better this way. "Just do me a favor and make your way out of here before someone calls to tell you someone close to you died. I don't think I want to see you beat down any harder and I can't afford to comp your entire bill."

5

This bed I am waking in feels strange. Maybe this is because I have ended up in some stranger's bed, or because I am fully clothed on the top of the bedding. I can't quite figure it out yet because I am either still drunk or so hungover that I am struggling to recognize my surroundings. Wait, there's my Echo Spot on the nightstand. Okay, the good news is I have ended up in my room. The bad news is I have no idea how I made it back here. I must have blacked out. I am trying to see what time it is, but I can't bring the clock face into focus. "Alexa. What time is it?"

"4:13 a.m."

Ugh. I somehow made it home and into my own bed. Why can't I just sleep this off? I am rolling over onto my side, closing my eyes to go back to sleep when I have the realization of the happenings of the previous evening. Though the memories of last night had slipped away from me, they now flood back in vivid detail and I remember how I humiliated myself in front of Rebecca. No, that's not right. I remember how I humiliated Rebecca. I also remember how I let Mr. Brown down and lost my job. Somehow, it seems that my head has begun pounding ten times as hard as it was a moment ago. I thought it couldn't hurt any worse.

My eyes open wide now and they come into focus for the first time as I see the apparent reason for my early morning awakening. I can see through my bedroom window that there is a spotlight in the distance. My initial instinct is to just go back to sleep. My eyes are once more closed. Who even cares anymore? It has become quite clear there is nothing I can do about it anyway.

My eyes spring back open. Something is tugging at me and before I can even think about what I am doing, before I have even made a choice,

I am bouncing out of bed and standing in front of the elevator. Before I know it, I reach ground level and I am running out of the building and down the block. A moment ago, I just wanted to give up, accepting that I have no purpose in this crazy story, or maybe in this life. But now I am deciding, or something is deciding for me that I am not going to just lie there and let that bastard keep killing innocent people.

I can already see that the spotlight seems to be shining on someone on the other side of DuSable Bridge. I am approaching my side of the bridge now and the illuminated figure is heading across in my direction. I don't see anyone else around at the moment and I don't think it wise to keep running at full speed towards this person. We are walking towards each other and I am scanning the area for some creep in a hoodie. There isn't anybody around, not even a car on the street. The hairs start standing up on the back of my neck.

The bridge is not well lit, but as I am approaching the star of this show under the glow of a spotlight, I can see he is a black man wearing a dark trench coat and he has both hands in his pockets. At our current trajectories, he will be closest to the bridge railing and I will pass him on the right, closest to the street. We are within about thirty feet of each other and as I am beginning to study his face, I can see that he seems equally interested in studying mine. In fact, he is so preoccupied with me, that he is completely unaware of the man barreling across the street towards him. However, I have sensed him just in time to pick up a pace that should get me to his destination at about the same time.

I am running forward with eyes focused on the hoodie-wearing figure bolting towards the railing, but I allow a slight glance to see the man under the spotlight stopped and looking at me, quite surprised. My eyes are back on the attacker now and some instinct tells me his intention is to launch the man over the railing, so I dive towards him at the last moment. It's like slow motion and in the blinks between my leap and the impact with the hoodie-wearing freak, I see one hand come out of the trench coat with a gun. I pile into the attacker and we tumble to the ground. At first, I feel my weight on top of him, but as my momentum takes me past him, my face meets the sidewalk while my feet race ahead of me in what must have been one wicked-looking scorpion pose.

It felt like every vertebra in my spine must have popped, but I am quick to my feet as I think about the gun coming out of the moonlighter's pocket, and I begin sprinting away without even looking back. A shot rings out and I allow a glance to see if the man is giving chase. He has already turned and is running in the opposite direction, and I notice the spotlight has disappeared. The hoodie man is several paces behind me and I am surprised to see he is not chasing his prey, but instead running in the same direction as me. I allow myself to think for a moment that he doesn't want to contend with a gun, but as I quickly round two corners and he continues to run behind me, it is apparent that he is now chasing me.

I am running faster now and have done so for a couple more blocks before I begin to wonder how this guy hasn't caught up to me yet. There was no way I was going to catch him last time, so why has he chosen not to take me yet. I chance a look back and see that he is still about the same distance behind me as when we left the bridge. I also can see now that there is a slight limp in his step. I bet he was hit by that gunshot. Wait, he is still keeping pace with me after he has been shot!? I feel like I am about to keel over after running these few blocks and this guy is not losing ground, even with an injury. I might still be in trouble here.

Where is everybody? I know it's pretty early in the morning but there should be more people on the street. This guy has shown a desire to hide his crimes. Maybe if I can find a group of people, he won't pursue me any farther. But everything is closed at this hour, and I have hardly seen a soul on the street. Now I see it though, almost like there is a spotlight shining down upon it, a cross at the peak of a steeple. Yes, there must be people in this Catholic Church. I just hope it is unlocked.

I release the deep breath I have been holding as I open the unlocked door and dash forward between the pews. There is a light on over the sanctuary, but I don't see anyone around. Now I suddenly feel like I have put myself in a box. I feel trapped. Maybe my only hope now is to hide. When I first entered, my eyes were drawn immediately to the confessional stall, so I bolt over and hurry into the side that I think would be for the priest. I have barely sat down and I hear the front door of the church open.

Now that I have slowed down, I feel how exhausted I am. I also realize this is probably the most frightened I have been in my entire life. It seems I have slowed my frantic gasps for air, yet, I am shaking so badly that I must be making some noise. I hear something resembling the sole of a shoe scraping lightly on a dirty granite floor. That was right out front, in the sanctuary. The next sound I hear is the confessional curtain being pulled open and then closed, and now someone is sitting down on the other side of the latticed opening.

I hear a couple of deep breaths from the other side and then a sigh. Now a much calmer and less sinister sounding voice than I would have expected begins speaking, "I have no interest in hurting you. Especially not in a house of God. I just want to know why you have been following me and trying to stop me from doing the Lord's work."

"The Lord's work!? I'm not much for religion but I am pretty sure it doesn't condone people murdering others."

"Murdering? Are you kidding me? These are the lowest people on Earth we are being charged to dispatch."

I am calming down as we speak, but even though I know I am the voice of reason here, I am the one with heightened emotions in my voice. Regardless of any emotion he is feeling, he seems capable of speaking with a radio announcer voice. Not the deep one, but his sidekick that generally has more knowledge to go along with the not quite as silky voice. "I don't know what shade of crazy you are to think that you are killing with a purpose, but all I see is someone who is killing innocent people in the street, or on balconies. And I am not following you. Something brought me to those places, but I have no interest in sharing that with you at the risk of you thinking of me as crazy as I think you are."

I think I heard a slight chuckle, "You are speaking of the exit lights."

This comment shocks my system and I am sure I let out an audible gasp. I want to run. I don't want to engage with this killer, but I also see my first opportunity to get some answers about the thing that has been destroying my life. "You... I guess, I just thought it was crazy and I was the only one seeing them. I've been calling them spotlights." I shake my head to snap out of the moment, "But you are still just murdering people. I don't see how a spotlight shining on someone means that you are supposed to kill them. You're a freak."

"So, what? Do you think that these amazing lights are shining down from the heavens with pinpoint accuracy on individual people so that you and I can watch them act out a play? Have you heard any of them singing opera? Have you seen any of them acting out Shakespeare? No, these are the scum of this world, the worst of the worst. The exit lights are a sign from our one true God that we are to rid this place of their vile existence."

"Just so you know, I am hearing you out because I have been dealing with this for months and you are the only one I have been able to talk to about these phenomena I seem to be caught up in, but you are not convincing me that you are serving some kind of justice. You look like you are murdering people, so I hear a murderer talking. Besides, you may be able to say these lights aren't for people who are performing some act on a stage, but who are you to judge that they are performing evil acts in their lives? You're right to think that I have no understanding of why this is happening, but you're wrong to assume you know they are evil people."

"This is where I can say you are wrong. I am able to understand the evil in these individuals where you apparently are not. For when I lay my hands upon their bodies, not only am I able to see the mortal sins of their past, but I also catch glimpses of the savagery they have yet to unleash on the good people of this Earth. You dare to call these people innocent, but you clearly have no idea how innocent the numbers are they stand to hurt if they are not dealt with promptly. I tell you now, you have no idea the ramifications of our failure to dispatch that man on the bridge."

It is just now that I remember the gunshot. "He hit you with that shot, didn't he? You should probably let me go and call an ambulance for you."

"Nice try. No need to worry about me, this is simply a wound of the flesh. I have had worse. And you do not need to bother plotting an escape from this booth or this church. I will be allowing you to leave this place unscathed. I do need you to leave me to my business or join me in the endeavors, but otherwise, I have no quarrel with you. Besides, there is no exit light shining upon you, so I have not been granted heavenly authority to send you on your way."

"Heavenly authority. You should hear yourself from this side of the confessional. You are truly bat shit crazy, but let me humor you for a moment. If you do know how evil these people are, then tell me, what had the man on the bridge done?"

"I do not know."

"Exactly."

"I cannot know because you did not allow me to put my hands on him. However, I can tell you something about the man on the balcony. He must have held some seat in government because I saw that he would be helping pass a major piece of legislation that would be opening our borders much more than they are now to immigrants."

"Give me a break. Yeah, he was a democratic senator from California who was in town to discuss the massive waste of dollars on border control. I read the newspaper too, ya know. And I don't see a mortal sin here anyway."

"Well, I generally do not catch the news and had not seen that, but believe what you want to believe. Now if you want to hear what else I saw, I will finish... okay. In his past, I caught glimpses of abuse and rape. In his future, I saw him kill one of a few prostitutes that must have been coming to his room that night. In addition, as I said before, I could see this piece of legislation passing. The problem with that was what I saw afterward. That man was going to run a human trafficking ring that would make any other look minuscule. You can't imagine the number of individual lives and families that were going to be destroyed."

Don't worry, I am not feeding into this psychobabble, but I can't help but be curious about what a mind so different than mine can be thinking to justify such heinous crimes. "And what did you see within the guy you killed on the street?"

"Which guy on the street?"

"*Which* guy on the street?! How many guys have you killed on the street?! The guy with the wool suit. The one you pushed in front of the bus." Now he has me thinking. "Jesus Christ! How many people have you killed!?"

"Jesus Christ didn't kill anyone. He graced this Earth to become what you see above that alter out there, a murdered sacrifice to cleanse this world of sin. Only, the sin still exists until we leave this place, hence the work we still have left to rid the most evil."

"You know what I mean—"

"Yes, I do know what you meant. But I do not think it wise to use the Lord's name in vain, especially in this place."

I couldn't help the sarcasm, "Well, forgive me father, for I have sinned. But aren't you being a bit of a hypocrite, Killer."

"Thousands by dozens."

"Excused me?"

"You asked how many people I have sent on from here."

"Oh, dear Lord. You have killed thousands?"

"No, I have saved thousands by ridding the world of dozens. I am sure there have not been one hundred, but I have not tried to keep count. Don't get me wrong, I have been working diligently, but it has only been a few months that I have been tasked to do this work for God."

It is not beyond me to realize he may have only been seeing the spotlights for the same amount of time as I have. However, his months might mean longer than my couple of months. Regardless, I am done sharing anything with this creep. I feel the need to keep some of this to myself. "So, what visions...," I can't help but chuckle at this ridiculous question, "did you see when you pushed the wool-suit-man?"

"Ah, yes. I was not aware you had seen him. In his past, I saw molestation of multiple young boys. Very young boys. In his future, I saw that he would become one of the most infamous serial rapists this city has ever seen. These glimpses showed him taking mostly teenage boys and vulnerable adult men."

"You say you get these visions when you touch these people under the spotlights. You couldn't have had your hands on that man for more than a split second. How could you possibly... I mean, hypothetically, if one could actually see such visions, how could you see that much with only a slight touch?"

"It all flows through my mind in an instant. I see what you are getting at, but it is not as if movie clips are playing to me in real-time. The information just becomes mine. Now that I think back on it, I can see these things playing out in real-time, but in those moments, it all just rushes in and I instantly know the evil that has come to pass, along with the evil that will come to pass."

"You say it all like it is factual. How could you possibly know for a fact that these things have happened or future events will happen? Again, if I were to believe you, and I don't, wouldn't you be worried that you were wrong? There is no way for you to know."

"I was hesitant at first. Even after I placed my hands on the first person I saw under the exit light and had a vision of her murdering her parents before going home to murder her three children, I did not do anything about it. I did watch the news though, and sure enough, within a couple of days I saw the exact incident reported, and I recognized the picture of the woman to be the very woman I saw under the exit light. Now I don't wait for news stories."

I have to get out of here. This guy is too calm and sure about all of this. He has me feeling the need to shake my head as if I need to snap out of a trance. "Well, these are all great stories and I am sure someone can write an entertaining novel about you once you're on death row. You said you were going to let me leave, so I think I will be going now. I can't promise to stay out of your way though, because we clearly do have something in common. While I may not believe in your God, I do see the same spotlights, or exit lights, whatever, and I guess I have no reason to think anything other than it meaning I am supposed to save these people from the real evil... you."

"You don't believe in God? Why would you find sanctuary in this place?"

"Well, let's see, I was just trying to find any place to get away from your crazy ass!"

"I think you will find we have much more in common than you think. I will pray that the Lord can break through and flow into your heart. Then maybe, in time, you will see the good work we have been tasked to complete."

I am laughing out loud now. "You are going to pray for me? Please, pray for yourself. You keep talking about praying, God, and sin. Do I need to spell out your sins?! M-U-R-D-E-R!" I stand and begin to exit the confessional. "I hope the next time I see you it is in handcuffs."

"Let me ask you one more thing before you go. How do you expect to get the law onto me?"

"You are murdering people in the middle of Chicago! There are hundreds of people around you when you do it. How crazy are you to think you are not being seen? I have seen you kill twice already!"

"Can't you see that God is protecting us during these missions? He gives us an easily identifiable target during a time when we can easily see an opportunity to dispatch them. However, He does not stop there. He also provides the protection we need to remain in the shadows, to do His work undetected."

"But I have seen you!"

"Of course you have. We are on the same mission, Brother! Tell me, do you know of anyone else who has seen the exit light? Or me for that matter?"

I am getting frustrated because I felt this moment coming. As easily as I could debunk the things he has said, I have no comeback for this because I know the spotlights are not being seen by others. I know he is not being seen by others. "I'll concede this one point to you. Nobody else has seen the spotlights, and it appears that you have been shifty enough to make your murders appear as accidents or suicides. But I have told the cops about you."

"So, tell me. What did they say?"

Stupid. Why did you even say that, Cotter? I have nothing to add here that will help me talk sense. "Well, they have told me there are no other witnesses who say they saw you. And, they shared with me that they haven't found any evidence to suggest the incidents were anything other than accidents or suicides."

"Exactly. This information does not surprise me. And that must be why you haven't called them for help right now, because I am sure you have a cell phone."

Right, because conversations with them have just been getting worse and worse for me, but I am not going to give him the satisfaction of even responding to his accurate revelation. Suddenly, I remember something. "In fact, I don't know when you had time to place the senator's cell phone on the balcony ledge, but that gave the detective a tidy little theory about how he must have accidentally fallen over the edge."

"Again, something to further explain God's protection, because I did not touch a cell phone up there. It must have been part of His plan to protect me, His servant."

I have the curtain pulled aside and am already walking away, "Whatever you want to believe." I don't know why I feel the need to show confidence, but I am just keeping a steady pace as I walk around the front of the pews and start down the aisle. I want to look back to see if he is pursuing me, but I am once again terrified and the thought of even looking is severely freaking me out. I also feel the need to see his face so I can identify him, but I just keep walking.

I have the front door open before I hear the other curtain on the confessional slide, and as I start to run through the door, I hear that sidekick announcer voice, "I will be praying for you." The tremendous fear I feel in this moment stiffens my spine in a way that almost sends me straight-legged down the steps, but I save my footing and pick up the pace as I begin to run home faster than I ever knew I could.

6

This morning I thought long and hard about going to the police with the events of last night, but I have decided there is no point. I have already put myself in a strange position with them because they have no understanding of how I could just coincidentally be at the scene of two strange deaths in such a short span of time. To introduce a third would certainly draw suspicions that I just don't need right now. Perhaps the only reason the thought lingered long enough to require a debate in my head was because I have an urge to see Detective Keller again. I feel bad about Rebecca, but I just can't help it. I keep thinking about that woman.

Even though I hardly slept during the night, I started walking from home quite early this morning without a clue as to where I was heading. Now I am standing on the sidewalk in front of the college, staring at the front door. I guess subconsciously I have not given up on my job. I don't think it's because I really need the job or that I even like it, but I think I can't live with how I let Mr. Brown down. It's actually kind of strange because I haven't even been working here that long, yet, I have made some kind of connection with Mr. Brown and he has been so kind to me that I just can't let it end like I did.

I found Mr. Brown getting a mop and bucket ready in the cafeteria. "Good morning, Mr. Brown."

"Cotter, what are you doin' here? Oh, let me guess. I suppose I can understand you not rememberin' all the events of the other night, so I will say again that you're fired."

"No, I remember you saying I was fired, but I just hoped you might give me a minute and just hear me out."

"You've had me downright pissed off, but I have to admit that I do still like you, Cotter, so what is it that you want to say?"

"Well, I am sure you feel like I was lying to you, but I actually was not feeling well that morning." Mr. Brown tilts his head and gives me that *don't you dare* look. "Not like I was physically ill, but I just was not okay, you know?"

He is starting back at his work now as he says, "Nope, I do not know, and I need to get to work with how short-staffed I am now."

"Okay, wait, the thing is that I have seen two people die recently." Now he pauses and shoots me a surprised glance. "And the second one was just that night before I called-in to you. I guess I did not explain it to you, but I was not simply bailing out of work, I really was not feeling myself."

"Well, that sounds terrible. But I am still not sure if it's a valid excuse for me to find you drunk in a bar after you had called in sick to work." He starts back into his work, but pauses again, "Or, maybe I can understand a little. I guess it's not like I never drowned my sorrows in booze before, but still, you've already had some poor attendance." He starts working again.

"I know, Mr. Brown, and I really do feel bad about how that went down in the restaurant. Mostly because I knew that I let you down and that mattered to me, so I am just hoping you'd reconsider so I could make up for disappointing you."

"Shoot, I hardly know you, Cotter. I'm not as much disappointed in you as I am pissed off that I can't keep people working here." If I was hoping for a warm, caring moment with Mr. Brown, it just flew out the window. "So, yes, but only because I am in desperate need of a body, I will let you come to work today." At least I got the job back and I don't have to feel like crap about one more thing.

"Thank you, sir. You won't regret changing your mind."

"Yeah, just take this mop and get to work. People already makin' messes with their breakfast this mornin'."

He wasn't exaggerating. It has amazed me in my short time working custodial at Loyola University how messy the students can be. I mean, these aren't exactly kids. They are adults now, and they still don't always take care of the messes they make. I know I have my own issues, but at least I have the decency not to leave my stuff for other people to clean up. It's easy to wonder what kind of squalor these students might live in, but then you have to realize how expensive this college is. These are probably individuals coming from upper-class families. Maybe they are used to maids cleaning up after them.

I guess this is something that has definitely gotten on my nerves with this job. What really irritates me is when I am around some of these students and it becomes apparent they intentionally leave something for me to pick up. I have watched and they don't seem to do it with the older custodians. I think they target me because I am around their age, and they like making me pick up after them. Like right now, a group is getting up from a table and a guy is looking right at me as he leaves his Styrofoam coffee cup right in the middle of the table. He chuckles and tips it over, spilling some remnants of coffee on the table as they walk away.

I think I am on my way over there to say something to this guy when I am drawn to the sounds I hear from the television I walk under. "Initial reports are that the man murdered seven people before being cornered by police and taking his own life. This was a crime spree that officials say started sometime after five o'clock this morning and did not end until police caught up with the killer around seven o'clock. The first five victims appeared to be shot at random as they sat in, or were getting into their vehicles. The last two victims were employees at a Starbucks where the suspect was cornered and committed suicide. The victims' identities are being withheld until the next of kin is notified. The suspect has been identified as Aaron Turay."

This sinking feeling started dropping in my stomach from the first words of the news report, and now I already know what I am going to see before I see it. A picture of the suspect pops up on the screen. Of course, it is the man with the gun on the bridge this morning. I didn't get a great look at him, but it's pretty clear that it's him. Regardless of how unsure I am about the face, my gut tells me that it is him. This can't be happening. I can't help but think of the possibility that the hoodie guy is actually telling the truth. No way, I push that thought aside as quickly as it pops into my head. It just has to be a coincidence.

***

Lunchtime arrived so quickly that I didn't realize the time and I missed the first part of it. I just could not get my mind off the conversation in the church and the news report I heard. I do not believe for a second that he is actually getting directions from God, but this is all so crazy. I mean, what am I thinking right now? I don't even think I believe in God and that creep has me wondering if he is getting signs from Him. I think I was at least feeling some relief after finding out that I wasn't the only one seeing the spotlights, but now this news story. *It's your fault all those people died, Cotter, because you saved their killer's life on the bridge!* I haven't even had time to feel like a hero or anything after that moment on the bridge, and now I am feeling responsible for a bunch of deaths. Wow, how the tables have turned.

Mr. Brown sent one of the other custodians to alert me to the fact that I was missing lunch. We are walking to the little break room in the back of our maintenance building and I am only interested in my own thoughts, but this guy wants to chat and he clearly hasn't caught on that I wasn't interested, so I engage just enough to avoid feeling rude. I had seen this guy around but hadn't really talked to him yet. "So how about you, Cotter, have any kids yet?" He's probably in his late thirties and had been talking about his wife and kids.

"Me? No, I'm only twenty-one, man."

"Hey, you never know these days. Young people think that getting to know each other means sexting and, well, having sex. So, I sure wouldn't want to just assume you haven't had kids yet."

"Wait. Is that seriously how the young people of today are viewed? I mean, I do realize how technology can interfere with social skills, but you painted that picture to look rather bleak. I don't see it as being that dark."

"Well, then consider yourself to be a part of the minority, my friend. I overheard a speaker on campus just the other day who laid out some scary statistics. And he also talked about how normal it is for young people to be sending each other nudes."

"Nudes?"

"You know. Dick pics? Twat shots?"

"No, yeah, I know what you're saying. I guess you're just

throwing me for a loop with this conversation."

"The worst part about it is they just don't know what they are getting themselves into. The speaker said this generation was just handed this technology without any real guide or anything, so being kids and all, they don't know the real ramifications of sending all this stuff electronically. He said that we are generating the statistics right now that future generations will learn from. Want to know a crazy statistic I heard him throw out?"

I sarcastically respond, "Yes?"

"He said that eighty-eight percent of teens' nudes get re-posted to parasite websites!"

"What? That is a pretty crazy number. Parasite websites? What exactly does that even mean?"

"That's the number he said and he seemed pretty official. The college must have paid him to come here and speak, so I would trust him I guess. He did kind of explain parasite websites. I think it was about them being shared. Like, if it was sent to a boyfriend, they would eventually share it with somebody and it eventually is posted or something. Oh! But he also talked about people being paid or making money by hacking into cell phones and stealing the pics and posting them on websites."

"Wait, holy shit. I hope all of that isn't true. But I guess there are plenty of crazy people out there who would do stuff like that. I mean, it's not that uncommon for celebrities to be hacked, but I would have never thought that type of thing would be so common with average people. What were the kids who were sitting in with this speaker doing, how did they respond?"

"Ha! Most of them were on their phones!"

"Nice."

Mr. Brown doesn't generally eat his lunch in here with us but he walks through at this moment. I snicker to myself as I realize I now know he is probably returning from Mr. Brown's Lounge. As he passes the table he says, "Sorry to hear about your uncle, Jerry."

"Thanks, Mr. Brown," I can tell he is waiting for Mr. Brown to pass through and leave the room before he adds, "but I wasn't sad that he died, son of a bitch got what he had coming to him. Only thing is, it was well overdue."

"Oh, you were the one at the funeral the other day then? You clearly weren't fond of the guy, so why go to the funeral?"

"I have been waiting for that bastard to be put into the ground for a long time. You think I was going to miss that? He was lower than the lowest scum of the earth and I am glad he is finally dead!"

"Jeez, man, take it easy."

"Don't tell me to take it easy! You have no idea what I've been through because of that man! No, not man, that is too good a way to name him. That monster!" He seems really upset.

"You're right. Sorry, Jerry. I don't know anything about what might have happened there. I just was curious and maybe I shouldn't have asked anything." He takes a deep breath and seems to move from anger to a deeper sadness.

"No, I am sorry for raising my voice, it's okay that you asked about it. It's something that I am not afraid to talk about anymore. I mean, it was a long time ago that I became willing to talk about it, but I just don't think I ever really had closure, so maybe that is why the emotion is bubbling over again like it used to. Now that he is finally dead, at least I know he can't hurt anyone anymore." He has tears in his eyes now.

"Did he abuse you?" Jerry nods his head. "Sexually?" Another nod.

"But it was so much worse than how that just sounded. He would come stay at our house every once in a while when we were kids. That's when he would always do stuff to my brother and me. I won't give you details, you don't need to imagine it in your head like I see it, but I will tell you that I am talking about full-on penetration."

"Oh my god! Well, didn't he go to jail or something?"

"No, we never told. He would say stuff to us that made us feel like we needed to keep quiet."

"I don't understand that. What could he possibly say that would get you not to tell?"

"You're right, you don't understand, it's not so easy for a child as you must think."

I realize my offensive comment, "Sorry, I just feel bad for you."

"He would tell us that our mom wouldn't love us anymore if we said anything, that she would be so ashamed that she would just send us to an orphanage. Sometimes he would say that he would just come back and kill our mom if we told anyone, and then he would be given custody of us and would do those things to us every night. That was all bad, but the threat he would make that always scared the shit out of me was saying that he would cut our penises off. I remember he would always follow that one up with the same joke. He would say, 'Actually, maybe you two sissies would enjoy such a eunuch experience.' I can hear his evil cackle right now. Boy, he would laugh long and hard at himself every time. Of course, I never even got his little joke until learning that word while reading the bible as an adult."

I can't imagine the look on my face right now. I don't even know what to say to this guy. This has to be the worst thing I have ever heard in my life, at least from a first-hand account. Finally, I am able to swallow hard and say, "Well, Jerry. You really seem to have come out of it well." He looked at me as if he was going to get mad again. "I mean, you told me about your wife and kids. That all sounded really good. I can imagine it's taken a lot for you to get to this point in your life is all, and it seems good. So, good for you, man."

"Yeah, well, thanks I guess. Too bad my brother couldn't be here, living a similar life, or a better life for that matter."

Like it can't get any worse, and I don't want to ask, but I do. "What happened to your brother?"

"He hung himself in the garage. He was nine years old."

What could I possibly say? "We better get back to it, lunch break has been over for about ten minutes." We both stand up and walk towards the doorway. "So, what ended up happening to your uncle? How did he die?"

Jerry still has tears welled up in his eyes, but he smirks and says, "The coward threw himself in front of a bus! I heard it squashed his head like a melon at a Gallagher comedy show!"

1

I've done a masterful job of avoiding my parents since our falling out. This evening I was able to slip in the front door and into my room without even feeling their presence anywhere nearby. It's not that I don't want to talk to them, I just don't think they can help me and I don't need the lectures on top of everything else I am dealing with. Mom has been quite intentional about leaving a plate of food out on the half-moon table in the hallway. I have not been so prideful as to not take these opportunities for sustenance. However, it does bring a sense of guilt since I refuse to soften up and speak with her.

I have been sending Rebecca so many texts, but she just ignores me. I can't blame her. Still, it leaves me with a deep sense of loss. The funny thing is that I don't even know if I want to be with her anymore, but I don't know that I want to lose her either. Really, everything is pretty messed up for me right now. I am actually having trouble thinking up one aspect of my life that isn't in turmoil. Detective Keller keeps popping into my head and I am guilty about that because I feel like I treated Rebecca poorly. But really, did I do anything wrong? If anything, I was honest with her about my thoughts. Thoughts that I just couldn't help.

I need to fix this before it drives me insane. I am calling Rebecca. This is the first attempt at communicating with her beyond the obsessive number of text messages I have sent her. It only rings a couple of times before it kicks to voicemail. Before she probably kicked me to voicemail. *This is Rebecca. Please leave a message and I will get back to you as soon as possible, unless this is the asshole formerly known as my boyfriend.* Well, that settles it. I am not even leaving a message because she definitely hates me. She would never want to have a voicemail message with her cursing. For her to put this out there for anyone she cares about to hear, she has to be loathing the individual responsible for making her want to say it. That individual is me.

***

I open my eyes to some sunlight slipping through the curtains and realize I am waking up from a full night of sleep for the first time in what seems like forever. *It is sad that you have to wake up being surprised it wasn't a spotlight that woke you up.* The next thought is almost an anxious one. I actually am feeling worried that I might have missed one. That I might have missed an opportunity to save someone. Or maybe this is becoming such the norm, such a part of my life that there is disappointment when a period of time passes without one. What a sick thought.

No work for me today, but I have to get out of here. I guess I will take some clothes down to Mr. Zetticci's shop. I open my bedroom door and my mother is standing there, apparently having just placed a couple of fresh cinnamon rolls on the half-moon table outside my door. They smell sweet and spicy and it's as if, for a moment, my mother is defined by a simple smell, and it's delightful. She looks at me with a softness that can't be denied, but I guess my posture and look is one of stubbornness as she seems hesitant to speak or move in for the hug that I know she wants.

I let out a breath that is so heavy it feels like I have released days' worth of air. I feel like I have let go of all the anger, sadness, confusion, pride and everything else that I am failing to understand about myself lately. My shoulders slump and it's in this moment that my mother steps forward and embraces me. We hold the hug for longer than normal as I release emotions I haven't felt in some time.

"I was just going to take some clothes to the cleaners. Is there anything you'd like me to bring down there?"

She pulls back and wipes some tears away from her bright blue eyes that are now also red from the tears. I can't help but wonder how I can be responsible for something so beautiful looking so much different. "Your father does have some clothes you could take with you, but would you sit with me for a bit before you go? I have some fresh coffee to go with those rolls."

I fight the flight urge that I am feeling and say, "Sure."

I pour my own cup of coffee and then sit down to start working at the rolls that apparently bring my sensory memory to some special mom place. "Cotter, I hope you know that I don't care if you are going to school in a college or working in a college. I just care that you are safe and well. I love you more than I could ever tell you and anything I say is truly out of concern for you."

"I know. There are just things that I can't even explain to myself, and, well maybe I should not have scared you by trying to tell you about it. All I can say is, as crazy as it all sounded, it's really happening. It's bizarre. It's scary. But it's also real and I can't explain it."

"I don't want to say the wrong thing right now... Please hear this statement and try not to take it out of context, Cotter. I believe that you have something going on that is, or seems, very real to you and I am willing to do anything in my power to help you."

I know the sigh I release is audible or visible. "You just can't believe it, can you? I should have never said anything."

"Honey, please don't get defensive. I don't know what to believe. I'll never be able to see what you've seen through your eyes, that's your journey. I just need to know what I can do to help you. Your father and I have talked a lot about what we should do. I am not sure we came up with anything great, but we would certainly help you find a good counselor." I feel my eyes impulsively roll a little as I look away and her voice sounds panicked. I can imagine she feels like she is losing whatever ground she has made up with me. "Or... or, whatever you need."

"If I thought I was going crazy, I would tell you." I feel a tinge of anger and I know I am getting defensive, but I don't want to hurt my mom. "It's probably best if I just grab the clothes and get out for a little while. Maybe that will be good for me."

***

I walk into the dry cleaning shop with a lot of attitude and it must have shown on my face because Mr. Zetticci doesn't even chuckle after he says, "Aye, welcome back, Cotter! Sun is shining today, why you look so down?" I shrug as I look around to see an empty store, which is rare.

"Well, I can't have you in my store looking like that, it's bad for business." I look around to signal to Zetticci that there is no other business in the store, but my gesture goes unnoticed. "How many flies does it take to screw in a lightbulb?"

"I don't know, how many?"

"Two, but I can never figure out how they get in there!" I guess I do think this one is kind of funny so I smile and chuckle. I wait for Zetticci to stop his wheezy little laugh and I hand the garments over to him. He snaps up from his doubled-over position, tears off the perforated portion of a ticket and hands it to me as he takes the clothes. Amazingly, I can see that he had already noted the garments on his half of the dry cleaning ticket. He must have been jotting it down as I walked in the door, but it is hard to believe that I didn't even notice. The man would be extremely annoying to me if I didn't find him so damn interesting.

Walking out of Zetticci's place, I have no idea what I am going to do now, but I just have no desire to go home. I can't handle these conversations with my parents. I have no doubt they care about me, but nobody is going to believe what is going on with me so I know any conversations with them will just be a setup for me to lose my cool and disappoint them more than I already have.

I think I am walking absentmindedly down the street, just heading wherever my feet happen to take me until I realize that my subconscious must have had something else in mind because I am heading right past Dark Cravings. No doubt to see if Rebecca might be around. I am almost in front of the door before I make this realization and I start to wheel back around because I don't think I really want to see Rebecca. I mean, she clearly wants nothing to do with me, and I just don't know what I want from her anymore anyway. Maybe I just don't like things ending so negatively.

I am walking away from the door now, but in my peripheral vision, I see a shadow through the window seem to hurry towards the door. Sure enough, I stop in my tracks as someone says, "Cotter, are you trying to avoid me?" Here it comes…

Wait, but that isn't Rebecca's voice. I spin on my heels, surprised, "Oh, Detective Keller, what are you doing here?" Idiot. She's going to jump on you over that question.

"What do you mean? Can't a professional gal let her hair down, go for a run and grab some coffee on her day off? Oh, did you not know that detectives were just people when they aren't working?"

It is funny how after only a moment together the other night I read her well enough to know she would be a smart ass with any ignorance that comes her way. However, while I expected a smart response to my greeting, it was a cold or defensive sarcastic comment that I expected. Instead, she said this in a soft and playful way and it surprises me. I also can't help but notice that she is wearing running tights and a rather slim-fitting top. Her hair is pulled back in a ponytail and her face is a little red still from running I guess, but she still looks really good.

"Ha-ha. I think I was just surprised to see you, but you're right, that was a dumb question."

"Well, you definitely looked surprised since you bailed at the door to avoid me."

"Wait, what?"

"You looked like you were coming in here and you suddenly turned and hurried away."

"Oh, it's not like that. You see, I thou—"

"Oh, don't worry about it. You don't have to explain to me. I wouldn't want to run into me if I were in your position either."

"No, seriously, I didn't even know you were in there."

"Well, it was clear you were turning away from something."

"Yes, you are a good detective." She tilts her head and makes a face that equally shows appreciation and distaste for my sarcasm. "I actually hadn't realized I was walking past this coffee shop and it is a frequent stop for my ex-girlfriend."

Detective Keller looks over her shoulder, through the shop window. "Oh, she is here."

"No. Well, I guess I don't know." I scan the tables. "She doesn't appear to be."

"Wow. You must really be dreading running into her if you reacted like that at just the thought of passing her favorite java hut. You must have really hurt her. Oh… or this is really recent I bet?"

"No… no. I didn't cheat on her or anything and, yeah, plenty of time has passed." I lied. It's only been days. Maybe because I've been pulling away for longer is why I think it's okay to say this. Or, maybe I just know it's going to sound better if it wasn't recent, like I have a chance with this woman or something. *You're an idiot, Cotter.*

"So, now that you know she isn't in there, are you going to come in and have a cup? You can join me if you'd like and we can chat."

"Detective Keller, I told you everything I know about that incident the other night, and it was all the truth. So I don't really have an interest in going over that stuff anymore."

"Whoa, defensive much? Did you not hear me say that I was not working? Do I look like I am working? I was just trying to be nice and see if you wanted to chat, but that's fine, I get it. It was good to see you and please take care of yourself." She scans me from head to toe and back up again, "You don't look so good." She turns and goes back through the coffee shop door.

That comment would have stung more if she wasn't right. I mean, I haven't been sleeping right, eating right, well… doing anything right. How could I look good? I only think about walking away for a split second and then I open the door and walk up to the counter. I can see that Detective Keller had her back to me as she walked back to her table and when she turns to sit down, she glances out the window. Apparently seeing that I was gone, her shoulders slump a little. She picks up her phone and buries her face in it without realizing I am at the counter.

As I finally walk over with my coffee, she is quite surprised looking up from her cup, "What? I totally thought you had left. What are you drinking?"

"A depth charge." I can see by her look that she isn't familiar. "It's just a shot of espresso in a cup of black coffee. Well, actually, I asked for an extra shot so this one has two shots of espresso."

"Jeez. So you are either a caffeine fiend or you need a pick-me-up. You are kind of intense, Cotter. I do like black coffee but I always feel the need to have something a little different when I go to a coffee shop. This is a mocha with toasted marshmallow and a little cayenne pepper." I can't help it, I burst out laughing. "What? Why are you laughing?"

"You call me intense when you have coffee with cayenne pepper in it!"

"What? It's a great combination." She smiles and laughs with me. "Here, try it." She hands me her coffee and I take a sip.

"Okay, I'll give you that. It is good, but still. I am not sure that there is much difference in our levels of excessiveness here. And, yes, if it was actually a question, I like this drink anyway, but I definitely need a little pick-me-up too. I have not been sleeping much at all. Maybe that's part of the reason you don't think I am looking too go—."

"Hey, I wasn't saying you don't look good."

"No, no. Now it's my turn to tell you no need to explain. And for the record, you did tell me I don't look good, but, I am not unaware of my current state of being. It's just been a lot for me to take in recently and I have been left with little time for sleep."

"Oh, I can imagine. I don't always do well with sleep after some of the things I have to look at. Fortunately for me, I am arriving on scenes after the events have unfolded. So while I can empathize, I guess I haven't had to bear witness to horrific deaths like you have."

"How long have you been a detective anyway? I mean, I'm not trying to be rude and ask your age or anything, but you must have worked your way up rather quickly because you can't be that old?"

"No, that's a fair question. I have been a homicide detective for less than six months. I was promoted shortly after I turned twenty-four. My time on the force had not been everything I was hoping for. Believe it or not, a female police officer doesn't just get sent out on the street to dig into all the important police work. I decided I needed to find a way to get out of the office and do something that felt... fulfilling I guess."

"Good for you. Did you always know you wanted to be a cop?" Her demeanor changes immediately when I ask this question. She looks like she is in pain.

"Well, there is a lot to that story, but the short version is that my father was murdered when I was young. So, yes, I knew from an early age that I wanted to be a cop. I knew that I wanted to try to stop little girls from losing their dads due to crime." She smiles. "And how about you, what have you grown up to be, Cotter Trespin?"

I let her evade that pain and change the subject. "Well, Detect… or…" I chuckle, "what should I be calling you? I don't even know your first name."

Straight faced she responds, "Detective Keller, just call me Detective Keller." We are staring at each other, she is stone-faced at first and finally, she lets out a laugh. "Okay, my name is actually Genesis, but you can call me Genny."

"Wait, your name is Genesis, like from the bible? Interesting."

"Yes, we can't all have your everyday, normal names," and she overemphasizes, "Cotter!" and we both chuckle a little.

"Yeah, okay. I get it. So neither one of us have household names. I guess that means we are special, and maybe there is a more in-depth reason why we have met."

"No, it's pretty clear why we met. Remember? You have been hanging around places where people die." She looks surprised by her own words. "I'm sorry, that just came out."

I chuckle for her sake. "It's fine. Not like that isn't accurate."

"I talked to Detective Banner about the other death you witnessed. He told me you were as adamant there with him as you were with me the other night about seeing someone that was responsible for the death."

"Okay, so now that you've got me hooked into a conversation you want to interrogate me. I see what you have going on. I guess this wasn't as much a day off as you sugges—"

"Stop with the defensiveness, please. I am talking to you right now because I want to, on my personal time." I feel my posture relax again and I take a deep breath. "Listen, you moved the conversation in that direction and I was just telling you a little about what I had done to further investigate the situation. In fact, I was about to tell you that it seems to me you clearly believe in what you were telling both of us, and that means something to me. I can't sit here and tell you there is any evidence to support your allegations, but I can tell you that I want to hear what you have to say about it and help if I can."

I was listening so intently that I hadn't noticed that Genny reached across the table and placed her hand over mine. I look at our hands touching and then up to her face and she pulls her hand away and says,

"Sorry."

She is looking away now and when she looks back I am seeing such a softness in these unbelievably beautiful blue eyes, and I know she is really being vulnerable and sincere with me. "No need to be sorry. I am sorry, but not sorry." She slowly smiles and we both let out a semi-embarrassed little laugh.

"Cotter, I have always believed that some people can just sense things, and maybe that is why you ended up in these places. I mean, have you ever been drawn to such things at other times in your life?"

"No, this is a new thing."

"So I was right? You do feel you were drawn to these locations by a feeling?"

"It's way more complicated than that and there is no way I can explain it to you. You'd think I was crazy."

"You should try me. I have seen a lifetime of crazy things already in my relatively short life. And not all of them were easily explained in my mind, so I might surprise you with some understanding." She has me so relaxed and unbelievably trusting in her.

"Okay, I see spotlights shining down on the people that get killed." Genny just stared for a split second and then burst into laughter. "See, I told you." She stops suddenly, seemingly realizing I might not be kidding.

"You're being serious, aren't you?" I just tilt my head and give her a little raise of a brow. "Wow, okay, sorry I just thought you were messing with me. I have heard a few people speak of having telepathy or sensing things in some way, but you are speaking of some kind of vision. Like, you're implying that you're having some kind of premonition before these events happen?"

I am surprised, but it seems that she is engaging in this conversation, as if she is trying to believe me. "Well, I don't know if I would call it a premonition or not. You know, I am just seeing these lights and tracking them down to see what they are shining on. Wait, maybe it would be considered a premonition though because it has woken me up in the middle of the night before. I guess I did sense that the spotlight was there."

"Are you saying that was the case the other night when you ended up at the hotel in your pajamas?"

"Yes! That is exactly how that scenario played out. I woke up sensing something and when I looked out the window there was another spotlight, so I went to it."

"How long have you been seeing them? How many have you seen?"

"It's been going on for months now, but never before then. I can't say how many I have seen. Sometimes it has gone a week or so between sightings, but sometimes it happens on consecutive days." Something registers to me right now. "Wait, do you believe me?"

"Well, I am trying to, yes. I have to believe you were at both these places for a reason, and I don't have a reason not to trust what you're telling me." I must have let out an audible sigh. "What?"

"Oh, it's just a relief to have someone hearing me about all of this. I mean, I completely understand how crazy it sounds because I have to live it, but I am living it and anyone I have trusted has just looked at me like I was crazy or tried to explain it away. Except for the other guy who can see it I guess. Oh, yeah," I am remembering the most recent encounter, "I ended up having a conversation with the hoodie guy."

"What! Why didn't you call me...or did you at least call the police?! How did you find him?"

"I followed another spotlight a couple nights ago and tackled him before he could push a guy off the bridge." The reports of the murders that guy committed after I saved him pop into my head. "Then the hoodie guy chased me into a church and we had a conversation through the screen of a confessional booth. Oh, and he was shot by the guy on the bridge. Maybe that will help you find him, but he said it wasn't bad."

"Holy shit, Cotter. This is a lot. Just slow down and tell me everything you can about him. What do you mean the guy shot him? Do you mean the guy you stopped him from doing something to on the bridge shot him?"

"Yeah, and that's the crazy thing he was telling me in that booth. He was trying to get me to believe that he is sent by God to kill the people under these spotlights. Wait, what did he call them... exit lights. Yeah, that's right, he called them exit lights." I'm distracted by my own thoughts as I remember how he referred to the lights.

"Cotter. What else did he say? And what was it about the guy on the bridge shooting him?"

"Oh... sorry, yeah the guy on the bridge shot him and he was so mad at me for stopping him from killing him. And he sounded so crazy how he was talking about being sent to do it, but then he actually had me thinking a little yesterday when I realized the guy who murdered those seven people was the guy from the bridge."

"What the hell? You are saying the mass shooting suspect, what was his name, Turay I think, was the man you saw on the bridge? You won't like this, but seven was only the initial report, and last night they found two more crime scenes from earlier. He had killed his family and then his parents so there were a total of twelve."

"Oh my god! I felt bad enough with seven!"

"Why would you feel bad, it's not like it was your fault?"

"I saved this guy and then he kills all these people. It sure feels like I had something to do with it."

"So you're telling me that you believe that he should be killing these people?"

"No! I think he is crazy."

"Then how can you blame yourself just because something bad happens after you did something good? It's not your fault, Cotter. You didn't pull that trigger for him."

"Well, I can't help it though. This murderer also said that he has visions, past and future, when he places his hands on these people. He told me about the two I had seen. The one who was pushed in front of the bus he said was a pedophile and was about to become a serial rapist."

"I don't think there was any kind of record on that guy though. He seemed like your average Joe."

"But that's the thing. I think he was just never caught before. Coincidentally, I had a conversation with that guy's nephew." She shoots me a confused look. "Because I work with him and I realized he was at his funeral. But he told me he wasn't sad because the guy had molested him, like in the worst way, when he was a kid."

"Wow. Still, could be a coincidence. Did he say anything about the

Senator?"

"Yep. That was even crazier. He said he was about to get laws changed on immigration or something, and then he was going to end up being like the worst human trafficker ever. I think he said there were prostitutes coming to his room that night, and he would have killed one."

Genny gasps at my last comment. "Hold on, did you see the prostitutes that night?"

"You mean on the balcony? No, I only saw the Sen —"

"No, I mean at all that night, like when you came back to the scene. When we talked or when you left."

"No, why would you ask that?

"Because three prostitutes showed up to the hotel and asked the clerk to ring that room."

"You're joking?! When was that? I didn't notice anyone but the front desk girl."

"This would have been later. I was already there so you must have still been away from the scene. They were probably still being questioned or maybe already gone by the time you returned."

"Yet another coincidence, you think?"

"Yeah, I don't know about that. Now you are talking about three events and there was seemingly information that could not have been known, or at least would have been very difficult to obtain. Maybe too many coincidences."

"So what does it mean. That guy makes it sound like I am stopping him from doing God's work. Hell, he acted like I was supposed to be doing it along with him."

"Well, I cannot advise that."

"Of course not. I haven't thought twice about any of this. He is a murderer and I certainly am not. It's just confusing that some of his crazy-ass claims are actually adding up."

"All I know is you have my heart racing right now."

"I tend to do that for women." She smiles and then laughs before I start to laugh with her. "Just kidding, of course. I'm not really that confident."

"Yeah, I think it was mostly because of what we were talking about and maybe just a little bit you." Wow, I am pretty sure she is flirting with me too. "Nonetheless, I do feel the need for some fresh air."

Disappointed at the abrupt end to this moment I say, "Okay, I'll let you get going then."

"Well I meant to allow you to walk me home, it's not too far. My apartment is just past Union Park."

"Yes, of course I can do that." Genny smiles and lets out a snicker. I realize that I had jumped up with what probably looked like more excitement than a kid skipping down Navy Pier. I feel my cheeks flush as I walk over and hold the door open for Detective Genesis Keller.

8

We slowly walked the two miles that got us as far as Union Park. We have talked about so much of our lives already that it seems we have known each other for a much longer time than we have. I found myself reflecting on how she was coming at me on the night we met. She seems so much different than she acted towards me at that moment. I guess a female detective has to be able to separate her professional and personal life. We are walking around Union Park now.

"My apartment is just on the other side of the park. Thank you for walking with me. It has been nice to have this time to chat more with you."

"It's no problem at all. Actually, it's been my pleasure. What a relief it has been to unload some of what I have been experiencing to someone who believes me. Well, I shouldn't assume you believe me, but at least you list—"

"I do believe you, Cotter. I mean, I should say that I believe you are experiencing these things. It is kind of hard for me to fully buy into things unless I can see some proof, but that doesn't mean I don't believe that others might have already seen that proof. So, yes, I do believe you are being honest with me about something you are seeing."

We are just past the park now and I can tell Genny is slowing down, implying to me that we are reaching the front of her residence. It is a nice looking house. "This is a great looking place you have here."

"Oh, don't think that it's my house or anything. I only rent an apartment inside part of the place. Did you think that young homicide detectives actually get paid enough to live outside of crime-riddled neighborhoods?" We both laugh. "I have decided it's actually a ploy to keep us in close proximity to our work to cut down on response time."

Another laugh as we reach the doorstep.

"You're a funny lady, Genesis. Quite different actually than how I pegged you to be when we met."

"Oh? And what did you think of me then, Cotter? You didn't like me at first? It seemed to me that you liked every inch of me, but then again, I only noticed you looking at every inch several times."

I'm really blushing now. Had I been that obvious? "Um... yeah, no, I definitely noticed you... your... yeah... everything."

"Well, if you can't use it to speak." She is leaning towards me and we kiss. This isn't just a peck on the cheek or lips. It is a full-on kiss and now I grab her around the waist and pull her body tightly to mine. I can't claim to have kissed many, but her lips are softer than any I have ever experienced. It feels like I am face down on a feather pillow. No, I don't practice kissing on my pillow. Her curvy body pressed against me is just about the nicest thing I have ever felt. With my arms around her, it feels like our bodies were made to fit together in this exact position.

The kiss finishes just when it feels like it should and she says, "I don't know what you thought about me when we met, but it sure feels like you like me now." If my cheeks weren't still flushed, they definitely are again now, but that isn't the only place my blood is rushing to. She has unlocked the door and as she steps inside it seems like she isn't even going to say anything as we part ways, but then she reaches out and grabs my hand and says, "Get in here!" as she pulls me inside and slams the door.

**

The first thought in my mind as I am waking up is about how hungry I feel. However, there is another thought taking priority at the moment. *Where am I?* It's pretty dark but there are street lights and now that I am looking around I quickly rollover to see Genny's bare back in the bed next to me. There is just enough ambient light slipping around the window shades for me to see several moles that remind me of tiny islands in an ocean of unbelievably smooth skin.

I am lightly touching her back, charting a course around the mole islands when she begins to stir and rolls over onto her back, exposing the mountains on her front side. Her body is as amazing as I had imagined it to be on the first night I saw her. I think it is more the norm that a lover's body ends up being much less than one might imagine through clothes, but Genny has certainly been an exception to that rule for me. It is only now that I begin remembering the events of the afternoon. *How many times did we lay here and make love in the moments between long conversations?*

Now Genny is opening her eyes and I can't believe how her blue irises penetrate the darkness. It's almost as if they are emanating some kind of force and I am so entranced by them that it feels like they are looking straight into my soul. She is such a beautiful woman. I can't believe this is happening. I think she is reading my mind as she smiles and says, "What did you do to me last night, Cotter? I am absolutely famished."

"And here I was thinking it was you that wore me out. I am hungry too, should we go get something to eat?"

"That's the best suggestion you have had since you asked to come inside earlier."

I start laughing, "What? You practically broke my neck jerking me through the doorway. So I am pretty sure that was your sugges—"

Now Genny is laughing and I realize what I misunderstood even before she says, "Sure, that's what I was referring too." She pulls me on top of her and we kiss with more passion than I think I have ever felt, even if you combined all the kisses in my lifetime. All of a sudden, her arms extend and I am flopped on my back as she jumps out of the bed and heads toward the bathroom. "I like you, Cotter Trespin, but a girl's gotta eat. Get dressed."

I expected Genny to take a little time to be ready but it feels like mere minutes and she comes out of her bathroom looking absolutely perfect. No words are necessary as she sees me scanning her body and probably looking like a grinning fool. She smiles and grabs my hand as we walk out her front door. We just start walking. I am not even sure who is leading so I say, "I know a place we ca—"

"I'll take us for some Chinese. I mean, I am not trying to be controlling, but I do need to keep a low profile with this."

I shoot her a look, "Wait. You mean you don't feel like you can be seen with me?"

"Now just hold on, Big Shot Cott." I cringe a little inside as that felt like a pet name Rebecca would have called me. "Just think about the situation. I interviewed you at a scene where a man died. A high profile man at that. It probably would not look too good if I was seen gallivanting around the city with you. So don't take it personally, but I have to be a little careful right now."

"You know, that is the most sense you've made since you said you liked me as you walked your sexy ass to the bathroom."

She smacks my arm before smiling. "You were looking?!"

"Um, hell yeah I was looking. When a man has a chance to view something so nice that it could be displayed in a trophy case… yeah, I was looking real hard." She smiles even bigger and hooks her arm inside my elbow as we cross the next street. I don't feel familiar with this part of the city but I see a bright sign embossed across a building front on the other side of the street. "King Wok, huh. I feel like I have heard of it but never been there."

"Oh, I suppose I should have asked if you like Chinese food. Where are my manners? Well, I hope you do because that's where we are going anyway."

"Well then, I guess I am in luck, because I do like Chinese food. Actually, I am not too fussy with food. You'll be hard-pressed to find food that I wouldn't eat."

"Great. Their egg rolls are awesome."

"I don't like egg rolls."

"But you just…" She looks and sees me smiling. We chuckle as she smacks my arm again.

"You're pretty easy to mess with, ya know. I am going to run to the restroom. Feel free to order if you'd like and I'll pay when I get back."

"What, you don't think I am a strong enough woman to pay for myself? Are you sure you trust me to order for us both?

"Wait, you were going to let me have a say in what we ordered?" And there is the third smack in the arm of the night as I turn and walk toward the restroom. Reaching the door, I turn the handle, but it is locked. I only have to wait a few seconds and the door opens.

The man exiting is looking down, scrubbing his eyeglasses with a cloth, as he exits. It's Detective Banner. I immediately think about Genny's thoughts of not being seen with me and I turn on my heels to look at the advertisement board on the opposite side of the hallway. I can tell that I turned too quickly and I know I can feel Banner's eyes on me. There is a quiet moment as I wait to hear him walking away or say something… "Hey." I pretend I don't hear at first. "Dude, are you trying to avoid me for some reason?"

I don't want to act any more suspicious so I look back. "Oh, Detective Banner. Hello."

"Yeah, like you didn't already see me."

I just move past that, "I wouldn't expect to see you in a dive like this." He lifts his hands to his face to replace his spectacles and I notice his tie tail hanging off to the side. Damn this guy, can't you just tuck the thing in the keeper. What the hell does he think that part of his tie is for?

"Are you kidding? Best Chinese food in the city. Actually, a new coworker told me about it and I haven't been able to stay away since. You frequent the place?"

"Um, yeah. I pretty much live here."

I see Genny walking through the sitting area with a tray of food as Banner starts to turn and says, "Well, see you later, Cotter."

"Wait!" He turns back a little startled while I think of what to say. "Sorry, it's just that I was curious if you ever had any other witnesses turn up who saw things as I saw them the other day."

"No, no I haven't. To be honest, I haven't had time to focus on a suicide. As I'm sure you've heard, some dude committed a number of murders and that means more work for me." A look of realization crosses his face. "Although, I did hear you met Detective Keller. She told me you said similar things about her accidental death case as you said about my suicide case. Very curious. I think I will give you a call when I have time so we can discuss you showing up randomly at these scenes."

"That'd be fine. That'd be great, actually. So, talk to you soon I guess." I start to go into the men's room but stop before closing the door as soon as I see him turn away. If he looks to the left, he is sure to see Genny. He doesn't, but turns to the right instead, towards the door. I assume he has already eaten. God, I hope he has already eaten. I realize my heart is really racing as I watch Banner walk out the door and turn down the street.

I wash up in the restroom and find Genny sitting with an extraordinary amount of food in front of her. "Wow, I am just going to go grab something for me."

"Stop it. Some of this is for you. Well, maybe one thing anyway. Here, you have to try these. They are actually my favorite."

"Wow, beating out the egg rolls, eh? Looks like a cheese wonton?"

"Nope, crab rangoon."

"Hmm, not sure that I have ever had it." I bite into one and savor it for a moment. "Wow, they are delicious."

"Told you."

"I believe you now, at least that you are probably only going to let me have one of these."

"Ha-ha, well, that actually might be true."

"So, if you want to keep me all to yourself, that is, a secret, you might not want to take me to places you have told the entire police force about."

Genny instinctively ducks down a little and begins looking around. "What!? Who is here?"

"Nobody now, but I had an interesting conversation with Detective Banner outside the restroom."

"Shit. I hope he didn't see me. He probably would have said something if he saw me, don't you think?"

"Relax. I watched him leave and he never even looked your way. I am certain he did not see you. Well, thanks to me, and you owe me for extending a conversation that I didn't want to have in the first place."

"Thank you."

"Extending that conversation gave him time to think and mention how he wants to have a meeting with me to discuss everything you told him about me." I might have said this just a little defensively.

"Come on, Cotter. It is my job to communicate with other detectives about cases. Especially when there are commonalities. Besides, he would have viewed all briefs on other cases and sought me out about you anyway. Oh, and even though I thought you looked pretty cute in your pajamas that night, I certainly didn't think I would be sitting here right now having already had sex with you...like four times." She smiles at me and I loosen up a bit.

"I thought it was more like nine times."

"No, you must be thinking of the total number of orgasms between us," and she laughs a little embarrassed.

"Okay, I know you have to do your job."

I feel a prickling on the back of my neck and turn towards the window to see a woman walking along the sidewalk, just outside the restaurant windows, under a spotlight. I am aware of turning and sliding my chair abruptly and now I feel Genny's hand on my arm. "What is it, Banner again?"

"No, do you see that woman in the light brown tweed coat and the blue scarf?" I am pointing at her as she is just on the other side of the glass from us.

"Yes, what about her."

"One of those spotlights I told you about is shining on her."

"What?!"

"Let's go. I need to stop this." I am already heading for the door.

"But what about my food?"

"Genny!" I must have given her the *WTF* look because she is jumping up now. "She is going to die if I don't do something!" I see her look around and I realize everyone in the restaurant heard me say this.

We are on the sidewalk in a heartbeat and it only takes a few seconds for us to be nearly on the woman's heels. This is the closest I have been to a spotlight. It looks like a draped veil hanging around her with a snowy film flowing through it. I am reminded of watching slightly fuzzy television as a child. We are just close enough that I instinctively wave my hand through it, not sure what to expect, but it feels like nothing. There are many other people around us but I still whisper, "You can't see it?"

"No, did you just try to feel it? Anything?"

"Nope, didn't feel like there was any difference in the air occupying that space. There is a filminess to it, almost like the smallest flakes of snow within the light. It's hard to see if that film is moving or if it just looks that way because everything else is." As if to answer my question, we all stop at a crosswalk. "It looks like the film is moving ever so slightly, like a light snow, but it is not really moving towards the ground, or in any direction for that matter." I look straight up and the light looks infinite. "If there is a source, or some starting point, my eyes cannot see that far." Suddenly I feel panicked, and I spin around to look in all directions.

"What is it?"

Still trying to keep my voice down, as if this woman would even have a clue what I am talking about, "I need to spot him. He will be coming!" We are all crossing the street now and I am seeing no sign of the hoodie man. Now I am also finding myself looking around for signs of danger, ways he could find to kill this woman. We are approaching the next street and everyone on the sidewalk seems to be stopping to cross to the right, but the blonde under the spotlight appears to be crossing ahead.

There is a stop signal on the crosswalk of this one-way street but there are clearly no vehicles approaching from the right and this woman looks like she is just going to cross. "She is not stopping so let's go, hurry." We had fallen a few paces back so I quicken my step, not wanting to be held up if vehicles come after she crosses. A woman is screaming somewhere behind us and I sense everyone on the block turn their gaze in that direction. Genny and I stop in our tracks and we both start to look back.

I barely look at the screaming woman long enough to see a man pulling on her handbag, but I feel a need to resist this distraction. I glance back to the street and see a speeding yellow taxi barreling towards the woman as she is trying to hurry across the street. "Look out!" It's too late. Everyone's attention is now on the blonde woman in the tweed coat and light blue scarf as she lay motionless in the street. I am not sure if they even heard the tiny yelp she let out after hearing my warning, but they certainly heard the crunching of the taxi as it made contact and they might have even looked in time to see her body reconnect with the pavement in a disgustingly soft thud.

I stare for a moment, confused. Many of the bystanders rush into the street to try to help, including Genny, while I stand here trying to figure out how the hoodie-wearing freak was able to pull this one off. Or is it possible this was actually just an accident? A coincidence? The taxi, which hadn't braked until screeching to a halt well past the point of impact, is just sitting diagonally on the side of the street. A thought pops into my mind and I rush towards the taxi just as some random driver slowly opens the door and steps out. It is not who I thought might be behind the wheel. I don't get it.

I am still approaching the taxi and the driver tearfully says, "Oh my God. I never even saw her. The light was green. It was not my fault. I saw a guy over there…" he's pointing, "…mugging a lady or something."

I don't understand that comment. "What? How could you even notice that down a side street? Maybe you should have had your eyes on the road, pal!"

"My fare pointed it out." He looks and points to the back of the taxi, but there is nobody there. However, the back door on the other side is wide open. "What the... I had a passenger. He must have taken off."

"Was he wearing a hoodie?"

"Huh?"

"Was your fare wearing a hooded sweatshirt?"

"Um, yeah, yeah he was. Did you see him get out?"

"Well, yes, I guess I must have seen him run off." Of course, I did not see him, but it's just better to not have to explain.

Genny is walking over and I move to meet her away from others. Her hands are covered in blood. "Well, I guess I definitely believe you now."

"She's dead?"

"Yes, she never had a chance." A confused expression comes across her face, "But hold on a second, I don't understand how the guy you speak of made this happen. You said he makes this stuff happen. And what the hell kind of threat was this lady posing to anyone?"

"Hold on. Remember that is his irrational explanation for murdering these people. She was just an innocent woman and he is a killer." I point to the back of the yellow taxi. "I didn't see him, but I think he was in the back of that taxi. The driver said he had someone in the back. I don't know how he could have known it would work, but the driver says he distracted him."

"Wow, it's going to take me some time to absorb all of this. Listen, I'm going to stay here and help work the scene and I can imagine officers who have seen you at the other scenes will be here very soon, so you should go."

"Yeah, that's a good idea. I think I will walk for a while and see if I can spot him."

Genny starts to grab my arm but stops just shy as she looks at the blood on her hand. "Be careful, Cotter."

"I will. Can you call me later?"

"If I get out of here I will, otherwise I will try to talk to you tomorrow. I am one of the detectives on call, so there is a good chance they will be having me investigate this." I try to squeeze out a smile and turn to walk away. "Just so you know, I won't be pushing about the passenger in the cab, but I will get a description and any other info the driver has about him."

"Yep, I understand that. You're not going to get anything more than some kind of vague description. He is elusive, and anything you say about it will just sound weird, so I get that you won't be saying anything. No sense in us both sounding crazy."

9

I don't know for sure how long I have been walking the streets, but the horizon is starting to show the promise of another day as the sun is creeping on me from around the corner of a building. This thought sends a chill down my spine and I shake my tired brain free of it so I can start looking again for my spotlight partner. The one who thinks about things in a completely different way than I do. The one who apparently believes more in God than I do yet breaks one of his greatest commandments one hundred percent more often than I do. The one who calls them exit lights, because he makes sure all the actors exit this stage through the vampire trap in the floor that presumably drops straight into Hell.

Not thinking for a second that I was actually going to spot him, I guess I have just been wandering aimlessly thinking about the intersection I am at in life. On one hand, Genesis allowed me to forget about spotlights that lead to murder for a few sweet hours. On the other hand, here I am again and there is no sign that this is going to stop before something gives. And, what is the thing that is going to give anyway? Can I find a way to get the law on the heels of this creep? Maybe Genny is going to be the key to making that happen. Will I have to kill him? Maybe he is going to kill me. Do I care at this point? I just need this to be over.

I have to tell you that part of the reason I have been struggling to focus on seeking hoodie punk out is that I spent the last few hours of bar time on a stool last night. I could not shake the feeling that I needed something to calm my nerves. It also didn't help that I never heard from Genny and she didn't answer the few times I tried to call. Now I am thinking that I shouldn't have been trying. Maybe I was being obsessive, but I just want to spend time with her. I think she might have been the only thing that could have calmed me, other than the booze. I am pretty relaxed now. Not flat drunk, but my cares have faded to the less active portions of my brain.

I feel my phone vibrating in my pocket and my heart starts racing as I think of Genny. I hope my dad doesn't hear any disappointment in my voice as I answer, "Hello."

"Cotter?"

"Hey, Dad."

"Where are you? It doesn't seem like you ever came home last night and your mom is worried sick."

"Um, no, I didn't." My parents really love Rebecca so I have no interest in telling him about my new friend. "Yeah, I never did make it home, no."

I feel judgment coming. "Hmm, you're drunk again aren't you?"

"I am not drunk, Dad."

...

"I might have had a few, but I am not drunk."

"Well, you certainly don't sound yourself, Son."

Shamelessly I grasp at whatever I can to sway things back in my favor. "Well, I don't expect you to understand my life right now."

"I raised you, Cotter, how about you give me some credit and try me."

"Well, you know, here's the deal, I saw another person die last night."

"What?! How is that possible, Cotter?"

"I tried to tell you how it is possible, Dad, you know, how it is happening, but I am pretty sure you and Mom just think I am crazy."

"You're talking about these damn lights again? Come on, Cotter! I will help you however I can but you have to tell me the truth!"

"Like I said, you just can't understand this I guess."

"Has any of this stuff even happened?"

"Wait, what do you mean? You have seen the news about these deaths."

"That's not what I am talking about. Have you actually even been at the scenes or has it just been an excuse for you to give us so you can cover up your drinking problem?"

"Wait! What! I don't even know how to respond to that. So not only do you not believe what I am experiencing, but now I am lying about the trauma I am seeing too?"

"Oh, like you never lie to us, Cotter?"

Now I really don't know what to say, because the pang of guilt I am feeling is admission enough of the constant lying I have subjected my parents to. "Well, I am not lying about this," and the timing is just right as I glance toward the sunrise and see a spotlight in the forefront. I hang up the phone and start running towards the quarter sun rising out of Lake Michigan. I am actually quite close to it already but as I quickly approach it is starting to move rapidly. Shit, it looks like it's shining on someone who has just gotten on a bus.

The streets are fairly busy right now during rush hour so I am just going to keep running and hope this person gets off the bus sooner rather than later. It has been unseasonably warm this fall but there is a stiff wind coming off the lake. Still, I am already working up a good sweat. I am sure the booze from last night, which was really only some hours ago, has something to do with it as well. You know, I am just realizing how much clearer my head seems. Probably a little help from my old pal adrenaline. We have become much closer in recent months.

Maybe my head isn't as clear as I thought. I am lost in thought, still looking at the bus a few blocks ahead of me, but now I can see that the spotlight has moved away from the bus, to the west. I don't think I should wait to head west so I turn on the next block. Maybe I can get ahead of it. Quickly I am heading towards the spotlight again and now it is moving further to the west. This time I run two more blocks to the north before I head west again. I turn down the next block and start heading to the north again and it appears that the spotlight has stopped.

I am exhausted but I continue to jog, moving as fast as I can. I am approaching the spot now and I can see it has moved just around the corner, which I am rounding now. I am stopped in my tracks as I stare at the spotlight shining in the middle of the street, with nothing under it. Confused, I look around thinking something has already happened, but there is no evidence of that. Now it registers. The subway!

I turn back around the corner and hurry to the stairs right in front of me. I am going so fast down the steps that I am stumbling now about halfway down. There is no saving this, I am going down so I turn to the side and my shoulder slams hard into the tile floor. Sharp pains shoot through my shoulder, but luckily, this maneuver prevents my head from hitting the floor.

With disregard for the stinging sensation deep within my shoulder, I am only on the floor for a split second before I am up. I am already rounding the corner and I hurdle the turnstile as I sprint toward the tracks. Though my eyes dart immediately to the side of the tracks, I am aware in my peripheral vision that everyone has turned to look at me running past them. I guess the freak standing near the man under the spotlight would say I was the distraction God created to protect his anonymity during the act about to take place on this stage.

I am almost to them but I hear the train screeching along the rail and it is likely concealing the throaty warning emitting from my mouth. The murderer's arms extend and the man is clearly jolted so unexpectedly that he must have gotten whiplash. I have reached them in this exact moment and I try to come to a halt so as not to propel myself in front of the speeding train while simultaneously reaching to grasp at the man's leather jacket. As if I have an eternity in this sensational moment, I feel my fingertips slide across the entirety of the dry and cracked leather, but this is as close as I get. The train collides with the man and I feel ninety-eight-degree wetness splatter onto my hand.

My instinct has me spinning on my heels to make sure my hand was out of the way, and because I am not sticking around to see the aftermath of this collision. Instead, I am already spotting the killer as he boards a train car on the other side of the tunnel. I sprint over just as the train's dwell time is ending and I am just able to slip through the doors before they close. There are only a couple of passengers to my right and I see the killer has looked over his shoulder while walking to the opposite end of the car. I am already following and I sit directly across from him so that we are staring at one another.

I am not sure what I planned to say in this first moment, but my jaw just drops open, my mouth will not form any words at this moment.

The reason for my being rendered speechless is quite clear, it's because I am staring into a mirror. Aside from a dark beard, it is easy to see that this man is a mirror image of me. I am so dumbfounded right now that I immediately wonder if he literally is me, and my brain wraps around an idea. "So is this what's going on? You... or I, time-traveled to take care of unfinished business?"

A confused look crosses his face, "What are you talking about?"

"I mean, what the hell is going on?! Did I figure something out about these people, like you've tried to tell me, and travel back in time to stop them from doing the things you've said they do?!" He looks even more confused for a second and then comprehension lights up his face as he begins laughing. "How is this funny? I mean, you are me, right?"

"Time travel? And you call me crazy? So, what's the deal here, do you not know that you're adopted." I can tell by his response now that I am the one looking confused. "Wow, I don't know how you are not getting this. We are twins."

"Bull shit!" Maybe my head did hit the ground back there because it is really spinning now.

"Why would that be so hard to believe? So you're more apt to believe in time travel than believe that we ar—"

"Shut the hell up!" I feel a rage coming over me. "My parents would have told me! You don't have a clue who I am, you piece of shit!"

I start to look around, panicked to find a way off this train, but that won't be happening until the next stop. And, as if that thought was played upon, the subway slows down and stops. A voice comes over the intercom, "We apologize, but all trains have been stopped momentarily to tend to an issue on another track."

"Well, that's just great! Now I have to sit here listening to your murdering ass feed me a line of shit."

"Hold on, so just a moment ago, it sounded like you were willing to accept what I've told you as truth as long as it meant that I was you because you time traveled, but now I am back to being a murderer? You might need to see a therapist."

"Are you just trying to piss me off?"

"Actually I'm not. I am just trying to reason with you so that you can help share this burden, or so that you'll at least quit trying to stop me from doing my part."

"Let me get this straight. It sounds like you're almost guilt-tripping me for not joining you in murdering people?"

"Well, that's not exactly what I was trying to do, but yeah. I guess it is my interest to help you see God's true message here, to help you understand that there is a reason why exit lights shine down from the heavens."

"You should hear yourself, talking about God this and God that, like if there really was a God he would be sending signs to have people murdered. I am not sure you'd be the ideal follower of any real deity anyway, but I don't know how anyone could even believe in one that allows so much suffering in this world. You add to that with how you hurt people."

"You know, many people struggle with faith for those exact reasons, because they can't understand the suffering. Here, *you* actually have more of an opportunity to see how God is at work to stop suffering. He is sending signals to a few special individuals, like you, so they can help to stop evil people from harming many. These exit lights are a direct response to your questions about suffering. Why can't you see that?"

"Don't preach to me, asshole. I will never buy into the thought of murdering people because a light shines on them, so you're definitely not going to be able to use that to convince me that God exists."

"What if you're wrong? Wouldn't you hate to know you could have saved innocent people?"

"You know, what if you're wrong? Even if you truly believe these people are going to do evil things, even if your visions are real, who made you the authority to say they can't be helped? Who told you they had to be executed?"

"I have faith that these obvious signs are truth. It all makes sense. And, I guess I also had the advantage of remaining connected to the previous generations who have also carried out this important work for God."

"Previous generations?"

"Yes, our father was task—"

"Your father…"

"I do understand this would be a tough moment for you, but you are adopted."

"Stop!"

"Anyway, I grew up being aware that our father," I choose to just let him get it out but I am sure my hot gaze is burning a hole in his soul right now, "and his father were both tasked with the same work. These are the men I have actually known to see these things, but I am also told that every generation experienced the same thing upon coming of age."

"Coming of age?"

"Yes, apparently it hasn't always been the exact same age for every generation, but the exit lights are not seen until sometime around adulthood. For me, it was shortly after I turned twenty-one years old."

"And when was that?"

"I don't know if your parents kept the same birthday for you, but we turned twenty-one on the sixth of June this year."

I try not to react. I am sure he could have easily found this information about me, but he is right. "I am not going to keep reminding you that I do not believe your theories, however, I will ask you a question about your make-believe world. If we were actually born as twins, why was I given up for adoption and you were not?"

"It was a mistake our father made when you were born. He chose not to kill you."

"What the hell is that supposed to mean?"

"There was an exit light shining on you when we were born and he chose not to kill you."

I begin to laugh. "Do you have all of this thought up before we begin the conversation or do you make it all up as you go along?" He isn't laughing, but I haven't stopped. "This is just a bunch of crazy bull shit and I don't know why I am even indulging you. I guess if this train ever moves I will get out of here so you can take care of the important business of making sculptures from your own feces, or whatever you do with your crazy ass."

"I am just giving you the information. Do with it what you will."

"Okay, again, hypothetically, if that is what happened, what vision was seen of me as a newborn," I can't help but laugh again at the ridiculousness of this, "what harm had a helpless little newborn caused?"

"Remember the visions are also about the future, but our father has never told me what he saw when he held you at that moment."

"Yeah, whatever. I am not doing this with you anymore." I get up and go to the door at the back of the car. I am surprised at how quickly I am able to get the door open and am immediately wishing I had tried it earlier. I climb down the steps and I am heading back to the station in a hurry. I look back and see that it appears he is still just sitting there. Though it felt like an eternity had passed listening to that wacko, I only round one corner and I can already see the lights at the station.

Climbing onto the platform, I see emergency personnel have arrived on the scene and I also can see someone pointing me out to a police officer. He begins walking toward me with his hand on his weapon and we meet in the middle of the platform.

"Just stop right there for a minute, sir. Why are you coming up from the track?"

I point behind me, "The train stopped and I just exited and walked back here."

"A witness just told me she saw you yell before this incident, and then she saw you run to jump on that train after that man committed suicide." He points in the direction. "Can you tell me why?"

"Because he didn't commit suicide! I was chasing after the guy who pushed him in front of the train."

"What? These people all stated he was standing alone and jumped."

"Wait, what?! Didn't they see the guy standing with him?"

"Nobody said that, but were you the guy causing the commotion prior to that. They said a guy came running and jumped the turnstile."

"This is what I am trying to tell you, yes, I was trying to stop the guy I am telling you about. Listen, he might have left now but he was on that train right now." The cop looks at me suspiciously. "Listen to me, can't you just go check? He was just there!"

He gives me a look like he is going against his better judgment. "Officer Peterson!" A female officer is being waved over. "Can you keep an eye on this gentleman? He might have something to do with this incident." He pulls out his flashlight, walks over to the edge of the platform, and climbs down.

Now he is walking down the tunnel but a voice comes across the public address system, "Attention. All trains are now back in service. Attention. All trains are now back in service." The officer is right back and up on the platform.

"Sir, I am going to need some more information from you."

"But what about the guy on that train?!"

"Calm down, sir. The trains are back in service but I will try to get an officer at the next station to check on what you have told me."

I am sure he sees me roll my eyes, "Well I am sure it will be much too late. That guy is quite sneaky."

"Oh? And how would you know that, you know the guy who is supposedly on that train?" There is judgement and disbelief oozing from this question.

Realizing that I am in deep enough on this one that he is going to at the very least take down my information, I just tell him, "I don't know the guy, but I have seen him do the same thing a couple other times."

"You've seen him push other people in front of trains?"

"Not in front of trains every time." I almost spill the beans on last night's murder, but catch myself as I remember that only Genny knows I saw that one, and, I don't want someone to eventually realize we both witnessed it. After all, though I wish we didn't need to be secretive about what has started between us, it does make sense for her to be careful. "I have seen him push one man off a balcony and one man in front of a bus."

"Yeah, okay." He doesn't believe a word I am saying. "How about you just show me your identification. I am pretty sure someone will be wanting you for further questioning."

I see no point in arguing with this guy anymore so I just pull out my wallet and give him my driver's license. He quickly jots down my information and hands it back. Turning to walk away now, I say, "Why don't you write down those other deaths I mentioned too. If you care to be a cop for a minute, you'll find the name you just jotted down in those reports as well."

"Whatever, man. Why don't you save if for your next therapy appointment." I just walk away while I still can. Wow, that guy's a real dick.

10

It's midday as I walk down what appears to be a deserted street. I don't remember the last person I saw and panic begins to come over me. I am not quite running but I am now hurrying to the next intersection, hoping to see someone, anyone. Rounding the corner, I can see that this street is also empty. It's only now that I realize there are no cars driving on the street either. What the hell is this?!

Now I start to jog down the sidewalk, looking in the stores as I pass. There isn't a soul to be seen. These stores and restaurants are always busy. Yet, in the middle of the day, whatever the hell day it is, I am beginning to lose track of that, here they are all completely empty! How are there not at least staff in these businesses? I try one of the doors, knowing it is going to be locked, but it isn't. I open it halfway and then let it go as I start to move on.

Just as it closes, I hear a phone ringing inside. I don't know what the hell is going on but this ringing gives me an overwhelming sense of relief. It was beginning to feel like I was the only person left on earth, but if that phone is ringing, it can only mean there is someone on the other end. All of a sudden, it hits me that I have to answer it. Maybe they know where everyone has gone. I fling the door open and sprint behind the counter to pick up the receiver. "Hello!"

How would you like to minimize your debt today and get those pesky creditors off your back? Please hold for the next representative so you can find out how low your new payment can be. It's a damn solicitation! *You are next in line, please hold.* There isn't anyone on the end of the line. Where is everybody?! I almost have the receiver back in its cradle and I hear, "Thank you for holding, sir."

I just catch it before hanging up. "Yes, hello! Can you tell me what the hell is going on please?"

"Well, sir. We would like to offer you better credit —"

"No, I don't care about that! I mean where is everyone?"

"I don't think I understand, sir."

What is that accent he has? "There are no people on the streets here. In the middle of Chicago. Wait, where are you talking to me from right now?"

"Well, let me first assure you sir that we are an American compan—"

"Stop! I don't care about your company! What country are you in right now?!"

"Okay, sir. Sorry, sir. This call center is in India."

"And are you the only person left there?"

"In the office? Well, it is actually night here, so, yes. My numbers are down."

"No, in India I mean. Can you see anyone right now?"

"Yes, my office is street level so of course, I see people. It is not that late here. The streets are full of people."

"I have to go, there is nobody here and I need to find out what is going on."

"Wait! Don't you want to lower your debt?"

"Least of my worries right now so unless you know what is happening to me, I have to go now."

"Well, have you thought that maybe the problem is you are a lying drunk who is only interested in self-satisfaction and pissing his life away?"

"Huh, what did you just say to me?!" But the phone had already clicked. He hung up on me. Is that really who I am? Wait, did this guy know me. *What the hell am I thinking, he couldn't know me, and that's not me... is it?*

I hardly feel myself leave the store and I am running down the street. The stores feel like they are whizzing past now, one after another, and I have yet to see any sign of movement. I pass a jewelry store and nothing. There is that local pharmacy my mom goes to, empty. A small deli is deserted. The Apple Store's lights are on but nobody's home. There is a flipping McDonalds that is barren! I press my face against the window because I can smell greasy fries cooking, but the damn place is empty!

I realize how scared I feel. I am frozen with my nose pressed up against the glass. I am lost for a moment thinking about how stupid my pig-nosed face must look from the other side. Now I hear ringing again and I press harder, turning my ear to the glass and looking for a phone inside, but the sound is from behind. Turning, I see a payphone on the other side of the street. What?! I didn't even know payphones still existed. This one looks like one of those old, red booths they had in England.

I sprint across the street as fast as I can in fear that I'll miss the call. "Hello."

"Where you at, Cotter?"

"Wait, how do you know who this is?"

"What on earth are you talkin' bout, kid? Why ain't you at work?"

"Mr. Brown? How did you know you could reach me on this phone? And where is everybody?"

"What are you ramblin' bout? Dammit, Cotter! You're drunk again, ain't you?"

"No, Mr. Brown, I am on the street and there is nobody around. I am not drunk."

"You can choose to waste your life, but you're done wastin' my time, Cotter. You're an alcoholic and you need help. You're fired." The phone clicks before I can plead for him to tell me what's going on.

It's so quiet without the hustle and bustle around me and already I can faintly hear another phone ringing down the street. Panicking to find answers, I run so hard and fast that my throat gets that metallic sensation. I slam on the breaks and my shoes squeak slightly as I skid a little at the door of what looks like some kind of sales business.

Hurrying through the door I can see phones lined up next to each other on long tables. Actually, this looks more like the call center you'd see on a public broadcast channel when they beg for your money, or during some disaster relief performance where celebrities pretend like the cause is more important than the publicity they are getting. There are dozens of phones and it takes a moment of focus for me to find the right one. "Hello?"

A woman is crying. "How could you hurt me like this, Cotter?"

"Rebecca? How are you calling me here?"

"Don't play dumb with me, asshole! What, were you expecting it to be some other woman? Like maybe the hot lady that turned you on the other day, or are there others now too?"

"No, Rebecca, I'm sorry, but I have a big issue that came up right now."

"Hmph, like she gave you a big issue? Don't flatter yourself, Cotter, the issue rising wasn't that big." And another hang-up.

The phone right next to it is ringing now. "Hello?"

"You're an uneducated piece of shit." The phone hangs up. Who the hell was that?!

The next phone in line rings once and I answer, "Hello!"

"You're lousy in the sack." I don't think I recognize her voice and I don't get to ask because another hang-up.

Now it sounds like all the phones are ringing and I just pick them up rapidly. "Hello!"

"Liars never end up happy." Click!

"Hello."

"Showing up to work is the least you can do for an employer!" Click!

"Hello."

"Your bar tabs look like car payments, you lush." Click!

"Hello."

"Who's your daddy? Oh, that's right, you don't know." Click!

"Hello."

"Why are you letting everyone in the city get killed, murderer." Click!

"Hello, and what shit do *you* want to say to me?!"

"Cotter?"

"Mom... is that you?"

"Of course it is, Honey." Her voice sounds so soft and kind, but then with what's been happening, I wonder what the catch is going to be here.

"What do you want to say to me?"

"Well, I just wanted you to know that I love you."

Thank god, I don't know how many more insults I can take. "I can't tell you how good it is to hear that from you. I am feeling so alone and all these people are coming at me with insulting and negative comments, but on the phones, because everybody is gone. Mom, the streets are empty!"

"Yes, I know, Sweetie."

"Wait, you know what's going on."

"Of course we do, Cotter. Your father and I are very sad about the things being said to you, because we know it's all true."

"What?!"

"It's sad but true. You lie to us about everything in your life, your alcoholism is hurting you and everyone around, and you're letting everyone get killed. That's probably why you don't see anyone around you. So, your father wanted me to tell you that we are extremely disappointed in you, and as of today, your adoption papers are being revoked."

"What the hell are you talking about?!"

"We don't want you anymore."

"You're crazy!"

"Careful now, Honey. In New York, the legal terminology of the third trimester has been pushed all the way back to age twenty-five, so you might just want to be happy that we revoked adoption instead of going with abortion." She hung up.

The next phone ringing feels like there is a rave going on inside my head. The rhythmic pulsing feels excruciating as I open my eyes and begin the all too common orientation process of figuring out where I am waking up. Okay, I am in my room and my cell phone is laying on the pillow right next to my ear, ringing and throbbing. I am realizing now what a brutal combination an annoying ringtone and hangover can be. Maybe that dream would be a desirable trade-off for this headache I have going on right now.

Desperate to stop one contributing factor to the headache, I pick up the phone, but stop right before I answer. What if it's some awful conversation like in my dream? This is just a momentary fear as I remember I am a grown adult that doesn't worry about dreams coming true. "Hello."

"Jeez, Cotter, you sound terrible. Are you okay?"

"Rebecca! I've been trying to reach you all night!"

"What? Cotter, this is Genny… remember me?" She chuckles but there is also a hint of annoyance.

"Um… of course, I know it's you… sorry. I meant I have been trying to call—"

"Who is Rebecca?"

"That's my ex-girlfriend."

"Nice… listen, it doesn't really matter anyway. I was calling because there was something I wanted to tell you. I would like to think I would do this out of respect anyway, but I also needed to have this conversation so you'd quit obsessing over me with all the calls and texts." Damn, she's right, I think I did a ton of drunk dialing last night. "Anyway, I just wanted to let you know that there is nothing between us. Well, at least from my end."

"Wait, what are you saying?!"

"I am trying to tell you that I don't want you to bother me anymore. Listen, I only hooked up with you so you could lead me to the killer. Now I have seen what I needed to see, so I just don't need to keep doing that anymore with you. Hell, one day was hard enough as it was. Well, kind of hard."

"I don't understand! Are you being serious right now?"

"Come on, Cotter, grow up a little." She chuckles. "I mean, it's like Rebecca told you on the phone, you hardly rise to the occasion."

"Huh?"

"You know, it wasn't that *big* of an issue, like she said."

Now she is laughing hard enough that it brings on a snort and Detective Banner jumps on the line, "Dude, relax, it's just a small dick joke!"

It sounds like he slams the phone as hard as possible when hanging up and this creates a jerk in my body, waking me up. Unreal, those are some of the craziest dreams I think I've ever experienced. I generally like remembering dreams, but that was rough and I hate the ones where you think you've woken up but you're actually still sleeping. I'm never taking tequila shots again.

My cell phone rings and it is right next to my damn ear! That rave *is* actually pulsing in my head now, but the hangover doesn't quite feel like I thought it did in my dream, it's much worse. I'm not letting this cell phone ring again. I answer without looking at who it is. "Hello."

"I'm trying to reach Cotter Trespin." Damn! It's Detective Banner.

"This is Cotter."

"Cotter, this is Detective Banner. It appears that you were at the scene of a potential homicide in the early morning hours today?"

"Today? Wait, you're finally admitting that this was homicide. That's a start."

"Potential homicide, yes, that is what we would like to speak to you about. And I am referring to the incident from the subway that happened today, this morning. The report has your name and says you were there?" Confused, I jump up and almost fall over with a spinning head. Out the window, I realize that what I had mistaken as the morning sunrise is actually a sunset. Wow, that's some kind of bender if it put me down and out and it's still the same day. I'm probably still drunk, oops. "Are you still there?"

"Um, yes, I was in the subway when it happened."

"What's the deal? You seem confused, or are you trying to avoid something?"

"No, I don't feel the need to avoid this stuff any longer. I am glad you are ready to look at it for what it is, murder. So, do you want me to come down to the station tomorrow or something?"

"Actually, we think it would be best to talk as soon as possible. Are you at your home address? I will send someone over to pick you up now." It doesn't exactly sound like he is asking.

"Oh, sure, I guess I can come in today. Just give me about half an hour to wrap up what I am doing and then I will meet you down on the street." I don't need my parents seeing this pick-up.

"Sure, a car will be out front in half an hour."

***

About twenty-five minutes passed while I showered, got dressed, and tried to make sure I didn't smell like booze. I open my bedroom door and hurry toward the front door, but not quite fast enough.

"Son, could you come in here a minute." I walk over to the dining room, where my parents are both sitting at the table. "We would like to talk to you."

"Listen, I can't do this right now."

His voice level rises, "You've been avoiding these conversations long enough! If not now, when? Let me answer for you, it would be never as far as you're concerned, young man."

"Okay, the truth is I do not want to talk to you about my life, but the truth of the moment is that I literally don't have time right now."

"How do you not have time?" My mom hasn't said a thing, but tears start to roll down her cheeks. "You aren't going to school. You don't have a job. What could you possibly need to be doing?"

"No, I do have a job."

Mom says, "Cotter, we know you were fired."

"Yes, but I got my job back."

Dad almost yells, "Since when?! In the last hour you managed to get your job back?!"

"No, this was days ago that Mr. Brown fired me, but I convinced him to give me a second chance right after that."

"Stop lying to us! He just called here today looking for you. He said you didn't show up for work today and he hadn't been able to reach you all day, said he left you messages. He also asked that if you didn't get the message that I tell you not to bother showing up there again."

Shit, I was supposed to work today. Looking at my phone now, I can see I have voice messages and the call list shows three missed calls from Mr. Brown. I don't want to let myself be distracted checking voicemails from him, I know what they are going to say, but I see there was also a call from Genny this afternoon.

Dialing into my voicemail, I turn to walk a few steps and out of the corner of my eye, I see my father put his hands in the air and hear him mumble to my mom, "Where is the respect?"

The first voicemail is indeed Mr. Brown and he is saying pretty much what I already know, so I just delete it.

The second voicemail is from Genny. "Cotter, sorry I haven't been able to take any of your calls, any of your many calls," Great, she does think I was obsessing, "but there is a lot going on right now, especially after this incident at the subway station. Listen, you are going to be questioned and I need you to play it cool when you see me and talk to me. Think of it as if we have only ever talked when I interviewed you the night we met, and nothing, I mean nothing more." Well, that wasn't the contact I was looking to have with her. The message was devoid of any emotion.

Closing my voicemail, I notice there is a text message, it's from Rebecca. *You know, sometimes a girl just needs some time to get over something hurtful. My aunt told me she saw you last night while she was picking up food at a Chinese restaurant. She said you were with a woman. You seemed to be getting along quite well. I suppose this was the woman you told me you were attracted to, or maybe there are already more! Unbelievable, Cotter. After years together, we've hardly been apart for a week!* I feel the hairs on the back of my neck standing up. That sounded too similar to what I heard in the dream from last night, or, I guess it was still today.

I guess because my head is still foggy I forgot the situation I am in, but Mom reminds me, "Cotter, can you please just give us a minute."

"What? Oh… no, Mom, I do have to go."

Dad speaks up, "No! We are worried sick about your drinking. Keep in mind you are still living under our roof! Your parents should not have to sit here at one o'clock in the afternoon and watch you stumble through the front door, puke all over the entry and piss in the corner!"

"Excuse me? That didn't happen, did it?" They both just nod and Mom averts her eyes.

Dad continues and points, "Look at the corner, you can see the stain still even from here. And what's worse, Son, we don't understand where all the lying is coming from."

I feel embarrassed and ashamed but all of a sudden it comes out in anger, "You want to talk about lying?! When were you two going to tell me that I was adopted?!" Dad's jaw immediately goes from clenched to literally dropped open and Mom just drops her head and begins sobbing. "So it is true."

They don't even react to that last comment, which gives me the answer I guess I was in denial about. We are all just silent for a moment until Mom tries to speak through the tears, "H... how... how could you... have found out?"

"I think the more important question is why did you feel the need to keep it from me all these years. I mean, what was your plan, to never tell me?"

Dad answers, "Son, it is completely normal for adoptive parents to not tell the kids they are adopted. At least until..."

"Until, what? Until they reach a mature age. I am pretty sure many are still kids by the time they are told. When did I have the right to know in your eyes?"

"You might not want to use the mature argument." I feel myself scowl at him and Mom shoots him a look too. "What? I mean, look at the wall." He points again.

Mom can still hardly speak but she does before I can go back at him. "I can understand you being upset, but I just want you to know that I love you." The hair stands up on the back of my neck again. "It's not like we never talked about telling you. It's just that we worried about losing you. And, well, there are circumstances we were scared to explain." Now it was Dad's turn to shoot her a look. "Well, he knows now, how can we keep it from him?"

There is an obnoxious rhythmic knock on the door, *shave and a haircut, two bits.* This tells me that I've missed my window to meet the cops on the street, and a gut feeling adds that it's Banner who would do such a corny knock on a door while investigating a murder. He said he would send a car, so why did he come on his own?

Dad starts for the door but I save him the trouble. "I got it. Listen, the cops want to question me because I witnessed another murder last night. And it was all the stuff that you don't want to believe that drew me to that location. I'll be back later and I would like to hear the rest of what you wanted to say, Mom." And Dad gives her the look again and shakes his head.

I am not surprised to see Banner when I open the door, but I am sure I am not hiding the surprise on my face as I gaze at Genny. She gives a nervous smile as she looks past me to my parents and quietly says to Banner, "We can do this downstairs."

"The hell we will. Cotter Trespin, you have the right to remain silent." It would be an understatement to say I am surprised. "Anything you say can and will be used against you in a court of law." Banner is patting me down while reading me my rights. "You have a right to an attorney. If you cannot afford an attorney, one will be appointed for you. Place your hands behind your back." And there are the cuffs. I look over and Mom has collapsed back in the chair, shock written across her face.

Dad is walking toward us. "Now wait a minute. On what charge are you arresting our son?"

Now, it's Genny who talks. "Please stop right there, sir. Your son will have every opportunity to get this sorted out."

"What's the charge?!"

Banner turns me around and I lock eyes with Genny. I don't know how I expect her to look, maybe a tear in her eye, but whether it is difficult or not, she appears to be quite composed as she says, "There was a death at a subway station early this morning and we have probable cause to arrest Mr. Trespin." Nobody says another word as the three of us walk out the door and down the hallway. Stepping into the elevator, I look over and see my parents standing outside their door. It looks like Dad is having to physically hold Mom up. What a sight this must be for a parent, even if they aren't really my parents.

11

I decided just to keep to myself during the entire ride to the station. They have walked me into a room that doesn't look much different than the interrogation rooms on television. Banner is taking the handcuffs off and Genny asks, "Can I offer you something to drink?"

I feel pissed off at her and that makes me want to say no, but I could use something to take the edge off right now. "Coffee would be good."

Banner says, "Yeah, dude, you smell like you could use a lot of coffee right now." I don't even look his way as Genny exits the room. "So do you want to talk to us or are you going to lawyer up?"

"Am I actually going to be charged with something?"

"You might be."

"Well, I guess I'd like to hear what you think you have against me before I decide what I should or shouldn't say."

"It doesn't really work that way."

"Doesn't it? How does it work then? Charge me or I can just leave?"

He seems to be getting a little irritated. "Nope, we've skirted that little loophole by arresting you for probable cause. So, basically, if you don't want to talk to us we will be moving you to a jail cell."

"Then I guess I would be getting a lawyer and I am sure he would have me out of here without you getting your interview with me, because it seems to me you must need something more or you'd be charging me with something already. And, you know, I've been nothing but cooperative with the police during all this crap I've had to go through."

He raises his eyebrows and sneers at me. "What you've gone

through?"

"That's right. I am certainly not the perpetrator of these crimes, but I might be a victim. After all, witnessing these things has definitely affected my life."

"Is that your excuse for smelling like alcohol right now, or did you already smell like alcohol at the subway station this morning?"

Genny walks in with the coffee and sets it down in front of me. I am guessing we both have a look of distaste on our face because she says, "Oh, have we started already?"

"With? Asking and answering questions?" My sarcasm is thick. "Nope, Detective Banner here has just been kicking me in the balls some more is all you missed so far."

She looks at Banner but he just glares at me, "Whatever, dude. Are you willing to answer some questions or not?"

"You know, I have no idea why I am even here. We all know I was there this morning because I willingly talked to the cops. I am sure you read a report that says I confronted the killer on the other train and I am sure it says I saw him push the man in front of the subway."

"You see, that's exactly what Detective Keller and I want to talk to you about. Unfortunately, there is a technical issue with the surveillance camera, but we were able to see what could potentially be a push before the man gets hit."

"That's right, the video! Well, why did we even need to go through this charade? And embarrassing me in front of my parents when you must have seen this guy in the footage?"

Now Genny speaks up. "Well, hold on, that's where we have a discrepancy. As Detective Banner was saying, there is an issue with the recording. More than half the frame is scrambled during the time this incident happened."

"I don't understand."

"It's a little bit difficult to explain." It is much easier to listen to Genny than her asshole counterpart. What is this guy's problem anyway? "Actually, why don't we just show you what we have and maybe you'd be willing to explain to us what we are seeing." She gives a head nod to Banner, motioning to a table behind them and he reaches back to grab a laptop.

He sets it on the table and just hits play. A scene pops up of the subway station from a trackside angle, with a view of the platform and the tunnel where the train would be coming from. I can see the man who was killed standing about where I remember he was, but there aren't many others around. I definitely don't see... well, I don't know his name but I can't deny anymore that he is my brother. That sounds strange in my head. "Wait, the picture looks perfect, you can see the entire platform all the way over to the other train."

Genny continues to lead. "Yes, for right now, but you will see what we are talking about in a moment. Do you recognize the man who died?"

"Yes, he looks to be standing in the same spot he was when I saw him."

"Can you show me on the screen?" I point to him. "There. Now you can see the glitch in the recording." The entire right three-quarters of the screen is scrambled now and the rest is nearly perfect. It looks like the way an old VHS tape would scramble a little on the screen, but these lines run vertical instead of how those usually seemed horizontal. And, you can't see a thing on that part of the screen. On the left side, I can see the man standing on the edge of the platform and the tracks to the left.

"Wait, that subway station still has a VHS recording system? A little behind the times I'd say."

Banner chimes in, "No, it actually doesn't. And that makes this a little bit stranger because this was a digital recording system."

"I am not really technologically advanced, but is the way it's scrambled really possible with a digital recording?"

Banner continues, "I don't know, but it is weird and we are having some experts look at it to see why it would happen, and hopefully they can clean it up so we can see the entire frame. However, initial opinions do not make that hope seem promising. That being said, pay attention to what we do have here because in a moment you will see that it still catches something."

"Isn't there audio to go along with this."

"No, it is just a video recorder. No audio." Banner seems to be a little less assy right now. I wonder if Genny taking over helped him chill out. "There! You missed it, didn't you? Here, I'll go back and slow it down. Watch the cadaver."

Genny frowns. "Really, Banner? You could show a little more sensitivity for the dead."

"Relax. You know he was a lowlife."

"Regardless."

"I hate to interrupt you two, but I am not really interested in seeing this guy get hit by the train if that is what your intention is, to try and guilt something out of me or something."

Banner again, "No, it will stop before you see any of that, but watch right here... there!" I see exactly what he wants me to see. The scrambling moved over half the man at what appeared to be the exact moment my brother shoved him. The man lurched forward, his head whipped back and the scrambling goes back away from the man just in time to catch my arm reaching for him. Of course, it is not completely clear if the arm was reaching... or pushing. "Do you see whose arm is in the frame?"

"Yes I can see an arm but I am not positive who it belongs to." I am thinking I might actually need a lawyer with this asshat manipulating what is seen here.

"Well, we can come back to that frame but let me show you the rest. Oh, feel free to look away if you don't want to see impact." I actually feel desensitized now so I just watch as the train hits the man and the scrambling immediately disappears from the screen, revealing me, the owner of the arm, running over to the other train. Well, there is no need to play dumb now. "Now do you see whose arm shoved the man?"

"Okay, it was my arm, but I didn't push him, I actually was reaching out, trying to grab him!"

Banner is ramping up again, "How in the hell do you expect us to believe that?! You have been chirping to us about people being pushed or thrown or however you've wanted to state it, and here we now have video evidence that actually does show the man's body looking like it was vaulted forward and you deny it. See, look here." He has rewound the video. "There! His neck is clearly whipping back as if he didn't expect to be lurching forward. Nothing at all like the neck of a man who willingly jumped in front of that train!"

Now I am angry. "Wait! I have been trying to tell you that every time something like this has been happening! But because I have literally seen the man doing it! All you have done is doubt me, but now half a video has you accusing me of something you told me wasn't happening?!"

"You seem to be confused, dude. There is enough video evidence here to crucify you. Look at the arm. That's your arm pushing—"

"No, you're the one confused! I know it's my arm! I admitted that already, but it isn't pushing anything!"

"You want us to believe so badly that this guy was pushed, and yet, when a video shows that you are the one doing it, you can't admit when you're caught red-handed. I don't know how you manipulated this video, but you've been caught, Cotter. Give it up."

"Wait, what? You're saying I also manipulated the video? How in the hell would I have even done that? This video evidence that you're so proud of also shows me jumping on the other train."

"So what?"

"What do you mean, so what? I am sure the rest of your footage shows the train leave and then me eventually coming up off the tracks after walking back from the stalled train. So, I don't know how brilliant you think I am, but I never was anywhere near the recording device, wherever the hell that's even located." He is just staring at me. Clearly, he can't argue. "And, you know, explain to me how I am the one who pushed that guy in front of a bus from across the street. Or, how did I throw the senator from the balcony while standing on the ground. Maybe I roped him with my lasso and yanked him down, eh, Cowboy?"

It doesn't look like Banner appreciates my last comment. "Oh, you think you're pretty smart, huh? You little shit!"

Genny steps in front of him as it looks like he actually wants to put hands on me. "Banner, back off!"

"No! I am not going just sit here and take his smart-ass comments. Maybe you have been obsessing over your little lies about how these accidents were something more and now you decided to make one of them true by doing the exact act that never really happened the other times!

Well, you won't get away with it on my watch!"

Genny still has an arm outstretched, holding him back. "Why don't you go cool off, Bruce?"

Regardless of the seriousness of my situation right now, I just can't help myself. "Wait, your name is Bruce Banner?!" And I burst into laughter.

"Great, thanks for giving him that, Keller." He leaves the room.

"Wow, your partner needs to control his anger a little better."

"Well, maybe you could help him out a little by not provoking him. Can't hardly blame the passion of a homicide detective who is convinced there is a murderer sitting in front of him."

I reactively tilt my head and give her a look of disbelief. "Come on, you know better than that though."

"Do I? I don't know you from Adam, Mr. Trespin." Her look reminds me that I shouldn't feel too comfortable with her and just to make sure I am aware, she looks back and up to a camera, "Everything is recorded in this room, so you don't have to worry about anything violent happening to you. Well, at least if something did you could rest easy knowing that you would have video evidence against your attacker. Speaking of which, I am willing to listen if you want to try to explain what we see in this video."

I don't really know what to think about how this is all playing out. It feels so strange to have Genny sitting across from me in an interview, acting so professional and like she doesn't know me. Part of me understands why it has to be this way, but it's just a bit surreal. I mean, it wasn't long ago she was pulling me into her home and absolutely devouring me. We knew each other pretty well that day.

But, I guess I better play along and see if there is anything I can do to flip this situation. "Yeah, can you rewind to the moment when my arm comes into view?" She is rewinding and though it goes by quickly, there is a sick moment when the man's body comes back together. "Okay, can you just play it a couple times as my hand appears?" This part of the video is so brief, I don't know how I can explain it to look any different when Banner has a preconceived notion about what he is seeing.

"Wait! Are you able to play this in slow motion?"

"Yeah, I should be able to. Here we go."

"Okay! Look at how you can see that my hand is closed."

"And? What does that prove?"

"Well, I was grabbing for him after he was pushed, like I said. If I had shoved him, my hand wouldn't be almost closed into a fist."

Banner bursts through the door. "Why are you listening to this? Clearly, he is just trying to think up a way to explain it away. There is nothing to say you couldn't have lunged and punched at him to launch him in front of that train."

"But that isn't what happened. If you'll just look for yourself, you will see that my hand looks like it is trying to grab. There! See how the video clears in time to show my hand closing in a grabbing motion?"

"Bull shit. You could have pushed him and then made that grabbing motion."

"Can you play it again, please. Okay, wait! Play it again in slow motion. Look! You can actually see my hand moving toward him and then grab as it pulls away!"

"That doesn't prove a thing."

"Actually it looks like it proves that I never touched the guy. Just try to explain to me how I could have shoved the guy with the kind of force necessary to snap his head back and then immediately have my hand moving back toward him with a grabbing motion that pulls back. I am pretty sure when you put that scenario in real-time, the physics of it would sound ridiculous to just about anyone."

Genny speaks up, "I think there is something to that."

Banner's face is red and he reaches in my direction as I flinch away, but he grabs the porcelain coffee cup in front of me and launches it at the wall. The cup sounds off with a hundred simultaneous cracks and disappears, leaving only a brown stain that instantly starts racing down the wall.

I am shocked, however, the sarcasm still flows. "Uh oh, Hulk smash!"

"Fuck you!" And he is turning and out the door he goes.

"Wow, that guy really does have an anger issue. He must really want to nail me with something."

"Do you blame him with how you go at him?"

"Hey, I wasn't the one starting all of this. He is the one who has treated me with nothing but disrespect."

"He is just trying to do his job, Cotter."

"Whatever. I have a right to defend myself here. I haven't done anything wrong. And honestly, I don't know how you could defend that. I mean, you saw him the same as me. That's how you do this job?"

"Well, even good detectives can lose control of their emotions when they badly want to solve a crime."

"Are you kidding me? Everyone ignores my claims and now I am being badgered like I am some criminal. If he was so passionate about solving murders, maybe he'd be looking for the real criminal." I think for a second. "You know, he was on the other train and they were all stopped. If anyone cared to listen to me, they would have at least tried to look into what I was saying."

"Yeah, the officers on the scene did say they were going to check, but the trains were back in service."

"Right, and it's not like a cop has enough power and resources to have them stopped again? One of them said he'd have the train checked at the next station, but I doubt that even happened."

"You know what, actually it did happen. I was on my way to the scene when it came over the radio that there could be a suspect on the train you spoke of and I cared enough to rush to the second station in line. I knew I wouldn't make it in time to the first stop."

"Nice. I am sure he took his first opportunity to flee that train and considering I've been sitting here getting harassed, I am guessing your passionate police force must have missed the opportunity to catch him before he jumped off."

I feel like I should have a hole burned through me with the look Genny is giving me right now. "Only so much can be done sometimes and I tried, so save your sarcasm for someone else!" She turns now and is also exiting the room.

I feel a little bit guilty for my snarky comments but I am also pretty pissed off that I am in this situation and that is what continues to come out, "Sorry, but not sorry." She doesn't even react like she heard me as the door closes.

Now I am left sitting in this bright white room all alone. Knowing that I could be on the verge of moving from this lonely locked room to a lonely locked jail cell, there is a feeling in the pit of my stomach that I'm not sure I've ever felt. I guess it must be anxiety. Well, probably something like a mix of three parts anxiety and one part hangover. I have reminded myself that my head hurts and I wish Detective Butt-munch hadn't painted my coffee on the wall.

As much as I want to get out of this situation, the realization that nothing seems like it can or will work out for me has me suddenly feeling like I actually don't care what happens right now. I was so excited about what was happening with Genny, but it seems like even that it is already unraveling. It has felt very strange since I brought her along to witness the taxi hit that woman. It's almost as though I could sense that she was already moving away from me. I get that fuzzy feeling again at the back of my neck as I think about the things from my dream that I have now actually heard this morning. Maybe Genny really was just using me to get closer to this case. *Talk about commitment to the job.*

The door is opening and there is that beautiful face with those penetrating blue eyes, but they don't look at me like they did a couple days ago. Wow, it was really less time than that. It feels like there is so much distance between us now that it had to be several days, or even longer, that we were so hot for each other. But no, it was quite recent and I can't wrap my head around how this can be or what the hell is even going on. She must sense what I am feeling or is reading my body language even before I ask, "You and I, are we oka—"

"Don't!" She looks extremely irritated. "Just listen for a minute. My captain agrees that we have no reason to hold you here any longer, but you may need to be questioned again. Now, Detective Banner disagrees and he is still angry. He was even pushing to have you charged for jumping the turnstile just so we could lock you up."

"Well, that would definitely be some kind of joke, but what does it matter to me how he feels?"

"I just want you to understand that you should be careful how you handle yourself when you leave here. If you want to alienate the people around you, that's your choice, but just know that it doesn't help you when you find yourself in difficult situations."

"Yeah, look, I am sorry if I was disrespectful to you."

Genny laughs, but it's one that says don't be ridiculous. "Um, I am talking about pitting Detective Banner against yourself."

"So what are you saying, that I should be careful so I am not targeted. What, because he wants to believe I have done something wrong I have to watch my back. It doesn't sound like how the system should work. It seems more like corruption than anything else."

"You know what, you can just go because clearly you don't get it or you don't want to help yourself." She stands up, opens the door and waves me through, but doesn't even look at me.

Stepping out of the interview room, there is a wide-open space where I can see several officers, or maybe they are all detectives, sitting at desks in cubicles. Directly to my right, there are a few more standing and just staring as we walk toward them to get to an elevator. One of them is Banner and his face is literally red right now. The scowl he is wearing is actually a little intimidating, but I still can't help myself from saying, "Hey big guy, sun's gettin' real low."

Genny snaps her head around and gives me a look of disdain, but an older guy standing amongst the group actually bursts into laughter. Banner turns and just walks the other way. The guy who is laughing calls after him, "Come on, Bruce. Where is your sense of humor? That's just plain funny, man!"

We step into the elevator and turn as the doors close. The guy is still laughing and he turns toward us just in time for me to see him nod to me and raise his hands up while moving them to feign applause. I realize I have a huge smile on my face as I turn to Genny and see that she doesn't. "Who was the guy laughing?"

"That was our captain."

"What?!" I start to laugh now. "I can't believe I got a rise like that out of your boss."

Genny chuckles, "Yeah, I do have to admit it wasn't easy for me to keep my composure. It surprised me how funny I thought that was. But it doesn't mean that I think it was a wise move for you to continue to push his buttons."

Walking out the front door now, "Are you giving me a ride?"

"Nope, there is an officer right over there who will give you a ride home." She points.

"Seriously? After all this humiliation I still get to endure more by being dropped off in a squad car?"

"That is not the intent, but yes, that's what's happening."

"Well now that we aren't being scrutinized under cameras, can we talk about *us* for a minute?"

"Listen, Cotter, I don't think it's a good idea for us to be talking about anything right now. I already told you I needed to be careful and now it is an even worse situation with you being questioned like this."

"But you know I didn't do anything. Right? You don't think—"

"I don't know what to think right now, okay? What I do know is that I can't be seen having any kind of discussion with you that looks anything but professional. That car will take you home. I have to go." She turns and just walks away.

Walking up to the squad car now, I go around to the front passenger side, but the officer motions with his thumb for me to get in the back. Nice. I close the door and glance over to the police department building as Genny opens the door and enters. She doesn't look back, didn't even show a hint of wanting to look back. That didn't feel good. This doesn't feel good at all. In fact, there is a bubbly feeling in my stomach that doesn't feel good. It might be due to a combination of things, but I have no doubt it is caused by either my addiction to Genesis or Guinness.

12

I walk away from the squad car as briskly as possible without running. What an embarrassing moment to be dropped off in front of our building by the police. I mean, I know people around here! I have moved so quickly that I am already away from the front door of the building and I realize I never had any intent on going home right now anyway. I pull out my phone so I can at least tell my parents I am free. *Free?* That sounded weird in my head. What a scary feeling to know my freedom could be taken away so quickly.

I am not going home because there is no way I feel like talking to them right now, so this notification process of my release back into the land of the free will be through a text message. I wonder for just a moment where I am going but then realize my feet are naturally walking me towards Mr. Brown's Lounge. I begin to slow for a moment, but just a moment. Running into my boss, well, my former boss, Mr. Brown, is not on the top of my list of things to do on this day, my second Fourth of July this year. But, I'll risk it because I just like that place.

My phone is ringing for the second time since I sent a text to my mother. There is no way I am answering. I will send a more detailed text once I sit down. Maybe after one drink takes this edge off. Surprisingly, I realize that the hangover has subsided greatly. I think I am starting to get good at this hangover stuff. I feel a slight grin turn up on my face. What a terrible thing to feel good at. Oh well, with everything that is going on, I don't feel like I need to worry about anything beyond simply feeling good right now. Who says instant gratification is bad.

***

If there were any remnants remaining from last night's, or more like this morning's hangover, they are certainly gone at this point. I also am not feeling too bad about life right now. Ten Island Rum Punches can help cure just about anything, and my Jamaican bartender friend is certainly not holding back on the liquor in my libations. Just now, he shoots a look my way and I realize I am laughing out loud.

"What's so funny, mon?" I don't know that the guy is actually from Jamaica, but either way, the accent adds to the character of the place and I chuckle some more.

"I don't know how I didn't notice this before but look at the mural behind the bar!"

He doesn't turn. "Yeah, I've seen it plenty. What about it?"

"All the people facing away from us, and the liquor bottles on your back shelf!" And I am chuckling again.

"What is it you see, mon?"

"Look again, the bottles are all just the right height that it looks like they are sticking up the Jamaicans' asses!" He looks back now and quickly puts his head down, shaking his head, but he does smile. "Is that just a coincidence you think, or were they intentionally placed?"

With a bigger smile coming up he responds, "Oh, I have no doubt it was on purpose. In Jamaica, the ole back door is the preferred method of contraception, mon!" Now we both are doubled over with some deep belly laughter erupting. I look around for a moment thinking everyone must be looking at us, but there aren't many patrons here right now. However, as I look over toward the restaurant area, my eyes lock with none other than Mr. Zetticci.

"Aye, Cotter! How ya doin? I didn't know you go here."

"Oh, hey, Mr. Zetticci. Yeah... um, I guess I like to stop in here every now and then. Can't say I ever see you in here though?"

"Every Tuesday I just have to stop by to pick up a couple orders of the jerk chicken for the old lady and me."

I glance at the bartender. "Is it still Tuesday... is this the longest day ever, or what?" He just shrugs at me as if he knows this was a rhetorical question.

"Jeez, Cotter. You okay? You look like you been here a while."

I don't even look at him and just wave him off. I really want to tell the old man to just go away and leave me be. "I'm good. Just trying to relax on my day off." He doesn't need to know every day is a day off for me these days.

"Well, my food isn't quite ready and I guess I could use a drink, so let me buy ya one." He is already sitting down and motioning to the bartender before I can even respond. "I'd like two of whatever Mr. Trespin here is having." The bartender was already getting my next one so he sets that one in front of Ole Zetticci first and moves to get another for me. "Ah, the Island Rum Punch. Certainly the thing to be having here!" He takes a big gulp, "Ahhh, yes, perfect refreshment late evening on a Tuesday in the Windy City."

I look over at him now with what must be a bit of a scowl on my face. I am not too drunk to sense that he might be throwing some shade my way. "Is that right?"

"What? You don't agree, Cotter? Listen, I am just trying to make conversation here. Sure, I have never been sitting next to you in a bar, but how long have I known you, Cotter?" I only shrug in response. "Well, the answer is pretty much your entire life. I can remember you walking into the shop when you were just a wee bambino. You'd have a handful of your mother's dress and you'd pull it up over your face anytime I'd say something to you." He chuckles. "Oh how I enjoyed those moments. You were pretty cute."

"Yeah? Maybe that was the case then, but it sure doesn't feel like it now."

"Come on, Cotter. You are a damn handsome young man. Listen, I am not going to pretend to know everything that is going on with you, but maybe you are in a place where you need to hear that it can get so much better. If you are in here to drink sorrows away, just be careful."

"I told you I am just relaxing on my day off."

He puts both hands up to signal him backing off, "Yes, I know, I know," yet I still feel the lecture coming, "but it is clear to me that you are down. You need to know that you have your entire life ahead of you and it doesn't have to be anything like it is now." My glance at him must show my annoyance because his face looks like one who realizes he is digging a hole. "Okay, here is the thing. I know you have had some tough stuff going on lately because your mother talked with me a little about it yesterday."

"Wait, what?! She told you stuff about me?"

"Well, yes, but it wasn't anything bad, Cotte—"

"Nothing bad? Everything that's been going on with me lately is bad, and I don't need my mother telling the local dry cleaner."

He looks slightly pained by my comment. "Please understand that I am not just the Italian shopkeeper on the corner to your parents. We have developed a friendship. Our families have dined together, Cotter. Yes, I am friendly with all my customers, but most are still just customers. Your parents are my friends and so you are my friends' son."

"And I still don't think I want my parents talking about my personal life."

"I get your perspective, and maybe they shouldn't, but everyone needs people in their life they can ask for advice."

"How are you the person to give advice? And what is she telling you? That I screwed things up with Rebecca? I have seen people die? Did she tell you about the spotlights?!"

"Spotlights? I don't remember her mentioning anything like that. What is that?"

Just keep your mouth shut, Cotter, you're drunk. You don't need to be talking crazy and drunk at the same time. "It is nothing. Forget it."

"I didn't know about you and Rebecca. I am sorry. Your mother was just asking me about how they can help you through the trauma after seeing people committing suicide."

I softly mumble, almost to myself, "They weren't suicides."

"What was that?"

"Nothing."

"Your mother also wondered how to help with your drinking."

I let out an irritated laugh. "Of course she did. And what is it again that makes you the expert on such things?"

"Well, I am guessing your mother was looking to lean on a friend who has had a son who battled alcoholism and who also committed suicide. Do you remember ever meeting my son, Angelo?"

I don't think I knew he even had a son, but I am not too drunk to soften up a bit after hearing this. "No, I don't think I ever met him."

"Oh, you met him before." I give a puzzled look. "But I wouldn't expect you to remember. You would not have been much older than the age you were when still hiding behind your mother's dress by the time he moved out of our place. Our pretty little Angelo wasn't quite eighteen when he left us."

"Pretty? Seems a strange way to describe a son."

He chuckles to himself and there is a glint of a tear forming in the corner of his eye. "Ah, yes. I can see how that would sound, but I guess it was just the way I always saw him, more of a pretty bambino than a handsome bambino. However, I made the mistake of only associating that look with his features and was somehow blind to the feminine mannerisms." He looks confused for a second. "No, I guess I chose to be blind to the way he talked and acted. He was always my pretty boy and yet I still was surprised when he told us he was gay. At least I acted surprised, and I did not handle myself too well.

"In fact, looking back on how things went, maybe I was partly to blame for the way Angelo started drinking. It was bad. I had to go pick him up a few times from house parties and one time from the police station. And I let all of those issues justify how I treated him about his sexuality." He looks at me with glistening eyes. "I was not nice to him, Cotter. Out of anger in those moments, I even called him terrible things. I called him… a faggot." Zetticci's voice breaks up a little during that admission. "I pray often these days that he was too drunk to remember the things I said to him."

I feel bad for him right now but I am also feeling uncomfortable because I don't know what to say. "I can't… um, imagine. That must have been difficult for you to deal with."

"You said it. That was the problem. I was too worried about how *I* should deal with it, but you see, it was not my problem. I did not realize then that it did not even have to be a problem. I wish to God that I were wiser then. The bottom line is that my son was dealing with some serious issues and I did him no justice."

"Hey, I don't think you need to blame yourself for struggling with something that tough to understand."

"If that were the only way I handled it poorly, maybe I wouldn't beat myself up. However, I let fear take hold and I treated him terribly. I never needed to think that homosexuality was okay, and I never needed to accept it. That is something that goes against my morals, my spiritual beliefs, but it does not mean for a second that I still cannot treat someone who thinks otherwise with respect. It does not mean I still could not respect, and love, my pretty bambino. His sexuality was not hurting me and I had no right to hurt him.

"Anyway, it wasn't long before we woke up one morning and he was just gone. He was respectful enough to leave us a note. No, that is not accurate, he left his mother a note. I even used that as justification for how I felt towards him. I remember getting angry, wondering how he could leave a note that was specifically addressed to his mother. How could our Angelo show me that disrespect? Well, why would he not? I got exactly what I deserved.

"The note told us that he was headed to San Francisco." I raise my brows and try to hold back a smile. "I know. How cliché is that?!" He starts laughing and so I allow my smile to morph into a laugh.

"Were you able to eventually reconcile with him, Mr. Zetticci?"

The smile on his face fades immediately. "Unfortunately, I never got that opportunity, and that is another hard lesson I had to learn. There is not always time to set things straight with people, because you never know how long any of us will be around. Over the next year, Angelo wrote to my wife a few times.

"He did make it to San Francisco, but he never wrote too positively about his situation there. It seemed a struggle to get work without a high school diploma, so it sounded like he was just staying with people he would meet. Angelo never wrote explicitly about his relationships, but it was clear that he was in vulnerable positions and those men were using him. None of it sounded good. He would write a little about partying, but never specifically spoke about his drinking. Still, we figured it was probably bad."

"Didn't your wife want to help him?"

"Of course she did, and don't get me wrong, I loved my son very much and deep down I wanted to help too."

"Sorry, I didn't mea—"

"No, it is okay, Cotter. I have told you how terrible I was. I know how it sounds. In any case, Angelo never left a return address and the one time he called his mother, he said he was doing fine and he did not want us to know how to reach him. Then the last letter we received from him was written in a way that didn't seem like him at all."

"How do you mean? Like he didn't write it?"

"No, it was his handwriting, but he must have been drunk, or on drugs or something. Angelo must have been dealing with depression at this point too, or maybe he had been for a long time, I can only guess because I didn't ask when I had the chance." He shakes his head as if needing to wake himself up. "Anyway, the next we heard of Angelo was from a police officer who called to inform us of his death. He jumped off the Golden Gate Bridge."

"Holy shit. That's crazy."

"Yep, holy shit. It sounded like an absurdity to me too, but by asking some questions, we learned it is the most common place for a person to commit suicide or something. Of course, one of the first questions we wanted answered was if he was intoxicated or not when it happened. And as we suspected, the toxicology reports suggested that Angelo's blood alcohol content was something like three times what the legal driving limit was at that time."

"So he was drunk diving?" Zetticci snaps around and gives me a look of shock. "Oh my God. I can't believe I said that. I'm sorry."

All of a sudden, he smiles and chuckles. "Don't worry about it. Had plenty of time for the wounds to heal a bit."

"No, that was out of line, sorry."

"Ah, if you can't joke around with me, then you can't joke with anyone!" He laughs even harder. "But in all seriousness, I think the hardest part of it all was knowing that he made the decision to end his life during a moment when he was incapable of thinking clearly. I mean, in a way it would have been worse I guess if he had jumped completely sober, but you know what I mean. It is difficult not to wonder if he ever would have taken that leap without the liquid encouragement.

"So, I guess you can probably see the additional interest I have in talking with you right now. Not that it's only because you're doing some drinking. I just care more than you know about your parents and that means I care about how you're doing."

"Well, I am fine."

He puts his hands up. "Okay, okay. I really appreciate that you and your family patronize my business, so the last thing I want to do is sit here and patronize you. Just know that I had to take this opportunity to talk to you. I will leave you to it, Cotter. Take care of yourself."

"Yep, see ya, Mr. Zetticci." His story, and the booze has really gone to my head and my eyes are downcast on the drink in front of me. I am only hazily aware of him walking over to the restaurant counter to grab his food that is probably cold at this point. Now that he is nearing the front door, a lightbulb goes off in my head that excites me and my head pops up. "Zetticci!"

Halfway through the door already, he steps back in and looks my way. "Yeah?"

I point. "Look at the mural of those people facing away and the liquor shelf. Notice anything?"

He looks curiously for a moment, "Ha! The bottles are up their asses!" And Zetticci lets the door swing closed behind him as he begins laughing, maybe harder than I've ever heard anyone laugh before in my life.

13

I am actually surprised to hear Genny answer the phone after only a couple of rings. "Seriously, Cotter. I need you to stop blowing up my phone. It's after midnight you know! What the hell?"

"Is it that late already? Jeez, time flies when you're having rum. Come have a drink with me, Genny. Come on, you know you want to."

"Um, even if I wanted to, and I don't, it's late and I just now got home from work."

"Oh, come on, honey baby. I'll treat ya to a good time and then walk ya home, if ya know what I mean." She's not laughing with me. "Maybe we'll stop in the park and dance in the spotlight."

"What? You mean dance in the moonlight."

"Whatever, sure, if that's what you'd rather do."

"Wow, Cotter, how drunk are you right now? Forget it. Listen, I need to go to bed and I need you to stop with the obsessive calling."

"What do you mean? This is the first that we have even talked, Genny."

"Yeah, this is the first time we have connected, but you called my phone at least a dozen times today, and there were even more text messages than that! Don't make me block your number, Cotter."

"Wait! How could you do that to me? Why would you do that?"

"Because you are crossing a line! I have made it clear that we need to keep our distance. You are putting me in a bad spot by not doing as I have asked. You're going to cost me my job if you keep this up, Cotter."

It's difficult to focus enough to make sense of this conversation right now, but I shake the cobwebs free and gain at least a slight understanding. "Right. You're right. I am sorry I am being so pushy, but

I'm not crazy. I'm not a crazy guy, Genny. I just like you."

"Yeah, I know, Cotter."

"Just promise me that we can connect when all the shit stops hitting the shit outta the already shit-caked fan." I laugh in what feels like a sad attempt to lighten things up, to pull her back towards me, but I still don't hear her laughing.

"I'm not promising you anything. There are no guarantees in life. However, I will promise that if you continue to pester me, this will be our last personal conversation. Good-bye, Cotter."

"Okay, bye." Well that did not go as planned. I try to click into my text messages to see if she was exaggerating, but it's more of a struggle than it should be to put my finger on the right app and I realize my phone is ringing her back again. "Shit!" I hurriedly start mashing at the red button and it hangs up, but now I've fumbled my phone and it smacks down on the sidewalk outside of Mr. Brown's Lounge. I bend down to pick it up and side step a couple times to the right in order to keep my balance.

I grab my phone and stand up. "Oh, perfect. Isn't that some shit." Cracked it pretty good. The top left corner of the screen looks like a little abandoned spider web. That jolted a little clarity into my head and I open my messages to see that Genny actually undersold it. There are at least two dozen messages going to her. Jeez, I hardly remember sending any of these.

Wait, there is a recent text thread to Rebecca too! Looks like a sent a couple messages. *I miss you,* oh that's great, and prior to that one, it reads *What's up, Sexy?* And she responded, *Oops, you accidentally sent these to your old girlfriend!* All I can do is shake my head. How stupid of me.

I walk back inside and put my hand up to the bartender as I approach. It's way busier in here than I last remember and the bartender somehow turned into a white guy.

"Yeah? You looking to pay your tab?"

"No... no way. I definitely need another drink."

"Listen, I cut you off an hour ago, I'm definitely not going to start you back up again, pal."

"What the hell are you talking about? I haven't even been served yet by you... pal."

He laughs a little. "You're definitely not changing my mind with comments like that." He continues to chuckle and then seems to notice what feels like a confused look on my face. "Hey, I took over at six o'clock, man. I probably served you for way longer than I should have, but you seem to have one hell of a tolerance. The last drink though was the one you sloshed all over that chick at the table behind you."

"Oh, come on. You must be talking about someone else. I didn't do that."

"Listen, it wasn't intentional, you fell off the barstool. It was somewhat funny until I thought her boyfriend was about to pound you into the ground. I had to run over to save your ass." His eyes light up. "Oh! And then while I was talking that guy down, I turned around just in time to see you step back to the bar and say something like, 'It's all good, baby,' as you pinched the ass of the girl next to you."

"Okay, now I know you're messing with me."

He glances down the bar. "That guy was here," he points. "Hey! This guy fell off his stool and then pinched that lady in the ass, didn't he?"

He responds, "Well, I don't think I would call her a lady, but yes."

"See, and he's right, I was actually more concerned that she might be the one to kick your ass."

"Right. You know, I am a little tougher than I look."

"I am not kidding, man. She jumped up and gave you a shove that put you back on the ground." I look at him in disbelief. "Trust me, considering the state you were in, she might have been able to take you. Her hair was shorter than yours, if you know what I mean."

"Whatever... so, you're not going to serve me?"

"Jesus, man. Did you hear a word I just said?"

"Okay then, keep your damn stories to yourself." I wave him off as I start walking away. "I'll take my business elsewhere."

"What about your tab?"

I don't look back. "Just charge it to the card I gave you." And I wave him off again.

"So no tip then, nice."

I already have the door open but I turn and respond, "Here's a tip for you. Don't tell a grown-ass man that you think he could have been beaten up by a lesbian and still expect him to tip you." I am already across the sidewalk and heading diagonally across the street. There is a bar at the other end of the block I have never been to, but I know it's just a dive bar so I am sure they will serve me. I have definitely sobered up from how that bartender described me being earlier. I can't believe it was even that big of a deal then. That guy was feeding me a line of crap, I bet.

Walking through the door I see that the bar is dimly lit and does not possess an inviting feel at all. The place feels way too small to have a live band, but there are some fairly young looking guys thrashing away in the back corner. It is extremely loud, but I don't mind with the heavy rock sound they are producing. It's actually pretty good. Currently, they are playing a song by Nothing More. I can't think of the title, but it's the song about some megalomaniac acting like he is Jesus Christ. Too bad my brother isn't in here. He could certainly stand to hear this one.

This place is like a giant can of sardines. People packed in here so tight that they must be breaking fire code. Though I am enjoying the music, I have little interest in spending any more time than necessary squished in the middle of this number of people. I begin swimming my way through the horde to make my way over to the bar. It's taking forever considering how small this establishment actually is. I imagine it can't be more than twenty-five feet from the front door to the corner of the bar and it has probably taken me a few minutes to cover that ground.

I am thinking it will take even longer for a bartender to get to me with this place hopping like it is, but there are several servers behind the bar. Clearly, they were expecting a busy night. Maybe it's because of this band that they knew people would be flowing in here. Almost immediately, a pretty, older woman with long black hair pulled into a ponytail looks my way and points to signal I am up. "Five shots of Patrón, please."

She doesn't say anything as she grabs the bottle from behind the bar and pulls plastic shot glasses from under the bar. She is pouring healthy shots in each glass and as she reaches the last one she says, "That'll be forty-five dollars."

I hand her a fifty. "Keep the change."

"Thank you, sweetie. Are you going to be able to carry all those?"

I give her a questioning look and then start taking the shots, one after another. "Oh, my mistake. I guess if I were paying that much for tequila shots that is definitely how I would carry them away from the bar too." I hold the third shot up as if toasting and then take it down. "Well played, young man."

I pause before moving on to the last couple of shots. "This band is awesome! That guy almost sounds exactly like the lead singer of Nothing More."

She tilts her head with a questioning look. "That is Nothing More."

"What?! No way!"

"Yeah, seriously, it is."

"That is crazy. This is such a small bar, how could you get them to play here?"

"It's a pop-up concert. Sometimes bands just like to give fans a treat by popping up in small venues. Let's just say the bar's owner is a friend of the band and that is how they ended up here."

"So does that mean the employees didn't even know they were going to be here?"

"Well, not all of us knew it would be going down and it didn't get advertised at all. So, basically, no customers knew they were playing here until the first song started. Actually, I saw some people recognize them when they came out. Everyone just started calling people and this place filled up in a heartbeat."

"Wow, I had no idea, I just needed a drink."

"You mean you needed five shots of tequila." She laughs. "I would say that is way different than *a drink*."

"Okay, you got me there." I take the next shot and now the last. She gives me an impressed look and some mock applause, so I bow for her. "Well, I sure am glad I stopped in here. What a treat to be able to hear this band live. If you talk to the lead singer, don't tell him I said he *almost* sounds like the Nothing More singer." That gets a good laugh out of her. She is really good looking when she is smiling. "And, I think I found a new favorite bartender."

"Well, I'm flattered." She does a little curtsey and we both laugh. "Hey, how 'bout I have a shot with you before you go."

"How can I say no to that?" She is already pouring the Patrón. We raise our shots and figuratively clink the plastic glasses together. "To a night that's all about new friends and Nothing More."

"Ah, I see what you did there." She chuckles and we down the shots.

"I'm Cotter, by the way." I offer my hand to shake, once again thinking about how pretty she is.

"Jenny." She shakes my hand and all I can think of now is Genny. I let go and turn towards the band as I am just now recognizing the current song as being *Sex & Lies*. This one is all about catching a lover cheating. How appropriate. Now I am thinking about Rebecca, and what I did to her.

"You okay, Cotter?"

"Hmm? What?"

"You just looked like your mood suddenly changed or something."

I feel confused for a second and try to shake the cobwebs, "Oh, yeah, sorry. It's just that I used to really like this song."

"Yes, I love this song! But are you saying you don't like it anymore?"

I pause for a second. "No, I don't think I do like it anymore."

"Why not?"

"Memories. I now have sour memories to tie to this song. I guess it just made me feel weird just now." I feel my head starting to cloud up again. "Anyway, it was a pleasure but I should head home before my brain starts absorbing too much of that tequila."

"Sure, I should be helping a little more back here anyway."

One of the younger female bartenders hears this comment and says with a smirk, "Yeah, just because you're the owner doesn't mean you can slack off."

Jenny snaps her with a towel she is holding and makes a face that tells her to shut up and move on.

I was already walking away so a couple of other patrons have already filled my space and bellied up to the bar. I stand on my tippy toes and yell, "So you're the one who knows the band? That's a pretty cool thing you didn't tell me."

"Maybe when it's a little quieter in here some time I can tell you about that. Be safe, Cotter!"

I turn and start swimming my way towards the door. It feels even more packed now than when I came in. It's so hot in here with all this body heat. I am starting to feel like I could be sick. I don't know if it's the alcohol or the anxiety from feeling like I am stuck in a log jam on a river of people, but things are starting to spin. *Just take a deep breath, man. Just make it to that door and you'll be okay. Just get to the door... you'll be okay.*

I instantly have a renewed vigor because there is a spotlight shining down through the ceiling on an older man near the door. The sickness I was about to transfer to the floor is all but gone with the shot of adrenaline shooting through my heart. I am moving easier to the door now as I strategically dip my shoulders in an alternating fashion to wedge my way between the people in front of me. I am out the door in what feels like an instant but the man under the spotlight is already a couple of blocks away, on the other side of the street.

I am running down the sidewalk but I need to get to the other side of the street. Looking back, the closest car is going through the intersection a block behind me. I can easily make it across before it gets here. The adrenaline has me a little more focused but I am still not clear-headed, so I keep my eyes on the car coming up from behind as I start running across the near lane.

A blaring horn and the screeching of rubber on the pavement draws my attention back to the right just as a black Mustang comes to a halt inches from my knees. My momentum carries me forward and my thighs slam into the front of the hood while my forearms slap onto two white racing stripes. I only faintly hear a muffled voice from the driver's seat, "What the hell is your malfunction, man?" I stand up, put my hands up apologetically, and start walking away. "Better not be bent or you're dead!"

A twinge of anger produces a reflex in my knee that brings my foot up and through the right headlamp of the black Mustang with white racing stripes. I hear the driver's door pop open as I reach the sidewalk, so I break into a run. The last glance I had at the spotlight it was moving beyond a building up ahead, but now it appears to have been snuffed out. I can't see it anywhere. A glance back shows me the driver just standing between his car and the sidewalk with his arms outspread. Now he is flipping me off with both hands.

I don't have a spotlight to chase down anymore, but I don't want to get chased down either, so I keep running. I turn into the alley on the left. It's much darker down here. Even if he does give chase, I should be able to keep to the shadows and put some distance between us. Crossing the next street, more carefully, I head into another dark alley. My stomach is turning again so I sit down on the other side of some oversized garbage cans. My heart is racing and my head is starting to spin again so I close my eyes. I'll just take a few minutes here and then I should be able to get myself home.

14

"Sir! You need to wake up, sir!" I am trying to open my eyes, but it is proving to be rather difficult. There is a bright light shining in my eyes. I don't know who is doing this but it is probably not helping me obey his command. I feel my mouth moving to bring this revelation to his attention. "What's that? Sir, you have to speak coherently. I can't understand a word you're saying."

I put my hand up to shield some of the light and now I am able to open my eyes a little more, but my vision is blurry. "I said stop with all the light and maybe I can wake up for you. Hey, why are you waking me up anyway?"

"The reason I am waking you up is because you are passed out in the middle of an alley."

Pushing myself up, I lean on an elbow and look to my side to see two large metal garbage cans next to a building. Looking down now I can see that I am laying on asphalt. "Ick." I am leaning in a puddle of puke. "Damn. I hope that's not my puke. Actually, I hope it is my puke. Ah, I don't know what's better right now."

"What's that, sir?"

"Oh, nothing, I don't think." It's only now that I look up and see a badge on the man holding the light. I know my speech feels slurred and my vision is still blurry, but I can think well enough to realize this is a cop in front of me and I am not in a good situation.

"You're not making any sense, sir. How many drinks have you had?"

I look down and start pointing my finger, "One... two... three... four... five... six..."

"What are you saying now?"

"Well, you asked me a question, officer. I am trying to count how many drinks in the puke." I hear him chuckling a little. "What? Is this not my puke? Gross!"

"Oh, I'm pretty sure it's your vomit, sir. But I am also pretty sure you can't count drinks from looking at vomit."

"Sure ya can. I mean, maybe not all of them, but look at all the worms. I can at least count all the shots of tequila I had."

I hear him snickering at me again. "Though I have no interest in dissecting it, I am pretty sure those are bits of noodles, not worms, in the vomit."

"Nah, they're moving."

"They may very well look like they are moving to you, but they are not. Enough shenanigans, let's see some identification."

"Shenanigans!" I laugh. "Now there's a good old-timey word. You ain't no spring-chicken-cop to be throwing around an old geezer word like that!"

"Identification, please." He shines the light back in my eyes again and I try to shield it. It's too dark in this alley for me to see his face or how old he looks. Patting my pockets now, I don't seem to have my wallet. I always have my wallet. "I don't have my damn wallet. Where the hell is it?" I am on my hands and knees now, feeling the ground around me. My hands hit with wet sounding slaps as they come down in the puke.

"Enough! That is disgusting! Just get to your feet." He hooks a hand under my armpit and hoists me up to my feet. I stumble a little and he grabs hold again.

"Ah, a little puke is nothing compared to what I've seen lately."

"Your wallet isn't anywhere down there and it's starting to look like you will be riding in my squad car, so I don't need you getting more of that on you than you already have."

"Wait, why would you need to take me in your car? I haven't done anything wrong."

"While public intoxication is not illegal in Illinois, you can't just be passed out drunk in the middle of a thoroughfare. And you don't even have identification to show me who you are."

"How do you know that?"

"You just checked your pockets and didn't find your identifi—"

"No, how do you know the word thoroughfare. You are coming at me with some crazy old words."

"Don't condescend me right now. Do you really think you're in a position to play a 'who is smarter' game?"

"I apologize. I was actually just impressed, and amused I guess."

"Well, I am not amused. We do not become cops because we are not smart enough to do something else, if that is what you were implying."

"Nope. Wasn't implying anything, but you should see some of the cops I've met lately."

"And just how many cops have you been meeting lately?" He turns me towards the wall. "Put your hands against the wall and spread your legs. Do you have any weapons on you tonight, Mister?" He draws out the mister to make it clear he is asking for my name and now he is giving me a pat down.

"Cotter Trespin, and I sure hope this doesn't turn into the cop scene from *Days of Thunder*. I mean, no offense, you're a good enough looking guy, but just not my type."

He turns me back around to face him. "And what's your first name, Mr. Cotter-Trespin?"

"Cotter is my first name. Trespin is the last." I am still not seeing or thinking clearly, but it seems he turns his head like he isn't sure he believes me. He takes me by the arm and we start walking. I see now he is taking me toward his squad car. "Please, officer! You don't have to arrest me. Please, please!"

"Just relax. You are not under arrest, yet, but if you don't pull yourself together, that might be what you are facing. Just stand here and lean against the squad if you need." I don't wait a second to take advantage of the offer to lean on the car. It's so hard for me to think clearly, to think straight at all right now. I am really messed up. "What's your middle name?"

"Seriously? Do you really need to know?"

"What's the problem? Unless you are lying to me, you should not have any reason not to give me your full name. I need it to check to see who you are."

"This is me, right here." I point to my head, touching my hair and I feel how wet and slimy it is. *Must be puke.* "It's the dumbest middle name ever. I hate it."

"Try me. I have heard some doozies. Besides, names don't have to define a person."

"Ainsworth."

"What's that?"

"My middle name! If you have to know, it's Ainsworth."

"Hmm. That is a new one, but it's not that bad. Just different."

"Well, I hate it." He sits down in his car and I am just barely aware of a typing sound on a computer. I am so drunk still, and tired. Man, am I tired.

"If you check out okay, maybe I will just get you home, Cotter."

I heard him but all I can muster right now is a head nod. My eyes are closed, just waiting for him to take me home, I guess. I hope.

"Cotter!"

...

"Wake up, Cotter!"

...

"Cotter Ainsworth Trespin!"

Okay, I felt like I was hearing my name being called off in the distance, but that last one registered right next to me. I open my eyes a little and I can see the officer standing over me. I mumble, "Don't call me that."

"What's that?"

"I told you I don't like my middle name, officer."

"Yeah, well, you fell down here, passed out again and I needed to get your attention. You did not have any outstanding warrants and it seems like you are probably who you say you are. Who could make up that name and have it actually turn up in the system? However, I have a strong suspicion that you are the one who busted up a car last night, so I am taking you in."

"Wait, I didn't do anything, please don't! I am sure I can prove my identity if you just let me make a phone call." I pull my phone out. "Oh yeah, here is my license. I have a slot in my phone case."

"I'm sorry, young man, but it's too late for that and you can't even stand. I'm not arresting you, but I am taking you in until you sober up and can answer some questions."

"No, come on." I'm trying to pull myself up and he is helping me. "You don't have to, I'm okay."

"I'm taking you in to sleep this off and I don't want to hear any more whining about it or I will charge you with something right now. Watch your head."

He has the door open and starts to push my head down. "Wait, I have to piss."

"Everything around here is closed. I am sure you can wait."

"I can't. I have to piss right now."

My eyes are half-closed and I feel almost out of it again. I hear him sigh and half see him look around in the alley. "Okay, just go here."

…

"Well?"

…

"Cotter?"

"What?"

"You said you had to urinate. I told you to go ahead."

"I did."

"What?!" His loud response helps open my eyes a little more. "Seriously?! Why did you stand here and piss your pants?!"

I look down and can't really see anything, but now that he says so, I do feel a wet warmth spreading between my legs. "Oops."

"Just get in the car! I guess it'll be getting detailed tomorrow." This time he isn't so kind as to push my head down or warn me and the top of my head clips the door jam. It felt like a pretty hard hit, but it doesn't really hurt. I guess I am feeling no pain right now.

***

"Good morning, dude."

You've got to be kidding me. Am I really going to have to deal with this guy now? I sit up and look his way for confirmation of the voice I

123

think I've heard. "What do you want, Banner?"

"Oh, I just wanted to see this for myself. You look rather rough, dude. I bet your head is just pounding away."

"Nah, I feel just fine."

"Oh, right, after registering a .238 blood-alcohol level still this morning, I imagine you're actually still drunk. The party in your head might not start until this afternoon."

Of course he's right. I am definitely still at least somewhat intoxicated. However, my head feels bruised on top and is already starting to pound a little, but I wasn't going to give him the satisfaction. "You're a homicide detective, so why are you here, Bruce?"

Instead of turning green, his face turns slightly red. "You can refer to me as Detective Banner!" We just continue staring at each other. "I am here because I want to be the one to inform you of the charges being brought against you."

"Whatever. I don't know why I am being held here now and there shouldn't be any reason for charges against me."

"No? You don't think busting out the headlamp of a Mustang warrants a charge?"

"That guy almost ran me over!"

"You mean when you were jaywalking across the street in a drunken stupor?"

"I wasn't jaywalking. I was running."

"You sure do have a smart mouth for a guy who is sitting in a holding cell. I wonder what it would take to humble you, Cotter? Maybe this next charge will. You're also being charged with sexual battery."

"Wait, what?!" My heart starts racing so fast I worry it might run right out of my mouth. "Why in the world would I be charged with that?!"

"You grabbed a woman's butt in the bar. That constitutes battery." He is grinning from ear to ear.

I want to blow up, but I don't want to give him any more satisfaction than he is already getting. "Well, I don't recall doing that at all." I'm not lying. In fact, there is a lot I don't remember from last night. Like, why are my pants and underwear damp?

"You don't have to say anything right now. There are reports and witnesses to all of this and you'll have your day in court."

"This is ridiculous. I have a right to make a phone call and I want to do that now."

"Oh, it doesn't quite work like you see on television. First, we will get you processed. You know, fingerprints, mugshot, that sort of thing. Then we will give you some fresh-smelling clothes to change into. We want you to fit in with the other inmates and of course, nobody wants you to get all raw from those urine soaked undies." Oh, look at him just basking in the glow of my embarrassment. "Then we will give you a cell amongst all the other criminals. It's okay though, don't worry, we won't make you mingle with the hardcore guys. Sometime after that, you will be able to make your phone call."

I am not saying anything more and I try my best not to show any kind of reaction. He turns and knocks on the door. It opens and I see him speaking with two uniformed correctional officers. One is walking in now. "Stand up and step out." I walk out the door. "Stop there. Step over to that counter." He points and walks behind me.

The other correctional officer opens an inkpad. I guess they are going to take my fingerprints. "Give me your right hand and just relax it." He puts my thumb in the ink and rocks it back and forth. Now he is placing it on one of five squares on a paper card. The officer rolls it from the left edge of my nail all the way across so that he finishes at the right edge of my nail. He moves on to my index finger and I assume he will continue with the same technique for each of my ten fingers.

"Why do you make it such a large fingerprint?"

"You never know which part of a fingerprint might get left somewhere, so we need to make sure we document as much of each finger as possible."

"That makes sense."

The other officer had walked away but now he is walking back with folded, orange clothes in his arms. "Walk this way." He is leading me into a room with a bench and a shower. "Take all of your clothes off."

"That line might work with other guys, but I'm a little harder to get."

"Just do it. Or do you need help?" I start to disrobe and he is just staring at me. Now I am standing in front of him in my birthday suit. "Pull up your scrotum."

"Oh, come on!"

"Okay, this is the standard strip search for everyone who comes through here. So, again, you can do what I direct you to do or we will help you, and that way will be much more invasive."

"I don't see how this could be more intrusive." He starts to move but stops when I do as I was told. Now he bends down a bit and looks.

"Turn around and bend over as far as you can." What is this nonsense? I can't help but react by raising my eyebrows and tilting my head. "Unless you'd rather I put a glove on and do a full cavity check?" I bend over and I guess he looks to make sure I don't have drugs or a shiv hidden up my butt. "Okay, you can put these on now."

"Wait, can I shower first?"

"No, just get dressed."

"But I have crusty puke on my arm and a puke hairdo."

He looks back toward the desk at the other correctional officer who answers the look, "Detective Banner was clear. He said no shower. Get dressed." I slip a pair of baggy underwear on and then the orange scrubs before I am led back over to the counter. "Now step here so we can get a mugshot."

"You know, I realize I messed up, but this is ridiculous." They don't even respond as I step to the spot. "So this is why so many people look so terrible in their mugshots. It's all just a setup. You just woke me up and I don't even get to clean myself up or fix my ridiculous looking hair."

"This isn't a glamour shoot. Look at the camera."

...

"I said look at the camera." I glance up and scowl at them. The camera clicks.

"Set up complete with an angry look. Well done, gentlemen. How about my phone call so I can get bailed out of here today?"

"You can call later, but you can stop hoping for that, it's Sunday. You won't be able to see a judge until tomorrow. Start walking." My heart starts jumping again and it feels like it's bouncing on my stomach now. He points me down the hall and they both walk with me. I have to spend the night in jail. I don't belong here, this is crazy and wrong. We buzz through three different doors before we arrive in a two-level cellblock. There are two more correctional officers at a desk within the cellblock. "He's all yours."

The officer who walks over to take custody of me is well into his years, with his gray hair combed to the side and an almost white, closely cropped beard. He is tall enough to look down on me, which is appropriate because I feel pretty small right now. His nose is long and sharp at the end, like it's pointing down at me. I didn't notice name badges on the other officers' uniforms, but his says, Brutus. What a perfect name to sum up a rather intimidating older man.

Considering the callousness the first two officers delivered to me, I am having a tough time imagining this guy will be a gentle giant. I mean, those two looked very average and yet they presented plenty of heat, and this guy has a presence to start with. Brutus says nothing as he directs me towards a cell. We start walking that way and I only now begin to look around at all the cells. Nearly every tiny rectangular window has a face peering out at me. Some are just looking inquisitively, but others are smiling grossly as I walk.

Glancing up to the second level, the faces look more heinous. Almost every man I can see is sneering and some are yelling derisively. And now I can see that most of them are not alone in their cells. A specific cell window has caught my attention now and I just barely catch myself before running into a table as I walk. One man with short, black hair is staring blankly, a little back from the window, and a second man must be pacing the floor. He has long black hair and his shirt is off. Every time he reaches the window, he glances down at me and yells, "FUCK!" Then he turns and repeats the round trip process in about five seconds.

Brutus must recognize concern or maybe terror on my face because he speaks now for the first time. "Don't worry about the rest of these guys. Most of them are here for a while and their time out of the cells will not be the same as your time."

"You let them out of their cells?"

I must look shocked because he chuckles a little. "Well, of course. You will all get a certain amount of time out of your cells so that you can

127

eat, shower, and recreate a little if you'd like. Oh, and make your phone calls over there."

"Oh, can I make a call."

"Sorry, son, but it doesn't work like that. I need to put you in your cell and you will be free to make calls when your time comes to be out of your cell."

We are now standing in front of a cell that has a paper placard saying C. Ainsworth. "My last name is Trespin."

"Really? This is what they sent down to me. I guess they got something mixed up, sorry." It strikes me that this man has spoken surprisingly gently to me thus far.

"Whatever. I guess I don't really care what it says on my jail cell. What is C. Ainsworth anyway? Just a part of my name that I hate, and I don't like myself much right now anyway. Perhaps it's poetic justice." I look back at him. "I guess your name is Brutus."

He looks down. "Actually, Brutus is my last name. First name is Anderson and you can feel free to call me that."

"Anderson, hmm. A last name first with a first name last."

He chuckles. "Yeah, I guess. Except I don't feel like I've heard of anyone named Brutus since Julius Caesar was assassinated."

We both laugh. "I suppose I would agree with that. Well, Anderson, I wouldn't mind you calling me Cotter instead of C. Ainsworth."

"Fair enough." He looks toward the desk. "Open number thirteen!" There is a buzz and he pulls the door open. "The tour is short. There is your bed. Take the top or bottom bunk. You won't have anyone in here with you." I breathe a sigh of relief. Brutus points down, "There's the toilet and here are a couple of toiletries for you." He looks me over and takes an obvious sniff. "Did you refuse to shower when they processed you?"

"I was not allowed to clean up at all."

He furrows his brow. "You should have asked if you could."

"Oh, I did! More than once I tried to convince them."

His face hardens even more. "Those bastards. That is not okay." He shakes his head and lets out a heavy breath. "That is *not* how we *all* choose to treat you guys. I apologize for their behavior."

"No need for you to apologize for them, but I appreciate it."

"Well, feel free to wash up in the sink and then you can shower when you have time out." He turns to walk out, but stops in the doorway and stands there a second before spinning back on his heels. "Screw that. Do you want to take a shower now?"

"Yes, that would be great."

He steps aside and points across the floor. "The showers are right there and you'll see a rack of towels just to the left. I only ask that you make it quick."

"Thank you!"

I start hurriedly across the floor and notice the younger correctional officer looking confused. As I grab a towel I hear him say, "What are you doing, Brutus? This isn't protocol."

"You don't need to worry about it. Something needs to be fixed and I am fixing it." He must have started to protest again because Brutus says, "Just keep your mouth shut, Reynolds. Act like all the other power hungry officers around here and you will never earn the respect of these inmates. But, if you want to learn how to treat people with respect and have things go easier for you, stick with me." This helps me smile as the hot water begins flowing and starts cleansing me of the filth, at least on the outside of my body.

15

It is finally my turn to have some time out in the commons of the cellblock. There are only a few other guys who are out here with me. The upper level was let out before us and I spent some time studying that berserker who was pacing in his cell earlier. He wasn't really acting crazy while he was out of his cell, but now as I listen to the phone ringing in my ear, he is back to the previous behavior within his cell. "Hello?"

"Hey, Dad."

"Son, why are you calling me from the jailhouse?! You told us you had gotten out."

"I did get out yesterday morning... well, I mean, I never was in. They had just questioned me."

"So what's the deal then? They decided to charge you with something?"

"No, I am not here because of that. Some things went down last night, or this morning. I guess I don't know what time it all went down."

"All of it? What is going on, Cotter? Were you drinking?" He must hear or sense that I am having trouble keeping myself composed. I can't remember the last time I cried openly. Well, when I have been sober anyway. "Son, it will be okay. We will figure this out. Just tell me what happened."

I take a deep breath. "They say I am being charged with... I guess he didn't say the first charge, but I kicked the headlamp out of a car on the street. And the other charge is... sexual battery."

Dad is probably really trying to be positive and supportive, but I do hear an audible sigh. "Okay, tell me what the sexual battery charge is for."

"I don't actually remember that happening."

"Meaning? You don't think you did anything or you had a blackout or something?"

"Um, yeah, I guess that's what it would have to be because I do remember the bartender telling me later that I did this. I didn't exactly believe it at the time but I see no reason why he would have made it up, and then this terrible detective said a similar thing this morning."

"Okay, what did they say happened?"

"Apparently, I pinched or grabbed a woman's butt. I think I was almost in a fight before that because of spilling a drink or something, but the bartender stopped that from happening."

"Okay, we can work with that. The other will probably be a vandalism charge. Tell me why you did that."

"I ran across the street and a guy in a mustang almost hit me. He didn't, but I fell on the hood and then he yelled some threatening things at me. Something about being dead if I damaged the hood I think. That's when I kicked his car."

"Okay, are there more accusations that will come with the charges? Make sure you have told me everything."

"Well, that's all I remember, or have been told. So, yes, I believe that is everything."

"Alright, I have a friend who should be willing to help."

"But you're a lawyer, Dad. Why can't you just help me?"

"Son, it doesn't work like that. For one, I am not licensed anymore. Secondly, I just was not that kind of lawyer."

"You were good, Dad. I am sure you could manage this."

"I appreciate the vote of confidence, but I was a business lawyer. Even if I was still practicing, I would not want to take the risk of representing you when there is someone with more specific knowledge of the law as it pertains to your charges. However, as I said, I know somebody, so just plan on meeting with him early in the morning. And tell him everything, truthfully, Cotter."

"I will. Thank you."

"Why did you say *terrible* detective earlier?"

"Oh, it was that same detective that came to our door. I guess he has it out for me."

"I thought you said all this has nothing to do with that situation. Aren't those two who met you at the door homicide detectives?"

"Yes, they are. And, this *is* all totally separate from that. I am telling you the truth about it."

"No, I believe you are, Son. I am just having a hard time understanding why a homicide detective was there delivering these charges to you. Hmm, there might be something inappropriate here. Make sure you mention all that in the morning with Mr. Johnson. If you are allowed to make another call home this evening I will confirm that he will be representing you."

"Johnson? Is that the black man who would come over for dinner sometimes?"

"Yeah, I guess he did come over when you were younger. I'm surprised you remember."

"How could I forget? He would have a different magic trick to show me every time he stopped in. I loved that. And he always wore one of those hats. I don't know what they are called?"

"Derby hats."

"Yes! And every time I saw him I swear it was a different one. It was either a completely different hat or a different ribbon on them. I remember thinking of him as one of the coolest guys ever. Wait, isn't Mr. Johnson really old though now? He seemed old back then."

"He is, but he is still very good at what he does."

"Well, beggars can't be choosers, I guess."

"Cotter, he is the best I can think of. It will be okay."

"Okay, thanks for trying to help. I guess I should get off here."

"You know, regardless of the things you've done, regardless of anything, I love you, Son."

"I know, love you too, Dad. I'll try to call later. Bye."

I hang up the phone and look around to figure out what I am supposed to do with myself now. A couple of the other guys are sitting in front of a television watching the Bears game and it sounds like the other guy is in a shower. I really have no interest in interacting with anybody in here, but I don't know what else to do. I slowly walk my way towards the chairs. I can't believe I have done this to myself. I don't feel like I belong in here.

"Interception! Yes! Take it to the house!" This guy is so loud it startles me and at the same time helps me realize how hungover my body feels. My head is pounding and I have that feeling of just being totally out of it. "Damn! How you gonna run all that way and come up five yards short of the goal line?" The loudness jars me again and I start to turn away but the Bears fan looks my way. "What's up, man?" He's a skinny ginger with a red mustache and tattoos pasted all over both his arms. The other guy, a heavyset black guy with a cleanly shaved head also looks my way.

"Not much. You know, living the dream in here." They both just keep staring at me, straight-faced. Now they both start laughing loudly enough that the correctional officers at the desk look our way.

The super white tattooed guy says, "That's funny, man. But you haven't really looked like you are enjoying yourself, so I guess you are joking." I'm glad this guy figured out I was joking. He is clearly more comfortable in this situation than I am. "You looked real rough when you walked in this morning. What the hell happened to you? What did you get nabbed for?"

"I looked that rough because I drank too much last night. I'm in here because I kicked out the headlamp of a guy's vehicle and grabbed a woman's butt."

They chuckle. "You mean to tell me you pinched a chick's ass during a traffic accident or something? That is the most savage road rage I ever heard of, bro!" Turning to the big guy, "You hear that shit? Kicking out bro's headlight wasn't enough. He went and fondled the girlfriend too!" He turns back my way, "Savage, bro."

"What? No, listen, it wasn't just a singular incident. Both things happened at different times, in different places." I chuckle, more due to an uncomfortable feeling than out of amusement.

The big guy says, "The other way sounds better, stick with that story." Oh boy, I would just like to get back to my cell. "And what kind of name is Cainsworth?" I look to see he is looking at the name on my cell. "Must be some kind of spiritual name? I don't get it though."

I'm sure I'm looking at this bald black man with a bemused look on my face. "Spiritual name? Are you talking Cain and Abel?"

"Well, yeah. I am guessing that's where your name is coming from, but I don't get it. What *was* Cain's worth?"

I consider this for a moment. "Hmm, I guess I wouldn't know how to answer that, but I can't imagine he was worth much after murdering his brother."

The ginger chimes in, "I disagree. I would say Cain was worth twice as much after murdering his brother. I mean, I don't know what Adam and Eve had during that time, but wouldn't you agree that Cain stood to inherit it all instead of splitting it with someone else."

The big, bald, black man comes back, "Inherit?" he laughs, hard. "What you think they had? Some diamond earrings and a Lexus?! Nah, just a bunch a dem apples!" They both chuckle now. "Besides, that isn't what happened anyway. God punished Cain to a life of wandering, so he didn't gain nothin' from taking out his bro."

Ginger responds, "True. But he did go on to build a life for himself. I think he built his own city or some shit and even had kids. So I would say the stronger one survived and his line lived on. There has to be something to that."

Jesus, these rejects know more about religion than I do. "Anyway, I should clarify that is not even my name. They put my first initial and my middle name instead of my last name." They both squint and look over at the tag by my door. "Sorry to disappoint, but I am not a player in some Bible story."

Baldy actually does look disappointed. "Ain't that some shit. How your momma gonna put a middle name like that on you?" He shakes his head and starts to chuckle before turning back to the game. "Ah, snap!" My head rattles once again. "There goes the Bears season. Shit!"

The ginger turns to the television, "What?! What happened?"

"Trubisky just blew his knee!"

"Oh, hell no! That better not have happened. Maybe he's okay."

"No way, you didn't see it! It looked nasty as hell!"

I look at the game just as the Vikings are celebrating a defensive touchdown.

Ginger yells, "And he threw a pick-six too?! What the hell!"

This was loud enough that one of the officers calls over, "Settle down, fellas." They just ignore him. "Okay then, fellas, free time is up anyway. Head back into your cells."

Ginger looks his way now, "Let us just see this replay, man. Trubisky got hurt real bad."

"Back to your cells, now."

We all start moving to our cells just lackadaisically enough to see the replay in slow motion. Mitchell Trubisky is rolling out to the right like he is going to run it into the endzone, but as the defense converges on him, he plants his right leg and throws a terrible pass back across his body. Trae Waynes put his shoulder right into Trubisky's knee and it hyperextends to a sickening degree.

Beyond the crumpling quarterback, you can see a wobbly pass land in the arms of Harrison Smith who must have taken it about ninety-five yards for the touchdown. Yes, this will hurt the Bears season, but it doesn't hit me like it does the other guys. I have never really had an answer as to why, but I have always been a Minnesota Vikings fan. However, I will keep that to myself while I am around these guys.

***

I was under the assumption that my last stint of free time had already occurred this evening, but there is a buzz and my cell door opens. The tall correctional officer with the long nose, Brutus, walks in with a cart. "Everyone else had already gotten to pick some literature from the cart earlier today, but I thought you might want something to pass the time."

"Thanks, but I don't think I could focus on anything right now."

"Sure. I can imagine you have plenty on your mind. I get that." He turns to push the cart back out.

"I don't belong in here with these guys."

He turns back. "Come again?"

"I don't belong here. This is so foreign to me and everyone else seems like they fit right in." Brutus nods his head, seeming to chew on my remarks. I can feel tears welling up in my eyes. "I just don't know how things got to this. It's going to change my entire life."

He nods again. "Listen. I see good people come through here all the time. This doesn't have to define you, but I can assure you that it is all going to come down to how you respond. If you don't mind me saying though…" I shrug and nod, fighting back tears. I look away. "Try to humble yourself and don't be so self-righteous." I think he sees questioning in my face when I look up. "I understand you don't feel you belong here. I understand those other guys out there seem different than you. But, try to understand that you are here, right now, for a reason."

I feel defensive. "I am not like them at all."

"Cotter, I am not trying to say you are. On the contrary, I am identifying that you don't seem like one that belongs here. I just think it will serve you to reflect on the choices that got you here and do what you can to make sure it doesn't continue to be an issue for you." He pauses for a moment, looking like he wants to say something more, but choosing his words carefully. "You seem like a bright young man. I have no doubt that God has much more in store for you than this."

"Wait, God? I don't see how God has anything to do with my life. Like, what has He done for me lately?"

He cringes, "Oh boy. I think He has everything to do with your life. I think you have life because of Him. I believe you can have everlasting life because of Him."

"I have no idea what you are talking about, but the only thing I've heard about God lately is some pretty crazy stuff. I'll spare you the details."

"I'd be happy to share with you what I am talking about if you want to know."

"I'm good." I wave him off and he starts to turn again. "Wait. Why are you being so nice to me?"

Without looking back, Brutus replies, "Because I have been doing this long enough to know when there is a chance to make a difference with someone who looks like they don't belong here. And I can't imagine finding meaning in this job if I didn't at least want to help make a change."

"Why can you say I look like I don't belong here, but it's a problem if I say it?"

He thinks for a moment. "Let me answer that with a question. Would it mean more if you told us how much better you are than everyone else, or if you showed us the things that would make us notice how much better you are?" I must be looking a little confused again. "It's the difference between pride and humility, Cotter. And too much pride is a dangerous thing."

"But, that would be difficult… or impossible, for you to know who I am if I didn't tell you, or even to know how I prove myself after moving on from here."

"Exactly. Humility might just be the more difficult path. Part of the point is knowing that you don't need to get recognition from me or anyone else. What matters is that you do right by you. Your family. God. But you don't need to tell Him anything because He is always with you."

"Hmph. Is He though? I mean, I don't feel anything letting me know that."

He has the cart out of the cell now and he turns back towards me. "I also have been doing this long enough to recognize a lost soul when I see one. Close cell thirteen!" The door buzzes shut before I notice a bible sitting at the foot of my bunk.

***

I actually had picked up the Bible for a time before it was lights out, but only because those weirdos implanted the Cain and Abel story in my head. It's not as if I have zero knowledge of Bible stories, but I wanted to see what the Bible said about that. I found there were very few details to be gained once I located it within the book. Actually, all I got out of it was my thoughts turning to Genny when I found the story in the first book of the Bible, the book of Genesis.

Now that it's lights out, I have spent several minutes trying to get comfortable on this bed, if you want to call it that. I mean, it is literally a metal shelf protruding from the wall. Sure, there is something you might refer to as a mattress, but only because that is what you should say when referring to a mat serving as a bed. To help you truly understand what I am trying to sleep on, I will refer to it as an old, one-inch-thick gym mat on a metal shelf. When I try to lay on my side, it feels like my hip and shoulder bones are teetering on two flat rocks.

Really, all I want to do is get to sleep. There was not even an attempt to sleep once I was in my cell early this morning, but my wanting to sleep isn't even about being tired. Time has all but stood still during my day in jail. I have experienced the worst feelings I ever have in my lifetime. Feelings I didn't know existed. Feelings I can't even put a label on. The one that constantly lingers, and I can put a name to this one, is utter dread. Having my freedom taken away is absolutely dreadful. And, not knowing when this nightmare will end makes the feeling even worse.

Something else I feel I have gained a true understanding of is the ole *watching paint dry* cliché. I guess I have always understood how boring or mindless times could be when this phrase was used, but it's an entirely different level when you are literally left to watch the paint on a cell wall dry. And then, it's a step to another level when the paint you are watching dry was never even wet when you began watching it. There is no doubt that this situation could drive a man to insanity. It is utterly dreadful and I don't know how I am ever going to sleep on this metal shelf. Perhaps I will count paint drops as they dry on the fleece of a sheep jumping over the hood of a Mustang.

My cell door buzzes and I sit up. The door opens and one of the dimwit correctional officers from this morning stands in the opening. "Your lawyer is here to see you, Cainsworth." I start to open my mouth to correct this, but I realize it doesn't really matter and he is likely trying to get a rise out of me anyway. I stand up and walk with him out of the cellblock and into an interview room.

He closes the door behind me and I sit across the table from Mr. Johnson. As I sit, the lawyer squeezes out a smile, looking ageless, nearly exactly the way I remember him looking when I last saw him during my childhood. Amazing. This leads me to believe it could be one of his old magic tricks so I open with, "Are you going to start by showing me a magic trick?" His brow furrows and he looks confused. "You know. You used to do magic tricks for me when you'd come to our house for dinner."

"Ah, yes, that was a long time ago, Cotter." His face shows recognition of that time and now he smiles and looks around for show. "And it seems to me that we are far removed from that moment of having fun with a magic trick," I avert my eyes for a second as it feels I am being shamed, "but, you know, I do actually have one for you." He slides over a folder and opens it. "Here is the requisition document and the written charges against you. Watch it closely. Keep looking at it."

I have my eyes cast down on the documents within the folder for several moments before I look up at a quiet Mr. Johnson. "Nothing is happening."

"Oh, it didn't disappear, did it? Well, that is because it will not just disappear. This isn't a game and I cannot just make these kinds of charges disappear, Cotter."

I feel sheepish as I sense my cheeks flushing. "Listen, sorry, I was just rememb—"

"No, Cotter, you listen. I am seventy-four years old and it is nearly midnight. I appreciate the fact that you remember me from your youth, but I do not have time for games, and furthermore, this is no time for games. I would not be here if not for your father. He is a great man and I would never say no to him. But, that does not mean I am happy about having to fly up from my home in Florida."

"Wait, you came from Florida for me?"

"Wrong! I came here for your father. As I said, he is one of the best men I have ever known, and your mother is just as wonderful. I still talk with your father on a weekly basis, even when I am not in town, so let's suffice to say I have in-depth knowledge of your situation and the reasons you might have found yourself at the bottom of this barrel." Barrel? That must have been an inference about my drinking. Clever man. "In a moment I will ask you to give me the details of these charges against you so we can be prepared to make a plea deal tomorrow."

"A plea deal?"

"Yes, your father has an idea and I will use that along with any discrepancies we can find to work out a deal with the prosecutor." He must have noticed me about to question because he waves me off. "I don't have time to explain, you'll have to trust we know the best way to handle this situation. I need to get information from you and then I need to go get some sleep so that I can be at my best for you tomorrow." His face softens, "Cotter, don't take my demeanor as though I lack care for you. I do remember those moments with you, I am just disappointed."

"I can totally understand that, Mr. Johnson." I feel even more sheepish now though.

"Okay, let's get down to the business of things."

"Wait, can I ask one question?" He flashes me an irritated look. "It's not about my case. It's just a quick question about you."

He softens a little again. "Sure, go ahead."

"I am just surprised you are not wearing a derby hat. I never saw you without one."

Now he really smiles for the first time and then bends down below the table on his side. When he pops back up, he has on a black derby with a bright yellow ribbon. He is smiling and I chuckle while mimicking applause. His smile quickly fades though as he plucks the hat off his head and tosses it back down to the floor. "Now, can we get down to business so I can get some sleep?"

My smile fades as well, mostly because I think about sleeping on a metal shelf. "Yes, sir."

16

I am growing so tired of hearing the buzz of cell doors. There goes mine again, but there is no excitement within me about a potential exit from this place. I have already had time out of my cell this morning, but I haven't been arraigned yet and it's already mid-morning. Brutus is back on shift and when I questioned him, all he could say was that sometimes judges have delays and he didn't know when I would go to court. Would you listen to me? I never could have imagined I would be in a situation where I was impatient to get into court.

I stand up as Brutus opens my cell door. I raise my arms to stretch out and I feel shooting pain in my lower back from laying on the metal shelf. The only way I could fall asleep last night was to lay on my side. I rub my hand on my hip. It feels bruised. "The sleeping conditions in this joint can't be humane."

"Well, the good news is that if you are sentenced to more time you will get a permanent cell with a little better bed." I turn my eyes up at him and turn away, continuing to stretch my body out. "The bad news is that the judge who was to see you today is out sick."

I spin back around on my heels. "What does that mean?!"

"It means he won't be in today. They are trying to fit you into another judge's schedule, but there is no guarantee at this point that you will stand in front of a judge today."

"What?! You're saying I just have to sit in here for another day! I have rights, man, this can't happen. I can't handle another day in here. It's been bad enough already!"

"Just calm down, Cotter. There are people doing what they can for you."

"Calm down, huh? What the hell do you know about what I am going through?"

"Hey, I've seen hundreds of Cotters come through this hard-ass-sleeping joint. I think I do know a little something about your situation. I'm sorry I can't help."

"Yeah, whatever, man. You're on the other side of the locked door. You don't know shit." He doesn't say a word as he closes the door and stands on the other side yelling for it to be locked.

***

It's afternoon by the time my cell door buzzes for the fourth time now. I was out again for lunch, which was the best of the meals I have received thus far, but still absolutely terrible. I have hardly eaten any of the food handed to me. I guess it would be fine if I was starving, but apparently, I haven't reached that point yet. From my position lying on this damn slab of metal, I see Mr. Johnson as the door swings open and I spring to my feet. "What's going on? Why am I still sitting in this hole?!"

"Relax, Cotter. Don't you think we have been doing everything we can?"

"Well, I can't sit here for another day. They said I might not get into court today!"

"And I don't have a lot of power over that, Cotter. Sometimes things happen that are beyond anyone's power, even lawyers." He's giving me a look that says I better back off. "However, luckily for you, I have worked you into another judge's schedule at the end of the day."

"Oh, thank you. I wish it hadn't taken all day..." He shoots me another irritated look. "But thank you. Really, Mr. Johnson, thank you."

"I have a feeling you having to wait this out all day is actually a positive scenario."

"What do you mean?"

"Did you do something to upset this Detective Banner you told me about?" I shrug but also probably give a look indicating I may have. "He really seems out to get you. This is actually the reason it took me all day to change judges. He must have been pulling some serious strings to fight us on that. I have to ask myself why he would be this involved, and aside from the satisfaction of you having to spend another night in this jail, I can only deduce that he has an in with the judge you were scheduled to see."

"What are you saying, that the judge is crooked or something?"

"No… no, not necessarily anything like that. But, some cops have relationships with judges and they are able to push a little harder to get the outcome they see fit. And, yes, there is certainly the possibility of some foul play, but I have no knowledge of that and I am not insinuating such a thing. Regardless, I do get the feeling that this has worked out better in the end." He looks up at my hair. "Would you comb your hair, Cotter. You'll be getting ready to head over there any time now, jeesh." He just shakes his head as he walks out and they close the door.

Well, that was interesting. Have I really pissed off Banner so much that he is putting so much effort into taking me down? I mean, I know I've taken shots at him, but I thought that stuff all came after he was treating me so disrespectfully. I don't know. Maybe I have been pushing a little too hard when I have been in front of the man.

Looking in the tiny mirror above the small sink, I can see that my hair is a real mess. I should probably brush my teeth again with this nasty toothpaste and my little three-inch toothbrush. I don't know how they expect people to use this stuff. I guess they don't want me to sharpen a toothbrush handle into a shiv and bring it into court so I can plunge it into Detective Banner's gut. But seriously, these things are ridiculous.

The cell door buzzes and this time I am excited and nervous. That was faster than I expected. I skip the two-finger tooth brushing and hastily comb my hair. As the door opens, I see it is one of my officer buddies from the morning I was processed. I am suspicious enough now that I immediately wonder if it is normally his job to move me during this transition or if it is another string that Banner is pulling to get at me. "Step out, Cainsworth."

"Oh, are we heading to court? I thought maybe you were coming in to check out my butt again."

He is walking behind me as we pass Brutus and Reynolds at their desk in the cellblock. "You sure do have a smart mouth. Someone is going to have to teach you a thing or two about that real soon, Cainsworth."

"You know, that is getting pretty old. I think you are well aware at this point my name is Cotter Trespin. But, whatever, it doesn't matter to me if you want to sound like a dumbass, wannabe proctologist."

"Listen here..." He slams me face-first into the wall with my arm twisted behind my back. "If I wanted to listen to grumblings from an asshole, I'd fart."

I can't help but laugh and he puts more pressure on my arm. "Nice job sticking with your proctologist theme."

Brutus has something to say now, "Release him and do your job or you will be reported!"

He listens but turns and responds, "You think I am just going to take this punk's crap?"

Again, I can't help but laugh. "You are really stuck on that anal fixation. Are you currently taking online proctology classes?"

Now Brutus looks at me. "And how about you help yourself out and just keep your smart mouth shut. He's not wrong about that," his eyes go back to the officer, "but this is not how we conduct ourselves as professionals. I will file a report against you if I see that again," and he looks back to me, "but if you want to continue your provocation, I won't intervene again."

The correctional officer pushes me in the back a few times as he leads me through some locked doors and back into the room where I was originally processed. The big black guy and the ginger are standing there with an older, gray-haired man. "Everyone face me and stand shoulder to shoulder." This comes from the other officer who processed me yesterday morning. The one who manipulated what must be the worst mugshot in the world.

It's only now that I turn and see a chain with multiple sets of handcuffs attached to it laying on the floor. Both officers start handcuffing each one of us to this same chain. "What the hell is this? How dangerous do you think we all are?"

"It's not our job to judge how dangerous any of you are, but it is your job to shut the hell up. This is how this works. In a minute, a bailiff will come through that door and lead you all into the courtroom. From there, all you have to do is stand there and listen for the judge to call your name. Then you can step forward."

Wow, this seems a little extreme. I feel like a real criminal right now. Part of a chain gang. Right on cue, a uniformed officer opens a door and just motions to the gray-haired man at the front of our line. He points us through the doorway and we are walking down a hallway with another open door at the end. I can see intricate dark brown woodwork on the walls as we approach the room. The jail must be attached to the courthouse. I suddenly feel an overwhelming anxiety.

We step through the doorway and sure enough, we have stepped right into the middle of a courtroom that is apparently already in session. The bailiff closes the door behind us and steps through another gate that locks behind him. He is now out on the main courtroom floor and I realize we are left in a jail cell barely big enough for the four of us. It looks like the outside has the same fancy woodwork as the rest of the courtroom, but there is no disguising the fact that we are dressed as inmates, chained together inside a small cell at the side of the courtroom. How humiliating.

I glance out into the gallery and notice there are not that many people watching this show. However, I do see my father and as our eyes lock, I feel tears well up in mine. I can't believe I am standing here in this state with my father looking at me from a courtroom gallery. I don't believe I have ever felt such shame and embarrassment in all my life. I can't imagine putting all the embarrassment from the rest of my life together would add up to the amount I feel in this singular moment.

I am temporarily distracted from my shame as the judge begins to speak, "Desmond Ennis O'Malley?"

The ginger starts shifting and moves to the opening at the front of our court cell. "Right here, Your Honor."

"Do you have representation, Mr. O'Malley?"

"No, Your Honor."

"You stand here today being charged with petty theft and possession of drug paraphernalia. Are you ready to enter a plea?"

Someone stands at a table to the left. I am assuming it is a prosecuting attorney. "Your Honor, we have a plea deal worked out with Mr. O'Malley."

"State the deal please for the court."

"As you have seen in Mr. O'Malley's file, he is on probation in two other states, but not in Illinois. He would be released today with time served and be placed on one year of unsupervised probation. He would also be asked to report back to his probation officers in Texas and Indiana."

"Asked? This appears to be a light sentence. How many days have been currently served?"

The prosecutor shuffles some papers. "Four days, Your Honor."

The judge looks over his glasses at the prosecuting attorney standing there and down the line at the others who are seated at the table. "Am I missing something?" They just stare back, making it clear there is nothing else to say. "Okay," the judge slams his gavel, "Mr. O'Malley, you will pay the court fee and then you will be free to go."

"But I don't have any money."

The judge glares at him, "Figure it out! Next on the docket is Ronald Everett James."

"Here, Judge." The big black man works his way around his chained neighbors to the front. I lock eyes for the first time with the old guy. He has the beginnings of a gray beard and wild-looking eyes. He gives me a menacing smile. I look away quickly but a shiver runs down my spine.

"Mr. James, do you have an attorney today?"

"No, sir."

"It says here you are charged with fourth-degree driving while impaired. How do you plead?"

"Not guilty, Judge."

The judge looks toward the prosecutors, "No plea deal?" He shakes his head and looks over to the court clerk, "Let's schedule a pre-trial hearing about a month from today. Mr. James, do you have the means to post bail?"

"No, sir. I ask that you release me on my own recognizance."

The judge scoffs, "That's not happening. I am staring at a lengthy rap sheet here. However, I will give you the option of house arrest, with a visual alcohol monitoring system. Will you take that option?"

"Yes, Judge."

"You understand then you are not allowed to imbibe at all and you will be required to blow into a breathalyzer installed in your home when called upon to do so?"

"Yes, Judge, but what is imbibe."

"Drink, Mr. James. You are not allowed to drink alcohol at all. Do you understand?"

"Yes, Judge, but I don't technically have a home."

The judge shakes his head and sighs, "Figure it out!" He looks towards the court clerk. "Get someone to help him identify a home of a relative or friend where he can serve house arrest and get him his next court date." He turns to the prosecution table. "Why don't you have someone work something out with Mr. James prior to his next court date? Next up is Cotter Ainsworth Trespin. Did I say that right?"

"Yes, Your Honor."

I just now notice that Mr. Johnson had been sitting at a bench along the wall. "I will be acting as counsel for Mr. Trespin, Your Honor."

"Mr. Johnson, it is quite pleasing to see a professional lawyer enter into our proceedings." The judge looks over his glasses at the prosecution table.

"Thank you for taking this case on this evening, Your Honor."

"Yes, get on with it."

"We have tried to work out what I would consider to be a reasonable plea deal, but for some reason, the prosecution has been quite unwilling to work with us." I only now think to look in the gallery for Banner. There he is with a smug grin on his face.

"Well, I see there are some serious charges against Mr. Trespin."

"Of course they are, Your Honor. However, I think as the details come forth you might find that they are at the very least, a little trumped up. And, the defendant has no prior record."

"Well this isn't a trial and we are already running late, so I am not interested in hearing the case. What is the deal this prosecution team was so unwilling to consider?"

"Mr. Trespin's father would like to see that his son enters a special facility so that he may receive treatment for alcoholism and post-traumatic stress disorder." I shoot a look toward my father but he does not look my way. Seriously? I wonder what else he wants to say is wrong with me.

"Has he been diagnosed with PTSD?"

"He has not, Your Honor, but we have every reason to believe recent events in his life have certainly caused him some instability."

"And what is this special facility?"

"Mr. Trespin is in the gallery today. If it suits you, I think it would be easier if he explains this part, Your Honor."

"Yes, that is fine."

Dad stands and starts speaking from where he is, "Thank you, Your Honor. If you would consider allowing Cotter to receive this treatment before the court reconvenes on this matter, I would personally take him to Naniboujou on the north shore of Lake Superior in Minnesota." I have no doubt the look I am giving Dad now is one of befuddlement. I don't know why they think I need this, but if it's just to get me out of here, I am sure there are facilities much closer. "I would drive him there and check him in myself. We could use the time together anyway."

The judge looks confused too. "I am not familiar with such a facility, and what makes you think I would grant an out of state placement when there are perfectly suitable facilities right here in Chicago?"

"Most people know Naniboujou now as somewhat of a resort lodge. However, it was built with the intention of functioning as an exclusive private club. I will not bore you with the prestigious names who have held membership, but I will tell you I was fortunate enough to be placed on that member list at birth because of who my father was. Now, as I was saying, while Naniboujou has transitioned in the public's eye into a hotel and restaurant, membership is still in place."

"Sir, this does not sound like a treatment facility, so if you have more to tell me, get to it before I shut you down."

"Yes, Your Honor. What I am trying to tell you is this. Naniboujou has the appearance of a lodge that is open to the public, and it is to some degree. However, it quietly functions as a top-notch care and treatment facility for its exclusive members."

"You're telling me this is done in secret? Wouldn't it be a problem then that you're saying this in open court right now?"

"Secret? No. Do they like to keep it quiet? Yes. Think of it as a place where celebrities can go to get help and have a chance for some privacy with the issue. And I did get permission from the board of directors to discuss Naniboujou in my son's court proceedings."

"Well, I can't pretend I don't find this interesting, but I am not sure I am sold on the idea of you taking the defendant out of the state. It sounds like the prosecution has already been presented with this plea bargain." He looks to them. "Why would you not consider it?"

This time an older woman with long and straight dark hair that shows some gray at the roots is standing. "Your Honor, we have the same issue as you have presented with the defendant being a flight risk."

"I never suggested he was a flight risk. Don't go on the record putting words in my mouth."

"Sorry, Your Honor. I mean to say a concern with him leaving the state. Additionally, the man who has been working a case involving the defendant, Detective Banner, has concerns that his behavior is escalating to violence."

"Objection!" Mr. Johnson jumps up so fast that he must have been waiting for this moment. "Why is this detective so closely involved with the prosecution on such a case as this one? Is he on some kind of witch hunt?"

The judge speaks, "Mr. Johnson, you've been doing this for a long time. Shouldn't the police be an important part of this judicial process?"

"Yes, Your Honor, but Detective Banner works in homicide. Can someone please explain to me why he is showing such an interest in these petty charges against Mr. Trespin."

"I can understand that point. Does the prosecution have an explanation for this?"

She stands up again. "Your Honor, Detective Banner's concerns leak over to this case because Mr. Trespin was considered a suspect in multiple homicides."

"Objection!" I can surprisingly see some red in Mr. Johnson's cheeks. "What homicides? Furthermore, he has not been charged in any other crimes than those presented today. He is not a suspect!"

She rebuts, "There have been multiple deaths recently in which Mr. Trespin has been on the scene and given a statement."

"Yes, as a witness! These are some of the reasons in which we feel Mr. Trespin is dealing with PTSD. Furthermore, these deaths have been ruled suicides and accidents!"

Banner flies out of his seat and I shake my head as the tail of his tie swings to the side. "Not the last one! It has been ruled a homicide!"

"Detective Banner! You know the rules of my court and I expect you to respect them or you will be removed!"

Mr. Johnson points back and adds, "This harassment may just be another cause of PTSD!"

Banner stands again but sits as the judge motions at him. "Mr. Johnson, I will also insist that you respect my court and those within it. At this point, I am still struggling to see why this specific facility is necessary. Does the defense have anything else to add before I make my ruling?"

"Your Honor, we want the best for Cotter Trespin. That means we would want to choose the best available treatment. His family has a unique opportunity to use this specific facility. Shouldn't they have the right to feel they are giving him the best opportunity to be successful?"

"Is that all?"

"No, Your Honor. I feel it is necessary at this time to inform you of a major flaw in the police work in this case against Mr. Trespin."

The judge sighs and looks over his glasses, "Go ahead?"

"I don't know why a homicide detective, Detective Banner, was interviewing and charging the defendant in this case, but I do know that he neglected to read him his Miranda Rights."

The judge shoots a glaring look towards Banner. "Is this true, Detective?"

"No, no way. I am sure I would have taken care of that. I'm sure."

The judge turns to Mr. Johnson as if that statement alone just settled it. "Anything to add, Mr. Johnson?"

He holds up an envelope and motions for the bailiff to retrieve it. "Yes, Your Honor. In this envelope, you will find a flash drive containing the videos I reviewed this morning. They show every moment of contact between Mr. Trespin and police officials over these last two days. You will see that at no point did Detective Banner read the defendant his Miranda Rights." The judge glares hard at Banner. "You will also see some other poor interactions from correctional officers."

The judge looks down, sighs, starts shaking his head and mumbles,

"Can't anyone just do their job appropriately." He looks back at Mr. Johnson. "How long were you suggesting the defendant remain in treatment?"

Mr. Johnson looks back at my dad before turning and saying, "No less than two weeks. Longer if necessary."

The judge looks at my dad as he picks up his gavel and points it his way, "You will drive straight from here to Nanibooboo, or whatever it's called. And his therapist," he shakes his head and sighs again, "or whatever they have there, will report back to this court."

"Absolutely, Your Honor. They do have certified thera—" The judge puts up a hand to signify he no longer cares to hear.

"The defendant is ordered to remain in treatment for no less than two weeks and will obtain some form of completion to report back to the court." The gavel cracks down harder than before. He looks over to the court reporter. "Are we done?" Without saying anything, she just points with a pen over to our little box. "Ah, yes, great. Could our John Doe please step forward?"

I barely get out of the way as the wild-looking man jaunts over to the front of the box with a creepy little two-step dance move. I can't see his face but he bends over and puts his elbows on the ledge of the window and props his face in between his hands. I can imagine he is giving the judge that wild-eyed grin I saw earlier.

"Sir, you've been making a mockery of my court for the better part of a week! I demand that you give the court your identity so a full investigation can be conducted and the court can proceed. Are you ready to tell the court your name?" He remains in his pose, but I see him nod his head. "Well, what is it?"

He takes a deep, audible breath and in a gravelly voice he growls, "Santa Clause."

The judge plops back in his chair and drops his hands down on his legs with a loud slap. Looking toward the bailiff, "There's a new one." Looking back to the unknown man, "You know, this is a serious charge against you. I would take your defense a little more seriously. Perjury is not a charge you want added to strangling a homeless man in broad daylight."

"You mean like this?!" Suddenly this insane old man has his hands around the ginger's throat. The pressure is clearly serious as his pale face is beet red. There must be some extraordinary strength within this man because just to get his hands up to the neck with us chained as we are, the remaining two of us were yanked right next to him. In fact, the big black man is pulled right against him with their heads nearly touching. Without loosening his grip, the man snaps his head toward him and licks his face as if it was a giant lollipop.

This all happens in just a few seconds and the bailiff is keying the door quickly. He charges in, pulling the Santa imposter away. Two correctional officers come in through the other door and they quickly have him off our chain and pinned to the ground. Facedown, he looks over at us and produces a guttural chuckle that makes the hairs on the back of my neck stand up. They yank him up with hands cuffed behind his back and they push him past us. Still with an insane grin on his face, he says in that same growling voice, "Don't get on my naughty list."

The door closes behind them and I look out and see everyone is standing with shocked expressions on their faces. I jump as the gavel slams down. "Court is adjourned." By the time I glance his way, the judge is already heading out through his back door. He slipped out so fast that his robe trailed far enough behind that it almost was caught in the closing door.

17

I was not thrilled when they brought me back to my cell after court. Apparently, it takes some time to get paperwork in order before you can be released. I figured this was just a last-ditch effort by Banner to keep me in here longer. In any case, my cell finally buzzed one last time after about an hour, and now I am finally walking out the door.

Brutus happens to be outside the back door I leave through. It looks like he must be on a smoke break and he says, "Good luck, Cotter. Hey, no offense, but I hope I never see you again."

"I share the same hope, Brutus, and thanks for caring about me in there. I am sure it could have been a lot worse if you hadn't helped me out."

"No need. That was the way it should have been. It's just too bad all the employees here don't treat everyone with respect. Anyway, I'll be praying for you."

I don't know how to respond to that, so I just turn and start heading to where I see my dad and Mr. Johnson standing in the parking lot. After a couple of strides, I turn back, "Hey, would God really want you wrecking your lungs with those cigarettes?"

He chuckles. "I never said I was perfect, but I also never pointed out your vices." He gives me a bigger smile.

"Touché."

I turn and continue walking and he preaches one more time, "Just remember what I said about not being too self-righteous. We are all sinners in the eyes of the Lord, and no sin is worse than another, so make sure you're not the one casting that first stone." I'm not sure I completely understand what he is saying. I throw a hand up to wave without turning back.

Walking up to Mr. Johnson, I see he is wearing a brown derby hat now. It has a baby blue ribbon and as usual, it accents his suit perfectly. "I can't thank you enough, sir."

"No problem at all, Cotter. I'm glad our plan worked. Really, you need to be thanking your father. Obviously, Naniboujou was his idea."

"Yes, thank you, Dad. I think."

Mr. Johnson lights me up, "Damn you, boy! This was something that worked and you should show your father some respect!" I know he is right and I just hang my head. "You'd probably still be in there if not for the help of your father. Furthermore, did you ever stop to think that you just might actually need a little help?" He cocks his head when he sees me ready to disagree or deny whatever I was going to do. "Boy, if this experience doesn't humble you, I just pray it's not something devastating that does."

"You don't think this was devastating for me?"

"I would have thought it should have been, but if you can't emerge from an experience like this a little more humble than you were going in, then I do worry that it wasn't bad enough to break that foolish pride."

"I'm sorry, you're right. Things just come out of my mouth most of the time before I really think about how it will sound." He softens up a bit. "Really, thank you. I'll find a way to repay the service."

"Don't worry about that. I wish the best for you, but this was something I did for your father. Take care, gentlemen." He tips his hat and gingerly turns around to walk away.

Dad comes around the car and gives me a hug. "I don't want this life for you, Son." His voice cracks a little and I feel some wetness where he has his face buried in my neck. "I know you can do better, and I just want to do something to help."

"I know. I am sorry, Dad. And I didn't intend to be disrespectful in any way. It's just, I don't think I need to go to a treatment facility."

"Well, the good thing right now is that you and I don't have to debate it. The court has ordered you to do so."

"There is no way around it? Can't we just have Mr. Johnson fight this another way."

Now he seems more irritated than sad. "What? No, Cotter. The only other option is right there." He points back to the jail. "If you don't want to go where the court has ordered you to go, you can march your butt right back in there. Is that what you want?"

"Not at all."

"Then sit your ungrateful butt down in the car." I can't help but think that was a little harsh, but I do as I was told.

***

We made one stop before starting out of the city. We went home so I could gather some clothes, and, of course, so Mom could see me. It was nothing but a constant flow of tears from her. Don't get me wrong, I am not without feeling through all of this, and the last thing I want to do is disappoint or upset my parents, but the situation ends up being so uncomfortable. I just do whatever I can to get through it so I can move on, and I guess that makes me look insensitive.

Before Dad drives too far I suggest, "Mom seems pretty upset. Maybe I should just fly to Minnesota so you can stay with her."

"Nice try, Cotter."

"What? Why does it feel like everything I say you take like I have my own agenda?"

"Because that is what you're doing, Cotter! If you need to hear it straight, then here it is. I respond to you like that because it definitely seems you are making a comment to get out of going to Naniboujou or at least riding there with me. There, are you happy?"

"Jeez, sorry I am such a burden."

"Stop! Just stop! I don't want to hear you trying to turn yourself into a victim! You're in the situation you are in right now by your own volition. Everything we say, everything we are doing is to try to help you, because we love you." I have never seen him this upset before. Maybe I am being self-centered. "I have my reasons for driving you there, and now it has been directly ordered to happen this way by the judge. So, quit trying to manipulate things into your favor and let me try to help you. Please."

"I don't know what's wrong with me, sorry, Dad. You must think I'm a narcissist?"

He shoots a surprised glance my way and looks ahead again before saying, "No… no, Son. I don't think you're a narcissist, you're just a young man. I do think you think about yourself a little too much. Now, I have no doubt that can change as you get older, and I hope it does. But, no, I don't necessarily think you are simply a narcissist." He is not very convincing.

"Wait, oh that's just perfect!"

"What? You asked, Son, I'm sorry."

"No, not that. There is a spotlight up ahead."

"What? Come on, Son. Please, no more attempts to derail this."

"That's not what I am doing. I don't care if you believe it, but this *is* happening to me. I see a spotlight up ahead and there is no question anymore what that means."

"What does it mean?"

"That somebody is going to die!" He just looks at me with concern. "Listen, every time I have seen where a spotlight ends, someone dies." It suddenly registers how much I haven't shared with my parents. "Oh, and by the way, how do you think I found out I was adopted? That was because I met my twin brother." Dad glances my way again and he looks floored. "Right, so I know that much too. Or maybe you didn't even know I was a twin."

"No, we knew that. In fact, that was part of the reason I wanted to do this like we are, me driving you out to Minnesota." Now it's my turn to look surprised. "But I am curious, how did you happen to meet your twin? Are you two identical?"

"I guess. He has facial hair but appears to look exactly like me. And I ran into him because he is the guy I have seen murdering these people under the spotlights!" Dad looks shocked again, or maybe he just still looks shocked. "Only, he refers to them as exit lights."

"What? I don't understand."

"My twin brother, I don't even know his name, is the one murdering people. Apparently, we both see the spotlights. Oh, and get this. He tries to tell me that this is happening because God is sending us a signal to kill evil people."

"How could other people not be seeing him if he is really killing those people."

"Oh, okay, this is rich too. Get ready for this one." I become aware of how excited I am as I say these things. Big, sarcastic hand movements are accompanying my words. "He says that God protects him. Like, He creates distractions that allow him to be unseen, making these murders look like accidents or suicides." Dad gives me a bewildered look. "I know, right?"

"If this is all fabricated for some reason, Cotter, you should turn it into a book."

"Yeah, I know you can't believe this, and I don't blame you."

"Actually, not that I don't think you are creative, Son, but I have a hard time thinking you could make it all up. At least I can't understand any reason why you would make it all up. So, you're telling me that if I drive us to where you are seeing this spotlight right now, I will see your twin kill someone?"

"Yes! Well, you will likely see somebody die, but you won't see my twin doing it."

"Why? Because he says he is protected and you believe that?"

"If you want to see what happens or maybe stop him, turn right here." He looks like he is thinking better of it, but at the last second, he does turn right. "I don't know what I believe. Nobody else has seen him do the things I have seen, even when there are many people around, so I guess part of me wonders how that could happen."

"Yeah, I could understand that being confusing."

"This guy also has told me that when he places his hands on these people under the spotlight, he can see the terrible things they have done in the past and also terrible things they are yet to have done."

"Now that's just plain crazy."

"I know, but…"

"But what?"

"You need to take a left up ahead. It's just that some things have happened where… I don't know how to say it. The thing is, he told me the visions he claimed to see when touching some of these people, and I actually heard the same things coming from others who knew the people."

"That's weird, but maybe he is connected to those people."

"No, I really don't think so. And, you know that guy who went on a rampage the other morning? You know, killed a bunch of people."

"Yeah, I read about it."

"He was under a spotlight in the middle of the night and I actually stopped my twin from killing him."

"You've got to be kidding. You're sure it was him"

"Yes, the guy actually shot at us right afterward. I thought he was confused because I had tackled my twin before he tried to shove him off a bridge. He actually hit him with the shot, but I guess he didn't get him good enough. Anyway, you can imagine what I was thinking when I saw his face on the news."

"Wow. I don't know what to think about all of this, Cotter."

"No! Turn here. Shoot, it looks like it's shining on West Grand, but you missed it."

"Should I go around the block?"

"No, it might happen soon, just jump on the I-90 ramp here and let me look at what I can see from the bridge."

"Okay, but you know I won't be able to get off the interstate quickly."

"I know, but something tells me enough time has passed that something will happen very soon. There he is! On the Grand Avenue Bridge. Stop!"

"Son, you know I can't stop here."

"Just pull to the left as much as you can! Traffic isn't that bad, people can go around." He grumbles but does pull over. "There, see the guy walking on the near side of the bridge?" He doesn't indicate that he sees him. "Stop worrying about traffic and look! There is only one person in the middle of the bridge. He is wearing something red and walking to our left."

"Yeah, I see him."

"Okay, just watch him." He only has a third of the bridge left to cross and I don't see any creepy twin brothers approaching him.

"I don't see how falling into the water here would even hurt someone. It's not that far."

"You're right. It might not happen here." A semi-truck blares its horn from behind us. "Look!" The man is tumbling through the air. My brother shoved him at the precise moment the man reached the edge of the canal. There is a sidewalk with a railing and it looks as though he slammed face-first into the railing and then crumpled into the canal.

"Oh my God! We have to call for help. Oh my God!"

"Dad, calm down! Don't bother calling anyone. He's going to be dead anyway."

"Son! We have to call for help!"

"No! I don't need to be linked to another one of these!"

"But, you're sitting here with me. You didn't do anything."

This hits me hard for some reason. "You're right. I didn't do anything. I should have done something to stop this." I notice he has his cell out and starts to dial 911. "Stop. It doesn't even matter, Dad."

"Maybe they need to know you were this far away and witnessed something again. They can't do anything to you."

"I don't know how this Banner guy might be able to manipulate things against me. So, no, I am not as confident as you that it would be positive to put myself here." He hasn't clicked call yet. "Look, I can see people down on the walking path looking over the edge. And that person, there," I point, "looks like they have a cell phone to their ear. There is no need to call." He reluctantly flips his cell phone closed and looks in his rearview mirror before pulling back onto the interstate. "Do you believe me now?"

He glances over with wide eyes and then focuses on the road. "I don't know what I believe, but it is clear to me that something is going on. I can't imagine it was a coincidence that you said something was going to happen to that specific person, and it did. So, I believe you know these things will happen somehow and your story makes as much sense as I think any other explanation could."

"Did you see him get shoved?"

His face twists into a confused look now. "No? I thought he jumped." I can't help it, I just laugh. "What? You're saying you saw that guy?"

"I'm not surprised you didn't. I told you this is how it happens. I am not saying I believe God made it so you didn't see him, but he was there and he pushed that guy, and you didn't see it."

"Seeing that just messed me up so much, I instantly forgot about all the other aspects of what you had told me about how these incidents occur."

"But you watched the guy that whole time? Saw him fall, right?"

"Yes, but now that I am thinking back on it, I didn't see how he left the bridge, I guess I looked in my rearview mirror when that truck horn blared behind us."

I chuckle. "Of course you did."

"What? There isn't even really a shoulder there and you had us stopped on the interstate, Cotter. I had to at least pay attention to that."

"No, it's fine. I just don't understand it, but I feel at this point you would never have been able to see that moment anyway." He glances at me questioningly. "I guess there was always going to be the proverbial truck horn to skew your vision." Without looking, he sucks in his lips and nods subtly. I think he wants to believe me.

***

We are well into Wisconsin by the time I convince Dad to stop so that we can eat. It's already late for supper so we decided not to search for anything special, eventually settling on a Perkins just off the interstate on the outskirts of Madison. I seem to recall us having meals with extended family at a Perkins occasionally when I was a kid, but I can't remember the last time I was in one. Something feels good about sitting down here though, like it reminds me of family.

"Thanks for stopping, Dad. I hardly touched any of the crap they served me during my time in the big house, so I am starving."

He furrows his brow and snickers at the same time. "The big house? Cotter, I hardly think you can refer to that place as the big house."

"Hey, that was terrible. You have no idea what that was like for me."

"Oh, I have no doubt it was an unpleasant experience. But you spent a small amount of time in *jail.* You were not in the big house."

"Fair enough, but it was the worst experience of my life." He swallows his lips again and his face softens as he gives me a couple nods.

We both turn our attention back to the menu. "What?! I thought this was like a family restaurant or something."

"Yeah, I guess it is, why?"

I scoff, "They have beer on the menu?"

"Cotter, you're not having a drink."

I tilt my head. "I am not saying I want one." Not that it hasn't crossed my mind. "It just seems out of place to me here."

Now he thinks on it. "Yeah, now that you bring that up, it does seem a bit strange."

The waitress is back with water and coffee for us both. "Are you two ready to order or would you like me to give you a moment."

Dad and I look at each other and I nod for him to go first. "This pot roast looks good. I guess I have to go with that." Of course, he does. Very predictable. It's the closest thing to a hot roast beef sandwich and that is always what he would have in a place like this. He's a man who likes to stick to his comfort zone.

She looks my way. "I think I will go with the country fried steak."

Dad chuckles, "I could have ordered for him! He always orders country fried steak when it's on the menu." I scowl for a second, but then realize there is some truth to what he said. Funny that I reflected on his predictability but had no conscious awareness of my own.

Just as the waitress turns to walk away I call after her, "One quick question." She turns back and smiles. "It seems strange to us that there is beer on the menu at a Perkins. Why is that?"

She turns her face into a pose of questioning or lack of understanding and responds, "This is Wisconsin. A restaurant without booze on the menu is a restaurant not in business." She finishes by raising her eyebrows and giving a slight headshake as if saying, *duh.*

She walks away and Dad and I can't help but burst into laughter. It feels good to have this moment, but as the laughter subsides, I am ready to ask him about something I've been chewing on since he mentioned it. "You said earlier that one of the reasons you wanted to drive me out here was because you wanted to talk about my adoption?"

He sighs like he doesn't want to get into it, but he doesn't object. "Yes. Your mother and I have been talking a lot about it since you confronted us. First, I need to tell you I am sorry we never told you. That decision truly came out of love… and concern."

"What do you mean, concern?"

"Well, so you know I am not trying to deflect, I have to admit that part of the reason was because we were scared that you might turn away from us. We were scared we might lose our son. I am admitting that, but there are other reasons why we were concerned about you potentially trying to find your birth parents."

"Like? What are you talking about? Did you know they were going to be the kind of people who would teach their son to be a murderer?"

"Well, I wish you were further from the truth than you are." He certainly has my interest piqued and I signal for him to get on with it. "We did worry about what might happen to you if you tried to meet them."

"What would happen to me? You mean, what would happen between us, you and me? Mom and me?"

"No, I mean what might happen *to* you. I don't want to hurt you or mess with your head any more than all this already has, but I think I just need to come out and say it."

"Yes! Please just say it already."

"What I am trying to say is apparently your biological father attempted to kill you immediately after your birth."

"Oh, no worries, my twin brother already told me this and it apparently wasn't quite like that. He said there was a spotlight on me, but our father decided not to kill me."

Dad looks like he is mulling something over, "You know… as creepy as it sounds, especially after what I witnessed today… my God, that was awful. I have seen some things in my life, but the way his head hit that railing was so devastating, I thought I was going to be sick. And then the way his body turned into a ragdoll. It didn't even look real as it tumbled into the water. Cotter, if you have had to see other stuff like that… I am so sorry for you. No young person should ever have to see such a thing. God, I don't think any person should ever have to see that."

"What were you going to say?"

"What?"

"You were saying something about even though something sounds creepy."

"Oh, yeah. I was just going to say, although it is creepier, if all this is playing out like you have told me, I do think it is more appropriate that these... lights, be called exit lights."

I ponder this for a moment. "Unfortunately, with what he is doing to people, it does seem like they are exit lights. You're probably right, but maybe I can do something to change all of this."

"And back to this guy, your brother, saying that your biological father chose not to kill you."

"Yeah?"

"That is not what we believe to know about the situation." I narrow my eyes with curiosity. "The way we came to adopt you, in Minneapolis, Minnesota..."

"I thought I was born in Chicago?"

"Now you know otherwise." He chuckles. "No matter how hard I tried to change your allegiance, apparently you were born a Vikings fan."

Man, does this make sense and as hard as most of this information is to take, I allow myself some enjoyment, "SKOL!" Several patrons give me a disappointed look.

Dad shakes his head, "Looks like they pulled an Anthony Barr and put Trubisky out for the season."

"I know, I saw that play when I was in the big house." Dad furrows his brow and then we both start laughing. "At least I can respect the Bears organization. Unlike in the case of the Rodgers injury, the Bears won't cry their way to a rule change. They might as well just hang flags off Rodgers' hips."

"Well, at least we can join in solidarity against the Pack, even if we aren't rooting for the same team. Anyway, we were looking to adopt a baby because your mother and I were not able to conceive. The agency notified us about you and we flew that night to Minneapolis. We fell in love with you the moment we saw you. Now that I think about it, we were overly excited before we even stepped on the plane. I don't think it would have mattered how you looked or anything, but you were beautiful and we were completely smitten when we met you."

The waitress interrupts as she delivers our food. "Can I get anything else for you two?"

We laugh, as we are both so anxious to finish this that we almost rudely say no in unison. "Sorry, ma'am, but we are fine. Thanks. Go ahead and start, Cotter."

"I can't, my stomach is in knots so let's just get through this and then eat."

"Well, there isn't much more to it, but I am sure it won't be easy to hear. You had actually been in the hospital for a day or two. We had to meet with an entire panel of people before we could finalize things and take you home. There were social workers, law enforcement and even lawyers."

This sounds confusing. "Is that how adoptions generally work?"

"No, I don't think it's anything like how they normally work. Everyone seemed well versed in the situation as they all took turns talking. Really, they were all awesome through the whole thing. I will cut a long story short. The reason so many people were involved was that I don't think anyone had encountered a situation like yours before.

"They basically were quite honest with us about the entire situation. We were told how this couple came in with false information, but they didn't realize all that until after everything went down. They went through the story according to the nurses and the doctor in the room. And the short of that story was that the father had attempted to murder you."

"But, I told you that's not the way it apparently was."

"Told by someone who witnessed this? Told by someone who you trust?" He tilts his head at me and all I can do is sigh. "Exactly. This story came from the people in the room, Cotter. More than one person corroborated this story."

"I hear ya. Go on."

"Now, this is exactly what we were told. I'd never forget it because it all sounded very sinister." He closes his eyes and grimaces like he doesn't want to remember what he does. "You were born... well, you and your brother. The father was right there and stepped up to the bed when you two were presented to your mother. He was said to be looking nervous when he mumbled, 'Okay, which one is it?' Then he picked up your brother and quickly gave him back.

"Next, he nervously rubbed his hands together and then picked you up. They said he almost immediately snapped his head towards the mother and looked terribly distressed. She picked up on this right away too and said something to the effect of, 'Does it have to be this way?' To which he responded, 'It is the only way. I told you before, you can't understand. Only I can understand what he will do.' The doctor was apparently very in tune to something being off and asked him what was going on.

"But before he received an answer, the father grabbed you by the legs and began to swing you down... from over his head..." My heart is racing and a sense of sadness envelopes me. My eyes are hot with tears. "... they said like the swing of an ax. Thank God the doctor was trusting his instinct already and tackled the father. You landed on the bed first, but then fell to the floor."

I am aware of tears rolling down my cheeks now. "Thank God? Really? The same God that was apparently telling him to kill me? How could you believe in a God that would allow an innocent baby to be hurt?"

"Cotter, you have already said you don't buy into that line of thinking, that they are doing God's work by murdering. You know I believe in God. And in your heart, I believe you do too."

I am feeling angry now. "Oh, I think not! What kind of God would rule a world like this?"

"He is not the one who has ruined this world. Man has ruined this world. He gave us free will, and we could not handle that. But because we have free will, there are people on this earth who do evil things, and it is not God's doing."

"Well, why wouldn't he stop it then?"

"Maybe I don't have all the answers to those questions. However, I do know what He *has* done. He sent His only Son to die on the cross for all the sins of man so that we could be free of this broken world."

I feel like I want to keep arguing this, but I know if I do that it won't end. "So, what is the rest of the story?"

"Unfortunately it doesn't end there, but you are pretty upset. Are you sure you want to hear more?" It hurts to think there could still be more and I can't speak without losing my composure so I just wave both hands at myself for him to give it to me. "Okay. Nurses had scrambled out the door and you fell to the floor, but I understand you weren't injured. Bruised in the end, but not injured. So, the father had flung the doctor to the side and he fell over an armchair in the corner. The doctor hadn't taken him to the ground or anything, so I guess he ended up being within a couple of paces of the bed... and you." He pauses, looks like he is going to be sick or something.

"Finish."

"I don't want to say this."

"Just get it out."

...

"Please."

"There must have been a security guard very near because he was being brought in by the nurses already. The father jumped up and over you. Everyone thought it was with the intention of stomping on you." I break, sobbing now. "But the security guard caught him in midair and slammed him down, hard.

"That move took a toll on the guard though and he was not able to subdue the father. Two brave nurses had scooped you up quickly and were already heading out of the room. The father grabbed your brother and yanked the mother out of bed. She apparently protested but he just took off with them, half carrying the mother. I guess just ripped the IV out of her arm and everything. And that was the last anyone saw of them, aside from others in the hospital who reported seeing them run by, but they had no idea what was going on."

"They just got away and disappeared, how is that possible?"

"I don't know. They just got away, and they said it became clear right away that they weren't who they said they were. They said they would let us know when they caught up with them. I guess they figured they eventually would figure it out, but we never did hear any more about it... until you broke the news to us that you knew you were adopted."

My sobbing has ceased but there are still large pools of tears puddled in my eyes, blurring my vision. Dad starts to come over to my side and I wave him off. "I'm fine. No, just sit down, please. I am getting hungry again. Let's just eat." I just keep my head down, forking food into my mouth as tears drip onto my plate.

18

We traveled well into the night after supper, only stopping at a hotel once we had crossed over into Minnesota. Dad insisted we get up early this morning to travel the rest of the way to my new home for the next couple of weeks. "Cotter, before we arrive at Naniboujou, I want to tell you another reason I wanted to drive you here. Knowing a little about how you process things internally, your mother and I knew that no matter what we tell you about your adoption and former family, you'd make your own way to find all the answers."

I smirk at him. "I don't know that I've ever reflected on how my ways come across to other people, but as I've had time recently to look more introspectively, I can understand why you would feel that way. Good or bad, I guess that is me."

He smirks back at me. "I'm glad to hear you are looking inwardly some. I think that's healthy, and I wanted to make it easy for you to explore this new area of your life. That's why I am going to be getting a ride to the airport and the car will be left for you to do what you need once you complete your time at Naniboujou."

"Really? You're not so worried about me that you're still willing to put me behind the wheel of this sick 2013 Electric Ford Focus?" He raises his eyebrows. "You know, I could really tear up roads along the countryside with this example of American ingenuity."

We both laugh a little at this thought. "Yeah right, Cotter. Good luck getting the tires to break loose. Probably couldn't even spin out on a dirt road." I look at him and we laugh harder. "And it probably isn't as American made as you might think."

"Well, in any case, I'll still try to find and take the governor off this golf cart."

He shakes his head. "Back to the point. The car will be locked and the staff will have the keys for you when you are finished up there. In the trunk is a file with all the paperwork we kept from your adoption. It should give you all the information you need to check into your adoption in Minneapolis."

"They will keep the keys? So you don't trust me enough to have the keys in my possession. Cool."

"It's not exactly like that, Son. Truth be told, it's part of the stipulation of the court mandate that you do not have access to transportation while here. In fact, I might already be a little over the line by even leaving the car, that is not completely clear."

"Well, can I at least just hang onto the file so I can look it over beforehand?"

"No. I don't think you need any distractions during your stay."

"Come on, it won't be tha—"

"I said no, Cotter."

The GPS says we will arrive at our destination in ten minutes. There is something I've been thinking about since court and I am running out of time. There have actually been several moments when I have thought to bring it up, but I have been so distracted by the views here on the north shore of Lake Superior. Starting in Duluth, the structure of the land turned into something that appears to be too rugged for the shore of a lake. The combination of water and rock have come together in places to create waterfalls like those that I've only seen through media.

I wanted to stop several times, but Dad denied me that opportunity. I felt a tightness in my chest every time I caught a glimpse of one cascading over and between the rocks. It wasn't a bad feeling, but rather one that made me feel like there is a peacefulness in this world that I do not know. And, there was a picturesque lighthouse positioned on the edge of a cliff. That scene looked like one that must have been snatched up from some ocean coast and simply deposited here, out of place next to such tranquil waters.

The GPS announces five miles to the destination. "Dad, I know you don't like talking about your father, but can you explain to me how you have a foot in the door at this place because of him?" He doesn't say anything right away, but just takes a deep breath and slowly exhales. "All I have ever gotten out of mom was that he died when you were still relatively young."

"Yes, that's true. I was only fifteen when he died. I consider him to be a dark part of our family history, that is why I don't speak much on the topic, but maybe it is time you hear about him."

He glances over at me and I try to nod in appreciation. I can tell in his voice it is difficult, I could tell every time I ever brought it up.

"He was a man with a dark secret that he nearly took to the grave. It wasn't until he was on his deathbed with lung cancer that he confessed this to your grandmother and me." It's almost scary with the buildup. *What am I about to hear?* "But he must have always known he would have to divulge all of this before he died so that his affairs would be in order. That's the one thing I've always been willing to give him. I think he did care about his family, and I do believe the things he did throughout his life were what he thought he needed to do for the betterment of our family.

"We are almost there so I am going to give you the short version of it now. That day before he died, your grandfather told us that he had spent years of his life working as a racketeer on the streets of Chicago." I don't know how bad I thought this secret was going to be but I think I am looking confused to Dad, because this is not as bad as my worst thoughts about what it was going to be, but still it's probably pretty bad. "Yes, if you're thinking mobster, gangster, or some other mafia-related term, that's what he was telling us."

"Wow, that sounds crazy. I bet you and Grandma were beside yourselves knowing the things he had... well, what types of things did he say he did? Like, did he ever kill anyone?"

"He only said he had hurt people, and we didn't get too worked up right then because we honestly thought he was just losing his mind as sick as he was getting. But, the truth is, deep down inside I think I believed every word he said, right away. And though we stayed by his side and loved him until he passed away, I do think I started hating him as soon as he said anything. I guess that is part of the reason I never want to share it with others. It's too easy for me to immediately go to those moments when my feelings for my father changed, and I don't want anyone to be influenced like I was."

"Wait, did he know Al Capone?!"

Dad has been somber since starting, but he does allow himself a chuckle now. "Actually, he did mention his name, but was clear he wasn't working directly with him or anything like that. He did say he had several conversations with the man though."

"That is unbelievable. I mean, really unbelievable. Didn't you and Grandma stop to think that maybe he was just out of it, or just pulling some cruel joke at his end?" I wonder what type of person would really end their life leaving a joke like that open, but I bet it happens.

"Well, that's the rest of the story. He gave us very clear instructions about where to find documents, stocks, money, and all kinds of other stuff he either said he had in banks or hidden around the house and in other locations."

He doesn't say anything right away and now I wonder if he is playing with me. "Come on! And?"

"After he died, it was all exactly as described in the instructions he left. There wasn't one bank or location that didn't have the money or valuable holdings he said would be there."

"Wow, so why were you so upset with him, he left you and your mom everything you needed to thrive?"

He shoots a glance of immediate anger. "He lied to everyone for his entire life! And what he left didn't feel like security as much as it felt like dirty, filthy, dishonest money." He softens a bit but glances my way again. "Cotter, he was supporting us with a lifetime of money he took through criminal acts... he hurt people. Like you asked before, maybe he even killed people."

"Right, I'm sorry, that was a thoughtless comment. But, you said you do believe he did all that for his family. Do you mean to say he was engaging in these activities during your lifetime? How could Grandma not at least know what he was doing?"

"I do believe that part of his life might have spilled over into my early years. However, his story was that he had gotten out of it years earlier, both because he had ridiculous amounts of equity built up and because that way of life had gone by the wayside. He claimed almost everyone else either had been put in jail or was already dead.

"I don't know how my mom didn't know something, but she maintains to this day that she hadn't the slightest inkling. Apparently it was always what he did from the time they had met, but as far as she knew, he was a driver for some prestigious businessmen." He allows himself a smile. "I always remember her saying when they were young he was the most well-dressed young man around. Dapper and proud of whatever fancy ride he had that day. That was his reasoning for all the different nice cars he was driving in those days, that they were clients' vehicles. However, in hindsight, they were probably his or produced through some unsavory activity he was involved in.

"He told us it all started as things led into the Great Depression. His claim was that he got into it to help keep his parents above water, as his father had already lost his job."

"Why did he stay involved after he made what was needed though, or after the economy recovered?"

"Well, he didn't really say and we didn't ask because we didn't even believe the stuff he was saying. However, it'd be easy to assume he didn't feel like he would be allowed to remove himself from that life, even if he wanted to. Remember that the Great Depression lasted for a decade. Regardless, I don't know why he truly chose to do those things or why he may not have been able to get out of it, but I've never had any interest in taking advantage of what he left behind.

"And I am not telling you I have never taken advantage of what he left. I am right now, to do something I think is necessary for you, and I have at other times when the need was felt. However, I wanted to make a life free of those ties and I've dipped into those accounts only on rare occasions."

"You don't have to convince me of anything, Dad. I see you as a self-made man and I also don't see a problem with you taking advantage of money that is yours, regardless of where it originated."

"Well, I do have a problem with where it originated."

"Clearly. I'm just saying I would never think anything negative of you because of things your father did."

He does let down a little with this last comment. "Thank you, Son. It seems we are here."

Pulling onto the lodge grounds, they look quite impressive, and the lodge itself is a uniquely beautiful structure. I can't quite place it, but much like the lighthouse we passed earlier, it looks like it is a design borrowed from a country in Europe. "Looks like quite the place."

"Yes, it certainly does look nice, and right on the shores of Lake Superior too." We get out of the car and Dad looks a little mesmerized as he looks around before closing the door. "Wow, I sure can understand why they would have chosen this spot when deciding to build this clubhouse." We approach the front door and he says, "Now, they claim not to be some kind of secret society, but at the very least, they operate with the utmost discretion. The place is somewhat open to the public, so there is a specific process to checking members in. Let me do the talking."

We walk through a door and we are in a room housing the front desk and a gift shop. I am immediately distracted by the dining room that I can see through another doorway. "Whoa, it looks trippy in there." I am starting to move that direction instinctively, but Dad grabs my shirt and gives me a look that tells me to stay right there.

A woman in uniform steps over to the counter, "Good morning, gentlemen. Do you have a reservation for breakfast?"

"Good morning, ma'am," he motions at me, "I have a descendant of a charter member who is in need. The Clubhouse has been contacted and has been awaiting our arrival."

"Very good, sir. I will have someone with you momentarily."

I lean into Dad, "What the heck was that?"

He whispers, "That's what they told me to say."

Almost immediately, an older man wearing a brown suit steps in front of us. The wavy wrinkles on his face tell me he is quite old, but out of the corner of my eye, I saw him walk up like a much younger man. "Good morning, gentlemen." He extends a hand to Dad. "You must be Mr. Trespin. I am Mr. Lardner. It is a pleasure to meet you."

"Yes, sir. Good morning. Nice to meet you."

He turns a bit on his heels and smiles broadly, as even more wrinkles develop on his face. "Good morning, Cotter." Strangely, I feel an overwhelming urge to trust this man, and yet, in this same moment, I am questioning whether I should trust him.

"Hello."

"You will have an extended stay," he looks back to Dad, "No?"

Dad answers, "Yes. He is to be here at least two weeks, yes."

The man looks at our feet. "Did you forget to pack a suitcase?"

"Oh yeah, I left it in the car."

I turn to head that way, but dad says, "I'll quickly grab it, Cotter." I get the feeling that he doesn't want me being in the car by myself.

"Great. Please do hurry, Mr. Trespin, it is our custom to get started immediately."

I also think Dad feels he has to kiss some feet here. He is out the door before Mr. Lardner even finishes his sentence.

"Can he come check things out with me? Like a tour or something."

"I'm sorry, Cotter, but we have our best results when we don't prolong the arrival and processing time of our club members."

"Well, could you at least show me the dining room while we wait?" I point to the room full of color and people. "I don't think I can settle in if I don't at least get to hear a little about that."

He looks to his left, "Oh, of course." We start walking that way. The closer we get, the colors are even more intense and broader ranging than I first saw. It looks to me like some Native American style, but something about the building gives me the feeling of France. Not that I have ever been to France, but I think that is the country I was trying to think of when we drove up to the place. "I don't mean to sound unwelcoming, but it is part of our process to introduce you to aspects of the property as you work through some of the reasons why you are here. So, actually, we do intend to be a little unwelcoming but we do so in the most positive of lights."

Um, okay. I am not sure if he made sense there or not, but it sounded like he was trying to find a way to tell me he didn't want to be overly hospitable. "Wow, that fireplace is unbelievable too!"

"Oh... why, yes it is. As a matter of fact, I was under the assumption that was what drew you to the room in the first place. Here you will see the largest stone fireplace in Minnesota." He waves his arm to present it to me as if it is a showcase on the Price Is Right. "And all the stones you see are native to Lake Superior."

"Wow, a sight to behold, no doubt. You said native, was this originally a Native American structure."

"It was not. I will save the history for later. Good eye with the paint style though. I will tell you that the artist used Cree Indian designs."

"Amazing color, how old i—"

"I see your father is back in the lobby with your suitcase. Let's get you settled in." This guy really wants to get started. I can hardly keep up with him as we quickly are back in the lobby. "Thank you, Mr. Trespin. I will let you say good-bye and we will take things from here."

"Wait, he can't even walk to my room?"

Dad puts a hand up and his facial expression tells me to relax. "Cotter, I already know their process, it's okay." He hands me my bag and now leans in and hugs me fiercely, but also more tenderly than I can remember for a long time. "I love you, Son. Please don't be too prideful to accept some help."

"I love you too, Dad. I will try."

He is at the door and waving before I could say anything more. "Alright then, this way, Cotter." Mr. Lardner walks over to the stairs and does another one of his Barker's Beauties waves, motioning for me to precede him on the staircase. I reach the base of the stairs and he simply says, "Shoes off, please, and place them on the rug."

I look at the stairway in front of me and though it is painted the color of the orange creamsicles I used to get off the ice cream truck as a child, there are black trails worn into both the right and left side of each step. But, there are a few pairs of shoes already on the rug so I choose not to question this and do as Mr. Lardner has asked. I begin to ascend with quiet feet and when I hear him start to follow with hollow-sounding footsteps, I look back to see him with his shoes on. "Wait, why do you get to keep your shoes on?"

Mr. Lardner just gives me that broad, extra wrinkle-producing smile and says something I had the feeling I was going to hear, "It's all part of the process. You will just have to trust me."

19

At least Lardner didn't go as far as my correctional officer friends and strip search me. However, delivery to my room was less than hospitable. He patted me down and then did a full search of my bag, confiscating a bottle of tequila I had packed when we stopped at home. Now I wish I wouldn't have resisted the urge to take a swig while Dad was in the shower this morning.

Lardner also went over a plethora of clubhouse rules. I guess even though it is housed within Naniboujou, they refer to this elite treatment facility as The Clubhouse. When I asked again about taking my shoes off, Lardner informed me this is a part of treatment where each of us starts at the bottom, having to earn privileges back. Apparently, beginning this process in a perplexing fashion at the bottom of the stairs is meant to be symbolic.

I was given a daily agenda that basically states meal times and therapy times, both individual and group sessions. Aside from the strict rules of conduct, it doesn't feel like we are in lockdown or anything like that. It seems that they will let us roam the grounds or even beyond as we please. I mean, where are we going to go anyway? The scenery is breathtaking, but it felt like we drove out to the middle of nowhere. It was stated though that missing mealtimes simply meant you didn't eat, so I am on my way down to supper.

I slip my shoes on at the bottom of the stairway. There are no other shoes left on the rug at this point. I guess all the other lackeys have already come down for supper. "Ma'am, could you tell me where I am supposed to go for supper?"

"Oh, certainly, sir." She walks to the doorway and points to a long table where many others are already seated. "The Clubhouse members always sit at that table during mealtimes."

"Thank you." I walk over to the table and see about a dozen plain-clothed individuals, all of them male. In addition to these men, Lardner is sitting at the table along with three others wearing the same brown suit as he is wearing. It is only now that I notice a round, yellow patch with an NC pasted to the breast pocket of each of their suits.

They all have a menu in their hands and Lardner, noticing my arrival, motions for all his colleagues to stand as he announces, "Gentlemen, please greet our latest arrival to The Clubhouse, Cotter." They all nod and offer a hello, waiting for me to take my seat before they sit back down. Quite official. One of them is still standing and Lardner adds, "Cotter, this is Mr. Anders." He walks around the table to shake my hand. "He will be your individual therapist and mentor, so look for him when you arrive in the lobby during those times."

This guy has one of the bushiest beards I think I have ever seen. It is ebony and matches his wavy hair that is long enough to cover most of his ears. He doesn't seem all that much older than me. The other men in uniform here are closer to Lardner's age and completely clean cut. This guy looks out of place in both age and the fact that he looks like he should be wearing a flannel shirt while wielding an ax.

Mr. Anders is back in his seat and as a waitress approaches, Lardner says, "You will see that we have a limited menu for The Clubhouse meals, but I am confident you will find all selections to be gourmet in both choice and preparation." I would say this is a sincere comment as I study the menu while the waitress makes her way around the table. It *is* limited to only a few choices, but they are selections I would expect to see only at the most prestigious restaurants.

I order the walleye dish figuring it has to be good in this geographical location and I hear, "Are you famous or the son of a famous person?"

I look up, not expecting whoever said this to be directing the question to me, but the speaker is looking directly at me. I hadn't noticed before, but this boy can't be out of middle school yet. "Um, neither."

A tall, grim-looking fellow across from me says, "Kid, not every member of The Clubhouse is a celebrity or even the son of a celebrity. I tried to tell you that yesterday at lunch. There are so many powerful people in this world who aren't celebrities. Some more powerful than any celebrity can imagine. My father, for example, is just a rich asshole real estate mogul. Yet, he holds enough power in this world that he seems to be able to find me wherever I am and deliver me here. Not until after I screw up, of course."

The boy responds, "Oh, yeah, sorry. It's just that my dad is an actor and the way he talked to me about this place, it sounded like everyone who came here was a celebrity."

The look of irritation the tall fellow gives him has me reconsidering my description of him. It is an evil look and the situation suddenly feels creepy as he growls, "Are you a celebrity just because the world has decided your father is?" The kid shakes his head, looking frightened now. "Exactly, so if you'd use your stupid little head, you'd know that one hundred percent of the people you know here aren't celebrities, because you're not even one." I don't even want to know this guy's name. He's just a big bastard as far as I am concerned.

I suddenly feel like I need to lighten the mood for the scared boy, and put this Big Bastard in his place a little so I say, "Well, to be completely straight up with you, I guess I am here because my grandfather was a gangster who was one of Al Capone's right-hand men." I might have embellished a little, or maybe I didn't. I am not sure Dad has the full story anyway. The boy's eyes light up. "That's right, none other than *the,* Al Capone."

The Big Bastard gives me a glare that implies he doesn't appreciate me minimizing his chastisement of the boy. "Hmph," is all that comes out as he turns his focus to the meal that has just been placed in front of him.

***

I have some time before my first individual therapy appointment, so I decide to check out the shores of Lake Superior and explore a little. It amazes me how often the landscape of this shoreline can change from place to place. Even as we drove this morning, it seemed if you were to randomly pick a spot at the lake, you wouldn't have greater than a fifty-fifty chance of guessing if it was going to be a craggy cliff or a small beach with little polished rocks. The area near the lodge is the latter.

I can't remember the last time I have done this, but I pick up one of these flat rocks and try to skip it in the water. Fail. I can see why the structure of the shore is the way it is in most places, like waves have chopped away at it for eons, because today there are rough seas and the rock just went straight into a wave. Still, I try again… fail. Defeated in this childish endeavor, I turn to walk away and the boy from supper nearly takes me out coming over the steep ledge of the lawn and down to the beach.

"Here, let me show you. Your form is wrong."

I chuckle, "No, I think it's just too wavy to skip them today." I haven't even finished my sentence and he launches a rock that skips high above the waves.

"See. You were just standing too upright." He has picked up another rock. "You have to reach down and really throw it side-armed, so you are almost releasing it right at the water's level. Like this." He launches the rock and once again it skips perfectly on the water.

"Nicely done. What's your name?"

"Joseph. Now you try."

"Nah, I don't think I can do it like you can. How'd you get so good at skipping rocks anyway, Joseph."

"I have just spent a lot of time around water I guess. My family owns lake homes and we vacation in other areas around water." He seems to lose a little of the pep he arrived on the beach with. "And, I have plenty of time to myself. I have never had anyone to play with and my dad is always working on a set and my mom is always working on improving her status."

His specific pinpointing of their busyness helps the resentment shine through. "That's right, you said your father is an actor or something? Who is he? Maybe I've seen him in something."

"He doesn't want me to divulge that information. I was told to only go by my first name while I was here. I guess so the public doesn't find out that their son has problems. That's why I'm here I suppose. The most secret place they could send me for help." He is growing even more somber now.

"Hey, man, everybody has problems. They just aren't all necessarily the same problems and we all deal with them differently. What is it you're here to get help with, alcohol, drugs?"

He snickers but his mood doesn't seem happier. "Nope, I bet my parents wish it was that simple a problem to understand. Depression I guess, and suicidal tendencies."

"Like, you mean you have thought about suicide?"

"That, and I have attempted twice. The first was pills, but they pumped my stomach in time. The second, well..." he looks at me and pulls his turtleneck collar down a bit to show a red line on his neck, "One of the hired hands cut me down pretty quickly, bastard."

"Damn!" The way he states this really makes me feel like he wishes it would have worked. "You sincerely feel as though you have nothing to live for? I don't understand how you could feel that way?"

"Well, you're not me!"

...

"Sorry, it's just that is the type of thing that everyone says to me, like that statement alone is supposed to make me choose to be happy."

"No, I'm sorry. I didn't mean to be insensitive. I think I just don't get it. I am sorry you feel that way."

"It's okay. I think I am starting to understand at this point that some people's brains just function differently. I guess it's like you said, we all handle things differently. So it's like, I don't know how thoughts work in your head, but in mine, the focus hardly ever strays away from all the negative things in my life. Even all the negative things in this world. The quickest and easiest answer that comes to mind is just to be done with this miserable existence."

I just chew on this for a moment. "I think you are really right about the thought processes being different in our brains. I won't pretend like I know what has gone on in your life, but interestingly enough, I have had plenty of negative aspects to my life lately. And, I have been feeling this impending doom, like I feel I am destined to die sometime in the near future." Joseph is looking at me with genuine interest right now. "Yet, through all of the negativity and dread about my future, I haven't thought for a second that I wanted it to just end."

He is really thinking about this. "That is interesting to hear."

"You know, I have zero interest in being here for therapy, but it sure has been a nice break from reality so far." I have a realization of how refreshing it is that I don't have to worry about exit lights popping up right now. "Looking around at all the different landscapes, and... I would say just breathing the air here is really rejuvenating for me. I think it makes me want to live more than I even wanted to live before."

"I appreciate you sharing that, but it's not how I look at things."

"Listen, I'm not trying to convince you of anything. I'm just letting you know how I am thinking."

"I get it, and it does interest me to know how someone else thinks, but I don't think I want to talk about it anymore."

Clearly talking isn't helping the boy. "Okay, let me give this a try."

"What?"

I grab a rock to indulge his earlier desire. "Skipping one like you do."

A grin pops up on his face now. "Okay, you've done plenty of talking. Let's see if you did any listening." I smirk out of annoyance with this comment, but also amusement. I think I like this clever boy. I throw the rock and it plunges straight into a wave. "Wait, do you have back issues?"

"No, why?"

"Because you aren't bending down to the water like I told you."

"Alright, alright, I hear you." I grab another rock and really lean down into it this time, giving it my best Pat Neshek sidearm fastball. It skips multiple times on the water. "Ha! There you go. That was even better than yours!"

He laughs, "Okay, now it's on." We both grab at rocks and it's rapid-fire rock skipping. Well, his are skipping way more than mine, but he is laughing and that success feels more fulfilling than any number of skips could.

***

I think I'd rather still be skipping rocks on the shore of Lake Superior with Joseph right now, but it is time to meet for my first individual therapy session so I am sitting in the lobby. I considered just skipping out and seeing what would happen, but Lardner was quite clear about this aspect of the rules. It didn't sound like anyone was going to track me down and drag me to the lobby, but I was left with the impression that this type of behavior would at least prolong my stay here.

"Good evening, Cotter."

"Hello, Mr. Anders." His voice is so much higher than the deep lumberjack voice I was expecting.

"Let's go ahead and head out." He walks to the door of the lobby.

"Oh, is your office in another building?" He is already heading through the door and I follow. The sun has set, but it hasn't reached civil twilight yet so I can still see fairly well.

"We don't have offices." He raises his hands into the air. "This is our meeting room."

"Maybe I should go grab my jacket."

"Ah, you won't need it. It's unseasonably warm for this time of year on the North Shore." He looks back at me as he walks, still dressed in his brown suit. "You have long sleeves on."

We are nearing the lake now and I look around to see if Joseph is still by the lake, but he must have moved on. I can see even better in the dim light now that we are away from the trees, but it is getting dark quickly. "How long are we going to be out here, shouldn't we have a flashlight? It can't stay this light for long."

"Wait until daylight savings time kicks in, then it will be quite dark at this hour. No need to worry, Cotter, you have everything you need. This won't take long and there will be a bonfire started shortly up there on the lawn." He points back toward the lodge. This has all been very strange so far and I am starting to worry about what *this* is actually going to be. "I can imagine you have many questions about The Clubhouse's treatment process."

"I was actually just thinking about that. Can you read my mind?"

We both chuckle. "Although it may seem this way, the point isn't to necessarily be secretive about how your therapy will take place. It's just that the process is for everything to unfold as you see it. I will never meet with you in a place with walls around us. The idea will be for us to be in nature and just let the process develop organically." Even in this dim light, I have no doubt he can see confusion on my face. "I will not prod you with accusations of what you are doing wrong in your life, or what you need to do to lead a healthy life. We will just spend the time together and have conversations about it all, and ultimately you will decide the best way to turn at this juncture in your life."

"So, we will always meet here on the shore?"

"No, not necessarily right here. It can be anywhere in nature. Well, within reason. It is not our practice to drive somewhere from here, but there are many different places to meet on the grounds of Naniboujou. It really is a beautiful place to be, and many people find the location to even be spiritual."

"Well, I am not sure I am interested in anything like that. Wait, is that what this is all going to be based on, God?"

"No, it doesn't need to be at all, I was just saying."

"Okay, good."

"So, this first session is mostly for us to just begin our dialogue. Moving forward, a large part of the success of this therapy will be your willingness to talk with me. Of course, completion of treatment at The Clubhouse will certainly require some openness about why you are here and some discussing of how things can work out more positively in your life. That part is something I just want you to hear, so there is no confusion if you feel your time is coming to an end but you are told you have not completed the process."

"This all sounds much different than I was expecting. I think I get it, but it also sounds somewhat vague. Like, I am not sure if it will be clear to me when I have done what is required of me to complete."

"No need to worry, it is not our goal to trick you into staying here longer than you need. I will be straight with you about where you are in the process. See, the idea here is that there is no definitive answer as to what specifically is needed for each individual to move on from here with a more positive trajectory than the one they arrived on. We believe this is where most therapy misses the mark. Too many over-educated clinicians think they have a right or wrong answer as to how people should live. We think there are too many individual variables to be so presumptuous as to direct people like we have one specific answer for everyone or every situation. This is why The Clubhouse mission is simply stated, *Therapy for YOU!*"

"Hmm, this all either makes a lot of sense or you are a hell of a salesman because I never thought I would even think about buying into therapy." He smiles. "And just so you heard me, I am only *thinking* about buying into this."

We both chuckle and I realize now that it is quite dark. "Good enough for me, I'll take you thinking on this as our first positive move." He clasps his hands together. "Well, that's it. Our first session feels complete." He turns and points toward the lodge and I see there is a large bonfire roaring up on the lawn. "Let's go warm by the fire where your first group session will take place in about..." he stretches his arm to extend his watch from his cuff, "five minutes. Now it is difficult to see, so watch your step."

We carefully step our way up to the ledge of the eroded bank and onto the lawn and begin walking toward the fire. I am pleasantly surprised by the soft way Mr. Anders is speaking with me. His burly look had me thinking this was going to be a much gruffer conversation. "Can I ask you a question that might be off-topic?"

"Go for it."

"Why do you seem so much younger than all the other... counselors? Are you all considered counselors?"

"Yes, we would be referred to as counselors, but it doesn't mean we are licensed therapists. To answer your other question, I am only here because I pressured my way into this position. I felt it was time to focus on a changing of the guard, so to speak. It was not easy because these old-timers are set in their ways and they expected mine to be different, which they are. But, they see that I am still working toward The Clubhouse mission and I have slowly been accepted."

We are at the bonfire now and I am very inviting of its warmth, so I bypass the chairs and stand as close as I can bear. There are already a few of the guys I saw at supper sitting around the fire and all of the counselors are here as well. One by one, I am seeing the other guys enter into the light of the fire and sit down, including Joseph and The Big Bastard.

Lardner stands and says, "It looks like everyone is here, so let's take a seat and start group." He nods at me, as I am the only one standing. I hesitantly move farther away from the heat of the crackling fire and sit down. "Okay. Cotter, this is your first group so you are not expected to participate, since you will only now be learning what you will bring to group each night. Everyone else understands the expectation of the circle is that you recount three things from today and announce them to the group. The three are something positive that was done for you, something positive you did for someone else, and something positive you are looking forward to tomorrow."

I am surprised when he looks to his left and one of the counselors starts, "I was grateful this morning to get an email from my grandson. He is in the service and stationed overseas. I haven't heard from him in some time." He pauses briefly. "There was an older woman who tripped and fell in the parking lot this morning. I was nearby, so I helped her up, but she had made a mess of herself in the mud. I couldn't fix everything for her, but I did get her coat and bag cleaned up while she had breakfast with her husband. Tomorrow, I hope to finally see a breakthrough with one of my mentees who is struggling to move in a positive direction."

There are some nods of affirmation but nobody says anything. Lardner looks to the next chair and it is Joseph. "I showed someone how to skip rocks at the lake today and he spent some time with me talking and skipping rocks. Well, trying to skip rocks." He looks my way with a smirk and I smile at him. Now he looks down and seems to be thinking. "And, tomorrow I am actually looking forward to waking up." This really gets a reaction out of the counselors as they nod their heads exuberantly. It feels like they know him well and are pleasantly surprised.

The next guy is a counselor, but I am not hearing much of what he says as I am thinking about what Joseph said. Did I make a difference for him today by simply throwing a couple of rocks? I am not looking for a pat on the back. I just can't help but wonder if there is an easy solution to what feels like such a hard issue for him. Maybe he just needs one person in his life who he feels is noticing him, caring about him. I would have thought a kid like him must have at least one. What the hell are his parents doing, or rather, not doing for him.

A couple more guys have spoken now as my distraction is broken by the troubling voice of The Big Bastard, "Well, let's see. One of the voices in my head was quite complimentary of the way I combed my hair this morning. Tomorrow, I hope to remember to comb my hair again so that I might coax some lady into following me to my room." So bizarre. What a weirdo.

He chuckles and looks to his left as Lardner says, "Not that I expect an appropriate response on this one either, but you forgot a positive thing you did."

"Oh, yeah. I didn't kill anyone today, so that was positive."

Now he erupts with a deep belly laugh and Lardner responds, "Right. Moving on then." The counselor to his left begins speaking but I am hearing none of it. My focus is on this creep as he continues to cackle to himself. My entire experience with him so far gives me this gut feeling that his comments shouldn't just be dismissed as jokes. I am not so sure he is just blowing this group off. He catches me glaring at him and turns the corner of his lip up into a grimace. I don't want to show fear but I can't help but look away. I think the three things he shared might have been shared with the utmost sincerity.

I barely hear Lardner commend everyone, specifically Joseph, saying something about a big step, which means he can now keep his shoes on wherever he wants. He dismisses us and everyone starts standing. I hang back so I am not too close to The Big Bastard as we start walking toward the lodge. Mr. Anders falls back and then alongside me. "Awesome what you did for Joseph."

I was still having the negative feeling from the end of group, so I almost feel like I literally shook my head to register what he said, but I don't think I did. "Wha... what? What makes you think it was something I did?"

"I could tell by your nonverbal reactions when he spoke. Come on, man. I'm sure everyone could see that. Anyway, it was clear to all of us who have gotten to know him that something important happened."

"He seems like a nice boy. Hopefully, he can have someone step up in his life."

"Right. Like you." I look his way in confusion as we approach the lodge. "What? You don't think you can make a lasting impression in a short time? Listen, Cotter. The goal is for things to happen organically here. That's what happened at that moment and it meant something. There is no pressure. Nobody asked anything of you, but you can be a positive influence in other people's lives. See you after breakfast tomorrow for our next session."

"Wait, where will we be going for that one?"

He stops just inside the doorway to respond, "Wherever we want."

"I noticed driving in this morning there is a waterfall down the road. I think it said Devil's Kettle?"

"Ah, yes. It is a neat waterfall, but I have to tell you it is a much farther hike to get to than most the waterfalls along the North Shore. And there are some serious stairs to tackle."

"Well, I wouldn't know how far a hike it is to any of the waterfalls. I am not from here and my dad wouldn't stop on our way up, so I only saw the ones visible from the road."

"If you are up for it, then that is where we will go. It is an awesome spot."

"I am good to go for a hike. Besides, didn't you say this area is viewed as spiritual by many people?" He looks at me sideways. "Is there a more spiritually named place than Devil's Kettle around here?"

He laughs as he starts up the stairs, "Nicely played, Cotter."

"Wait, are you staying here too?"

He looks back, "Yep, The Clubhouse is a little like a convent for guys," he chuckles, "except we aren't sworn to celibacy and we can have families here." He starts back up the stairs as he says, "Don't forget to take your shoes off."

20

We had to walk a decent piece on the highway and down a drive before getting to the actual hiking trail this morning. Now on the trail to Devil's Kettle Falls, it is some rugged terrain, but there is a well-established walking trail. There is enough of a chill in the air that we can see our breath this early in the morning. However, it still feels surprisingly mild, especially considering the potential for some lake effect on the weather here. In any case, right now it feels amazing to be out in the open air of such a beautiful landscape. The trees are mostly coniferous in these rocky areas, but in areas where you can see a rolling hillside, there are innumerable hardwood trees with yellow leaves that flow vibrantly amongst the rest of the flora.

"What are those yellow-leaved trees?"

Mr. Anders stops ahead of me and looks where I am pointing to a hillside. "Oh, those are just the autumn leaves of the poplar trees. Of course, they are green until they change and fall."

"*Just* poplar trees? I think they look awesome set against the rest of the forest."

He seems to chew on this for a minute. "Well, I guess I can't disagree with you. Maybe I take them for granted because they are numerous and somewhat plain compared to the other deciduous trees of the North Shore. You should see the hillsides before their leaves fall. Now that is something truly worth gazing at." We start walking again but I notice him look that way a couple times and mumble, "Hmm."

"Hey, what is the deal with taking our shoes off before going upstairs at the lodge?"

He doesn't look back and continues walking, "It is one of the things we consider to be a privilege in The Clubhouse, and privileges should be earned. It is one of the simple, yet meaningful symbols we carefully slip into your treatment."

I am sure if he was looking at me he would see me rolling my eyes. "I guess I can understand the privilege part, but I am not sure I get the symbolism aspect."

"Well, think about every step you take in a day. I bet when your shoes are off you tread more carefully than when you have something on your feet. During the infancy of your treatment, we want you to work on treading carefully. Every misstep will potentially set you back, so we want you to remember how to make decisions with some caution."

"How could anyone really mess up here? You give us nothing and there is nothing around us."

"If you really allow yourself to think about it, you have way more here than you might in some other treatment facility. Maybe you haven't seen other treatment settings, but I know you've been in jail. I would say that is also a form of a treatment facility. Here, we don't even take your cell phone away. We don't check on you during the night to make sure you have the lights off, or that you are even in your room. Sure, we lock the outer doors to keep everyone in the lodge safe at night, but they definitely aren't locked on the inside. You could choose to walk out anytime you wanted."

Now I am the one chewing on a thought. "Okay, I hear you, but I still am not sure I am buying your attempt on symbolism with the shoe thing."

"It's all about the steps you *choose* to take in your life. Yes, you really have all the freedom in the world when you come to The Clubhouse, but the choices you make regarding that freedom do not come without consequences. This is one of the simple stipulations we put on you to help you see when you are either making better choices for your life, or maybe to show you that you are finally maturing to a point where you should be. The shoes are symbolic because we are either telling you that you're still taking baby steps or that you are ready to not have to worry as much about every little step you take."

I am getting what he is saying, but when he looks back at me, I still am giving him a look like I need to hear more.

"Listen, I have made it clear that we function on a level where we just want to assist you while you understand what you need to do in order to live a positive life for yourself. We try to keep things simple in that regard. There is a reason why stipulations on members are so minimal. It's because we know all too well that people will not change habits unless they want to. This is one of the little things we do to help you know when we believe you are choosing to move in a positive direction. You saw it last night. Joseph earned the privilege because he chose to simply think something different than his normal self-destructive thoughts."

"Alright. I get it. It's not like you weren't explaining it well, I just needed to hear more because I thought it was all kind of silly, but it does make sense."

"Fair enough, but what about you, Cotter?"

"What about me? What do you mean?"

"You said you thought having to earn the right to wear shoes upstairs is kind of silly. I would assume that means you think it's silly you've lost the right to wear your shoes while taking those steps. Does this mean you feel silly that you made choices in your life that placed you on the path you currently find yourself on?"

"Well, no, I am quite enjoying the current path I am on. I actually feel excited to see this waterfall."

He pushes his eyebrows up as he glances back at me, but also snickers, "You know what I mean, Cotter."

"Yeah, of course I have felt silly, and many other feelings along the way."

"Okay then, I challenge you to truly think about which part of it is silly. Is the reality that we have taken your shoes, or have you lost your shoes?"

Damn, he is pretty good at this and I don't have a response. I am guessing he is okay with this being a rhetorical question anyway. "What about you, Mr. Anders?"

We are still walking. He wasn't kidding about the hike. "What about me?"

"How did you come to live at Naniboujou with your family?"

"I don't live there with my family."

"But you said... er... I guess I am confused. You implied you lived there going up the stairs last night."

"I do live there, but my family doesn't."

"Oh, sorry, you said *our* families and I thought that included you."

"No, I was just including myself in what was allowed for the group. To answer what brought me here, that does have to do with my family. The short version is that my wife was having an affair and left the kids and me. I allowed my life to spiral out of control, losing a great job and not doing my best for my children. I went to Naniboujou for help and I never have left. I believed in what they were doing here so much, that I pushed my way into serving at The Clubhouse."

"What about your kids? Is that normal for someone to be placed in servitude after treatment?"

"It's not servitude. I could leave anytime I wanted, so I guess that is another way it is different from a convent. It is my job now, but there are also stipulations to holding the job. One of them being, we live in The Clubhouse. Though my kids do not live with me full time, they do come and stay with me. That was just another consequence of my regression back to infancy. I left the door open for their mother to come back into the picture and convince the courts that she was best suited to care for our kids. It was a dark time for me and I made mistakes, but my time at The Clubhouse brought me back to God. I was so grateful for that time and it motivated me to become a part of the system that helped me wake up."

"Why does everyone keep bringing up God? I feel like everyone is conspiring against me to manipulate me into religion."

He stops now and laughs. He is just straight up laughing until he sees my scowl. "I'm sorry. It's just that you are definitely misunderstanding me. I don't know what all the other situations are that you speak of, but I am not trying to manipulate you into anything, especially not religion. Did you ask a question about me?"

I just want to be done with this part of the conversation but I do nod my head to him.

"And I answered you by telling you about *me*. That was the journey that brought me to this moment right here, with you. I would be remiss if I did not tell you about the biggest part of it all for me, getting back to God. But it's not about religion for me, it's about spirituality."

"What's the difference?"

"Everything. Religion is about the system and how the group or leaders think Christianity should be practiced. Spirituality is all about my relationship with God. It's not about what others think I need to do to serve God. It's not about how much I go to church, if at all. It's not about how much money I give to the Catholic Church, and it sure as Hell isn't about needing to confess my sins to a priest. My spirituality is about *my* life with God, and that is preferably where I like to keep it, between Him and me."

"So you don't even think people need to go to church?"

"Need is the key word. I actually do think people need to go to church, that I need to go to church, because it is helpful for one's spirituality. I have a problem with that word when a religion is saying an individual *needs* to attend church to have a relationship with God, or to have faith, or for God's sake, to even earn their way into Heaven." Mr. Anders is more animated than I have seen him so far and I think he is recognizing this as he looks at me and takes a deep breath. "Seriously, that is how some religions, or at least some churches function. They would say you have to do certain things to get to Heaven. On the contrary, the one thing needed to get anyone into Heaven has already been done for every one of us. Jesus Christ was crucified to cleanse us of sin. All we need is to know that truth. It's much simpler than any religion."

"Wait, how could you not be resentful of a God that would bring so much suffering into your life? I mean, how your wife treated you and the time you lost with your kids, doesn't that upset you?"

"Well of course it was upsetting, but I know that I can maintain my relationship with Him because I know it wasn't His fault. God gave humans free will and that is why my ex-wife chose to do the things she has done and seeing my kids less is a result of all that as well. The way I handled all the turmoil in my life was a result of my free will. I made choices too and they didn't work out positively for me. If I had turned to God, things may have gone better in the end."

"How can you say God doesn't make bad things happen, but what, He might have made good things happen after the bad thing if you would have just turned to Him?"

"You're missing the point. Having faith in Him helps me through the tough stuff. So, no, I am not saying He might have made something good happen, I am saying I believe I am better knowing He has me. Knowing that He can lift me up in the darkest moments. Knowing I will be in His Kingdom when things are done here, because He already paid the ultimate price for me, for all of us, so that we too can have everlasting life."

I can appreciate his passion for this, but I don't know why I engaged him on this. "Yeah, I am not sure I understand everything you're saying. Can we start walking again?"

He simply nods and turns back to the path. "I can help you understand if you'd like, but I will move on if that's what you want. The bottom line is this. I am at a place where I am ready to face Him in Heaven. I am not saying I want my time on this earth to end. I love my kids and I want to be with them. I love my job and I want to help you. But, if things were to go so awry that I lost my life today, I believe I am okay with that because I know God."

I just let this last comment sit in hopes that we may be done with the conversation. However, I have the slightest twinge of guilt. I actually like this guy. I think I really like him, and I almost feel like I am letting him down by not continuing the conversation. Instead, I deflect my way to a new one, "What can you tell me about Devil's Kettle Falls?"

"Other than it's a really cool waterfall? Not much." I suspect he might be acting a little cold towards me, but now he adds, "It's just that there is some mystery surrounding the waterfall, so I won't necessarily have all the answers for you, but it will probably be easier if I tell you about it when you can see it. We are getting close so you won't need to wait much longer. Maybe you can talk about why you think you are here until we get there."

As if he timed it this way, and maybe he did, we stop at wooden stairs that head down for what looks like forever. "Wow. When you said a lot of steps, I didn't even know you literally meant steps. Clearly, you weren't exaggerating. Is this why they call it Devil's Kettle? It looks like a descent into Hell."

"No, it is not, but there must be something like two hundred steps down and back up, so I could see where some people might view the effort as hellish. While we traverse them, why don't you answer my question? Unless you have another deflection strategy?" He gives me a wry smile and starts down the wooden steps.

"Ha, ha," I say sarcastically, but he probably does have me pegged. "I think I am here because it was the best strategy to get me out of jail."

"I'll just let you keep telling me reasons why you think you're here until you hit on one that you actually believe. So don't wait for me to speak when I don't respond, just keep digging for the real, honest reasons you believe you are in this spot right now and I will indicate when I think you've told me something you truly believe. You can look at that as literally this place, or this place in the span of your life."

"Yeah, yeah. You have all the answers, don't you?" At this moment, I feel the desire to start liking him less, but at the same time, I feel like I have to respect his ability to call me on my bullshit. "Okay, I have a lot of difficult situations going on in my life right now and I have struggled to deal with them."

...

I guess I'm going to need to be more specific. "My girlfriend broke up with me. My parents never told me I was adopted and I just recently found out. Another girl I cared about cut me out of her life."

...

"Hmph." I am starting to see the rocky bottom of a small canyon area. We must be at least halfway down. "I have seen multiple people die over the span of just a couple weeks and there is this hateful detective who wants to pin crimes on me. I even spent some time in jail because of him."

...

I think I'll take a risk with him. He won't believe me anyway. "Okay, try this one on for size. I have been seeing exit lights. They are like spotlights coming from some unknown place in the sky. They shine on the people who I have seen get killed, and I found out that it's my twin brother who is killing them. Oh, and get this, he tells me that God, your God, is using the exit lights to give him a signal to kill evil people. He even suggests that is also what I am supposed to be doing."

...

"I don't know what you think you're going to hear before you actually believe me, but that was actually all true, so whatever." We are down now, but it looks like the trail goes back up on the other side of a valley. You can see some of the falls from down here. "That does look amazing up there, wow. We don't have to go up there if it's the same as what we can see here."

"Oh, there is much more of it to see up there. You'll want to see why they call it The Devil's Kettle. And about everything you said on our walk down, remember that I'm not waiting for you to convince me of the truth, I'm waiting for you to convince yourself."

I am a little snappy, "I don't know what you want! Everything I said was truthful."

"I never said it wasn't, although I do think you started playing with me a little at the end." He turns and looks me in the eye now, "Cotter, you know better than anyone the reasons you are here. Stop being dishonest with yourself by deflecting with a bunch of excuses." I start to open my mouth but he puts a finger up. "It doesn't matter if everything you've said is true. At best, it was nothing more than a bunch of things you're choosing to blame for the choices you made."

He turns and starts up the steps. I want to argue with him, but I just bite my lip. The way up from the river bottom is nothing compared to the way down from the trail and we are almost to the top. I realize I do know what I should be saying and I decide that I am going to trust Mr. Anders and maybe take advice for the first time in my life, or at least the first time in a long time. "Okay, I'll really try one more time to say what it is you think I need to admit to myself, but only if you agree that we don't need to talk about it anymore during this session."

"Fair enough. Deal."

"Here it is then. I may be suffering from PTSD because I really have seen many people die. I generally stuff my feelings and don't want to talk about it and that has probably helped to hurt relationships in my life." We are at the top and he looks at me and takes a deep breath. "I know there is at least one more thing, I'm working on getting it out…"

...

"I drink too much. I think I told myself the drinking was helping me get past all the stuff I didn't want to talk about, but deep down I know it wasn't helping anyway. And, many of the problems I have had were caused by the drinking anyway. It all became cyclical then I guess. I drank and it caused me problems, and then I just wanted to drink again to forget about those problems. Of course, I never have forgotten anything except more stupid stuff I might have done when I drank excessively."

"Nicely done!" He slaps me endearingly on the shoulder. "Now check this out!" He has turned now to face an awesome looking waterfall, but I am distracted.

"Wait. That's all you have to say after I finally drop that bombshell on you. Or was I dropping it on myself."

He turns back. "Cotter, you made me agree not to talk about it anymore."

"Well, yeah, but I didn't expect you to necessarily do that I guess."

"I'm asking for complete honesty from you. Of course, most importantly honesty to yourself. How could I expect that of you if you can't expect honesty from me?"

"No, I get it, and I appreciate it. I think I have just been caught up in too many lies, my own lies, to trust others."

"Besides, I only have to wait until the next session." He winks at me and I grin. "Now, look at this amazing waterfall. See how the river flows to this rock ledge in two different locations. The water that divides to the right flows over just like a typical waterfall would. On the other hand, see how the water on the left flows into a hole in the rocks, or The Devil's Kettle."

"This is definitely a beautiful place to be standing at this moment." Mr. Anders did not oversell this waterfall. It is truly stunning. Just the typical side would have been worth this hike. It must drop about fifty feet to the new level of the river below. I close my eyes and just listen to the sound of the rushing water. Now the sound of water crashing into water down below drowns out the river up here with its hellacious roar. Together, it is all quite mesmerizing and I feel as though I could stand here forever. Opening my eyes now, the other side of the falls comes into focus. There really is simply a hole in the rock that half the river appears to dump into. I

195

study the two falls individually and then together, and then I glance down at the water flowing away at the bottom. "Wait, where does the water flowing into The Devil's Kettle come out?"

"I thought you'd never ask."

I start looking around us, away from the river and waterfall. "Does it exit somewhere else because it doesn't seem as though there is the same amount of water flowing away at the bottom as there is flowing up here?"

"Great observation. This has been the mystery of this place for probably as long as it has been known to man, but there has never been any other exit flow found. A common misconception was that it might even exit all the way out somewhere under Lake Superior, but that isn't the case either."

"So this is why it's called Devil's Kettle. The water just flows down into the Earth? Some people probably think it is a gate to Hell?"

He is chuckling. "Yes, I guess that would be yet another theory of what is happening. Do you believe in Hell?"

I think for a second. I don't think he says much of anything without a purpose and I get the feeling he is setting me up. "I guess I do, why?"

"I am just curious if you think someone can believe in Hell without believing in Heaven? If a person believes in Hell, then they have to believe in Satan, right? So, wouldn't it make sense that if a person believes in Satan, they have to believe in God?"

I should have trusted my gut. I knew better. "You know, I guess I am just not sure what I believe in, okay."

"Sure. I was just wondering what you did believe. I don't want you to feel like I am trying to convince you, but could I just ask one more thing?"

I am hesitant but he has a way about him that I have trouble denying. "Go ahead."

"Is part of your disbelief a science thing? Like, you believe in the Big Bang Theory and stuff like that."

We have our eyes on the waterfall as we continue this uncomfortable conversation. Something about being in this spot seems to make it more acceptable for me. "I certainly am a believer in the science of things. I think there is something to be said about the Big Bang Theory I guess, but I wouldn't say I worship such things or anything like that. I guess I mean to say I don't think there is enough proof to make it a hard truth for me."

"Sounds like a fair stance. Have you ever heard of irreducible complexity?"

"It almost sounds familiar, but I can't say that I have."

"Okay, so, I am not an expert on this, but the idea is to say that it would have taken astronomical odds for the life on this Earth, from organisms all the way up to humans, to have risen up from goo."

"What do you mean, risen from goo?"

"Like with the Big Bang Theory. If an individual believes that the Universe started there, then they would have to believe that the first organisms rose up from the elements on this Earth after it was formed into a planet from the particles that shot out across the Universe."

He looks to see that I am following. I do not take my eyes off The Devil's Kettle, "Go on."

"From there, I guess you look to Darwinian evolution to explain how we evolved into what we are today. If you're following me, you should see what I mean when I say rising up out of the goo."

"Yes, I get that now, but explain the irreducible complacency."

"Oh, there is always room to reduce one's complacency, but I am talking about complexity." I look at him sideways and of course, he has a smirk on his face. "Sorry, I know you only heard it once but I couldn't resist the joke."

"Yes, I totally get that feeling, so I should be able to take it. Maybe I need to add hypocrite to my list of faults.'

He waves me off, "Don't worry about it. Back to the topic. Here is the main concept to grasp. Something is irreducibly complex when it is complicated enough that taking away just one part of the machine reduces the thing to nonfunctioning. Not sure if that made sense."

"No, I think I hear you."

"Then here is the thing, organisms much less complicated than humans are irreducibly complex. Meaning, if you take one part away, it just isn't what it used to be. It doesn't work."

He is looking at me as if he solved some cosmic puzzle. "Couldn't all of those parts just have evolved together?"

"Could they have? That's where the math comes in. What are the odds that all of these things could develop independently and then come together to create something so complex, through random design? I mean, come on, aside from just saying it would be impossible, I'd have to say the odds would be against it on an astronomical level. And the human body, I won't try to explain the biology in detail because I'd butcher it, but we have extremely complex mechanisms that come together only at certain times, like to fight illness or something, and individual parts that are entirely meant to function as something else come together to create an entirely new mechanism with a different function. It really does seem impossible to have happened through random processes."

"Oh, it is certainly an interesting concept, and not that I don't believe you, but it sounds like something I'd like to see research on."

"I completely understand that, but it does make sense that this is how our bodies are made up even if I didn't explain it well, right?" I nod. "So, to me, it would be very hard to argue these bodies weren't created by some intelligent designer. At the very least, I would have a hard time saying it is possible they magically came to their current complexity through evolution."

I nod again and think for a minute as the sounds of bubbling and thrashing water flows back into focus. "You want to know what I think is crazy?"

"What?"

"The thought of this river flowing to Hell brought up a conversation about the impossibility of evolution."

"Oh, speaking of which," he laughs pretty good for a couple seconds, "that is one of the more ridiculous theories and they recently determined the water does come out somewhere at the bottom of the waterfall." He laughs even harder as he starts heading toward the steps. "Let's start heading back. We have a long hike and I don't want to miss lunch."

I look back at the different sections of the river in disbelief. "What?! It doesn't look even close to the same amount of water down there." I pull out my cell phone and quickly take a selfie with the waterfall in the background. He hasn't stopped so I hurry to catch up.

Without slowing or looking back, he says from up ahead of me, "Apparently it's just an optical illusion. They have proven there is about the same amount of water flow on the lower level as there is on the upper level. Still, a cool illusion to go along with a neat little waterfall, right?"

"Well, yeah, except you let me go on about thinking maybe it flowed straight to Hell… and there were other people standing up there."

He chuckles, "I know, pretty funny, huh?" He looks back and I am scowling. "Hey, remember not to be too hypocritical when others joke with you." He looks back again and we both start laughing. "See, it was funny and I proved intelligent design at the same time."

"Proof is too factual a word."

We are at the base of the longer set of wooden steps now as he says, "Last one to the top buys lunch," as he starts darting up the stairs.

I catch right up to him and pass. "Wait, I thought the meals were free for members?" I continue to speed up the steps, all two hundred, or however many there are. Getting to the top now, I am exhausted and my legs ache. I look back and he isn't even halfway up, and he is walking now. *Quitter.* I sit on a nearby bench and wait as he slowly makes his way up the remaining steps. "Jeez, not moving as good as you used to, eh, old-timer. Man, did I smoke you. Looks like you're buying lunch."

Mr. Anders just chuckles and starts walking before he says, "Cotter, all meals are free for members."

"What?! That's what I thought. You had me running all the way up those stairs for nothing? Now my legs are wasted, man."

"I know, pretty funny, right?" He laughs and looks back to see my scowl before turning back. "Don't be a hypocrite, Cotter," and he laughs some more. Actually, *we* laugh some more.

21

The day passed with little happening to compare to the extraordinary experience I had at Devil's Kettle Falls. I don't know if there are waterfalls near Chicago, but I have never had the opportunity to see them, and I guess I never really thought much about how much more astonishing these natural landscapes can be in person. My session this evening with Mr. Anders went by easily for me. He is a very likable man, and our time passed so quickly that I couldn't believe we were done in the end. Honestly, I found myself feeling a desire for our time together to continue a little longer.

Right now, we have all taken our seats around the bonfire for the group session. I shouldn't be surprised by the chill in the air this time of year, but it has been so warm this fall that I did not bring enough appropriate clothing for the season, so I was once again reluctant to leave my post next to the fire when the time came to take a seat. I hear some of the guys talking about snow flurries in the weather report for tomorrow. A chill runs down my spine. I may need to get some warmer clothes.

Lardner calls the meeting to order and looks to the individual on his right to start tonight. It is Joseph. "Let me see. It was a nice surprise that my mother called me this morning. My parents are always busy with their own stuff, and I don't usually know if they care or not, so to be honest, I usually don't care when I do hear from them. But, it felt nice to me this morning. Hmm, does the other thing have to be something positive I did for a person, or can it just be something positive, like for an animal?"

Lardner seems impressed with what he is hearing from Joseph and he replies, "No, no it doesn't have to be specific to a person. Something positive that wasn't just for yourself is what is important."

"Alright. This afternoon, I was reading in the back room of the lodge when a bird hit one of the windows rather hard. I looked out and it looked like it was dead. However, when I went outside, its eyes were open and it stood up. When I stuck a finger out towards it, the bird actually stepped onto my finger and just perched there. It was shaking its head a little, so I was figuring that it probably knocked itself out. Anyway, I found a bench and sat there with it for about an hour before it finally decided to fly away. I did a little research on my phone and determined it was a chickadee."

The Big Bastard lets out a growl of a laugh and says, "That's the most common, plainest looking shit-bird around. Way to waste your time helping to keep another one of those around, kid. They're a dime a dozen."

It feels like every one of us tenses and is about to defend Joseph, but before the profanity in my head spews out, he defends himself, "I wasn't worried about the number of thriving members of its species, I only cared about the one that needed something."

"Bah! The weak have no place here anyway."

The staff seem content to let this play out for now at least. "How weak do you think it was to take a blow like that and then fly off? I saw several dead birds laying under the windows over there, so I would venture to say they were the weak ones. I guess this was the one that fell on hard times and chose to get back up. Perhaps a great example of it not being about what happens to people as much as it is about how they respond. Doesn't sound like weakness to me, more like strength."

"Says the suicidal kid!" He starts his growly laugh and now it turns to a hyena pitch. This must be the laugh when he really thinks something is funny. Sick.

All our feathers are ruffled and we sit up, ready to have at The Big Bastard, but the boy stands strong, "And look," he spreads his arms wide, "here I sit. I've bounced off more windows than you can imagine, and here I sit. Actually, I didn't think that chickadee looked plain at all. It had a black cap on its head that made me think of a black cloud. Like, maybe it always had this cloud over its head that created rough conditions for it. Yet, there it was, in another stormy situation and still persevering. I can identify with that. Maybe I am a chickadee."

201

The Big Bastard looks like he wants to say something, but either he knows we are all sticks of dynamite around this bonfire and he is dangling our fuses dangerously close to the flame, or the boy has shut his nasty ass up, because he just grinds his teeth, silently.

"And, you know what, I would much rather be one chickadee amongst a thousand others who are struggling to stay in flight than a big, ugly, lazy buzzard circling overhead as it waits on the weaker of a species to bounce off a window."

"Why you little…!" He jumps up in a flash, but his butt is back down in his chair even faster as every other Clubhouse member pounces on him. It all happens so quickly that he didn't have room to throw a punch or anything. "Get off me, you sons a bitches!"

Lardner is standing, but not amongst those of us pinning him down. "We will let you up as soon as you calm down, and then you're going to get up and report straight to your quarters."

"The hell I will! I'll do what I damn well please, you king fuck!"

"And we will call the cops to come deal with you, Dwight. Then we will notify your probation officer." He immediately lets up a little at this time. "You know exactly what will happen and where you will go. Now, if you don't want to be here, I suggest you get with the program and complete your treatment. We can do this every night, I don't care. This is what we do. We aren't going to give up and throw you away, and we aren't going to just pretend like you've completed and cut you loose. This is as simple a treatment you can go through, but it's up to you." He doesn't feel like he is resisting at all now, and I see Mr. Anders give a nod to Lardner. "Now, the guys are going to let you up slowly, but if you make any kind of negative move, I'm sure they will control you again. So get up and walk to your quarters."

We all slowly release any hold we have of him and slowly step back. He is glaring at each one of us, but as soon as he has room, he stands up and marches toward the lodge, knocking his chair over with the jerky motion. I move to sit back down, thinking Joseph is going to be pretty rattled, even though he displayed some serious strength, but he just finishes as if nothing happened, "I am actually looking forward to the cold and snow that is coming. I think I will get up at sunrise and walk to the waterfall. The only real snow I have been around has been up on ski mountains when the weather is warm. I don't think my parents would ever book something when the weather isn't warm."

He just looks to his right and we all are quiet for a moment, shocked at the activity of the evening and maybe more shocked with Joseph's ability to stay composed. The next in line, a counselor, begins speaking but I am just staring at Joseph. The thought repeating over and over in my mind is, *what an outstanding young man, he is going to be just fine in this life.* A knee jerk reaction causes me to glance quickly to the lodge, thinking The Big Bastard is lurking and about to launch his hulk back into the bonfire ring. However, I see his dark form standing next to the lodge, apparently peering back at us. It surprised me to see him hurry away from the bonfire, but I am not surprised now to see this creep gawking at us from the shadows.

Looking back toward Joseph now, I see he had finally glanced back to the lodge. Of course, he is not unflappable, but that display of courage was something I won't easily forget. He is a neat kid. Turning back to the group, we make eye contact and he makes a rock-skipping throw with his arm as a huge grin pops up. I smile too, remembering how much better I did today when we threw some after lunch.

I snap out of my trance as I hear Mr. Anders taking his turn, "Although I generally feel I am self-actualizing in my daily life, this morning I was reminded not to miss some of the simpler things in life. Cotter pointed out something I apparently always overlook. I think I would have considered all the leaves to be down right now, but they aren't. The yellow leaves of the poplar trees are still bursting on the hillsides and I was overlooking them. I just needed a new perspective and Cotter presented that to me."

Hmm. I didn't realize how much attention he was really giving me, but this guy is for real. I don't think this is just a job to him. Mr. Anders actually cares about me, and what I think. Still, as I sit here believing I can trust him, I am simultaneously wondering when he is going to be done with me and throw me away. What is my problem? Maybe I need to start a running list of my issues to add to our conversation from this morning. I have some real trust issues I guess.

"Cotter?" It's Lardner letting me know I am up.

Crap, maybe I should have been thinking about what I need to say instead of everything else that I have been pondering. "Sorry, I was just reflecting on the excitement of the evening." I get some snickers and nods. "Maybe this is cheating, but Mr. Anders pointed out something I did for him today, so there's that. And... tomorrow... oh, I noticed on the menu for breakfast tomorrow that there will be eggs benedict. That's something I always love having, so I am looking forward to that."

It's Mr. Anders who says something, "Okay, Cotter, quite an acceptable start, but go after this last one. It's like you're walking up the stairs when we know you can run up all two hundred steps." I start a scornful glance at him, but now we both smile.

"Yeah, okay. Even though I thought I was getting the best of you, Mr. Anders, you were actually getting the best of me. I just didn't know it at the time. So, clearly you were pushing me without me knowing... many times, now that I dwell on it." He chuckles, surely about leading me along during our hike. "Yes, Mr. Anders challenged me to be honest with myself and figure some things out. He helped me move away from all the excuses I presented as the reasons for my being at this pivotal juncture in life. In the end, I finally admitted to myself that I have some issues that I need to change if I want to live a more positive life. One of many that I will say out loud to you all is that I have a drinking problem."

I have many heads nodding to commend my statements. I feel uncomfortable, but good too. Lardner speaks up, "Okay, that puts an end to our group for this evening. Nicely done everyone. Jeremiah and Cotter, it appears to me that you both took steps today that warrant you receiving the shoe privilege." It seemed so dumb to begin with, but hearing that I can now wear my shoes upstairs actually makes me smile broadly.

***

Walking back to my room, I decided I should give my parents a call tonight. I am lying on the bed as the phone rings in my ear. My gaze is down to the foot of my bed where my shoes are still on my feet and firmly planted on the bed. I don't think I have ever kept shoes on when I have climbed on a bed, wait, I probably have when I was drunk, but this has to be the first time I have felt privileged to be on a bed with them on. Even as I notice some dirt I am getting on the blanket, a satisfied smile curls up.

"Hello."

"Mom, hi!"

"Cotter! Oh, I am so happy to hear your voice. Is everything okay?"

"Yes, actually. It isn't as bad as I expected it to be."

"Hold on, your dad wants me to put the phone on speaker but I don't know how... oh shoot, here," her voice gets muffled, "you do it. Okay, hopefully he hit the right button, can you hear us still."

"Yes, I can hear you, Mom."

"Oh my, these cell phones can do so much but they sure do confuse me."

"Hello, Son! Is everything okay there?"

"Hi, Dad. Yes, I was saying it is actually better than I was expecting. I guess I might even have to say it is going well for me here."

"That is great to hear, Son! Are you speaking of how treatment is going, or about the accommodations? I knew I wasn't going to be able to go around with you, but I worried your room or the food maybe wouldn't be too nice."

I inadvertently snort, "Oh, nothing to worry about there. I almost feel as though they treat us like kings here. It's like I am a member and they are providing me with a service. The room isn't large or anything, but it does feel extravagant. And the food is really top-notch."

Mom speaks, "Well that doesn't sound like any treatment facility I have ever heard of."

"Yeah, it's nothing like I was expecting, but they do still hold us accountable. However, they do it in an extremely respectful way. I don't know how to explain it exactly, but their process seems to be all about letting us figure out what we need to do. They have said things about it not meaning anything unless we decide to make the change."

Dad says, "Hmm, I am not sure I can fully wrap my head around it, but what you just said sounds like a smart way to conduct treatment. Maybe that is the way it should be done. Interesting."

"Did you get the photo I sent of the waterfall?"

Mom answers, "Yes, it looked amazing! What a beautiful place for you to see."

"It is so awesome. I have been thinking about it constantly. Really, since we drove past the sign coming here, Dad. It's like I am just being drawn to that place. And could you see how half of it goes down into a hole in the rocks?"

Dad responds, "Yes, that must be a unique formation at a waterfall."

"Yeah, I would think so, but I guess I don't know what most waterfalls are like. Do we even have waterfalls over there near Lake Michigan?"

"Well, there is nothing that I have really noticed, but maybe if you get into the Upper Peninsula."

"It's weird because I don't think I have ever really thought about checking something like that out, but it's so cool that I wish I had cared about stuff like that before."

Mom says, "Well I think it is normal to not be as concerned about things like that when you are younger. It's all a part of growing up when we begin to care more about nature and everything around us."

I'm sure she means well but I think she was calling me immature. "Anyway, it's because of this big caldron looking side that this waterfall is called Devil's Kettle Falls."

"Ew! That makes it feel more creepy than beautiful."

"Well, I don't know about that. It seems like a creative name to me. Especially considering the enigma of that hole. They don't actually know exactly where that water flows."

"Hmm, that fact just made it even creepier for me."

Dad adds, "But extraordinarily interesting at the same time." I picture him giving her a look as he says this. "I think it's great that you appreciated the opportunity to see that place. Is it close, will you get to see it again if you want?"

"Well, it's actually in close proximity to Naniboujou, but it was an exerting hike, hundreds of steps to descend and of course the ascension back up those steps is the really taxing part. I could go anytime I want though. As long as we are on time for our groups, they really give us all the freedom in the world. Another interesting aspect of the process here."

Dad agrees, "Yes, that is surprising, but then again, maybe it is the best way to make this work for people."

"I don't know, but I am happy it's going this way. You know, I even have some say in where my individual therapy takes place. The selfie of the waterfall I sent was actually during a session with Mr. Anders. He's a neat guy, very easy to talk to." I snicker to myself. "But he looks like... Dad, what is that show you used to watch, it was set in the backwoods and had the guy with the beard?"

"Are you talking about Grizzly Adams?"

"Yes," I laugh, "He looks like Grizzly Adams. But only if Grizzly Adams wore a suit every day." I hear them chuckle through the phone. "Alright, I'm going to let you go now. I just figured I should give you two a call to let you know how things are going."

Dad says, "Yes, we are glad you did."

"Oh, before I go, it is starting to get cold up here now and I didn't pack appropriately. Do you mind if I put some Naniboujou clothing on the credit card?"

"Um, yeah, that's fine, Son."

"Oh, if it's a problem I'll be fine with what I have, no worries."

"No... no, it really is fine. That card is always available to you. You just caught me off guard because you have been using it a lot lately and you never ask, and just leave us to pay it off."

"I know, sorry."

"It's fine. I appreciate you being respectful enough to ask about it now."

"I can pay you back when I am able."

Mom chimes in, "We aren't worried about it, Cotter. Just get what you need and be warm. We love you."

"Okay, love you both. Bye."

I had felt the urge to talk to my parents for the first time in a long time, but as the phone clicks, I have an overwhelming feeling of loneliness. The realization sets in that my parents are all I have in this life. I've done nothing but burn bridges with the few people who had been in my life. And then there is Genny. I don't even know where I went wrong there. Maybe that is one that wasn't my fault. Or, maybe it was the way of this world. Genny hurt me like I hurt Rebecca. Tit for tat.

Now Rebecca is on my mind. We were good together for so long. I can't believe I could be so stupid as to lose a girl like that. She is beautiful, smart, and was always good to me. Now that I am thinking about it, maybe I never deserved her. But, why did she even respond to my text the other night. Perhaps that door isn't completely closed. I don't even know if I had accidentally texted her, as she suggested, because I can't remember that time, but it might have been the only good thing I did that night. All I know is she responded and that might mean I still have a chance to fix this.

I surprise myself as I look down to see I have already begun a text message to Rebecca with the selfie from the waterfall. I only take a moment to second-guess myself before I start typing, *Hi, Rebecca. I am sure you don't want to hear from me, you probably hate me, but I wanted to let you know I am trying to get some help. I am at a treatment facility in Minnesota. That's where I took this picture at a waterfall. It's beautiful here and it has me thinking of you. I just want you to know I am so sorry for what I did to you. If there is any way you can forgive me, I would very much appreciate an opportunity to talk with you when I get back to the city. If not, I totally understand.*

I click send and then plug my phone into the charging cable on the nightstand. I am comfortable and don't feel like getting up to brush my teeth, but I head that way. Looking into the mirror, I think this is the least hesitant I have been to face myself in some time. Not that I am completely happy with myself right now, but I have loathed to look into these eyes for so long. I guess there has been a sense of guilt that I was unwilling to admit to myself, but also quite unwilling to stare in the face. It probably didn't help that I was usually drinking or hungover. Oh, the great denial that has been my life. Hopefully, I am done with all that.

I walk back to the bed and reluctantly kick my shoes off. It just wouldn't be comfortable to keep them on when I slide between the sheets. Slipping off my AG jeans, I think about how cynically I have been thinking about my life. I have neglected to recognize the positive influences impacting my life here, at Naniboujou. Mr. Anders and Joseph have interacted with me in ways that have brought me more happiness than the bottom of any bottle. Sure, I've screwed up plenty of positive relationships in my life, but maybe I am not hopeless. Perhaps I just need to realize I am at my best when I am not self-medicating with booze.

I lay down, click off the bedside lamp and close my weary eyes. It was a long and exhausting day. A good day, but also tiring, both physically and mentally. I have no doubt that sleep will find me soon and the rest will do me some good. My phone vibrates on the nightstand and I sit up to see Rebecca's name on the alert banner. My heart begins to race excitedly out of hope for a positive response, but also out of fear of a negative response. I slide the banner and put my thumb on the home button to open it.

I am pleased to hear you are taking steps to better yourself, Cotter. I don't hate you. How could I after all the love I have showered you with over the years. Ouch, I don't know if it was meant that way, but it delivers a zap of a guilty feeling. *I don't know if I want to see you, but you can reach out to me when you have completed treatment and I will let you know at that time. I do hope you find yourself and I appreciate you letting me know you are okay. I have been worried.* I think I will just take this message as positively as I can and not respond. Pushing her any further than this right now may not be beneficial. I close my eyes again and realize I don't feel as exhausted as I did a moment before, but I am thankful for this. It's because there is hope in my heart.

22

I startle myself awake. It was one of those moments when through a dream or for some other reason I actually made what felt like a huge kicking or throwing motion that vaulted me out of sleep. My head tells me this happened shortly after falling asleep, but the clock on the nightstand tells me it's already 7:30 a.m. I don't need to get up yet so I close my eyes, but something has my eyes open again and I find myself glancing towards the window. No! Not here! Not now! Why is this happening here?

I slip out of bed and quickly slide on the pants and t-shirt crumpled up on the floor and then step into my shoes. I traipse over to the window and pull the curtain aside to reveal what I suspected I was feeling, an exit light. I am surprised I can see it through the falling snow, but there it is, some distance to the west, as plain as day in the predawn light. My mind tells me I can just ignore this, but my body is already closing the door to my room behind me. I fly down the stairs, consciously slower than I did when I biffed it in the subway.

I zoom through a mostly empty lobby, out the door and tear across the loose-dirt parking lot before gaining firmer footing on the highway. I can see the exit light above the tree line up ahead and to the right as I run down the highway. It must be shining on someone who is on The Devil's Kettle trail. I slow my pace but continue jogging. My instinct tells me I could be on the move for a while before I catch up with this person. My mind has stopped racing as fast too and I notice the snow more now. It's a bit more than the *flurry* they were predicting. Big, wet snowflakes are plopping onto my face and already wetting my clothes. The ground must still be warm enough though to keep it from accumulating. The highway is wet but no slipperier than it would be during a rainstorm.

I turn onto the dirt road and there are areas with a skiff of snow now, not able to shrug the snowflakes off as easily as the asphalt highway. I focus on the exit light above the trees and I'm mesmerized for a moment at how it looks in the snow, and how I can see it through the snow. If there were an actual artificial spotlight shining down that far away in this snow, there is no way it would be physically possible for me to see it. In fact, I couldn't imagine seeing an artificial light that was even seventy-five percent closer than this exit light. As if I didn't already know this, I imagine how magical this force must be.

I physically shake my head from its momentary hypnosis and veer onto the footpath. Amongst the forest of evergreens now, I can only see the exit light in the spaces in between some of the higher treetops. It seems clear that the person must be on their way to the waterfall because I am barely making up any ground. I hasten my steps only a little while trying to remain cognizant of my stamina. I don't want to burn myself out and get there even later than I already will. I round a bend of the trail and can see the wooden stairs up ahead. The trail within the woods has no snow cover, but as I approach the stairs, I am already telling myself to *be careful, despite the traction on the asphalt, the wood will no doubt be slippery.*

I am hurrying down the stairs, doing my best to focus on each step. I risk one glance up to see that the exit light appears to be shining over by the waterfall. Even though I traverse the steps at what I think is a meticulous pace, I am at the bottom in a flash. Down here, at the base of the falls, I can see to the top until I begin to ascend the steps up to The Devil's Kettle. The precipitation has lightened into a flurry, but I still should not be able to see the waterfall at this distance through the snow. However, under the mystical film of the exit light, I can see The Big Bastard standing on The Devil's Kettle side of the waterfall.

I can't see anything outside the exit light up there, but The Big Bastard appears to be talking, or arguing with someone. I can't hear anything, but it feels like I am watching him act out a solo scene on Broadway, all dark with the only light in the theatre shining on him. He is quite animated as he speaks, stepping back and forth and waving his arms emphatically. I start running up the steps as I just now remember that Joseph said he was planning to hike here this morning. *Oh no! Is he up there with that Big Bastard?!*

I reach the top and slow down as I survey the scene. There is nobody else up here that I can see, yet The Big Bastard is engaged in the same activity as before. He hasn't noticed me as I walk up on the opposite side of the falls. I take a moment to look around and down the waterfall. Could he have done something to Joseph before I arrived? "Who are you talking too?"

He nearly jumps, like he was startled out of a trance. "Ah... nobody. What the hell are you doing here?"

"What do you mean? This is a public place. Who were you talking to?"

"None of your damn business! You'll get the hell out of here if you know what's good for you!"

"Settle down, man. I'm not bothering you." Though he is turned my way, I wouldn't say he is looking at me as much as I would say his eyes are just burning through me. His face is full of rage. "How did you get over there anyway? Bet it looks even cooler over there."

His face actually loosens a little as he looks around. "Oh, yeah." He points upstream. "You just have to pick a spot and walk across the river. Go ahead, you'll make it just fine." A tight grin envelops his teeth. "Don't worry, if you slip and the river snatches you up, I'll grab your arm before you get flushed down the Devil's toilet." His grin turns into a heinous laugh.

I want to just walk away, but I'm already moving carefully upstream, looking for the easiest place to cross. A relatively shallow spot draws my attention and I gingerly begin stepping across the river. It is numbingly cold on my feet, but I continue. Halfway, I chance a glance in The Big Bastard's direction and see him staring with an evil grin on his face. I'm caught by his sinister gaze and I don't look down before footing my next step. My shoe doesn't quite gain purchase as it slips off a large rock. I stumble to catch myself with the other foot, but the current of the river has swept me off my feet. Slapping down onto the water, I am immediately scrambling with my hands to grasp something, anything.

I panic and roll to my back to see where I am going and I'm most of the way to plunging down The Devil's Kettle. I roll back over to my stomach and luckily the sole of one foot slams onto a rock. Purely out of instinct, I bend the knee, push my upper body off the rocks on the river bottom and spring towards the shore. Just enough momentum was created to close that distance and I scratch and claw at the rocky shore. Sharp pains shoot through some of my fingers as I pull myself onto dry land. With a cheek down on the ground, I see my other shoe speed over the waterfall. I hadn't tied them when I rushed from my room.

"Oh nooo!" He draws this out like the fading voice of someone plummeting off a cliff. "Whoopsy, there goes a shoe. Oh, how fun! Let's see if it comes out somewhere down below in the Devil's cesspool." I'm on my feet already, shivering, and I look at a throbbing right index finger to see the fingernail bent back at the halfway point. The big bastard is giggling like a child now, peering over the waterfall when I walk over. "Hmm, I didn't see it come up down there. I guess the illusion hasn't been shattered by your clumsiness," he points down on this side of the river as he continues, "you should have just come up the path I used on this side," and he erupts into a roaring laugh.

"Yeah, that is absolutely hilarious. More than my shoe could have died just now. You realize that, right?"

He snaps his head around and looks me in the eye with the straightest of faces, "Like I give a shit. If you don't scram right now, I am going to kill you anyway."

I don't know what this guy's deal is, but my gut says to believe him. "Relax, man. I am not going to bother you."

He growls, "You're already bothering me. Get the hell out of here!" He lunges at me and grabs for my arms. I was already in a bit of a defensive stance so I am able to grab his forearms as he grabs mine and then pulls.

In a split second flash, my mind cycles through several scenes of The Big Bastard killing people with his big, murderous hands. The hands currently holding onto my forearms. He looked younger in the first images and they vividly depicted victims being shot, stabbed and even strangled, as was the case in the final image that showed The Big Bastard choking the life out of Joseph... "Wait! You killed Joseph?! Is that what you were doing up here?!"

A look of complete shock forms and he releases me as he staggers a couple steps back, "What? How could you know that... what the fuck is going on!?" My blood is boiling and I feel a rage inside me that I've never known. I scream something incoherent, as I am the one going after him now. He looks vulnerable when he yells, "Get out of my head!" My rage isn't enough to overpower his raw strength when I grab hold and he muscles me around so that I am the one closest to the ledge now. Before he can make another move though, like I had been practicing Judo my entire life, as opposed to never at all, I pivot to the side, slip my right leg between his and launch The Big Bastard over my hip. He yelps as his head smacks the rock on the rim of The Devil's Kettle and he instantly disappears. I watch down below, expecting to see him pop up in the water below cursing at me wildly, but I see nothing appear in the water.

I am just standing and staring when everything that just happened actually hits me square in the face. "Oh my God! What the hell did I just do?" *Killed him. That's what. You killed a man. But he was a killer himself. A serial killer. And poor Joseph. Did he really kill Joseph?* I feel the tears welling up in my eyes and they turn into waterfalls before I can even think about suppressing them. *What does it matter anyway? If you can't cry when a boy is murdered and you've killed a man now yourself, maybe you couldn't consider yourself human, Cotter.*

The shock subsides a little and now the adrenaline is pumping. *You've got to get the hell out of here! Move it!* I spot the trail on this side of the river and I shuffle my way down the steep bank. There are no steps and I have only one shoe, so it takes me longer than it would on the other side. The trail continues on this side, so I decide to stick to it with the hope that I might get out of here without anyone seeing me.

The terrain on this side is less aggressive so far, so I am able to move quickly. Voices from atop the hill on the other side of the river send me hunkering down under an evergreen. I sneak a look at what appears to be a random couple. I can't imagine why they are out here in weather like this, but at least it isn't someone from The Clubhouse. The adrenaline must be wearing off some because I am chilled to the bone right now. The couple is not quite comfortably past me, but I take off anyway. I have to get back to the warmth of that lodge before it's too late. Even if I get back safely but have to get medical attention, the explanation will be so much more difficult.

It is awkward running with one shoe and it hurts my foot at least every other step, but I am sprinting right now. The exertion and cold air is leaving my throat with that metallic feeling. I keep pushing hard and I am at the highway sooner than I expect. The trail on this side skips the dirt road, but that means I have to risk a longer distance of being spotted in this condition on the highway.

I get on the highway and use the bridge to cross the river and the road. I start running down the shoulder, but it sounds like a vehicle is approaching from up ahead so I take off toward the lake. The Clubhouse should be just through the trees and this might be a better way for me to make a discreet entrance anyway. I quickly spot the buildings of Naniboujou and maneuver so that I run onto the open ground to the side of the closest building. I peep around the back corner of the building, thinking this side is my best bet of slipping in without detection, but I am shocked to see numerous people out and about in the snow.

Freezing my butt off, I quickly make a decision to race back to the trees. From here, I weave my way down to the shore of Lake Superior. It doesn't look like there is anyone down here so I start sprinting down the beach. The bank up to the lawn is quite high, but I still hunch down as I run in front of the resort buildings. I stop running when I get out in front of the lodge and casually walk up the bank.

A thought comes to mind and I nonchalantly turn and walk back down the bank. Once out of sight, I take off my other shoe and sling it sidearm, as high and far as I am willing to risk so as not to be seen by anyone who might be looking out a window. Upon release, the numbness in my hands isn't enough to hide the pain in my finger as the damaged nail rips back a little more from the nailbed. The shoe splashes down and I feel satisfied with the distance. I watch it disappear before I turn back and scramble up the bank. Walking toward the lodge, it strikes me that I may not have executed that throw well enough if Joseph hadn't helped me with the rock skipping, and tears well up in my eyes again.

I fight them hard this time so that I won't be crying if I run into anyone while entering the lodge. I am preparing different stories in my head as I go through the back door of the lodge, just knowing there will be somebody who will speak to me. However, in an astonishing stroke of luck, I am into the lobby and the employee at the desk is turned when I bolt up the stairs. I pass nobody in the hallway and I slip into my room under the assumption I might have actually been undetected the entire time I was out of my room.

I frantically try to rip every piece of clothing from my body, but it is a slow go with my fingers failing to function properly. They are both cold and tender from my catfight with the riverbank. When I finally get my jeans unbuttoned, I hang all the clothes on the shower door in the bathroom. I push my damaged fingernail down as best I can and then quickly wrap some toilet paper around it to stave off any bleeding. It probably doesn't hurt because my fingers are numb.

Hurrying to the closet, I grab both extra blankets and jump into the bed. My hands can't work fast enough to spread out the blankets and I am cold on a level that has ice cycles piercing my brain. I curse under my breath about the struggle to unfold a blanket, about everything from the last... hour? The clock says 8:40 a.m. How could a lifetime worth of pain and guilt unfold in an hour? I curl up in a fetal position under the heft of blankets and close my eyes hard. Maybe if I squeeze hard enough it will all just go away. Maybe if I fall asleep and wake up it will all just have been a nightmare. Maybe I will just lay here, unable to sleep knowing I have killed a man and poor Joseph is dead. Maybe I am just being too cynical and I should be thankful for my only warmth right now, the hot tears welling up under my closed eyelids.

***

The snow has lightened now and I am able to see clearly while I gaze at the spot where the Brule River enters into Lake Superior. I seemed to walk right to this spot, knowing The Big Bastard's body would surface here, and there it comes, floating in jerky motions as it encounters tiny rapids in the river. The only surprise comes to me as the body nears the mouth of the river and suddenly stands up. He turns to look straight into my eyes with that menacing grimace on his face. There is a gaping gash on his brow from hitting the rocky rim of The Devil's Kettle, and a glint of sunlight peeking through a cloud shows the white of bone in the center.

The Big Bastard starts taking labored steps toward me looking like he is simply emerging from a casual, but tiring swim. I am frozen by cold and terror. No words, just a dedicated march in my direction as he holds my gaze with that psychotic smirk. I can't move my feet and I look down to see that I have no shoes and my feet are now frozen in big chunks of ice. I move my arms up in a position of defense, but he doesn't raise a hand when he stops in front of me. Instead, he draws my attention to his foot by pointing and lifting it up as he says in a more cheerful voice than I've ever heard out of him, "Check out my new shoe."

The phone ringing on the nightstand breaks this image. I am thankful it was only a nightmare, but thankless for the reminder of what I have done. I don't want to answer this call. A gut feeling tells me they found his body and they want to confront me about murdering him. The nightmarish image of him wearing my shoe comes to mind. The evidence is right there to put me on the scene. Wherever his body ends up, my shoe will be there too.

Another thought has me reaching for the phone. If they don't find the shoe, I'm going to look guilty anyway if I am also missing in action. "Hello."

"Cotter, what's going on? You missed our morning session." It's Mr. Anders and I can't believe I didn't hear an accusation of murder.

"Um… yeah, I know. I'm sorry, but I am not feeling well."

"I see, and no breakfast either? So you haven't gotten up at all yet today?"

Damn, damn, damn! Why didn't you figure out a story before you answered the phone? Can't risk saying you haven't left the room because someone must have seen you… and you've lost your shoes. "No, I actually got up this morning and tried to get going, but I ended up in a position where I felt even worse, so I came back to my room and laid down again."

"Oh, so you did make it to breakfast. I didn't know because I was offsite this morning."

"No, I wasn't at breakfast." My mind is racing to come up with something that makes sense. "The thing is, and this was really stupid of me, but I thought I'd feel better if I got some fresh air, so I went out and walked the beach. I didn't pack the right clothing for this cold weather, so I was definitely chilled."

"That happens, you don't have to think yourself stupid for not predicting the weather."

"Well, that wasn't the stupidest part of it. When I got to the river, I wanted to keep going. I attempted to get across in a shallow spot and I fell in."

"Cotter, that water must be freezing and there are no spots shallow enough to keep your feet from getting wet anyway. That was not smart at all."

"That's what I said. And to make matters worse, one of my shoes came off and was swept away."

"What? Were you able to recover it?"

"No." He sighs into the phone. "I tried to look for it, but I couldn't even see clearly in the water. It wasn't very bright out and then I was really chilled so I knew I needed to hurry back and warm up." I'm half impressed with myself. As dumb as the situation sounds, maybe it is believable.

"Shoot, that sucks, Cotter. You have another pair of shoes?"

"No, I was planning to buy some warmer clothes in the gift shop, but I can't imagine they have shoes?"

"They don't," he is quiet a moment, "but things get left behind all the time by guests so maybe I can round something up for you. What size shoe do you wear?"

"Eleven."

"Okay, I will check with them. If they don't have anything, we can take a look at the mouth of the river. There's a good chance it would be pushed up where the river meets the lake."

"I wouldn't bother with that."

"Why not?"

"Well, because I was so pissed off at myself and the situation that I launched my other shoe into the lake."

"Jeez, Cotter."

"I know, but I didn't think for a second the other shoe could be found."

"Doesn't mean you needed to leave a second footprint on this environment by polluting it with the other shoe."

"Good point. I guess I wasn't thinking at all."

He breathes heavily into the phone, "But I get it, man. Weird and annoying situation you found yourself in. Why don't I get a doctor out to see you if you're feeling so badly?"

"No, I don't think it's that bad."

"Listen, if it's bad enough that you can't make your sessions, that's a problem. So, if you are going to be missi—"

"I think I can make the evening session."

"Are you sure?"

"Yeah, I think a little more rest will do me good and then I will be down."

He pauses before speaking, "Well, okay, but if you don't make it to lunch I think we will need to have someone look at you."

"How about I promise I will make it to supper, or you can send someone."

"Alright, but you still have some time before lunch, try to make it."

"I will. See you later."

"Oh, hold on. Have you happened to see Dwight at all this morning?"

"Who?"

"Dwight. You know, the big guy we had to hold back at group last night."

"Oh... him. No, I was only out of my room early this morning and I didn't really see anybody."

"Hmm, okay. It's just that he hasn't been seen this morning either and he didn't answer his phone. I guess someone will just have to go up to his room. See you soon, Cotter."

"Okay, bye." Hanging up the phone I realize the feeling has come back to my fingers and it prompts me to survey the rest of my body. I push the covers down and nothing looks black from frostbite, just a redness to my feet. My body is fairly warm now, but a little stiff and sore. I hadn't realized before, but there is a huge black and blue knot just under my right knee. I bend my leg a couple of times to confirm it is only a nasty looking and painful contusion. Unwrapping the toilet paper on my finger reveals the worst injury. Approximately two-thirds of the fingernail is popped up, exposing the raw-looking meat of the nail bed.

I climb off the bed and walk over to my bag. A tenderness on the sole of my left foot, the foot that was shoeless on the return trip this morning, causes me to stop and hold the dresser as I lift my foot and turn it upwards. There is a fine, but deep slice across the meaty ball of my foot. It's one that doesn't seem like it bled much, but the tissue is puffy red and tender. I find the nail clippers in my bag and gently clip off the upturned portion of fingernail on my right index finger. It was going to come off anyway. Now, at least it won't snag and bend or tear anymore.

I hope that Mr. Anders or anyone else isn't thinking there is any connection between the two men who missed breakfast and sessions this morning. Then I just have to hope a body doesn't bob up next to a shoe somewhere in the river or the lake. Images of the morning flash through my mind. I recall the sight of Joseph with huge hands placed around his neck. If I am lucky and there is any justice in this world, maybe The Devil's Kettle actually does flush straight down to Hell and that Big Bastard is right where he belongs. But, if that is where it leads, it would also mean the Devil has a shoe that I will one day have to try on in some twisted Cinderella-like moment of justice.

23

More sleep and a hot shower did me some good. While I am still left feeling extremely paranoid about how things are bound to play out, at least I don't have hypothermia and my body feels relatively normal. Mr. Anders had a pair of shoes sent up to my room, so I am not sitting in the dining room without shoes on. They are actually a pretty decent used pair of Saucony running shoes. Quite a comfortable fit, but the breathable mesh won't provide any warmth outside. That being said, I guess beggars can't be choosers, and though I'd like to be able to say I don't know how uncomfortable it would be to run around out there this time of year without any shoes at all, unfortunately, I do.

Most of the counselors and members were already at the supper table when I sat down, but a few have yet to arrive. Of course, I know a couple of them will never sit down at this table again. "You must be feeling better, Cotter?" It's Lardner.

I shake the thoughts that have me on the verge of tears. "Uh, yes. Thanks."

"We totally understand these things come up sometimes, but just know any sessions you miss only delay the completion of your treatment." I guess this is the best way he is able to suggest I not let myself get sick too often. You know, part of me wants to like Lardner, but he is just impersonal enough that I can't fully get myself there.

I am having a hard time making eye contact with anyone, but I see more of the guys arriving in my peripheral vision and Mr. Anders speaks as the remainder of the chairs fill up across from me, "Those shoes fit you okay?"

I'm already looking down and I glance at the shoes. "Perfectly, thanks for finding them and sending them up. I'm surprised this nice of a pair of shoes would be left behind."

"Well, they actually didn't have anything close to your size. I just gave you my running shoes." Surprised, I look across in his direction and I am unable to speak as tears well up in my eyes. "Cotter, it's really not that big of a deal. I'm happy to help you out. Please. Don't worry about it." He has no way of knowing that my emotions are because Joseph is seated across from me.

Tears race down my cheeks before I smile and drop my head, quickly wiping my face with the sleeves of my new Naniboujou Lodge sweatshirt. I chuckle a little out of pure joy and look up at Mr. Anders. "Sorry, I am just really thankful right now."

"No need to apologize for showing emotion."

I look to Joseph, "Have any time to skip some rocks after we eat?"

He had looked concerned or maybe surprised by my tears I suppose, but his face brightens into a smile now. "I could probably spare a couple of minutes to help you hone your skills."

I sigh deeply. What a relief, but what does this mean. I hadn't thought much about the vision I had, or maybe it wasn't a vision at all. Either it was something real my brother would label as a vision of some future evil that Big Bastard was going to commit, or it was just my overactive imagination. I don't believe the crazy things my brother has said, his reasoning behind him murdering people, but I also am not sure I want to think I murdered a man who didn't do the things I imagined.

Supper is being ordered at the other end of the table already and Mr. Anders looks that way, "Still haven't caught up to Dwight?"

Lardner responds, "No. We entered his room and he was not there, but his things were still there, so I think he is around somewhere and just skipping out on his responsibilities. Or, who knows, it wouldn't be beyond him to happen upon an opportunity to abscond and just leave his belongings behind. This is not necessarily abnormal behavior for him."

**

We have been throwing rocks for several minutes when I finally ask something that was weighing on my mind. "How did you like the waterfall this morning?"

Joseph has a look of confusion when he looks my way, "What are you talking about?"

"You said you were going to the waterfall." The confused look does not fade. "At group last night you said you were looking forward to the cold and snow and you were going to get up early to take a hike to Devil's Kettle Falls."

"Oh, that's right. I didn't go. I mean, I did intend to get up and go, but I just shut off my alarm and went back to sleep." He shrugs his shoulders and chuckles.

"I see. It is an amazing site, so you should check it out another time."

"Oh, I've gone a couple times already since I have been here. It is a sick sight. I think last night I was just feeling pretty good about myself and I did feel inviting of the cold, and I thought the waterfall would be cool to see when it was snowing, but then when my alarm went off, I had no desire to choose the cold over the warmth of my bed."

"I hear ya, I'm sure it would have been quite frigid."

"You mean to say it *was* quite frigid?" I am not sure what this comment means but my heart starts pounding. I don't say anything as he gives me a *duh* look and finally explains, "You would know what it was like outside this morning because you were outside. I saw you on the beach from my window."

I swallow hard and try to recover as I say, "Well, I was out here, yes. I guess I meant to confirm your thought that it would have been cold going all the way to the waterfall."

He gives me a suspicious look that says *sure that's what you meant.* He throws a rock that skips several times and I throw one that fails to skip. "Oops, that one skipped as many times as your shoe did this morning." He smirks at me as I try not to show a reaction. "Why did you throw your shoes in the lake this morning?"

I give him my best fake laugh and his smirk turns into a laugh. "I only threw one of them and that was because I was pissed off about a dumb situation I put myself in this morning." I study his face while I give him the brief version of the story I told Mr. Anders on the phone. He shakes his head and chuckles at what I say I had done. I think he believes me completely, and that makes me feel guilty. But, I don't know if there was another way to play it.

"That is pretty crazy, Cotter. I don't know what you were thinking." He launches another rock.

"I better go meet Mr. Anders for my session. I already missed one this morning when I was trying to thaw my feet." He looks up chuckling and shaking his head. "Thanks for hanging out with me, Joseph. I needed this."

He looks at me surprised. Maybe not realizing I am not just hanging out for him. "Sure, no problem. I'll see ya later." I am already up the bank and I wave at him as I hurry away.

Mr. Anders is walking up from the parking lot so I connect with him at the front door. "Are you feeling better, Cotter?"

"Yes, but is there any way we could meet inside. I just have a chill that I'm struggling to shake."

"It's not how we like to do things. Like I said before, we believe there is something therapeutic about nature."

"I hear you, but aren't there individual circumstances sometimes? I mean, I've had plenty of new experiences with nature today." I see I need maybe one more twist to convince him. "Plus, I would hate for the cold to make me feel bad again and set me back."

"Fine. This one time we can hang in the lounge, maybe play a game." We walk through the door and head towards the lounge at the back of the lodge. "I had a special hike planned for you."

"Oh yeah? And what was that going to be?"

"We were going to head back to Devil's Kettle Falls." I swallow hard, more paranoia setting in. "A new perspective. There is a trail heading up the other side of the river. It's neat because you get to see into The Devil's Kettle much better when you get on top of the falls on the other side of the river." I want to tell him it's awful over there, but I just feign interest as we sit down and he digs out a cribbage board. "You know how to play cribbage, right?"

"I mean, I guess I know how to play, but I don't really play."

"I can help you along, but don't expect me to be easy on you."

"That sounds like a challenge. Let's do it." He starts shuffling a deck of cards and my attention is drawn to the snow that is beginning to fall again outside. The view from here is special. Looking out the window, I can see snow like little cotton balls floating down around evergreen trees with Lake Superior whipping up white caps in the background. In the other direction, I get to look over from the warmth of this inviting lounge to see the glory that is the dining room. I can see much of the psychedelically painted room from here. I have yet to grow tired of the look in that room.

"Hello. Cotter, you have to make the first play."

"Oh, right. Um, seven." I play my card.

"Fifteen for two. You see, you may not want—"

"Twenty-four for three."

"Okay, okay. I guess you don't need my help. You can keep announcing the game if you need, but unless we disagree with something, let's play it in the background of some conversation."

"Sounds good."

"What was going on today, Cotter? I guess it just surprised me at supper how emotional you were, and then I wondered if maybe it was more than me giving you a pair of shoes."

We just finished scoring the first hand and I am already shuffling. "Why didn't you want your point for nobs on that last hand?" He thinks back as I flip the turn-up card after dealing. "Two for his heels."

"Apparently you know the game very well, Cotter. I think you were trying to hustle me... oh man!"

"Jeez, it's not that big of a deal. I said I knew how to play."

"Not that. What the heck happened to your finger?"

I swallow the lump in my throat, "Ah, it's not a big deal."

"Not a big deal? Most of your nail is gone."

"I had to clip it off because it got bent back when I fell in the river."

"Man, that looks painful."

"It's not really as long as I don't hit it on something."

He has a disgusted look and shakes his head as if he is trying to shake the image away. "I guess now I changed the subject for you, but how about what I asked. Why such emotions today?"

"I don't know. I think I was just overwhelmed at that moment. Not feeling well, your kindness, and many surprises that have come up at this place that I never expected."

"Yeah, surprises? Anything specific you want to mention?"

I am quiet for a moment, counting my hand. "I guess I probably had some expectations when I was traveling here, and I was coming from some serious chaos in my life. Not only from my relationships, but also from witnessing some extreme trauma."

"What you told me about seeing people die was true, wasn't it?"

"Yes, it was. And I think it might have been so shocking for me that I charged through the emotions of it all, especially when I saw things again and again."

"How did you come to see this stuff so many times? I mean, I know the extraordinary circumstances you described in that moment from our earlier conversation were not real, so how were you ending up in these locations where people were dying."

I chew on this for a minute. I never expected him to believe that and I see no benefit in trying to suggest it again, even though it is the truth. "That is the unexplainable question I guess. I really have no explanation as to how I ended up in those places at the wrong time."

Now he seems to chew on it, "Hmm, I get the feeling you do have more thoughts on how you ended up there, but you'll tell me if you want. What did you mean about having expectations when you came here?"

He counts first and pegs out. "Well, apparently I didn't know the game enough to beat you."

"You made me really focus there. You clearly know how to play, it's just that your cards started to suck. I'll give you another chance."

"Okay, I'm warmed up now so good luck." He chuckles. "So, about coming here. I didn't want to as I can imagine most don't, and I also expected to hate every second of it, but I haven't. I didn't think I would like any therapist or want to talk to anyone, but I have liked talking to you. Really, aside from today, it's been a great experience."

"Maybe you shouldn't be so hung up on today. Sure it sucks that you feel sick today and that you fell in the river, but I think it could be worse."

If he only knew how bad it actually is. "Maybe you are right, because like I said, aside from a moment in time, it's really been a positive experience." I think about it more deeply for a moment. "I still kind of have a hard time understanding the benefits of this process. Don't get me wrong, I like how easy it has been and I think I get the idea of me needing to work through things, but is it really helping in the end?"

"You tell me. Actually, maybe if you think about it, haven't you just been telling me how things have changed?"

I do stop to think. "Well, yeah I guess, but I almost feel like I am on vacation. Shouldn't a vacation be enough to put people in a better mood, or have them thinking more positively?"

"That might be one way to think about this place. But let's look at exactly what you just said from a different perspective. Couldn't it be argued that if vacation makes people feel more positive, then vacation actually is a type of therapy?"

"So, vacation is therapy, and therapy is vacation?"

"Why not?"

"I guess, why not. So I should stop obsessing over the process?"

"I don't know, perhaps that is what you should be doing? Maybe that is all part of your process. You might be understanding how you want your life to be through those thought processes."

"You're getting pretty deep there, but I think I hear you. One last thought on it all. How does this type of therapy help a guy like The Big Bastard?"

"What? Who is The Big Bastard?"

"Oh, my bad, before I ever knew his name I started thinking of him as The Big Bastard. Dwight, I guess is what I heard his name was."

Mr. Anders starts really laughing at this. "Yes, Dwight. I am sure I could have guessed that is who you meant. Well, I can't talk too much to you about other members, but one like Dwight might not ever find his way, you're right. I am sure it looks like we are just letting him do whatever he wants, and in a way we are, but that type of guy will often get sick of messing around and figure something out. I won't lie, it probably isn't going to be to the depth we hope most of you will achieve, but something *can* happen. With him? I just don't know. I've already seen him come multiple times in just the time I've been working here, so I just don't know, but here is what I believe I do know. He or anyone else being forced through a type of therapy is unlikely to be productive. If people don't *want* to change themselves or things in their life, they won't. A simple reason why I believe in what we do. It's really all up to you."

"Okay, one more question I just remembered."

"Shoot."

"There are no women in The Clubhouse?"

He chuckles. "Ah, yes. Another one of those age-old traditions here I am working on changing. The original idea was to build an elite, private club for men. The membership has never changed from that, even as it morphed into an elite treatment facility for members. However, as I said, I believe women should benefit from what we do here as well. Unfortunately, I believe I have a long, uphill battle still to fight before making that happen."

"You certainly sound intent on making it happen. I agree with you and hope you make it work out."

"I can be very convincing." I smile and nod to that. "Well, we should call this one and head out to group."

"Group will still be outside with it snowing like that?"

"Yes, Cotter. I told you we would still be out there in the rain. I see the fire is already going, you'll be warmed by it."

"Let's play one more hand real quick. I have a chance to skunk you."

"You do not, come on."

"I easily could. I peg first and you're stinking like a skunk this game."

"All right, show me." He deals.

"Ten."

"I'll bite, fifteen for two."

"Twenty for two."

He eyes me suspiciously. "Okay, twenty-five for six."

"Thirty for twelve."

He snickers. "Damn, go."

"Thirty-one for two."

He laughs now, realizing I am going to be able to peg out and skunk him. We finish it out. "Alright, alright."

"I'll admit that was a strong finishing hand you dealt me."

"I know, right. Still, you got me fair and square. Well done, Cotter. I am thinking you should play the game more."

The board is put away already and we are out the back door and onto the snow-covered lawn. "Maybe I will. That was rather enjoyable taking it to you."

He shoots a glance at me, "Slow down there big guy," and he laughs as we get close to the fire.

He stops laughing when Lardner says, "Sure is nice for you boys to show up. Why don't you have a seat so we can get started?" It's only when we sit down that he takes his beady eyes off us and looks to the counselor on his left, but a thought makes him look back up and instead say, "No, we will start with you tonight, Cotter."

Great. You'd think I would have figured out by now to have what I want to say ready before group starts, but no, I'm not ready. I would like to express my thanks for what Mr. Anders did for me with the shoes, but if some don't know about my story with the shoes, I don't want to put it out there further. Even finding a shoe with The Big Bastard's body might not get me caught if people don't know I lost mine. "I'll start with something I am looking forward to tomorrow. Mr. Anders told me about a trail that goes up the other side of Devil's Kettle Falls. He said you can see into The Devil's Kettle a little better and that he would take me there." I know, like I've never been there, but it dawned on me that I might as well pad my story a little. I'm not okay with what I did, but it was at least somewhat in self-defense, so maybe it's okay for me to try to get away with it. I have to get away with it. What other option is there?

"I helped to remind a man today about a cause that was important to him. Something that if changed, would help a group of people who have been excluded from receiving benefits." Mr. Anders gives me the *tread lightly* look. "And for something that was done for me today. There is a young man who might think all the time I spend with him is something I am doing for his benefit." Joseph looks at me curiously. "But, the truth of the matter is I needed him today, and he was there for me. And, you know what the best part of it all is, he didn't need to know that I needed something in order to be there for me. He was just there. It's not something I feel I deserve lately, and I am not sure I could have appreciated such a situation before today."

Lardner seems hesitant, but he gives me an impressed nod before he looks to the next member. I look to Joseph, give him a smile, and nod. He looks proud and that makes me feel good. Not more than two days ago, he didn't even want to be a part of this world. Yesterday, he might have been more alive than he ever has been. He has no clue that his life could have been taken from him this morning and though it may be at the cost of my mental health and my future freedom, tonight, I am just happy the boy is still alive.

24

I took a long and hot shower before getting ready for bed. It was lengthy because the warmth felt like it was pushing the last of the day's chill out of my body, and also because I feel dirty in a way that had me scrubbing hard, too hard, trying to cleanse myself. I caught myself in a moment of continual scrubbing on my chest, only realizing what I was doing after my skin started to sting. I had been repeating one phrase over and over in my head. *I killed a man, I killed a man, I killed a man.* Of course, the scrubbing did nothing to help. You can't expunge the sins of the soul with a washcloth.

Sitting down on the bed now, I notice my cell phone plugged in on the nightstand. It strikes me that I was in such a distracted state today that I never even thought about my phone. I suppose I have felt attached to it for a long time, but more so lately because I had been obsessed with constantly checking to see if Genny was reaching out to me. I pick it up and the spider web in the corner of the glass reminds me of how stupid drunk I am capable of getting. If there was any question in my mind as to what my future path needed to look like, this moment has me thinking total abstinence from alcohol might be my best bet for a positive outlook.

The only notification on the screen is a text message from Rebecca. Seeing this brings the slightest flutter of hope to my heart. It has been a hopelessly difficult day and now I hope there is at least a glimmer of positivity in this message. I open the text that came through at 8:03 a.m. as nerves start to make my heart jump out of rhythm. *I just wanted to let you know I am thinking about you. I awoke this morning with you on my mind. An instinct told me you were struggling with things there and that you may not have all the support you need, so I wanted you to know that I want the best for you, regardless of how things end up between us. I am praying that you are moving in a positive direction and I would like to meet up with you when you return.*

My heart flutters happily back into rhythm and I feel a broad smile turn up. I can't imagine expecting anything more positive from her at this point. I decide to reply with something short and simple. *Thank you for sending that, Rebecca. It was a particularly tough day, and you were right, I needed that. I look forward to seeing you soon. It may be the only thing I am looking forward to right now, so again, thank you.* The timestamp on her text pops into my head and I can't help but imagine the possibility of her text coming at the exact moment I killed The Big Bastard.

I switch the lamp off and pull the covers up to my chin. Laying in the dark now, my mind has shifted back to the events of the early morning. Now I can't imagine sleep coming easily, and definitely not without nightmares. Then real nightmares tomorrow when I have to revisit The Devil's Kettle. My heart feels out of sync again as I think about what we might see during that hike tomorrow. A body? My shoe? I have to get out of here. I can't just sit here waiting for one or both of those things to bob up somewhere in a body of water. My mind flits to the nightmare of that grinning lunatic actually wearing my shoe. I shiver and close my eyes, more out of need than want.

***

Joseph is already seated at our table in the magnificent dining room. I still look up, astonished, every time I enter the colorful room. I pat Joseph on the shoulder as I walk past and quietly say, "Can we chat after breakfast?" He looks up at me while I continue to the chair at the end of the table. He nods and smiles.

No nightmares last night. Well, at least not any that I remember. I have no doubt that any dreams I had were nightmares, but I must have been so exhausted that the night passed in the blink of an eye. It was one of those nights when it felt like you hadn't even been asleep, or maybe had been for only minutes when you open your eyes, but in actuality, the morning had already come. I had closed my eyes feeling such dread about potential nightmares that I smiled and sighed in relief the moment I woke realizing I didn't remember any dreams.

I look down the table and realize only a few members and no counselors are sitting at the table. I get up and move the two chairs down to sit next to Joseph. "Ah, there isn't anyone here to hear us. Let's chat now."

"Sure. What's up, man?"

"I just wanted to ask if you have ever seen an office, like, Lardner's office?"

He looks at me curiously. "I don't know if he even has an office." I immediately feel dejected and I guess Joseph sees it, "Just tell me why you need to know that. Maybe I know something else that will help."

"I just need to figure out where something of mine is and I figured Lardner has to be keeping it somewhere. If he doesn't have an office... I guess I don't know."

"Oh, maybe it's in the same place he was keeping my cell phone."

I perk up. "Wait, what do you mean, he had your cell somewhere?"

"Yeah, my parents wanted me to have it, but didn't want it to be a distraction, so they gave it to Mr. Lardner when I first arrived. He actually just gave it back to me last night after group. He told me I have taken big steps and he thought it was time I earned that privilege."

I try not to hurry past his achievement, "Good for you, Joseph." That's as slow as I can go, "Did you see where he had it?"

"Yep. He talked with me as we walked up to the lodge and then he just went behind the front desk in the lobby to grab it."

"Really? Was it locked up back there or something?"

"Uh," he turns his eyes up, thinking, "no, I don't think he used a key for anything. I think it was in a drawer and he just opened it and grabbed it right away."

Now I am the one thinking, "Hmm, I bet he had it secured somewhere else and put it there knowing you were about to earn it back."

"Why do you think that? Where else would it be if he doesn't have an office?"

"That's just it, I don't know. Maybe in his room and that's a place I am sure I can't get to."

"But why do you think it wasn't just always at the front desk?"

"Well, if there wasn't a key, then that isn't secure at all. I doubt they would risk member's belongings being stolen. Or, why wouldn't we just grab our stuff whenever we wanted if it was unsecured."

"But it is secured." I give him a questioning look. "That desk is manned twenty-four hours a day."

"Is it? All night?"

"Oh yeah. I have been down here in the middle of the night quite a few times. There is always someone standing there."

"I suppose that makes sense. It is also a hotel and I can imagine members might also arrive in the middle of the night." Another thought comes to mind. "You're right, but that means it might as well be locked because I can't get to it with someone always standing there." A better thought now, "You know, if you were willing to help me out by distracting the clerk somehow, I bet I could get into that desk."

Either his eyes brighten at the thought of something exciting or being able to help me, "I would totally be willing to help you."

"Great! You willing to try after the breakfast crowd clears out this morning?"

"Absolutely!" A look of recognition crosses his face. "What is it that Mr. Lardner has?"

"I have a car here and he has the keys."

The happiness fades from his face instantly. "You're going to leave? I don't want you to leave." He looks like he might cry.

"No... no, there is a file in the car my dad didn't want me to be bothered with while I was here. Kind of the same as your cell phone situation." He staves off the tears and his spirit is lifted slightly. Even though this was truthful, I realize there is another truth that I am withholding and I don't want to fall right back into my pattern of lies. Especially not with people I care about. Especially not to Joseph, so I tell him the truth, "But, I do need to get out of here, Joseph. One way or another, I am sure I will be leaving soon." He sighs and his shoulders slump. "I like you man, but you know we aren't both going to be here forever anyway. We will have to part ways."

"Please don't treat me like a baby. I am very well aware that you are not always going to be in my life. Probably better that it ends before you just lose interest in me like everyone else does."

Great. *Say something meaningful, Cotter. You're in the middle of the next moment of doing something to help yourself. Be this kid's one person. Right now!* "You know, this is something that has crossed my mind several times since we first connected, because I care about you and I don't want this to be only a brief friendship either. You said you got your cell phone yesterday, do you have it on you?"

"Yes."

"Okay, unlock it and let me see it." He gives me a suspicious look. "Come on, hand it over." He holds it out and I take it for a moment. "There you go."

Joseph takes the phone back. "Whoa, who do you have it calling?"

My phone rings in my pocket and I pull it out and hold it to show him his phone number. "Now we have each other's phone number." He grins. "I think you are a cool guy and I would like to stay connected with you. So, now it doesn't matter when our time ends here, we can continue to be friends."

Joseph is still smiling, but tears well up in his eyes again, "Thank you. I can't tell you how much that means to me." I pat him on the back and give him a side hug.

***

I don't know what distraction Joseph came up with, but the man at the front desk darts from his post, sprinting into the dining room. I am through the back door and quickly behind the counter where I open the first drawer. Many random-looking personal belongings, but no keys. The second drawer has multiple sets of keys, but none are mine. I am looking in the third drawer in a matter of seconds from the time I first pulled up to the counter and there are the keys to the Focus. They are right on top of another pile of personal items.

I turn to make my escape, but my eyes are drawn to a cabinet door next to the drawers. I open it and see my bottle of tequila on a shelf. There is a brief moment where I desire to grab the bottle, but I don't. I quietly let the door close and walk briskly to the back door while slipping the keys into my pocket. I won't risk going to the vehicle in daylight, so I head down to the lake to wait for Joseph to finish with whatever distraction he is engaged in.

I have skipped several rocks before I start to worry that Joseph may have gotten himself in a bind. I skip a couple more and then look towards the lodge. I breathe a sigh of relief when I see him walking my way. He reaches the beach and just casually picks up a rock, skipping it across the water more times than I could even imagine pulling off. We glance at each other and burst into laughter, finally able to release the nerves that had bound us.

"Did you get the keys?"

"I did, thank you." He smiles and nods. "What did you do? It seemed to work pretty well."

"I climbed on top of the fireplace mantel."

"What?!" We both burst into laughter again. Joseph sits down he is laughing so hard, and he emits a snort that makes me laugh even harder. "Dude, did you just snort?"

"Stop, I'm dying here."

"How did you even get up there?"

"Easy. Those big, round lake rocks were easy to climb. I called out to the clerk and he came running, and I couldn't see into the lobby so I didn't know if you were done. I kept him until he started to follow through on his threats to call Mr. Lardner. When he started walking toward a phone, I climbed down. And check this out." He pulls his phone out and shows me a selfie of him standing on the mantel with a pissed off man standing on the floor in the background. We start laughing again.

"Nice photobomb! You'll have to post that to one of the lodge's social media pages after you get out of here." We chuckle some more.

"Yeah, it was definitely an epic moment. I don't think I have ever felt a rush like that. And how many people do you think can say they have stood on the largest fireplace in Minnesota?"

"I'm gonna guess not too many."

Our laughter is suddenly staunched by the arrival of Mr. Anders. "There you are, Cotter. It's time for our session."

"Oops, sorry. I guess I lost track of time."

"Ahh, it's not a problem. I saw you come down here after you grabbed your keys." Joseph and I shoot shocked looks at each other. "Well, let's go check out the other side of that waterfall." He just turns and starts slowly walking.

A look of worry is on Joseph's face now. I just put my hands out, palm down, to settle him as I walk past and up the incline heading towards Mr. Anders. I have the keys out and extended to him as I catch up, "Sorry, Mr. Anders."

He puts his hand up, palm towards me, "No need, hang onto them. It doesn't matter to me that you have them." I feel surprised and confused, and I'm sure it shows. "Mostly, I am glad you didn't take the bottle of liquor."

"Does Mr. Lardner know?"

"I didn't tell him, and I don't plan to, but he will know when you leave." We are to the highway now and turn towards the river.

"Oh, I really just wanted to grab something."

"Let me stop you there before you maybe feel a need to lie. We both know you are likely to leave here soon." I start to defend but he waves me off. "Cotter, I had already seen this in you, and that feeling was confirmed with you getting the car keys, but it's okay. I am confident you will be ready when you do decide to take off. I intend to suggest to Mr. Lardner that he complete your treatment at that point."

Still surprised, "Well, I appreciate that, but I can't imagine that will help me in court anyway."

"Court?" He chuckles. "What makes you think we care about what the court says? Regardless of how long the courts say you need to be here, our concern is that you leave here in a better place than you arrived. So, you don't need to worry about the courts."

We have crossed the highway bridge over the river and now we are on the path I ran down yesterday morning. A chill goes down my spine and I shiver. "But what control do you have over the judicial system?"

"Who said we needed control over the judicial system?"

"Well, how else could you tell me not to worry about court?"

"Who do you think is going to appear in court for you? Me. If I think you have done what you needed to do here, that's what I will be telling the judge. I don't care if he thought you needed to be here for two weeks or not. He will hear what he needs to hear if that is what I decide."

"Wait, what are you saying? Don't get me wrong, I am not asking you not to do that, but what about all the talk about honesty?"

"I believe there are times when it is necessary to say what needs to be said for things to work out in one's best interest. When systems choose to handcuff themselves with policies that remove all opportunity for individual circumstances, they are cornering people. They sometimes inadvertently cause more harm than the good they intended. Maybe they aren't the leading experts they think they are. So, if I believe something has moved in a positive direction, I wouldn't necessarily think I was being deceitful by saying in some way that the process was completed. Who is that judge to say it needs to take a certain amount of time when he has nothing to do with this process. I am the one walking this path with you right now."

"Um, yeah. Wow, that really makes a lot of sense to me, and I am not just saying that because it could potentially benefit me." We quickly reach the lower end of the waterfall and we start the more aggressive climb up on this side. Even though I was intently listening to Mr. Anders' justification of deceiving the judicial system, my stomach was turning more and more as I nervously scanned the river for a body, or blood, or a size eleven shoe. Now my stomach is in knots as we approach the top. I can't look into the falls. I fear I might puke.

"Look at this view, Cotter. How amazing is that, to be able to see right into the mouth of The Devil's Kettle."

"Yep, it truly is something."

"Right?" In my peripheral vision, I see him look my way. "You're not even looking at it."

I know I shouldn't act too suspicious so I look. "I did already. I just want to take everything in." Now I can't look away as I stare into The Big Bastard's twisted face deep down in the Kettle. Shoelaces are stuck between his clenched teeth and my shoe is moving back and forth under the strength of the swirling water. It finishes every circular motion by kicking The Big Bastard right in the place where his head had been split open. The wound takes up most of his forehead now, but the blood has ceased to flow. Now it's all white bone and gray tissue that appears to be waving to me as the powerful water loosens it from the skull.

"You okay? Your face is extremely pale, Cotter. Maybe you should sit down."

I look up at him as I fight to keep my breakfast ingested. "I'm fine, but I guess I'm still a little sick, not quite back to one hundred percent." I'm thankful to look back down at The Devil's Kettle and not see what my imagination had developed a moment ago. "Maybe it would be best if I just head back down."

"I'm not risking taking you down that incline at the moment. Clearly, your equilibrium is off. Just have a seat."

I make sure I pivot to face away from the waterfall before I sit down on the rock behind me. "I'm feeling better already." I think I might jump out of my skin if I have to stay here much longer. This place is too much for me right now. A knee jerk reaction has me up and I just start climbing down.

"Cotter, take it easy! I told you to take a rest."

"I'm fine. Really, Mr. Anders. Let's just head back so I can rest a while." He begins following me down, but his face shows me a mix of concern and irritation. I reach the bottom faster than I know he wanted me to, but without incident. "See, like I said, I'm okay."

He is down quickly behind me, "Yeah right, what is going on with you?"

"What do you mean? I can't help feeling sick and I just think I should get to a place where I can actually rest." He just glares at me and starts to walk ahead of me down the path. "I can go faster than this, it's fine."

"Just relax, Cotter. If you're sick, then you don't need to exert too much energy or you might get worse again."

We continue along the path, at his pace, and I hear a muffled voice from behind and towards the river. Mr. Anders doesn't react and I look at the other bank expecting to see someone walking, but there is nobody in sight. I barely have my eyes forward again and the garbled voice sounds like it says my name from directly beside us. Again, Mr. Anders doesn't appear to have heard, but this time I do see something when I look. The Big Bastard is floating down the river on his back, keeping perfect pace with us. He holds my shoe with a straw coming out of it and he is taking a sip from it. With his head wound gaping open and an eye swollen shut, he looks like a drunken redneck taking a casual float down the river after a bar fight. The one open eye focuses on me and he stops drinking from the shoe solely to raise it in my direction, as if saying, "Cheers."

25

Group is dismissed and I make sure I am the last one to stand up. I shuffle over to the fire and hang back while everyone else moves towards the lodge. The snow is coming down steadily tonight. I would be hurrying indoors if I didn't have another agenda. All of the guys generally head up to their rooms after group and I am counting on that tonight so I can go get my adoption file without being noticed. I can't see anyone lingering outside the lodge, so I begin to head that way.

Near the windows of the lodge, I don't see anybody inside except for the front desk clerk. I start towards the woods where I will be able to go to the parking lot in the cover of darkness. Though it would be difficult to see very far through this snow, I don't want anyone to be in their room already and see me go to the cars in the splash of light from the lodge. I'm confident I am cloaked in the night now so I hurry directly to my dad's Ford Focus. He keeps the car meticulously clean, so I don't have to search at all. The file is literally the only thing laying atop the coarse gray carpet lining the trunk.

I quietly close the trunk and quickly start making my way back the way I came. I tuck the file slightly into the back of my pants and cover it with my sweatshirt. The clerk looks my way as I come through the door, but she just nods to me like we are doing business as usual. I hurry up the stairs, partly because I feel like I am going to be caught, but mostly because I am anxious to discover what is inside this file.

I hardly get my room door closed and locked and the contents of the file are scattered across the bed. I could feel how thin the file was the moment I picked it up, but the amount of information spread out on the bed is quite disheartening. My initial thought is that there isn't going to be much more information here than what my dad had already told me. However, my next thought is that he wouldn't set up this situation if he didn't know there was something in here for me to investigate.

The first item I pick up is my birth certificate. This is a post-adoption document with my current name on it. I scan the few remaining documents and I am slightly confused there isn't another birth certificate from my birth parents, but I guess they weren't around long enough to complete something like that. Dad did tell the story like the chaos started rather quickly.

There are two pages stapled together that appear to be some documentation of a police report. I immediately worry about how emotional it might be to read it, but it is actually quite vague. The details basically say that the victim was assaulted by his father, that he attempted to hurt the baby. *Yeah right. More like tried to commit infanticide.* Now I almost feel wronged that it didn't contain the grotesque details of his behavior, but at least it confirms that my brother was lying, or at least wasn't told the truth when he told me our father couldn't bring himself to kill me.

A news article clipped from the *Star Tribune* has yellowed significantly. The headline reads, "Attempted Infanticide in Minneapolis Hospital." *Exactly! Maybe the officer who wrote that report should have read the newspaper first!* The article doesn't offer anything other than what I already know about the incident. The headline is perhaps the only part that goes farther than the police report.

The last three pages look like notes written down by my parents. Skimming the first two, they seem to consist of the adoption process and legal steps my parents needed to take. The last piece of paper I look at appears to be the most informative and after seeing some names I yell, "Yes!" I pause and look around, as if anyone in the lodge who might have heard me would even know what I was excited about.

I look over the page more slowly now and it is clear that this is a list of names of the people who my parents met with when they arrived at the hospital to get me. Amongst others, there are the names of a police officer, a lawyer, a social worker, and most importantly, the name of the doctor who was in the room, Dr. Jack Alterman.

My excitement continues when I flip the paper over and see the name of the hospital, Hennepin County Medical Center. There are also a number of medical professionals' names listed. There are notes written about the description of my birth parents and how they entered the emergency room in a panic. Apparently, after having tried to have a natural birth at home, it became obvious that there was something wrong and that is why they ended up in the emergency room. The names listed are nurses who were in the delivery room, and others who were in the hallways when they entered and fled with my brother. A security guard is also mentioned.

The same name, Jack Alterman, was listed to confirm this was indeed the doctor who delivered me and was in the room when the subsequent events unfolded. There are many people here I could track down and that is a little overwhelming, but I quickly decide that the doctor is the person I want to talk to. If there is anyone I can hear the first-hand story from, I believe it's him. I can decide from there if I want or need to talk to others. Maybe he can even give me information my dad couldn't provide.

What do I do now? I think about going to bed. I should go to bed, but there is too much adrenaline flowing right now. There is no way I could go to sleep right now. I grab my cell phone and a quick internet search gives me a number for the Hennepin County Medical Center. I hold the number on the touch screen and it is quickly ringing. My heart is pounding by the time a female voice answers, "Emergency room."

"Hello, could you connect me with Dr. Jack Alterman."

There is a pause. "Can you hold one moment please?" Hold music comes on that makes me feel like I am on an elevator in a movie. I'm pretty sure I have never heard music in an elevator, but I've seen plenty of movies that have elevator music. Maybe it's only on elevators in Hollywood. "Sir, I did not recognize that name, but I did ask to make sure for you and I was told that doctor has not worked here for at least a decade."

I'm not surprised. "Shoot. Can you tell me which hospital he went to, or if he retired?"

"Even if I knew that, I don't think I could just give you that information, sir. I'm sorry."

How am I going to find him? "Well, I was a patient of his once, and… well, my current health may rely on me finding him."

"I'm sorry, sir."

"How about if I give you my name and information and you can look me up in your system."

"Sir, I wouldn't be able to confirm anything about you over the phone anyway and I certainly could not give out information to you about others."

"If I was able to come there and prove my identity, might I be able to talk to someone who could give me something… anything?"

"I don't know where you are, so I certainly would not want to tell you that would be an option and have you travel very far for nothing, but you could speak with someone about your records and go from there. However, I am not sure there would be any information for you."

"I understand, thanks anyway."

"Hold on, sir."

"Yes?"

"Why don't you just search his name on the internet?"

I chuckle to myself. "That's a great idea. Thank you, bye."

"For sure. No problem and good luck, sir."

I hang up the phone and Google for Dr. Jack Alterman and Minneapolis. There are hits, but everything is linked to that hospital and nothing from recent years. This confirms that she did hear from someone that he has been gone from there for a long time, but where did he go. There are news articles involving him in various events, but nothing about a retirement. I think Dad said he wasn't that old and he doesn't look very old in the pictures I see of him online.

Facebook doesn't seem to have an account for him either. There are some men with that name, but none of them looks like there is the slightest chance it could be him. Checking other social media sources, there are even fewer results with that name than Facebook, and none are him. I'm just starting to frustrate myself as I search different variations of keywords between his name and the Twin Cities.

I don't know what to do next, and yet my instinct is telling me what I should do next. I open the map application on my phone and punch in Minneapolis. "Oof." Four and a half hours. I thought it would be closer than that. I'm not even tired anyway and I know I won't sleep if I stay here. Besides, I need to get out of here before a body turns up, and I know I am going to leave before I am supposed to, it might as well be now.

***

I assumed I wouldn't make it out of the lodge without being seen, at least by the clerk, but that is exactly what happened. I was willing to just walk out even if someone questioned me, or knowing they would alert Lardner, but I am pretty sure I made a clean getaway. I don't even know where the clerk was when I came down the stairs, but there was nobody at the front desk so I hurried around the corner and just slipped out the back door. Well, after I ran to the cabinet and grabbed my bottle of tequila. It's not like I am drinking it, but I just don't like that Lardner took my stuff. And it's a damn expensive bottle of tequila.

There are a couple inches of snow on the ground and the car needs to defrost, but I wanted to get away from the parking lot, so I just quickly scraped a small box out of the ice on the windshield using my credit card and slowly drove out to the highway. I could hardly see where the road into Naniboujou was in some spots and it felt like I drove off it a couple of times. Luckily, the snow isn't deep enough to get stuck, even in this beastly Ford Focus.

The highway doesn't look too bad to drive on, but I have hardly ever driven, so I'll just take it slow. I'm pulled onto the shoulder right now, just letting the car warm up so the windshield can fully defrost. Dad didn't let me down. There was an ice scraper in the floorboard of the back seat, but even after fully scraping the windshield, it didn't help with the moisture fogging up the inside of the car. Probably my moisture. As cold as it is outside, I was so nervous I worked up a good lather while making my way out of the lodge.

The clock in the car says 11:15 p.m. and I am finally on the road. I still don't feel tired, but I don't know how much driving at night is going to tire me out. I guess I haven't driven enough to know what to expect of myself. There is something in my gut that tells me this might not be a great idea, but I am confident I can both stay awake and navigate the snowy roads if I take it easy.

I turn on the radio and try to find a loud rock station. I don't have to hit seek too many times. Not because I found a good station, but because there are so few frequencies that it hardly stopped on any station. I start to take my phone out of my pocket and the lack of concentration has the car veering onto the shoulder. I let go of the phone and correct back towards the road but the wheels break loose on ice. I hold my breath as the rear end kicks out slightly and then settles back in line. Maybe grabbing my phone is not being careful enough in these conditions.

I pull onto the shoulder and plug my phone into the external jack on the car stereo. Okay, now I can get some loud tunes on to keep me alert. Speakers start thumping, well… Ford Focus style anyway, and I pull back onto the road. I definitely think jamming out will help get me through this drive. I am feeling good about where I am right now. I am hopefully on my way to get some answers about my birth parents. Rebecca might be willing to come back into my life and I am getting further away from Naniboujou and that damn waterfall. *Shit. Why did you have to think about that place? It's never going to be okay. You killed a man.*

The music cuts for a second and when I look down at the phone, I realize my dad is trying to call. Part of me doesn't want to answer, but maybe it wouldn't hurt to talk to someone while I drive. I'm eventually going to have to tell my parents I left The Clubhouse early anyway. I clearly can't handle any added distractions with my limited driving experience, so I hit the speaker button, "Hey, Dad."

"What is going on, Cotter?"

I'm caught off guard so I step around even though I probably know the reason for the agitation, "What do you mean?"

"You know what I mean, have you left treatment?"

"Did they call you?" Shoot, I was sure I left undetected.

"No, but I have a GPS tracking device on that car."

Old habits die hard. I instinctively deflect, "Oh, so you can't trust me enough and you pu—"

"Stop, stop, stop!" He yells, "You can't always turn stuff around on people, Cotter! I had that on the car long before now and I wouldn't need to justify it to you even if I hadn't. When you do something you know you aren't supposed to, you have to just own it. You don't always get to find a way to get mad at somebody for the simple reason that they are mad at you. Take ownership! Take responsibility!"

"I know, you're right. You're right, Dad. I'm sorry I did that just now but will you just listen to me about why I left."

"Just turn around and go back, Cotter. It's not too late to make the right decision. I don't want you to go back to jail."

"I'm not going back to jail. Everything is okay if you'll just listen for a minute."

"Okay, I'll hear what you have to say, but I want you to go back."

"I've done quite well and it's going to be okay with me leaving right now."

"It hasn't even been a week yet, Cotter!"

"You said you would listen."

He releases an audible sigh into the phone. "Yes, go ahead."

"My counselor knows that I felt the need to go and he told me he thinks I was ready. Their program is a unique one, and he felt I had made the progress necessary for treatment to be considered complete."

"But it doesn't matter if he says that, Cotter. The court determined you needed to be there at least two weeks."

"I know that, and I don't know exactly how he is going to express this, but Mr. Anders said he will tell them in court that I completed treatment. They don't seem to feel they are governed by the courts. Actually, I get the feeling that they don't care for our judicial system." Dad scoffs at this. "Mr. Anders made a great argument about it. He said the judge leaves no room for individual circumstances when he says something like two weeks. He isn't involved with my treatment, so how could he know how long something like their program is going to take? Could be longer, could be shorter."

"Yeah, I just don't know about this, Son." It seems like he is softening a little.

"Dad, I am doing really well. My head is clearer than it has been in a while. I need you to trust me when I say I needed to get out of there. It's time for me to do what you set up for me to do. I'm headed to the Twin Cities to search for answers, and then I'm coming home. Everything is okay, seriously."

"Okay. I can tell I am not going to sway you in the other direction, but for the record, I don't think it's right that you left early."

"I hear you. I'll talk to you soon."

"Okay, bye."

"Bye."

Rebecca sent a text message during the phone conversation. I carefully tap the banner so that it opens. *I am glad my words mean something to you again and it does make me feel good that you are looking forward to seeing me. I am going to try to trust this means that other woman is out of the picture, but it is hard, Cotter. I guess I just don't know what to expect and it scares me to think about trusting again and then being devastated again.* Oops, drifting outside of the white line again. I need to read in smaller chunks. *I can't go through it again, so please stop talking to me now if there is any part of you that can't be fully invested. If you really are turning back into the Cotter I used to love, then I also look forward to seeing you soon.*

What a rollercoaster of emotions these last couple of days have been. Something negative, something positive. Something negative, something positive. Things would be feeling so good if I didn't just have that conversation with Dad. If I could have just got a hit on this doctor and known where he was. If I hadn't killed a man. *Stop! You have to stop ending up back at the bottom with that thought!*

Alright, back to the positive stuff. I need to text Rebecca back something to assure her I am all in on her. I must be getting nearer to Duluth though because I am meeting other cars on the road more frequently, so no distractions. I'll just do it voice to text. I try to push the microphone button out of the corner of my eye and I accidentally hit call. "No, no!" It's not the right time to call her while I am fleeing treatment. I hit the red button quickly so hopefully it doesn't show I tried to call.

My eyes flash back to the road and there is a man and a boy in the middle of the road. I slam on the breaks but there is little stopping power as the car slides on glare ice and the antilock brakes begin to shudder. The scene before me is in slow motion now as I am about to make contact with them. My eyes lock with the man. It's The Big Bastard. He stands there looking dead, except with the one eye locked on me and that psycho smile on his face. The boy is Joseph and his eyes are beginning to bulge out as The Big Bastard squeezes his neck so hard that veins are popping on his hands and arms.

I hold my breath as our paths cross, but of course, there is no impact because they were never really there. Except now, something very real has me continuing to hold my breath as I slide through a corner and my dad's Ford Focus slams into a sheer rock face. Everything is instantly blurry with a constant horn sound quietly going off in my head. The horn grows gradually louder as I begin to regain my faculties and realize what just happened. I am staring into a deployed airbag and a crumpled hood.

Glancing in the rearview mirror, I expect to see my face twisted up, but surprisingly there isn't even any blood. I start moving my appendages, one by one, and everything seems to be intact and maybe even pain-free. I unbuckle my seatbelt and try to open the door, but I can't. Vision is still a little blurry and I feel confused about exactly what is going on. I press the auto-lock button and try the door again. It won't open and my head is spinning now. I start to feel chilled and I cross my arms as I begin to shiver.

Thankfully, there is warmth from the flames that are just beginning to lick over the dashboard from underneath the crumpled hood. I uncross my arms and put my hands out towards the fire. Much better. Reminds me of those bonfires up there at Naniboujou. I can almost see the crew sitting around it in a circle. Why be so negative about things when you have so many positives to be thankful for. Yes, be thankful for the life still in that sweet boy, Joseph, instead of feeling negative about your dad's car being on fire. Something is wrong here. My hands are getting hot now and I shake my head. I have to close my eyes from the pain in my head, but now I open them and really take in the scene for the first time. "Wait, what in the hell is this!"

"Hey! Get out of the car!" I look over my shoulder to see some lady running from another car.

"I'm trying! My door is jammed."

"Here, come out this door!" She has the passenger side door open, but I feel pinned.

"The steering wheel is collapsed in on me. I can't get around it with the center console!" I try moving around and up the left side of the steering wheel but the door is too tight to me on that side.

"Try moving the seat back!"

Yes! Thank you, lady! "Shit! It's electric and it won't move!" I reach up to try to start the engine, but the flames are on the column. The key is on anyway, so it would work if it could, but it doesn't. Is this the end? The flames are so hot now and I look over at the woman with pleading eyes. She is sobbing. I hear the back door open and suddenly my seat flops back and I am being dragged into the back seat and out the door. I am pulled up to my feet and I scramble away from the car with my arm around someone's neck. I lean against a rock face and look into the eyes of a middle-aged man standing next to a semi-truck. "Oh my God, thank you."

"Exactly. It is thanks to God you didn't just burn alive."

"How did you get me out? I was pinned in there."

"Um… I reclined your seat." I let go of the rock and start to step toward him, but extreme dizziness hammers my head and everything goes black.

26

Thoughts of pain and dizziness in my head have me opening my eyes very slowly. The sunlight coming through a window is abrasive, but I work my eyes all the way open as I realize the pain isn't too much. Hospital room. Now that I understand where I am, memories of the accident come to mind and I look at my hands, expecting them to be burned. They look normal. Maybe a little red and there is a slight stinging sensation, but they don't look burned. There is a nurse working quietly to my right. She seems to have been here since before I woke, but I only now notice as she turns in my direction. "Oh, good morning, Mr. Trespin. How is your head feeling?"

"Morning," I feel like the pain is bound to come again, but I gingerly turn my head from side to side before answering, "actually, I think it feels okay. How bad is it? Do I have any other injuries? My hands?" I hold them up to her.

"Your hands? I am not sure about that. I wasn't told anything about your hands, but I will let the doctor know you are awake and he can discuss everything with you. I can tell you that you are very lucky and you are going to be just fine."

"Thank you." Something besides my health comes to mind. "Oh no, my stuff!"

"Your stuff? What about it?"

"It's all gone. I guess I don't care about my bag, but my phone and... the file." I feel tears coming up a little. "No, my file, that information probably can't be found anywhere else."

"Just relax, Mr. Trespin." I don't care what she says to try to soothe me, she doesn't have a clue what I lost. "A woman showed up here to check on you after you arrived by ambulance and she dropped off your bag and cell phone. She said she grabbed them from your car after you were pulled out."

Now she has my attention. "Oh, thank goodness. I wouldn't know how to get a hold of anyone without that phone. Maybe I should have some phone numbers memorized now that I think about it."

"Oh, don't think you are alone. I think the memorization of personal information is something that is lost in today's society. I think the only phone number in my head is the home landline from my childhood. That is probably only because my parents still have it. Can you believe that? They still use a landline." She seems very kind. A middle-aged woman who isn't a beauty queen, but quite pretty in a down-to-earth kind of way.

"But the file? It wasn't in my bag. I bet she didn't grab that." I am not as upset with this realization. I think I have already felt the emotions of losing it. "Where is my phone?"

"I think you should talk to the doctor first. I do not think he wants you focusing on that screen just yet because of your concussion."

"I do have a concussion then?"

"Yes, but I will let you talk to him."

"Can you just look in my bag and see if she might have put the file in there?"

"For sure, I can do that." She walks over to a closet and pulls my bag out. I can see that she has it wide open and has searched thoroughly, but she looks my way and shakes her head.

"Perfect. The entire reason I was even on the road last night, and my dad's car ruined, all for naught."

"Can I ask what was so important in this file?"

"The short version is simply that it had names with whom I might find answers to my past, but now they're gone."

"Oh, I am sorry to hear that. Maybe you can remember some of the names if you had looked at them already? There is a pen and paper there on the bed tray if something comes to mind and you need to write it down."

"You are very kind. I had only just seen them, so I won't be expecting that, but I do have the most important name from the list in my head, so there is that at least."

"Well, that is good. There, maybe that will be enough to provide what you need." I must look defeated to her. "What?"

"It's just that it is feeling like it might not be possible for me to track him down. Hell, maybe I'm here because I'm not supposed to get to him. I don't know anymore. I don't think I'll make it to the Twin Cities now to even search. And, you know, I was really looking forward to seeing U.S. Bank Stadium too." I force a grin and she smiles back.

"Oh, a Vikings fan. Well, I hope something works out. Do get some more rest. The doctor may not be available to come in right away." I just nod and close my eyes, but her voice sounds off again, "Oh, well would you look at that. Here he is."

I open my eyes again and smile at the doctor. Now I just begin to laugh and he gives me a puzzled look before popping his doctor's coat collar and wittily remarking, "Is what I am wearing funny?"

"You may think I chose a difficult path to get here, but I hoped we could talk, Dr. Alterman." He is much older than any pictures I saw online, but he really looks very much the same. The nurse gives me a questioning look when I glance her way. I point, "This is the one name in my head." She still looks confused. "Dr. Jack Alterman."

The recognition of what I am saying comes across her face, "Are you serious?! Oh my gosh. So maybe you are actually here because you *are* supposed to get to him. This has to be a God thing."

Dr. Alterman looks from me to her with his own confused look. "I'm lost. What's the deal?"

She responds first, "I will let you two talk." and she walks out.

He looks back to me, "Mind filling me in on the joke?"

"Well, I was laughing because it feels very unreal, but it is definitely no joke. How I am going to say this might sound blunt, but I will just cut to the chase. Do you remember being in an emergency room a little over twenty-one years ag—"

"You're that baby, aren't you?" I guess I am not surprised he picked it out right away. That must have been a significant moment in his life as well. As if to confirm that thought, he grabs hold of the chair to balance himself. Now he sits down and a distraught looking solemnness dulls his features, and I suddenly feel sorry for him. "I thought I recognized something in your name, and somehow I always felt we would come face to face. I think I knew it would be either you… or him. I'm glad it's you."

"I'm sorry to remind you, I'm sure it was traumatic for you?"

"I nearly quit medicine. I had already seen plenty of things at that point in my career, but this was something so sinister that I really struggled to accept what I saw that night." Recognition comes to his face and he says, "Oh, I'm sorry. This has to be hard for you too." He stands up. "This isn't a therapy session for me. Let's talk about why you're here."

"No. No, this is why I am here. I was looking for you to hear this stuff. Wait… I mean, I am *here* because I accidentally found you, but I was actually on my way to the Twin Cities to try and find you."

"What? I have been here for… probably a solid decade." He sits back down, shock on his face. "This is crazy. That night was crazy, felt like something more was happening than what we were seeing in that room, but I had no clue what. Now this? How can it just be a coincidence that you would end up here after a car accident?" He thinks a moment. "Maybe if we happen to live around the same area now it isn't too crazy. It is actually a small world. You live in Duluth?"

"No, Chicago."

He was sitting on the edge of the chair, but now he slumps back. "Pardon my French, but this is some crazy shit."

"Agreed. But, somehow we are here now. Could you tell me about that night?"

"I don't really want to, but yes. I want to run out of here right now, but I can't imagine denying you this moment." He kind of shakes his head. "But how is your head feeling? Let me just look you over first."

"I feel okay, really. I remember my head feeling pretty messed up after the crash." He is shining a small penlight in my eyes now. "Dizziness and some pain, confusion."

"None of that this morning?"

"No, I feel surprisingly clear-headed at the moment."

"Well, you definitely have a concussion, but I don't think it's serious."

"What about my hands, are they burned?"

"Your hands? It wasn't mentioned when you came in. Let me

look."

"They just sting a little. Kind of like a bad sunburn."

"Yes, I can see the redness, but it doesn't look bad. I can write you a prescription for the pain, but I don't think anything else is necessary."

"Nah, it's not that bad. Can you tell me about that night?"

He sighs deeply and sits back down. "What do you know?"

I briefly explain to him what I read in the report and what my dad and brother had told me about it.

"You know your twin? And what about the parents?"

"No, I guess I don't even know where they are." I think about how much I should even say about my brother. "I just happened to run into him in Chicago."

"You've got to be kidding me! What are the chances of all this?"

"You're right, it's crazy. Anyway, I don't really know him. In fact, our encounters have been quite confrontational." I pause in thought. "Jeez, I don't even know his name."

"Abel."

"What?"

"Cain and Abel is what they called you two."

"Wait, what?!"

"Well, I know you're adopted and that isn't your name, but what I am trying to say is that is what I remember them calling you."

"They filled out birth certificates?"

"Oh, no. Everything went down in a matter of minutes. I just remember them verbalizing those names."

"And you're saying he was Abel, and I was Cain."

"That's what I remember, yes."

This is something to take in. *Why would they call us those names... Cainsworth!* "Did my parents know that?!"

He thinks about this for a moment, "I remember meeting with them, as part of a team. I don't think so, but I'm not sure." He leans forward now on the edge of the chair. "Listen, why don't I just tell you what I remember because I do need to see other patients."

"Oh, of course. Please, do tell me."

"I'll skip to the part I think you want to hear about. They came in very late in the delivery. I believe they were trying to deliver at home, but your brother was turned around so it was never going to happen without help. At least it wasn't going to happen with a positive outcome. Anyway, as I said, it all happened quickly. Once she was prepped, I had to push him to the side and you were born. By the time you were cleaned and handed to the father, he was born."

"So I was first born?"

"Uh… yes, I think I can say that with relative certainty. Your brother was handed to the mother, and that is when I stepped back and the verbal exchanges began between the parents. It was as if the mother was asking him which one was to receive which name. He said something to the effect of, 'I think that one is Abel, and this one, the first born, Cain.' She kept asking if he was sure and he didn't respond. The more she asked, the more panicked she seemed about him being sure. Now that I verbalize it, they did seem confused, but that is what he said about your names, I remember.

"Then they exchanged the two of you between them. I remember him shaking his head and they exchanged you two again. Then the moment came that has confused me and tormented my mind. Like I said before, it seemed to me that something was happening that I was not able to see, because a look crossed your father's face that really confounded me. It was the biggest eyebrow-raising look of surprise I had ever seen. I think he verbally gasped and his look twisted into one that told me he was both horrified and angered at the same time. Then the look was only rage as he… well, you know what he did then. I don't want to talk about that and you already indicated you are aware."

"Right. He tried to kill me?" He just nods. "Not like my brother explained it with him only verbalizing, but as my dad said, with him attempting to murder me, right?"

"Correct. After the security guard tackled him and some amazing nurses rushed you out of the room, he grabbed your mother and fled. But not without parting words."

I was looking down, trying to keep my composure, but this catches my attention. "He said something? I haven't heard that."

"Oh, yes, I'll never forget the fear it instilled. The security guard and I were the only ones in the room. As he gathered your mother up, he said, 'You have no idea the harm done here today, but still, you've only delayed the inevitable.' Then turning back at the door, with a look of hatred on his face, he said, 'The mark of death has been placed upon that boy by God. Now you've placed a burden on his brother to rectify this!' I felt like he wanted to kill me for stopping him, and I have feared seeing him ever since."

***

I don't know what I expected to learn from anyone who was in that hospital room on the night of my birth, but I feel like I got more than I could have hoped for from Dr. Alterman. He came back before I was discharged and tried to apologize for how he reacted. I assured him that he was nothing but helpful and I appreciated his openness. We chatted for a while longer then, more about the other parts of my life. He said he had been fearful that I had already been tracked down and killed by my own father, so once he got over the shock of our initial talk, he realized how happy he was to have seen I was okay.

Now I am already on a flight home. Dad was pretty upset about his car, but of course, they were both just happy I was okay. They had blown up my phone all morning when Dad noticed the GPS was not working. Some of the messages were him expressing anger that I would destroy the device, and the rest were of him expressing his worry about where I was and if everything was okay.

There was also another text from Rebecca letting me know that she was really thinking about me. I responded the same and also decided I needed to give her a little information about what was going on. I didn't want to worry her, so I just said I was done with treatment and had a minor accident, and that I would fill her in when we could talk. That will be tomorrow afternoon, a lunch date.

The pilot just came across the intercom saying we would be making our descent into Chicago in a few minutes. Our cruising altitude is well above the clouds and I have been watching the sun plunge into the marshmallow field. It is still quite light above the pink and white blanket, but I am still able to see an exit light when it pops up. It doesn't even surprise me. What surprises me is that it doesn't even surprise me. What kind of life has this become that it is normal for me to see a sign that signifies someone dying? The exit light goes out and all I can do is imagine my brother snuffing the life out of some poor soul.

It's only a matter of minutes before another one pops up. This time I look up to see if I can see anything more than I have seen from the ground, but I can't. It is just a different vantage point of the same thing I have been trying to figure out for months. From this distance, it is just a narrow beam of light that punctures the marshmallow clouds like a roasting stick. And above, it just extends to some point that my little insignificant eye is not capable of seeing. If God is really in control of what I am seeing, then he must be controlling the spotlight from Heaven. But I don't think that is the source of these sadistic little shows.

There goes the light. Either that moment of opportunity passed, or my brother helped mutilate another body. The airplane breaks through the surface of the clouds and the marshmallow illusion is no more. Everything is white for a moment, and now the landscape comes to life below us. Chicago is ahead of us still, and another exit light comes into view. Now I am a little surprised. These few came in quick succession. And another one pops up. This is the first time I have seen two at once. They look like they could be close together. I can imagine my brother plotting a double homicide right now. Thinking he is David killing two Goliaths with one stone. Both lights extinguish at the same moment. Sick.

27

When my parents picked me up from the airport last night, I had the feeling they weren't happy with me. It's not like they didn't hug me, and show their love, but it was as if they were just relieved I was okay, and then they were irritated with me. We didn't talk much on the way home and I told them I was exhausted when we got there. I *was* exhausted.

This morning, I have other things I need to do before my lunch date with Rebecca, but I feel I owe Mom and Dad some time. I know I have avoided having to talk with them too much. I felt they were judging me, and maybe they were, and I was probably defensive because I was feeling guilty. But, deep down, I knew I was living in a way that needed some judging. I don't know if it's in me to be any different than that, but I feel like I have to try. I may not have respect for myself, but I do respect men like Mr. Anders, and I know my parents deserve my respect too. They are good people. They are my family. Those with biological ties to me will never be my family.

Mom has put out quite a spread on the table. "Good morning. This looks like a delicious breakfast, Mom. You didn't have to on my account."

Dad chimes in, "What, you don't think I get a high-quality breakfast like this every morning?"

I snicker, "You know what I mean. Besides, I didn't think you had more than coffee most mornings."

Mom brings coffee over, "Oh, would you leave him alone." She scowls at Dad, but then grins and turns to me, "This is all for you, Cotter."

"Thanks, Mom. Really, it smells amazing."

"I just want you to know how much I love you." A tear rolls down her cheek.

"Don't, Mom, I know. I am sorry I have made things difficult on you both." I am not good at this. It's uncomfortable for me to express feelings. I am used to the habitual hugs and terms of endearment, but when it's a real expression full of feeling, it's difficult. I push forward, "You want to know the most important thing I learned while searching for answers about my family?"

Mom says, "Yes, please do share."

"I learned who my real parents are," Mom is holding her breath and Dad puts his hand on hers, "and they are right here. They were always right here." Mom lets out the breath and a quiet sob along with it. "They always support me. They've always loved me, and I love them. Thank you for wanting me."

"Son, we will always love you, no matter what."

"I know, Dad." He grabs my hand now too and Mom comes around and hugs me. Now she sits down to eat with us. Well, to eat with me and drink coffee with Dad. "So, I did learn something though that I was curious about. Did you know what they named me before you gave me my name?"

They both appear to be sincerely surprised and Dad speaks, "No. I didn't think they filled out birth certificates. I was told they ran off only minutes after your birth."

"Yeah, I didn't learn anything different than that, and they didn't get to the birth certificates, but the doctor told me he heard them referring to me as Cain, and my brother Abel."

More sincere looks of surprise and now Mom, "Those are interesting names. I wonder why they would choose that."

"That's what I was thinking, been wracking my brain wondering why, but then I remembered I can't think logically about a couple of psychos. I guess I just thought you two must have known because of the name you gave me."

Dad frowns and says, "I don't think I follow, Son."

"Come on, you know... Cotter Ainsworth." He still looks at me questioningly. "C. Ainsworth... Cainsworth... Cain."

"Oh, okay I understand what you mean. Yeah, that is a strange coincidence, but maybe a bit of a stretch."

"So, seriously? You named me that without any knowledge they were calling me Cain?"

"Son, we have no reason to be dishonest with you about anything, and I'd see no need to lie about something like that anyway. So, yeah, seriously."

"Okay, sorry. I just had a hard time thinking that could be a coincidence."

"I get it. It is definitely interesting. But I think we have told you before that Ainsworth was your great grandfather's name, on your mother's side."

Mom nods and smiles, "Yes, he was a great man."

"That's right. I do recall hearing it."

"And I believe your mom just thought up Cotter. I don't think we had ever heard it."

"Oh, come on. *Welcome Back, Kotter* ring a bell?"

"Oh, right, your mom was in love with John Travolta."

We chuckle and Mom chimes in as she rolls her eyes, "Uh-huh, because Travolta would really be interested in someone like me."

I can't help myself, "What? A woman."

Dad and I really laugh now and Mom chastises me, "Stop that. I hear he is a nice man," but a smile slips and she chuckles a little with us. This is nice. I should give them my time more often.

***

My parents didn't ask me to pick up their dry cleaning, but I am standing in Mr. Zetticci's shop nonetheless. There is only one customer and he is already being helped at the counter. It looks like he has his clothes in hand, but it seems Zetticci is telling his daily jokes.

The radio is on in the background, so I choose to tune in to that and drown out sexist jokes. "… Judge's decision on the last appeal in what has been a month-long attempt to save a section of old freight tunnels. A demolition company has been waiting to bring down three condemned buildings above the freight tunnel. Today's ruling will allow that work to begin as early as tomorrow.

"Comments from the structural engineer in charge of the project have caused outrage amongst historical purists. After the ruling, he commented from the steps of the courthouse, 'This is a great win for the city and its taxpayers. It's an economical win. The implosion collapse mechanism I have planned will allow the buildings to fold right into the freight tunnels below, where the debris will settle and become the foundation for new construction. Listen, I understand there are individuals who believe these tunnels are a part of the city's history, but they are of no use and it's time that they become history. Have your cameras ready. We are planning to start the buildings' descent into the underground at noon tomorrow.' When asked if he was planning the blasts right away so he could beat any further legal delays, Mr. Driscoll simply smiled and walked away."

I tune back into Zetticci's voice just in time for a punchline, "Because they're ugly and they smell bad!" Both men laugh hysterically before the customer waves and walks past me to the door. "Aye, welcome back, Cotter!"

I step up to the counter, "Do you think my parents actually named me after that show?"

He laughs but then senses I am waiting for his answer. "I guess I don't know, Cotter, but I would rather it be that instead of you being named after something that latches onto a round shaft." He goes back into his laughing state, but I stay serious. He calms himself and looks at me, "You know, a cotter pin."

"Oh, I got what you meant, I just have my mind focused on something serious." He stops smiling and waits for me to say something. "That day in the bar, I believe you implied that you'd like to help me if you could."

He pauses and looks at me with interest, "Uh, yes, of course. I would be very happy if I could help you in any way, Cotter, but what is it you think I can do?"

"Well, before I ask, I just want you to know I feel my life is in danger." His brow furrows, but he keeps listening. "Things that have been going on in my life had already given me a feeling of dread, a feeling that I might not have much longer to live on this earth."

"Come on now, Cotter." He leans onto the counter, resting his forearms there.

I put my hand up, "Just hear me out please." He sighs and nods. "Now I have learned my life has probably been in danger for a long time, and there is someone who has come back into my life now who might be the one to follow through on the threats against me."

"Threats? What's going on, Cotter? Who's threatening you?" He looks sincerely concerned.

"I don't have time to explain it all, but I know what I need to do if you can just help me with one thing."

"Okay, I am hearing you. What can I do?"

"I need you to get me a gun."

His eyes get wide and he stands up straight, "Hold on now. I can't do that, and what makes you think I could even get a gun."

"I know you can, Mr. Zetticci. Dad recently told me that he first met you as a child, when you were working alongside my grandfather, and he told me a lot more about that work." He stays straight-faced and doesn't respond. "You know what kind of work I am talking about, so please do me a favor and don't deny it. Now, please help me. I need to protect myself."

He half turns away from me and scratches at the back of his head with one hand while twisting his handlebar mustache with the other. "You are putting me in a very tough position. It would be so irresponsible for me to do this for you."

"I understand, but I also understand you wouldn't want something to happen to me."

"What if something happens to you because I got you a gun? Huh? What if you kill yourself with it?!"

"That is not at all what I want it for. I have no desire to do such a thing, Mr. Zetticci. I just need you to trust me. You are the only person I could think to come to, and believe me, I would not have if I didn't think it was absolutely necessary."

It appears I may be persuading him. "Doesn't your father have a gun you can use?"

"He doesn't. I don't think he has ever wanted to be around them, especially after finding out about the activities you and my grandfather were engaging in back then."

"Hold on now, I didn't do half the things your grandfather did."

I put both hands up in apology to keep him on my side, "I'm not implying you did, Mr. Zetticci. I can't pretend to know that. All I know is that you're the only one I feel I can safely turn to with this request. If you can't help me, I'm afraid I will have to search Chicago for someone who can get me what I need."

"Wait a minute. You can't just go put yourself in situations like that on the streets of Chicago. That's dangerous, Cotter."

"Continuing to be as vulnerable as I am right now is more dangerous in my eyes."

"Okay, okay." Now he is putting his hands out to slow me down. "Here's what I am willing to do. I will think about letting you hang onto one of my guns for a while."

"No, that's not going to work. I need one as soon as possible, preferably by tonight." Zetticci's eyebrows shoot up. "And, I need it to be untraceable because I do fear I will have to use it."

"Aw, come on, what do you expect me to do? I close the shop at noon today."

"Perfect then, and I can pay for it. Can you help me?"

He looks defeated, "I don't feel comfortable at all doing this, but I guess you can meet me back here this evening. Let's say, uh... around seven o'clock."

"Great, thank you, Mr. Zetticci."

He scoffs as he turns toward the back of the shop, waving me away, "Don't thank me for something you're guilt tripping me into doing." I start to open my mouth to apologize or something, but I decide I don't need to give him any more time to change his mind. I leave the shop so I can meet Rebecca for lunch.

***

It is hard for me to understand how I could forget just how beautiful she is, but that seems to be exactly what happened. And she is so sweet. Even now, after everything, she greeted me so caringly and is speaking with me like everything is okay. *How could you have treated such a lovely young lady like you did, Cotter?*

"Cotter?"

…

"Hello?"

"Oh, sorry."

She chuckles, "Where were you just now?"

"Honestly, I was just thinking about how beautiful you look." She blushes. "And, about how nicely you're treating me when I don't deserve it."

She reaches across the table and holds my hand. "Let's not do any of that. It's not necessary. Nobody is perfect and I have forgiven you, so there is no need to dwell on it."

"Okay, but I guess I just don't understand why you would forgive me."

"I don't know. Maybe I wouldn't be able to if not for the grace of God." I must have made a look. "What?"

"Nothing."

"No, this is one thing I am going to ask of you. Communicate with me. What is it?"

"Just that you know I don't buy into the religious stuff."

"Well, maybe it's time that you do. You just expressed that you have trouble understanding how I could have the strength to handle something difficult. Did you ever think the reason you can't understand is that you don't have Him in your heart like I do? It's important to reconcile differences in any relationship, regardless of how big or small those relationships in your life are. Sometimes it might mean just forgiving someone so you can move on without them in your life, but sometimes it means forgiving because you love them," She smiles at me and I smile back, "and you know it's worthwhile to still have them in your life."

She is such an amazing person, an amazing woman, one that's way more amazing than a loser like me deserves. We are quiet for a moment and I try to change the conversation, "Anyway, what was it you were trying to ask me before?"

"Oh, I asked how you got out of the car when it started on fire."

Now that we were face to face, I had told her the entire story. Well, except for the part about killing a man, or that I was driving to find out about my biological father who tried to kill me at birth. Oh, and I haven't told her that I have a twin brother, or anything about adoption at all. Basically, I only told her about treatment and Joseph, and that I was driving home when the accident happened. I just don't want to spend this time on a bunch of things that will concern her. "Some guy finally reclined my seat and pulled me out through the back door."

"Oh my gosh. It's scary to think how close you were to being trapped. Who was the man who saved you? Did you get his name?"

"I didn't actually. I passed out afterward and woke up in the hospital. I did ask about him, but all I learned was that he left the scene before responders arrived. Another lady who tried to help me spoke with him and he said he didn't want to be labeled a hero, so he was leaving."

"Wow, what a nice man."

"Yeah, I do wish I could have had a moment to thank him though." The waiter walks up and offers us dessert. "No way, I am stuffed." I turn to Rebecca.

"No, thank you." I pay the bill and we walk to the door. The unseasonably warm weather has finally submitted to the normal blustery November chill and Rebecca is underdressed. She wraps her arms around herself and I drape my jacket over her shoulders. "Oh, thank you, but you only have a t-shirt on now. I'm okay."

"No, it's fine. You know how I stay warmer than you anyway."

She smiles at me and there is a twinkle in those beautiful hazel eyes. She looks like she might cry, "What a kind gesture. I've missed you, Cott."

"I've missed you too, Sweetheart." I crane my neck in her direction and our lips lock in a kiss much more passionate than I can ever remember. It is soft and tender and even though it lasts several seconds, I didn't want it to stop. "I don't want to leave you right now."

"I don't want that either."

"Can we hang at your place?"

A sheepish look comes across her face, "My parents aren't too happy with you right now. Maybe that's not a good idea." A feeling of shame punches me in the gut. "Don't worry, they will get over it. I just don't think the timing is right is all. Can we go to your place?"

"That doesn't really sound appealing. You know how restricting the space is there. We'd end up sitting with my parents all day."

We chuckle and she defends them, "Oh, but I love your parents!"

"I know, but it's not really the kind of time I feel the need to spend with you right now."

"Yeah, I know. I agree."

"Hey, let's get crazy and rent a nice hotel room!"

"What," she giggles, "are you being serious?"

"Yes! Why not? It's not like we've never done that before."

She giggles some more as she thinks for a moment while biting her lower lip. "Okay, let's do it."

"Great!" I pull out my phone. "I'm going to find us the best room."

"Whoa, what happened to your phone?"

I tell her I dropped it, but spare her the details of what I was doing when it happened. No need to change the mood.

***

I am all smiles as I stroll towards the dry cleaning shop. I imagine I might be strutting like Travolta did in *Saturday Night Fever,* and my smile turns into a laugh when I link this thought to the conversation I had with my parents earlier in the day. A couple of passersby give me funny looks and I stop laughing… and strutting.

It was such an amazing afternoon with Rebecca. It was like we were getting to know each other all over again, like we had just met for the first time. Sex felt new and exciting as well. The first go-round didn't last long because I was so excited, but she assured me that it was still amazing. Regardless, I made up for it the next couple of times. Initially, Rebecca had been concerned we didn't have a condom because she had just started taking her birth control again yesterday. Thankfully, I convinced her the two-day waiting period had pretty much passed.

It also took some convincing not to order room service when she got hungry. I needed an excuse to drop in on Mr. Zetticci, so I am officially on my way to grab us some Chinese take-out as I stop at the dry cleaning shop and knock on the door. He unlocks the door and lets me in, locking the door behind me. "Before you say anything, I'm not going to pretend that this is some mutually agreed upon deal. I'm going to give you the gun, make sure you know what I think you need to know so you don't accidentally shoot yourself, and then you are going to pay for it and leave, since you were never actually here tonight anyway." He looks at me with a face more serious than I thought I could ever see on him.

"I understand, and I am sorry."

"Oh, stop, just stop! You don't get to apologize in the middle of this manipulation!" Obviously, he is not happy with me. He unfolds a blue towel on the counter, "This is a Glock 42. It's a slim .380 ACP."

"What does ACP mean?"

"Automatic Colt Pistol, but I am not here to teach you the history of guns." Jeez, he's pissed. "This is how you eject the magazine." He pulls it out of the gun handle. "You can see I already have it loaded. You can buy more ammunition yourself if you need more." He slams it back into the handle. "This is the slide, and racking it like this loads the handgun." He pulls straight back and lets it slide back into place with a thin clinking sound. "Now it is ready to fire. The only safety is right here on the trigger." He points to the front of the trigger.

"It's pretty small, but it could kill someone?"

He sighs and glares at me, "Yeah, Cotter, it would kill someone if that is what you aim to do." Without looking down, he ejects the magazine, ejects the round from the chamber into his hand, loads it back into the magazine and slams the magazine back into the gun. He hands the gun to me, "There isn't a round chambered right now, maybe that's how you want to carry it since you have no clue what you're doing. If you fire the gun, the next round will automatically load into the chamber so you can just squeeze the trigger again to fire."

"Again, sorr—"

"Just get out." He points to the door and I start towards it. "Cotter." Maybe he is softening. I turn back to see him twisting his mustache nervously. "I meant after you give me one thousand bucks."

"Jesus. That much?"

He gives me an incredulous look. "Are you serious? Go apply for a purchase permit and get one legally then."

"No, I've got it." It's exactly how much I withdrew, but that was just in case. I didn't think for a second it would cost that. I hand it to him and open the door to leave.

"I hope you understand how devastated I would be if you got hurt in any way due to this gun. I shared a story with you about my own son that you must not have the ability to understand. Maybe someday you'll think about what your actions do to other people before you choose a path."

I do feel guilty and I want to say something, but I don't think he wants to hear it. I had to get this gun. It's the only way I think I can kill my brother, and that's the only way I think I will be allowed to live. I close the door behind me.

28

I can't tell if the Chinese food from last night isn't sitting well with me, or if my stomach is turning due to nerves. I am grateful Zetticci delivered a compact gun for me because I didn't think about a holster or how I would need to carry it. This gun is small enough to fit nicely in my front pocket. Still, I went home to grab one of my larger hoodies so it would hang down to cover the pocket of my AG jeans. The handgun really is sleek enough that this is probably overkill on the coverage, but at least it allowed for a slight decrease in my anxiety about carrying the thing.

I've spent the better part of the morning waiting for an exit light to appear. I have no idea how to find Abel any other way. *Did you seriously just call him that?* It feels strange to give that monster a name. Even more so when I realize admitting such a thing means accepting that I was called Cain. What kind of weirdos would it take to name their twins Cain and Abel? I guess it's no small wonder that a murder plot was accompanying their sick little naming ceremony.

Cainsworth. Where did that come from? What does it mean that the parents who actually love me coincidentally put a name on me that shares such similarities with my given name, Cain? It must be that it's my destiny to kill Abel, my twin brother. Wait, that's too good a title. Abel, the serial killer tormenting this city. *He told you he is a prophet of God, tasked with taking out evil people.* Yeah, right. If there was a God, I am pretty sure he wouldn't be directing these death scenes. Abel is simply a murderer who needs to be stopped.

Enough. I curse the day I first saw the exit lights, and yet, here I am desperate to see one so I can be finished with this nasty business. I need to calm my constantly firing brain, but there is nothing to do but think as I meander through the chaos of these streets. I catch myself pulling a door open and look up at Mr. Brown's Lounge. I immediately release the handle like it was something too hot to touch. I start down the sidewalk in such a hurry, as if lingering too long would give the bartender time to come out and pull me in. *You'll never stay sober. It's only a matter of time so why not now, you lush.*

I stop so abruptly that someone bumps into me as they pass. "Sorry." She just shakes her head without looking back. Maybe I can just have one shot. It will help to settle my nerves and I won't stay in there. I feel a force urging me to turn back. Spinning on my heels, I see a spotlight in the distance. *Saved by the bell.* It's show time. I instinctively hail a cab, realizing this one is a good distance away. I climb into the back seat, "I am in a hurry."

"Where to?"

"Just go straight."

"It'll be easier if you just tell me where you need to go."

"Please, just head straight, and hurry. I can't give you an exact destination."

"Okay, boss." I sense his irritation. The traffic on the street is light and we are moving at a pace that should get me close in a hurry. This driver is trying to make small talk but I am too focused to comprehend what he is saying.

The exit light appears to be only a block or two west of this street now. We are closing the gap even more quickly than I could have hoped. "Turn right." I slide over to the driver's side window so I can keep watching it ahead and to the left, but I see nothing, it must have gone out. "Shit!"

"What? You told me to turn right."

"Yeah, I did. Just go straight one more block and turn left, please." He follows my directions and we turn onto the block where I think the exit light was last shining down.

I am scanning the streets for Abel when the driver says, "It looks like there is a commotion on the next block so I am going to turn off."

"No! I mean, please drive down that block."

"Yes, sir." The sarcasm confirms he is annoyed with me, but I can't care about that right now. "By the looks of it though, we will have a delay, and you're in a hurry, remember?"

"It's okay. Just keep going." There is a cloud of dust concealing something that must have transpired on the sidewalk. It's out in front of the skeleton of a new building in the infancy of its construction. The cars ahead of us have eased through the white fog and we approach the spot where pedestrians and construction workers are beginning to gather. The cloud encroaching on the taxi is leaving a thickening white residue on the windshield. "What is that?"

The driver hits the wipers to clear his vision. "I have no idea." I can't see much of anything peering out the side window. "For the love of God! What the hell?!"

"What do you see?"

"Look!" He inches ahead and a couple people move as the dust clears enough for me to see a pile of concrete mix. It was likely stacked nicely on a pallet at one point, but now it is just a disheveled pile of white powder and burst bags. Everything here is coated with concrete dust, making it a scene from a black and white movie, but with one exception. The color red is bleeding into this still frame as blood from an unseen person creeps a distance from beneath the pile before slowly coagulating with the concrete mix. Further settling of dust reveals white stocking feet that are starting to develop red stripes. The ruby slippers must have been forced off by the weight and impact.

I look up and see the swinging cable of a crane several stories above. The arm of the crane indicates that the crane itself must be positioned up ahead somewhere. I'll get there faster on foot. "Let me out here."

I throw whatever wad of money was in my pocket as I open the door and slide out. It must have been substantial as I barely hear, "Jeez, thanks, man!" I could care less how much was there. My attention is drawn to the slowly hardening red concrete one more time before I move on. How in the hell did he pull this one off? I hustle toward the end of the street and the dusty air gives way to the large cabin of a crane, but it's empty.

"I don't get it." A white-dust-covered man wearing what used to be a yellow hard hat stands with his arms outstretched and wet eyes. "I had all the brakes set, and nobody was near the crane when I walked away."

Instinctually, I lie, "There *was* someone who got in the crane and did this. Tell the police to check any security cameras in the area and look for a man with his hoodie up." I have already started running down the next street.

"What? Hold on! You saw that?!" I hear him yell, but I just keep running. He has to be around here somewhere. The block turning to the right now is really quiet. Something tells me this is the way and I bolt down the street. At the corner, I don't see him in any direction. Damn! *He is too quick for you.* I'll have to wait for the next exit light. Defeated, I continue in the direction I had been heading. After crossing the street, I start to turn left onto the adjacent block, but my peripheral vision catches a flash of movement to my right. I have already moved passed the building on the corner, so I peek back around the corner and see someone crossing the street at the end of the block, and he is wearing a hoodie.

Yes! That has to be him. I peek again to confirm he continued onto the next block and not towards me or away from me. With nobody in sight, I sprint all the way down the block and then quietly slow to a stop at the corner. Feeling like a stalker now, I peek around this corner and he looks back at about the halfway point of the block. Wait, it's not him. That guy doesn't have a beard. Shit. I lean back with my head against the wall and close my eyes to think for a second. *No, you're wrong.* It is him, just clean-shaven.

I peek around the corner again just in time to see he has crossed the street and he disappears after turning right. I sprint down this street now and cautiously peep through the two corner windows of the vacant building. Much like his mind, Abel's shape is warped by the wavy old windows. I see his crooked form head down the stairs of the subway entrance and I hurry around the corner and across the street. It appears he is clear of the stairs so I quickly tiptoe down.

Crouching, I hurry behind the turnstiles and when I peer at the platform, I barely catch a glimpse of him jumping onto the tracks. Shoot, how can I keep following him in the dark. After crossing the platform, I sneak a quick peek down the tunnel and quickly pull back. It's pitch black down there. I can't see a thing. My mind registers that there was a light, but it was a significant distance down the track.

I crane my neck and look down the tunnel. I can watch until I see him pass under that light, and then I can feel safe to follow. I set my eyes on the spot under the light and wait to see him move under it. Too much time is going by. He should have entered the light by now. The creepy thought of him standing only ten feet down the tunnel, just watching me, pops into my head and causes me to shiver and pull back.

Okay, unless he lured me down for some reason, he is down here for something else. Either I go back up and wait for the next exit light, or I take a chance and see what is down there. I was lucky to see him this time. How long until I am lucky enough to be on his trail next? I take a deep breath and climb down to the track as quietly as possible. I start moving as quickly as I can while still remaining stealthy. I have to keep telling myself to breathe because the sense of dread has me holding my breath.

I am just waiting to be grabbed by Abel, or perhaps to stumble over him in the dark. Halfway to the light on the near wall of the tunnel, I notice an opening on the right wall that is emitting the faintest of light. Aha, so that is why he never crossed under the light. As I pass through the doorway, I am cursing myself for the head start I have given him now. *You should have gone right after him. You're going to need more guts than that to do what you came down here to do.*

I carefully round two corners, really watching my step now so I don't make any noise. I am in a longer hallway now. There is enough ambient light that I can see it has a brick pattern on the walls and an arched ceiling curves overhead. At the end, I only have to go around one corner before I can see another larger tunnel. Peering out at the doorway, I see the light source a short distance to the left. It might be a small flashlight set down on the track, but nobody is around.

I step down into the tunnel and survey my surroundings. *Is this an old subway?* The cement tunnel is shaped like an oval, but with a dirt floor that fills the bottom curve. It must not be more than ten feet wide and the tracks on the dirt are much closer together than it seems they are in the new subway system. I wonder how much smaller the old subway train cars must have been, but I quickly shake the thoughts so I can be aware of my surroundings. *Pay attention! He could be anywhere.*

I am at the flashlight now. It's set in a place where the tunnel curves around to the right. I bend to pick it up, but I jump up at the sight of a moving light not much further down the tunnel. It looks like someone is waving another flashlight around, but not directly from this tunnel, maybe he is in an adjoining tunnel. I quickly scoop up the flashlight at my feet and switch it off.

I don't feel the need to move too quickly as the light doesn't appear to be moving closer or farther away. I start to hear whispers and then a louder voice, "We need to move, now!" When I get to the other tunnel, I see it isn't an adjoining tunnel at all, but rather a small alcove. I see a doorway and suddenly a splash of light shoots past me from a window on the wall, and now it settles directly on me. I choose not to move because it is clear that I am no longer shrouded by the darkness. Instead, when the light darts toward the doorway, I pull the Glock from my pocket.

"What are you doing here? You followed me?"

The flashlight isn't a strong one, but it is still hard to see when he shines it in my eyes. "Yeah, I did. I saw the result of your most recent handiwork. You probably didn't even kill the person under the exit light."

"On the contrary, I did. God doesn't set this stuff up for innocent people to die."

"I didn't come down here for more of your bullshit. And I can't imagine anyway that God set up such a convenient situation as what happened up there."

"That's exactly what a job like this takes, a little imagination. What can I say, the timing was right." I click on my flashlight and shine it in his eyes. His hoodie is actually down and not only is he clean-shaven, but his hair has been cut shorter than it was before. In this lighting at least, he really looks identical to me. He appears to glance down at the gun in my hand. "Look, I can see you feel the need to unburden yourself. Why don't you just leave and ignore the exit lights from now on. You will not stop seeing them, but you do not have to seek them out. Do not worry. I'll take care of it."

"But that is the burden, you understand? I can't ignore what you do, so I am going to unburden myself and anyone else who lies in your path of terror, Abel."

"What?" I have the gun leveled at his head and my heart leaps into my throat as I pull the trigger, but it only clicks. I wait for him to lunge at me but the confused look on his face must not be about my gun. "I'm not..." Someone else moves in the doorway and I remedy my prior mistake by racking the Glock and aiming it in the direction of the movement. My flashlight now illuminates another man as Abel says, "Dad! I told you to stay back there."

I move the flashlight back to Abel and then back to the man. My heart is pounding now. "It is *you,* isn't it?"

"Yes, it is." He starts to shuffle to his left. "I cannot let you shoot Cain, Abel. It is not the way it is meant to be."

What did he say? "Wait, you called me Abel, you're confused."

"No, you are the confused one. You are confused about a lot of things, Abel."

"I'm Cain! I'm supposed to kill Abel."

"You are right that Cain is supposed to kill Abel, was always supposed to kill Abel, but you are Abel."

"I don't know what weird shit you and your wife were into, but if you wanted to play this biblical name game, you would have known that the firstborn was Cain."

"Yes, you got that right too, but you only came out first because of complications and the doctor had to push your brother aside. Twins do not change fates just because the wrong one came out first. He was always Cain and you are Abel. My brother came first too, but I had already killed him in the womb."

I hear a guttural growl bounce around the walls before I understand it is me. I also realize I have started sobbing. I let out another slobbery growl as I point the gun up toward my biological father's face. "If that even is true, and if Cain is supposed to kill Abel, then why did *you* try to kill me?!"

My brother, whatever his name is, speaks up, "He didn't try to kill you, he thought about it but couldn't."

"Lies! Everyone in the room saw him *try* to commit infanticide!"

"He is right, Cain. Let me explain." He has one hand, palm out towards me, and one towards my brother. "For generations, Abel had been slain by Cain so that the work of God could take place."

"What do you mean, 'for generations'?"

"I mean, since the dawn of man. We are, all of us in this tunnel, the direct descendants of Adam and Eve."

"Right." I doubt he could see me roll my eyes.

"That is the truth of the matter. Every generation produces another Cain and Abel. I am Cain, as was my father and his before him. Things changed though as mankind changed. People have gotten weaker and somehow it affected our bloodline as well. There came a time when Cain did not kill Abel, and more evil people than ever were allowed to negatively affect countless more innocent lives. That is when it was decided, by God, that each Abel be terminated at birth, before he could affect the prophetic work."

"By God, by God, by God! I'm sick of hearing it. You're crazy, and by God, I'm about to put an end to this *bloodline* right now."

"I do not know how else I can explain it to you, Abel. It was decided by God, because the exit light began to shine on each Abel when he was born, instead of later in life. That is what happened with you. If the light had not shined on you, if I had not seen all the death that you were going to be responsible for, I would never have tried to—"

Drinking fountain. That's what comes to mind. It looks like a drinking fountain spout is springing from his forehead.

"NOOO! Dad! No, no, no." I didn't even hear the gunshot ring out. The Glock slips from my hand. Cain is on the ground, cradling him. "You killed him!" The outflow of blood weakens as I suspect his heart quits pumping it. Though I feel nothing but hatred for the man, I'm still grateful the blood stopped shooting from his head. Still, it's streaming down his face now and I double over and empty my stomach. "You dare call me a murderer, a freak?!" I look over and see Cain has lost his composure for the first time. He's irate. His eyes look maniacal. "It's you who is the murderer!"

I can feel him moving towards me. I don't even look up, just start to run. I realize immediately that I started in the opposite direction I came, and I don't have the gun. *Why did you drop it?!* I don't have any idea where to go, but it's too late now. I risk a glance back and see that Cain is in pursuit. The tunnel is straight but there is some debris scattered here and there. The flashlight is just luminous enough for me to see in front of me, but I fear not being able to see something in my way quickly enough to sidestep at my current speed. Almost as soon as I think this, I stumble and flop onto the track, my forearm slamming onto the rail as I try to catch myself. There is a pop and excruciatingly sharp pain. I know it's broke.

Still, I gather myself up quickly, driven by the fear of what is coming up from behind me. I hardly get started again, holding my arm against my chest so it doesn't flop around, when I pass a ladder going up the side of the wall. It looks like there is a manhole cover above it and a twinkle of light blinks through as I run underneath. I slide to a stop and scamper up as fast as I can with one arm. Right at the top, I drop the flashlight, but Cain's light is only a matter of feet away from me so I let it go.

Something tells me this cover is not going to open and he is going to yank me back down. I put my shoulders and the back of my head into it and take the next step up with all of my might. I almost lose my balance and grip as the cover surprises me by popping up easily. I drag myself out of the hole with my right arm and realize I am in an abandoned building. A quick scan shows me that every opening on the ground level is boarded up. There is a staircase directly in front of me and light pours from the landing at the top. I hurry up the stairs, not knowing how I can make an escape from the upper floors, but knowing I can't escape down here with a broken arm.

Shit, the building is only two floors. There is nowhere for me to hide here, it's wide-open space. I run to the window and continue around the edge of the floor, looking for a fire escape.

"Don't waste your energy. There is no escape from this building unless you want to take the thirty-foot leap from a window." He is standing at the top of the stairs, having caught me as I was crossing the middle of the room to circumvent a large void in the floor. I am hardly closer than he is to the windows behind me, but I pivot and take off toward them. "Oh, no you don't!" I clearly heard what he said and I choose to take the chance at launching myself through the window. "I'm not going to let you kill yourself!" I must have had one burst of adrenaline left in me because I sense I am beating him to the window. I plant hard with my right foot and take the leap, but the soft board beneath me lacks the integrity to spring me and Cain impacts my body with a highlight caliber blindside hit.

There is a split second where I expect to look and see us flying down the rotted hole in the floor, but I see we are several feet short of that target. Cain still has arms wrapped around me when we hammer down on rotten floor, hard. It gives way underneath us and I hold my breath in anticipation of my plummet to the first floor, but I open my eyes when I feel a swinging sensation. He still has one arm around my waist and the other forearm is hanging on the floor. "Grab the floor."

"I can't. Just let me go, my arm is broken."

"Then use the other arm." I reach up and grab the firmest part of the wood I can. I pull, but I am too weak to get up. "Pull up again, now." I do, and I feel Cain pull at the same. I am shocked when I scramble and get my elbow up on the floor. "I am exhausted; we are going to need help. Grab your phone and call 911."

I don't understand what is happening right now. Is he just helping himself or is he actually trying to help me? I don't get it. "I told you, my arm is broken. I can't grab my phone and hold myself up with one arm."

"Which pocket is it in? I'll grab it."

"The left front, right next to your right hip." He seems like he can easily hold himself with the left arm as he pulls the phone from my pocket, flinging it up to the floor. I am wondering what he is going to do when a bright light shines from somewhere and distracts me. I look up to see that an exit light is shining on him. "There it is."

He looks at me, "There what is?"

"Your exit light."

A look of confusion wrinkles his face. "It's not shining on me, Bro." He reaches over and grabs hold of my arm and a look of sadness crosses his face. I am waiting for him to yank me from my hold and let me fall. Instead, his right arm is back to the floor and he easily pushes up to get a knee above so he can climb from the hole. He is on his feet quickly, and after picking up the phone, he kneels and grabs my left hand, putting my thumb on the phone.

"Ow! That hurts. I told you it's broke. What are you doing?"

"I need to unlock it."

"It's facial recognition."

He looks at the phone and I hear it click. I guess we are completely identical. "Are you going to call 911?" He just looks down at me. "Or how about just pulling me up. You didn't look as exhausted as you must have thought." I manage a chuckle. "The exit light is on you, Cain. You must be on God's list now."

"What vision of me did you see?"

"What?"

"You insist I am the one under the exit light, so you would have seen a vision when we touched. What did you see?" I didn't see anything and I don't say anything. "You did not see anything, because I was seeing what you have done, and what you were going to do. If you thought you could just kill me and our father and then you would live a blessed life, let me ease your mind. After killing me, you would accidentally kill your own child in a drunken rage and then your wife to cover it up. Driving drunk would then end your life, but not before wiping out an entire family in the other car. That all goes without mentioning the countless lives you would prevent me from saving."

"Whatever, I don't believe you."

"You do not have to." He turns to walk away. The exit light does not follow him. *Ignore that, it's a trick!*

"Where are you going?"

He stops and looks at my phone. "Trust me, I wish this could be different, Brother, but I have to go. Only five minutes to implosion." He hurries toward the stairs. It only now registers what that tunnel below was. The freight tunnel they spoke of on the radio, and by Cain's comment, this is one of the buildings that are about to be buried there.

"Wait, can't you just save me?"

Still moving away, he says, "It is not something within my power. But remember that God can save you."

"Right. After what I just did down there? I committed patricide, remember."

He stops on the landing and turns, "No sin is worse than another and it is never too late. All you have to do is accept Christ into your heart. We have been given the chance at everlasting life, the gift of salvation. Just let Him know that you believe He sent Jesus Christ to Earth to die so you could be cleansed of all your sins."

"How can you not seem angry with me right now? I killed your dad."

"God would want me to forgive you, so that is what I choose to do."

I can't understand how calm he is right now. "But why didn't you just let me jump, or fall? Why go through this little fiasco, only to leave me to die now?"

"The light was not on you. I would never just let my brother or anyone else die if it was not God's will." There is no happiness on his face. He looks like he feels sorry for me. Cain holds up the phone in a good-bye wave, "Plus, I needed your phone." He is off, racing down the stairs.

"Wait!" He knows what he is doing right now. I won't pretend to understand the details, but this was clearly planned. He knows I am about to die in a place where my body will never be found. This thought brings a panic as I realize the culmination of the impending dread I have felt for the last few months. I thought I felt death coming, but instead, I was the one knocking on its doorstep. Maybe this wasn't something Cain could have planned. Maybe it *was* God's plan. I try to move my broken arm and lean in to push myself up, but I only slip further away from escape.

I have never felt as fearful as I do right now. Knowing that the blasts are imminent, my heart is pounding so hard I can feel the pulses in my head. My only thought is to focus on some of the last words my brother said, and maybe really listen for the first time in my life. Closing my eyes, I begin praying, I think, for the first time ever. *Okay, God. I am ready to end my great denial. You must really be there. How could all of these things happen if You weren't. I've been told you made a great sacrifice to cleanse us of sin. You know... I know I am not deserving. I can't understand how You could give a Son for us... for me, but thank You. What an amazing gift.* My heart calms and I feel something inside me that is quite foreign. A feeling that fills a void, calms the fear and soothes my soul. I'll call it hope. I feel so peaceful at this moment that was previously filled with dread. *I am so sorry for all the things I have done wrong. I wish I had accepted You sooner, but thank You for loving me anyway.*

It's not instant death as the first charge lets loose. I am briefly aware of charges going off a distance from me and then all around me. It is startling, but the fear never returns. I only have one thought on my mind, *Oh, God, I love You.* I feel a quick freefall before the light goes away. I don't feel dead, but I must be by now. The air is filled with smoke and dust, but I can see myself in the rubble. No, that's not right. I can only see rubble, but I know my body is under there. It feels like I am floating, looking down from the place where I had held tight to the floor, but I am not actually here anymore.

I have the urge to look behind me now, but there is no physical aspect to this moment. I use my mind, my heart, my soul to turn and look up. The whitest light shines down. This is no exit light. I can hardly see anything in the brightness, but seeing it gives me the same feeling that came when I prayed and invited Jesus into my heart. I thought it was hope, but it was love. I move closer to the light and it begins to be eclipsed at the center. As I get close, I can see His outstretched arms. They envelop me and I fall into the hug I had been waiting an entire lifetime to receive, I just didn't know it.

Epilogue

Cotter's phone vibrates and bounces on the dining room table. The spider web of cracks zigzagging down from the corner is not enough to obscure the banner stating, *Rebecca, Text Message.* He picks the phone up and unlocks it with his thumb. *Hey, Cott, I need to see you after class. Can we meet at my favorite spot? Say, around 2:30?* He enters a response. *My parents are home, so I do not think my bed would be the best place to meet right now. Where is your second favorite spot?*

Cotter's father must have seen who sent the message, "That Rebecca?"

"Yes, Sir. She wants to see me in about an hour."

"That's great. I can't tell you how pleased your mother and I are to hear you and Rebecca have been spending time together again."

Cotter's mother chimes in from the kitchen, "Yes! You know how much we love her. I hope you've started treating her like the princess she is."

"Yes, Ma'am, I am trying my best."

Cotter's father looks concerned as he leans in, "Listen, Son, we really appreciate the added level of respect you've shown us lately, I mean, I truly appreciate you offering to repay your credit card debt, but you don't have to do all the sir and ma'am stuff."

"Yes, Sir."

He chuckles, "Well, like I said, we do love how hard you've been working on these changes. It all seems very positive." He looks down at the phone as it threatens to vibrate off the table again. "Are you sure you don't want a new phone? Or at least a new screen?"

"No, Sir, it's no big deal. Besides, it's nobody's fault but my own that it got cracked." He picks up the phone and pulls a credit card out from under the driver's license in the slot on the back of the case. "Why don't you just take the card, or we can just cut it up."

He seems surprised, "Oh, no. That won't be necessary. We would be more comfortable if you just hang onto it for when you need it, especially now that you are enrolling in classes. You will need a way to pay for things and we are happy to help. Remind me what you said you wanted to study?"

"Spiritual Training to start with. Then I might go ahead and seek out a pastoral degree. And you two said you will go to church with Rebecca and me on Sunday?"

Cotter's mother calls out from the kitchen again, "Absolutely! We will be there."

With a shake of the head, Cotter's father smiles and says, "Hmm, sorry to seem so surprised. It's just that is such a reversal from what you have always seemed to believe."

He opens the text from Rebecca. *LOL, you are a funny man. Okay, I will meet you at Dark Cravings.* She ends the message with a kissy face and he returns one. "No need to apologize. I do understand why this would all seem like a change. Let's just say, there have been significant changes with me and you can expect me to be a completely different person."

***

Rebecca is already sitting at a table when he enters Dark Cravings. She puts down her coffee and stands up to greet him. They embrace with a hug followed by the tenderest of kisses. "Sorry, am I late?" He waits for her to sit back down before taking a seat across the table.

"Nope, I was just so anxious about talking to you that I had to leave class early."

He looks concerned. "Is everything okay?"

She smiles nervously and then says, "I guess I don't know, but I hope so. It all depends on you."

He reaches across the table and takes her hand in his. "Just get it off your chest. You can tell me anything. We can figure it out together." He gives her a smile that instantly provides some soothing to her anxiety.

Her smile looks less nervous as she looks at their intertwined hands before gazing back into his eyes. "Things have been so much different since you went to treatment. I do feel like I can tell you anything right now. That being said, I am sure you can understand why I still hesitate because it hasn't always felt that way to me."

"I assure you, Rebecca, I completely understand why you feel this way. I wish I could explain the change to you, but I am probably the only person on Earth who could understand exactly how different I am now. So, while I do get it, all I can offer you right now is a promise that I will listen and work through this with you."

Her smile shows a touch of relief now. "Okay, I have two questions to ask you."

"Please, go ahead."

"Are you ready to be a father? I'm pregnant."

She tightens up again and holds her breath, anxiously awaiting his response. A huge smile stretches across a face she finds more handsome than ever. "Yes. If it's a journey I get to take with you, then yes, I am absolutely ready to be a father."

She exhales a sigh of relief, "Oh my God. I can't begin to tell you how relieved I am to hear that kind of response from you. I'm sorry, I know how spiritual you have become and this doesn't go along with either of our belief systems."

"No need to be sorry. It takes two to tango. We both did this and it will be okay." His smile hasn't wavered. It appears to be as genuine as can be. "What was the second question?"

"Oh, yeah. Are you ready to be a father to twins?"

Still, there is no fluctuation in his smile, not even a glimpse of surprise. "Why not? The best way to save you from the pain of giving birth twice would be to have two children at once." Now a questioning look does cross his face. "So you have already been to the doctor?"

Rebecca is giddy with excitement after his positive response to the news. "No, it's still early, but I can feel it. I mean, I've taken several pregnancy tests, so I am definitely pregnant, but I can't explain how I know I am pregnant with twins. Sorry if I am wrong, but that is what I think I am feeling for some reason."

"It does not matter. We will find out soon enough and it matters little whether we have one child or two. We will just focus and pray about a healthy pregnancy, for you and the babies."

"Yes, I couldn't agree more." She squeezes his hand and shows him the most beautiful smile he thinks he has ever seen. "Well, what do we do now?"

Without hesitation, "We should get married."

She is still smiling, but with added surprise, "Yeah? Like, you mean eventually?"

"The sooner the better. Do not get me wrong, I do not mean so we can lie about the order of things, but I do think it would be best to get things back in order as soon as possible. We can rid ourselves of at least some of the guilt."

"And, you'd be okay with us having sex again once we are married!" She realizes too late that this comment was loud enough to draw some looks from other patrons. She looks back at him, "Oops, sorry." They both chuckle now out of embarrassment and excitement. "So, when were you thinking?"

Rebecca sees a spark of love twinkling in his brown eyes that she is sure she has never seen in him before, and he says in a most sincere and tender way, "Well, what does the rest of your afternoon look like?" She smiles so big that her face hurts, and she answers the question by leaning over the table and kissing him.

Made in the USA
Monee, IL
27 January 2021